Erica Munro lives on the Black Isle in the Highlands of Scotland, with her husband and three children. After studying Law at Edinburgh University she worked as a property lawyer for six years, in Fife and Inverness, before leaving to care for her young family. On returning to paid work she set up one of the first home search agencies in the Highlands, working from an office at home, and travelling around the countryside checking out other peoples' curtains.

She often escapes with her laptop from the hurly-burly of Highland life, to write in the peace and tranquility of her in-laws' central London flat. *Guilty Feet* is her first novel.

Guilty Feet

Erica Munro

To Joan
With very best wishes

Erica
K

PIATKUS

Grateful thanks to Miles, Mum, Dad, Don, Tessa, Cynthia Rogerson and Jenny Wilson for all of their help in its many forms. Thank you to my agent, Jenny Brown, and to Gillian Green and everyone at Piatkus.

First published in Great Britain in 2004 by
Judy Piatkus (Publishers) Ltd of
5 Windmill Street, London W1T 2JA
email:info@piatkus.co.uk

The moral right of the author has been asserted

A catalogue record for this book is available from the British Library

ISBN 0 7499 3492 1

Set in Times by
Action Publishing Technology Ltd, Gloucester

Printed and bound in Great Britain by
Bookmarque Ltd, Croydon, Surrey

For Eric and Helen

Chapter One

It was when Esther Smith (Magnus, two and a half) advocated war in the south of England to reduce overcrowding on the roads that I realised there was more to her than met the eye. After all, she reasoned, war did the trick in Third World countries when populations got out of control, but did anyone ever consider it as a measure to cut congestion in the Home Counties? Far from it! They just built bigger roads! Housing estates with parking for four cars! Out-of-town shopping centres called World of Stuff!

Furthermore, when just for a second I caught myself thinking that she might have a point, I had to acknowledge that here in our midst was a woman with definite strengths in the complementary fields of power and leadership.

We were gathered in the kitchen annexe of the Mackenzie/Holland Room in the Brodie Wing of the Loch Martin Memorial Hall, to form a steering committee to decide on the venue for the Midsummer Charity Toddle and Dance. This was an annual event which, due to the unusually high proportion of mothers with time on their hands (as the amounts of money brought in by their spouses meant that for them to also go out to work would be just plum silly), had become one of the hottest fund-raising tickets in the Highlands.

Only four of us had turned up. We sat on orange plastic chairs around a gouged trestle table, surrounded by sage Formica kitchen units plotting their style comeback and no doubt hoping to emulate the success of the rickety wooden floorboards beneath our feet.

A two-bar electric heater glowered at us from each wall, switched on by Mr Jack the caretaker, a boiler-suited wisp of a man who had pre-arranged with Esther a precise time for our departure, before reversing out and softly closing the door. We were to leave the chairs as we had found them, switch off all of the heaters 'as soon as we were warm enough', take the plug out of the kettle, leave our exact coffee money in the ice-cream tub and deposit any rubbish in the big green bin outside the back door.

The drill was familiar to me as I had listened to Mr Jack instruct hall-users on hall-use for most of my life. His ritual conjured visions of Gilbert and Sullivan: 'And-Deposit-Any-Rubbish-In-The-Big-Green-Bin' ('We'll depositanyrubbishinthebiggreenbin'), and I nursed the hope that one day he would run through it in full naval dress, sharply indicating the whereabouts of the big green bin with a nasty little switch.

Actually the four of us didn't know each other all that well, despite the fabled Loch Martin community spirit which the *North Courier*, our local paper, trumpets all the time. Cynics say that you have to keep your voice down hereabouts or somebody'll be round finishing your sentence for you, but the fact is that unless you're either a sixth-generation local, a member of the drama, flower or snooker clubs or one of the many lunch-bringers, lift-givers and fence-menders (the types who get shock MBEs in their seventies), then you either have to hatch your own

2

community, or else do without.

And this is where toddler groups come into their own. There can be few working childless women anywhere who don't think of the phrase 'toddler group' without thanking their lucky stars that they have the brain and the good sense to work themselves clear of the sort of environment where nappy contents and how to get people to eat *more*, rather than less, are the main topics of conversation, but Loch Martin Mother and Toddler Group has over the years been the social saviour of countless lost, new mothers. From the wealthy superstratum of committee members who currently drive the group to the most hard-up of bewildered teens-with-tots, there's something about the comradeship of a toddler group which makes the tough years of raising tinies just a bit more bearable. Factions? Oh yes. Bitching? Absolutely. Petty niggles and mis-understandings? Yessiree, but surely even that's better than being stuck in front of daytime TV all day every day sobbing, eating breakfast cereal straight from the box and wanting to murder your kid?

But so to business. Esther turned to Susannah Grant (Abigail, three, Isabella, seven months) on her left. 'Could you be an absolute sweetie and take the minutes?' she asked, in the sort of voice that wasn't really a question at all. Susannah made a fluttery show of not being up to the task before looking round at us all and saying, 'Well, OK, sorry, as long as nobody else minds!' and rummaging in her bag. Flipping heck, she was chuffed. Then Esther was off again:

'Would you start by recording disappointment of those present at the low turnout this evening, and move that the matter be raised at the next meeting of the full committee? If Sarah, Amber and Claire don't get off their butts and start coming along to meetings, their positions on the committee may be in jeopardy. Time to kick some executive ass, no? No, no, sweetie, don't put that last bit in.' She laid a restraining hand on Susannah's knee.

Which was odd as none of the rest of us had said anything about the fact that there were only four people present – in fact I was quite pleased as, for one thing, a small turnout means fewer mums crowing on and on about their children like they're interesting or something, and for another I had only brought one packet of Jaffa Cakes. Still, once she was given the go-ahead from Esther, Susannah set to with her pen.

I watched her write a neat heading in capital letters; LOCH MARTIN TODDLERS – CHARITY TODDLE – 26 JUNE. Then she reached into her handbag, produced a small plastic ruler and double-underlined it, before entering the first of her sub-headings two lines beneath: Disappointment at Low Turnout. It looked as though Esther had found the top woman for the job, and no mistake. For a start, Susannah seemed to be the only one to have brought anything to write on – I don't know about the others present but a visit to the bottom of *my* handbag would yield up four confiscated small toys, a tampon, fifteen Austrian schillings, forty thousand supermarket receipts and a corkscrew. To be equipped with a *ruler* definitely denoted presentational skills of the highest order. During the pause, I pondered what else might equip the super-handbag. A small whisk, perhaps, in case one was abruptly called upon to make an omelette? Maybe a head collar, for those awkward moments when runaway bullocks need restraining?

The other person present apart from me was Val Gruber (Eden, six, Struan, five, Rowan, two and Charity, four months). Val attended everything. Meetings, concerts, evening classes, discussion groups, you name it. As far as

I was aware she didn't *do* much at any of them, but her gentle, baking-y presence was now not so much expected as taken for granted whenever any sort of public forum took place. This evening she had brought her cross-stitch with her: a thatched country cottage festooned with flowers, which she had planned to give to her friend Stella as an engagement present, but now it would have to be a wedding present as it was taking her so long. Irritatingly, she had also brought Charity, who snoozed comfortably in the carrycot at her feet.

I'd noticed Esther and Susannah eyeing Charity up as Val brought her in and wondered whether we were all thinking the same thing. After all, we'd all managed to shake off our smallest fry for an hour or two, so why the heck couldn't Val? But, with protocol to be observed, we'd stooped over the sleeping child anyway, noting how cute she was and how good she was to be asleep and was she always like this, and how did Val do it – because that's the drill, isn't it? And you think of your own children at home and of how *infinitely* nicer they are, and then you hope to goodness Charity won't wake up because then the chorus of admiration would have to start all over again and we'd get bugger all done.

'Can we go on?' asked Esther.

'Yes – so sorry – slow writer!' replied Susannah, her pen poised for her next sub-heading: The Toddle!

'Well, not so much "the Toddle" as such, perhaps more, "Arrangements for the Venue for the Toddle",' Esther corrected. 'The Toddle itself can be finalised once we've got details of the route, don't you think, girls?'

'We' didn't really mind one way or the other. Susannah, who in her enthusiasm had already written 'The Toddle', looked crestfallen and again reached into her bag, this time for her correction fluid. 'I do hate having to Tipp-Ex,' she grumbled.

'But don't you just love the smell?' said Val dreamily, her eyes rolling upwards into her head.

I'm Gail Macdonald. My children are Thomas, who is seven, and Emma, who to her complete indifference will be two tomorrow. I'm thirty-two, happily married to Stuart and currently sitting very, very quietly hoping not to be volunteered into doing anything.

Esther refers to me as 'the local girl', which made me feel kind of uncomfortable when I first heard it, even though she was factually correct. I certainly pass the 'born and bred' test, which on paper makes anyone a local here-abouts even if they flee Loch Martin the moment they sprint out of the gates of Loch Martin High School for the last time with no intention of ever returning. Stuart describes a local as the sort of person who gives directions to places by referring to landmarks which aren't there any more – and then we realised that that included me, too. My mum – a local – thinks you're a local if you can look around the married female population and, try as you might, only recall their maiden names.

But surely being a local should bring with it some sort of sense of *belonging* – some, some possession of space, or something? Oh, I don't know. Local, schmocal. It's that thing 'outsiders' imagine I must feel as I live out my life in the tracks of my ancestors, but I reckon that being a local just makes you feel under-travelled.

Anyway, I'm a darn sight more local than just about anyone else on the committee, that's for sure, as the cuteness of the village, its nice little school and its proximity to Inverness has attracted dozens of commuting yuppies whose arrival, as far as I can make out, made a lot of the other young locals cover their ears and move to Inverness.

Esther cleared her throat. 'Now, last year's Toddle was far and away the best yet, and I know it'll be a tough one to top!' Her cheeks were aglow. 'Lord Brankin was so kind to us, letting us use the Daffodil Wood at Invermartin estate out of season ...'

'And graciously charging us fifty quid for the privilege,' I couldn't help adding, still cross at the memory. Esther was momentarily thrown, her face clouded over and she shot me a dirty little glance.

'Well, yes,' she said tightly, 'but the weather was so glorious, and he didn't charge us any extra for putting the marquee on his lawn for the post-Toddle dance, even though it made a terrible mess ...'

'Which we fixed,' Val reminded her, stitching placidly. Well, *most* of us fixed. Val had been nowhere to be seen the following morning when a hungover bunch of cagoule-clad stalwarts squelched up to our knees in mud after an overnight downpour, filling bin bags with soggy litter and picking empty beer bottles out of rhododendron bushes.

Susannah hadn't minuted anything else yet. I guessed that, with her new heading set in stone, she wasn't going to write *anything* underneath it until it was directly relevant to *this* year's Toddle. Well, good for her. If she were a cutter of crap as well as a neat writer with a full set of stationery in her handbag then I'd employ her myself. Had I needed a secretary. And had she needed a job. Which neither of us did.

Esther continued, 'Anyway, we made money, which was the main thing, *and* we moved the venue up a gear, which was, um, also the main thing! I don't know about the rest of you,' (I don't think she cared much, either) 'but we simply must rise to the challenge of outdoing previous committees' efforts, don't you think?'

'In what way, exactly?' I asked timidly.

'In every way, Gail! Bigger venue, smarter event, more lovely money! The Toddle's got bigger with each successive year, hasn't it, and I'll be buggered if my year's the first one to drop the standard!'

This was certainly true. A flick through Loch Martin Toddlers' minute books (just how sad would you have to be?) would show that the whole Toddle event had grown in size, scale and status, all things of course being relative, each year since the first one, six years before. Which meant that now, with the sort of meteoric rise in popularity usually reserved for teenage pop stars who fall out of their tops on live TV, you have to understand, if any of this is to make any sense whatsoever, that amongst a certain slice of Loch Martin residents, and I don't necessarily mean the locals here, the very word 'Toddle' no longer merely defined tiny children using pudgy legs to take experimental steps. It was 'The Toddle'. Like 'The Derby', or 'The Wedding', 'The Toddle' was turning into an event for the diary to make you cancel your shooting, postpone the summer ski break, invite friends north for, buy new clothes and dogs, and be seen – with your shades on your head – at.

The year one Toddle had taken place around the weed-covered gravel of the Hall car park, ten laps, finishing up sheltering from a downpour in the Hall vestibule drinking juice and eating crisps. It raised a hundred and four pounds.

In year two, when my Thomas was a member, we Toddled round the football field, got our picture taken for the local paper with the manager of Loch Martin Wanderers, our perennially struggling Highland League footie side, got told off for scuffing the newly painted sidelines, had a picnic in the optimistically named 'Grandstand', and raised a hundred and ninety-six pounds.

By year three, with Thomas still a card-carrying toddler, some of the fathers had begun to show up. This time, we had a Welly Walk in the Woods. There was a treasure hunt, where the children had packets of half-hidden chocolate coins pointed out to them by parents, who then had to restrain their offspring from looking for others, as each child was only allowed to 'find' a single packet. Despite the heavy parental presence two children got lost for a while and their panic-stricken parents called in the police. Luckily the children were quickly discovered, long before the three panda cars had screamed up the drive, digging a molehill furiously with their bare hands, hoping to discover buried treasure and most miffed to be returned empty-handed to their mothers. Still, thanks to the resulting publicity in the local press ('Good Cause Nearly Ends In Tragedy'), and the raffle at the post-Toddle eighties' disco which shook the rafters of the Memorial Hall with the likes of 'Agadoo' and 'The Birdie Dance', over five hundred pounds was raised.

For year four, capitalising on the notoriety generated the year before, the committee invited national press and TV cameras to the 'Safety Toddle', where there were uniforms galore as firemen, policemen, an ambulance crew and a traffic warden jostled with the lollipop lady, the dog warden and a lifeboat crew to be seen on camera guiding the children safely round the Forest Park Nature Trail. Some of the dads did a jailbreak, where they were sponsored per mile to see how far they could travel in twenty-four hours with no money. Val's husband Janusz made it to Bahrain, which helped to bring the total funds raised, after taking into account the post-Toddle dance and raffle at the Loch Martin Arms Hotel, to just over six thousand pounds. We found out later that Janusz's neighbour had to take out a bank loan to service his open-ended stake of fifty pence a mile.

So, although marred by the disappearance of one of the

other jailbreak fathers, who phoned from Brighton to tell his wife he had decided not to come back, the year four Toddle set a standard which Esther, who took over the reins of the committee at the end of that year, was determined to exceed.

Thus the year five Toddle, last year's one, went further upmarket by Toddling round the Daffodil Wood in the middle of the gloriously scenic Invermartin estate, accompanied by the Invermartin Pipe Band (who had been instructed by Esther to 'try and play quietly'), and a small flock of designer sheep. The sheep, Esther explained, were to provide pastoral cuteness for the assembled press, and of course to also give the children an important message about the countryside, i.e. that it contained sheep, presumably. A tiny but tasteful fête was organised on the lawn in front of Invermartin House for the afternoon with a bottle stall (always a money-spinner), tombola, candyfloss, home baking, bric-a-brac, etc, and later on that night the ceilidh and raffle, held in a pink chiffon-lined marquee which looked like a brothel inside, brought the total raised to an impressive, if frustrating, five thousand six hundred pounds.

'Right then,' Esther went on, 'what are we going to do this year? I've got a few ideas, certainly, but I want to throw it open to the floor first, to hear your input. Anyone like to make any motions?' She looked round at us all with glittering eyes, reining in her own ideas with the effort of a child on an itchy racehorse. A pause. I stared at the roadkill that was her thrown-down challenge and realised that as neither Val nor Susannah appeared moved to move anything I'd have to say something pretty damn quick before we slithered helplessly into the thrall of the local landowner once more.

'Well, there's no way we're approaching that bugger

Brankin again,' I began, more firmly than I felt. 'I mean, I know last year's event went well, Esther, don't get me completely wrong, but, well, I felt he made us feel so, so *cap-in-hand* about it all, what with the fifty pound charge, and the five-million orders about where to toddle and where not to toddle, and having to go to the *back* door if we had any questions, and doing that sort of fly-past thing at the dance when he paraded in with that huge cigar and spoke to all of the committee and ignored everybody else ...' I tailed off before I reminded everyone about how I'd been a bit drunk and had followed him on my knees with cupped hands, shouting, 'Flick your ash here, your worship!' until Stuart had picked me up and taken me home.

'Hear hear,' whispered Susannah, who then turned pink and resumed her very, very neat writing.

Esther didn't seem to mind the criticism one bit. 'Fair enough, girls,' she said brightly, 'although Joffy Brankin's really quite a sweetie once you get to know him, ectually.' Something strange happened to Esther's vowels as she spoke of Lord Jonathan Brankin. *Joffy*! I'd forgotten he was known to his friends as *Joffy*! Joffykins! Joff the Toff! I bit my lip. 'It's always good to get feedback on one's ideas, what? Anyway, if no one's going to come up with anything, I've decided ....'

'Erm, sorry, but I've thought of something, Esther,' said Val, laying her cross-stitch down on her lap. If she'd been in a rocking chair she would have stopped rocking. We all would have, actually, so rare was it for Val to contribute anything other than her soft presence.

'Val!' squeaked Esther in alarm. 'Great! Let's hear it!' If a voice can turn pale then Esther's definitely did just then.

'Well, it's more of a feeling, an instinct, than an idea,

11

I suppose,' Val began. 'I just have this really strong feeling that we should be lending a more spiritual aspect to this year's Toddle, sort of, a more back-to-nature approach? I thought we could introduce some ritual, some sort of meaningful ceremony for the children, what do you think?'

'Ye-es? In what way, precisely?' said Esther, just a teensy shade menacingly.

'Well,' Val went on, 'dressing up, for a start. Girls as fairies, boys as elves. The mums and dads could dress up too, and we could have flowers, hundreds and hundreds of flowers, and instead of calling it a Toddle, we could call it a Procession, up to the Stone Circle on Pulpit Hill ... something like that, anyway.' Val's eyes were shining. She seemed bathed in karmic mystique. I thought of Stuart done up as a six-foot-one pixie and began to warm to the idea.

'And which child would you propose ritually sacrificing?' Esther sneered. Val didn't seem to hear her.

'Eden's got this wonderful fairy castle Janusz made her for her fifth birthday,' Val went on. 'It's feng-shui-compliant and everything. We could put it in the middle of the stone circle, and the children could toddle round and round it strewing petals, and the ones who have begun to talk could do a little chant, while the adults dance round and make wishes for the children and the earth! It'd be a real departure, I know, but so, so *symbolic* for the young people and their early steps in the world, don't you think? Stone? Flowers? Life? Birth? The eternal cycle?'

Twenty-five pounds ... twenty-five pounds ... this'll only raise about twenty-five pounds ... Speaking of chants, this one was almost visible in a little think-bubble above Esther's head as she closed her eyes and pinched the bridge of her nose. There was a hippy-induced silence as we contemplated our own mundane lives and ideas, and tried to connect with Planet Val, who had picked up her cross-stitch and resumed metaphorical rocking.

'Wow,' I said at last. 'Spooky.'

'But sweet,' added Susannah. Spooky and Sweet. Weren't they . . . oh, nothing.

Esther retrieved her normal voice, sharp and dominating. '*For Pete's* . . .' she began before pausing as though to manually adjust a volume control knob in her head. What came out next was far more conciliatory. 'It's a lovely idea, Val, sweetie, but, well, don't you think you have to be just a wee bit, urm, *broad-minded* to embrace it? It sounds very *pagany* to me! What do you think, girls?' Susannah had her head down and was writing hard, but I could see her eyes bulging. I squished my lips into a line that wasn't a smile and wasn't a frown, making my cheeks ball up like a hamster. Esther went on, 'Wouldn't it get right up the nose of the Church? Wouldn't the press think we were all a bit strange? Wouldn't they?'

None of us said anything quickly enough, so Esther continued, 'But thanks, Val, jolly well done! Anyway, I thought this year we should really go for something a little bit special, now that we know the things that work, and those that don't. Raffles, yes, the Toddle, *obviously,* parties, *definitely.* But some things are, erm, not quite such money-spinners and therefore perhaps not such a good use of our time?'

'Meaning?' Susannah narrowed her eyes and glared at Esther. Susannah was an artist, and she had volunteered the year before to do face-painting at the fête. In fact that had been my first encounter with her. But unfortunately she set herself such a high standard of excellence that she only got through four children in the entire afternoon, raising two pounds towards the grand total. I remembered

13

how Thomas nodded off while Susannah painstakingly turned him into a perfect little replica Spiderman, only waking up when she tearfully scrubbed all the paint off to start again because she had smudged a bit of web. The queue of waiting children got so fractious that they had to be given free ice cream.

Esther returned Susannah's look. 'Well, quite honestly, *yes*, Susannah, the face-painting was *really* lovely, but the sheer attention to detail you invested in those little faces was maybe a wee bit wasted on the day, don't you think?' Before Susannah could open her mouth Esther ploughed on. 'So I was thinking hard about how best to use you, and wondered whether you could maybe dash off a couple of your absolutely *fantastic* watercolours for us to auction off in the evening, perhaps?'

Susannah's little blonde-framed face whooshed from miffed, to mollified, to face-splittingly chuffed to bits in seconds. Her hands trembled as she said, much too quickly, 'Oh, OK then! Fine! Although I never actually just *"dash off"* anything, Esther, there's a lot more to my work than that, but, sorry, yes, fine!' She bent to minute the 'decision' before it ran away.

'In fact,' Esther continued, 'fêtes are such hard work, and so crashingly weather-dependent, that I've decided we probably don't need to bother with one at all this year, what do you think?' Like she cared what we thought. 'I've got one or two ideas up my sleeve which should more than make up any loss of revenue from baking our arses off and getting horrible village kids to do lucky dips, so can I take it that we'll proceed on a no-fête basis and save ourselves a ton of faffing around? OK?' Judging by the ensuing silence it appeared to be a fête accompli.

She had a point, though, as Val, Susannah and I must have sensed immediately, which explained why none of us

14

rushed to say anything. Baking my arse off to produce goodies which sold in polythene bags for sixty-five pence a throw was one of the things that made me crossest of all about being a stay-at-home mum. I'd hurl traybakes and sponges into my oven, muttering darkly about exploitation and hating myself for being traybake and sponge woman in the first place, then I'd hate myself even more for my subconscious desire for praise when I handed the stuff over, then I'd absolutely despise and loathe myself when I felt compelled to buy someone else's gritty fudge and evil-tasting boiled tea loaf.

Esther continued. 'But we're getting ahead of ourselves, girls! No more details until the venue's settled, OK? Now I thought . . .'

'Gottit!' I squeaked, suddenly inspired. 'We could go to Loch Ness and have a *Monster* Toddle!'

'No, Gail, we couldn't.' Ah.

'But . . .'

'Too tacky for words, sweetie!'

'Ah. Rightio.' Just a flipping thought.

'What about the Lottery?' put in Susannah. 'Didn't we apply to them a couple of years ago?'

'Yes, and they turned us down, Susannah,' I reminded her. 'We're not a good enough cause, or something.'

'My proposal not a goer either, then?' enquired Val.

'No, Val. Of *course* it bloody isn't!' Esther had one of those throbbing neck-vein things which shouted *back off, she's gonna blow!* so the three of us tacitly complied.

'All right then, I'll get the kettle on. Four coffees, yeah? Gail?'

'Great, cheers Val.'

'Susanne?'

'Only if it's no trouble, thanks, just half a spoon please. It's Susann-*ah*, actually. Thanks. Can I give you a hand?'

'I'll just about cope, I think. Esther?'

'Touch of milk, no sugar, and use one of the white cups if you can find one, they're at the back. I can't abide those minging brown mugs.'

Val moved into the kitchen like a liner leaving port. The last time I'd encountered Val she was returning from Casualty, fresh from watching Struan having a black-eyed bean extracted from his ear. The time before she was fretting about radon gas emissions from her new granite worktops. She returned a little later with our coffee, in four of the minging brown mugs, and I offered round the Jaffa Cakes (everyone, without exception, said they shouldn't really, before furtively grabbing at least two). Charity woke up, as children do when their mother is showing signs of relaxing, screwed up her eyes and opened her mouth to wail. Val scooped her up in the nick of time and tucked her under her rust-and-orange mohair jumper, from where faint slurping noises could be heard almost straight away. Then, underlining the maternal superiority of the mother of four, she placidly retrieved her cross-stitch and resumed sewing.

'Aww, isn't she just adorable?' ventured Susannah.

'Can't really tell from that angle,' I said, as we gazed at the baby's stout legs and odd socks, which were all that could be seen protruding from the bottom of the mohair.

'OK,' began Esther, draining her mug and wiping her mouth with her forearm. 'I have decided that, this year, the Toddle is going to get royal!'

'Pardon?' Susannah enquired.

'What do you mean, *royal*, exactly?' asked Val.

'*Balmoral!* Balmoral, of course! I'd been worrying about how to top last year's Invermartin House Toddle, which was such a' (looking directly at me) '*huge* success, and then it just came to me in a flash! The Queen spends

16

all summer there, doesn't she? So I realised we could take the children to meet her and then have the Toddle and dance at the castle! Just think how brilliant it would be!'

We all sensed Esther's excitement, while at the same time trying to absorb the fact that she wasn't having a laugh. *Surely* she couldn't be serious?

'Erm, I don't think you can just, well, *book* the Queen like that, Esther,' I said, trying to look solemn and picturing Her Majesty in a headscarf, sitting on a shooting stick in a field collecting sponsor money in an old ice-cream tub while pointing the way to the loos.

'I know that, poppet.' Esther smiled, trying to be patient. 'I'm not an imbecile, you know! These matters need to be approached delicately, using royal protocol! Royals don't intimidate me in the slightest, Gail – most of them are pretty brainless, actually, so I did my homework, and sent off this letter a couple of weeks ago, asking if she could fit us in! It's all just a question of *pitch,* you see.' And as we sat, spellbound, she reached into her bag and produced a copy of a letter, which she began to read out.

'"Madam, With my humble duty" – don't snigger, Gail, this is straight from *Debrett's Correct Form* – "I would like to respectfully ask if the renowned Loch Martin toddler group could come and hold its famous and worthwhile sponsored Toddle and ball at the beautiful grounds of Your Majesty's gracious Balmoral Castle" – Gail *please* – "on the afternoon of Saturday 26th June of this year. Furthermore" – stop writing, Susannah, I'll give you a copy for the minutes – "we would be honoured by Your Majesty's presence at the event, accompanying the children or perhaps welcoming them back at the end of their efforts. We would also beg Your Majesty's gracious permission to hold our post-Toddle ball within your gracious home or if that is not to Your Majesty's liking in a marquee on Your Majesty's lawn, at which, needless to say, Your Majesty's gracious presence would be most gratefully appreciated, together with any members of Your Majesty's royal family who would like to come too. We would be obliged if Your Majesty" – Susannah, are you crying? – "would honour us with a response as soon as possible as Your Majesty, of all people, will understand the amount of organisation entailed by such events. My telephone number is at the top of the page if Your Majesty requires any further details. I have the honour to remain, Madam, Your Majesty's most humble and obedient servant, Esther Smith."'

'Wow, that's some pitch,' I managed to say, after the deafening silence which followed threatened to make my brain cave in.

'You've actually *sent* that?' asked Val in disbelief.

Esther nodded smugly. 'Two weeks ago. I wanted it to be a surprise!'

'It's a surprise, all right,' I muttered.

'Bags first shot of William,' said Susannah, tears of mirth glistening in her eyes. We all looked round at her, and she shrugged gaily. 'And has Her Majesty said yes and enquired about the dress code yet?' she went on.

Esther ignored the sarcasm. 'No, not quite, but she hasn't said no yet, so I'm very hopeful.'

'Well, mate, ten out of ten for sheer brass neck,' I said, 'but, without wishing to pee on your chips straight away, mightn't it be an idea to have a contingency plan just, you know, in the unlikely event of getting a reply of the "bog off, peasants, 'er Majesty's on 'er break" variety?'

'Covered, ectually.' Oh no. The vowels, the vowels ... 'Joffy's delighted for us to hold the bash at Invermartin Hice again if the Balmoral idea doesn't come off. Funny, really, how the sniff of royal competition has him virtually pleading with me to bring the event beck to his place! I know you won't approve, Gail sweetie, but listen, he's not going to charge us a penny this year! Apparently last year the publicity surrounding the Toddle increased gate numbers at his Open Days by two hundred per cent, so he's letting us put on the whole shebang for nothing!'

'But he's a *git*!' I sensed the weakness of my final argument before I opened my mouth, but there you go.

'I went to the Royal Garden Party at Holyrood Palace in Edinburgh when I was sixteen,' said Val, catching us all off-guard. Charity had lolled out from under the rust-and-orange mohair and was lying flat out on her mother's lap in a shiny-faced state of bloated bliss. 'Years ago, before the princes got hitched,' (*'Temporarily,'* I mumbled) 'anyone who got invited and who had single female daughters at home got to take them along too! It was a sort of Festival of Crumpet. My three brothers had to wait in the car in a muddy car park until we came out. Do you know they actually *did* serve cucumber sandwiches? And some people brought little stepladders so that they could see over the crowds. Princess Anne had *such* skinny legs ...' She spoke the last bit in a whisper to her baby, then tuned out again.

'Gosh, amazing, Val. Now, so that's a decision, yup? Balmoral as Plan A, Invermartin as Plan B. OK with you, Susannah?'

Susannah's head shot up from her notepad. 'Me? Yes! Fine! Sorry!'

'Great! Shall we move on? It looks like we've got time to discuss the post-Toddle ball tonight too, now that the venue's agreed. Now ...'

I risked an interruption. 'Yes, I thought you'd mentioned the word *ball* earlier on, Esther. Don't you mean disco? Or dance? Or at a push, dinner-dance?' Somehow I knew she didn't.

'Gail, please, *hello*? Just take a moment to think it through, hmm? If we get Balmoral, then obviously it'll have to be a ball, won't it? The Queen's not going to turn up at an event that'll have her doing the Birdie Dance, now, is she?'

'No, Esther, I suppose she's not.' I answered solemnly, wondering if perhaps Esther was mentally ill, or on drugs, or something.

'And if by any chance we end up back at Invermartin, then holding a ball and grand raffle is the perfect way to trump last year's Toddle!' Esther sat back, thrilled by the elegance of her argument.

'*Grend* reffle?' I mimicked. 'What on earth's the difference between a grand raffle and a bog-standard raffle, then? I mean, surely if you win a prize in a raffle then it's grand, and if you don't, it's crap, whatever you decide to call it?' Oops, I'd gone too far. Val and Susannah were studying the floorboards. Esther looked like Jeremy Paxman facing Dimwit Polytechnic on *University Challenge*. We were officially in different worlds.

It was time to beat a retreat. 'Sorry, Esther. That didn't come out right. You mean humungous prizes like Rolex watches and trips on the Orient Express, rather than bottles of Lambrusco and boxes of Petticoat Tails shortbread, don't you? Excellent! I'm lucky in raffles! Well done, Esther! That sounds ... *grand*!'

Chapter Two

'How exactly does one go Looby Loo?' Stuart asked when I got back to the house that evening. We had a strange way of communicating sometimes.

'I'll show you on Saturday night,' I said, falling onto the fat red velvet sofa beside him and curling up like a wasps' nest in the crook of his arm. The fire was crackling behind the gigantic guard mechanism Stuart had rigged up to prevent Thomas and Emma from diving in and being burnt to a crisp.

'Good meeting?'

I sighed. 'I feel like I've been run over by a steamroller which reversed to flatten the gristly bits.'

'Esther there, then?'

'Yes. Most definitely.'

'Ah. Want to talk about it?'

'Not really. You wouldn't believe me.'

'Great, because . . .'

'You're going to have to dress up as a fairy and have tea with the Queen.'

Stuart frowned, then nodded slowly. 'I knew two guys at university who used to do that sort of thing. They started off by saying it was for charity but then I saw them holding hands in a jurisprudence tutorial. Actually, I should have guessed something was up because they were both in the Drama Club.' He gazed ceilingwards, lost in memory.

'Really. Can I speak now?'

'I thought you didn't want to? OK, I'll put the kettle on.'

'Cheers.'

So I told him all about it. In a fantastically one-sided way, as you do, which had me as the voice of reason, and Esther as some sort of crazed Tasmanian devil who by rights should have been hopping around in miniature in the fireside cage in front of us, spitting and snarling and waving a three-pronged fork. And when I'd finished with Esther, Susannah and Val got it in the neck for just, just *being*, which seemed to me to be completely and utterly fair. Then I fumed about Invermartin, hooted with laughter about Balmoral, snarled about the grand raffle, talked about the ball in a pathetic posh accent, bitched about Val, wondered whether Susannah had a dark side and decided that Esther had probably been bullied at school. And afterwards, just as I was starting to feel a bit better, I remembered that Stuart had spent the entire day on his feet in court in Inverness defending a man on trial accused of murdering his wife's lover. *Oops*.

'How'd it go today?' I asked, suddenly the very benchmark of the concerned wife, as he handed me a mug of tea. He shook his head and lowered himself and his tea onto the sofa. 'Oh, well, you know, not so great, actually. We came second. He got life. He's gone down. *Way* down. So far down, in fact, he's probably going to have to reach up to wipe his own arse. The judge recommended a minimum twenty-year term and called him the most worthless scumbag he'd ever had the misfortune to encounter. Said he hoped he rotted in an underground cell and that they threw away the key, leaving the worms and maggots to feast on his soft bits. Said . . .'

'Bad result, hmm? Poor you. Poor him. Poor, *poor dead guy*.' I put my head on his shoulder and tried to think of something positive, which wasn't easy under the circumstances. 'But, well, you know *you* did your best, though, don't you? You spent *Beanos* on that guy's defence' (Thomas measures time by the arrival of his weekly *Beano*) – you're not blaming yourself, are you?'

'Oh, I don't know. Yes. No. Maybe.' He rubbed his eyes. 'I mean, it didn't seem to matter how much defence I threw up about his friendship with the victim, or his happy home life, or his total amnesia on the day of the crime and all that stuff, I just never seemed to get past those four cops and seven neighbours who watched him throw the bloody knife out of the window shouting, "That bastard had it coming, right? I'll do time for him no problem!"' Shaking his head, he slurped his tea noisily.

'Mmm.' *Where were the positives? Where were the positives?* 'Those things were just so, so, *circumstantial*, weren't they?' I soothed. 'Just goes to show it's a mad, bad world. But you'll be able to get your bill out now, won't you? Anyway, can we talk about Emma's party?'

'And then there was the DNA evidence. And that so-called "confession".'

'My hero,' I said, snuggling further into his neck. 'My Champion of the Underdog.'

'Wasn't he a horse?' asked Stuart, perking up. 'Anyway, I like balls.'

'Sorry? Oh yes. Mmm. Me too,' I purred, in my up-for-it voice, nuzzling into his – overworked-smelling – armpit. 'Do you? You've never been to one, have you? Apart from at university, that is.'

'And they don't count because I can't remember anything about them. God, that cider . . . but I like the idea of a real, grown-up ball, though.'

'Or maybe you just fancy yourself in a white tie and wing collar peering down your nose from the edge of the dance floor saying things like . . . like, "In truth, old fellow, I'll wager a bottle of claret I've never seen Fanny look *quite* so agreeable!" and all that sort of stuff, don't you, Mr-Darcy-in-the-closet?'

'Yup. Well, there are worse ways of spending an evening.'

'I know. I've just done it. And I've got a bad feeling about this event. The Toddle's all very well, and a bit of a boogie afterwards, well, yes, that's fine too, but a *ball*? Who are we trying to kid? I think Esther's got her knickers in a twist about the whole thing – she's determined to outdo all the previous years' events, and her competitive streak is clouding her already suspect notion of reality. Somebody should have a word with her about keeping things in perspective before it's too late.' I folded my arms and added, very firmly, 'Bags not me.'

'Oh, come on, Gail, it'll be a laugh,' Stuart said, squeezing me tightly. 'God knows I need cheering up. You don't know how it feels to hear a judge hand down a life sentence in front of you . . .'

'No, but then I haven't killed anyone,' I replied unhelpfully. 'Yet.'

'Come to the ball with me, Cinders,' he wheedled. 'Bring Fanny if you like. You could get a new dress?'

I looked up at him and smiled patiently. Honestly, men could be so slow. 'Stuart, my love, I *know* I could get a flipping new dress! A new dress is the absolute, barest, most minimum requirement for my presence at any event organised by that woman! New dress, new bag, new underwear, new hairdo, new coat, new car, new tiara, well, yes, *then* we may just about have a green light ball situation, whether it's at Balmoral, Invermartin or the flipping Moon! I *know* I could get a new dress! Are you mad?'

'What happened to the simple tastes of the girl I married?'

'I didn't say "new husband", did I? There you are then.'

'Fair enough,' agreed Stuart, 'but anyway, it *is* going to be a proper Highland ball, isn't it, not just a dance by any other name?'

'Oh, never fear, it'll be a no-holds-barred, pumpkins-at-dawn, all singing, all dancing Highland ball, all right. We're going to have to fill out dance cards, and dance the undanceable until our ringlets drop off. Oh, except Esther says apparently at proper Highland balls you're meant to have breakfast in the wee small hours instead of dinner, but we all thought that was a bit pervy so we've ditched that idea in favour of a buffet supper at the start.'

'Sounds sensible,' agreed Stuart.

My gaze roved over the glossy magazines in the wicker rack beside the TV. 'God,' I murmured, 'next thing we know Esther'll be contacting *Hello!* and trying to scare up some celebrities to grace the event – who do you think we'd get? Cameron from *Big Brother* would be nice. Maybe some of the presenters of *The Beechgrove Garden,* if we're truly lucky? A whole *crop* of them? *Dug up* by Esther? Coming to our *hoe*-down?' My brain wasn't really directing my mouth any more and Stuart was too knackered to humour me. Anyway, I'd started thinking about my dress. Probably green, to match my eyes. Or red. No, plum. Black? Yeah, why not. I look sexy in black.

'So do you think there's any chance it'll actually be held

at Balmoral?' Stuart yawned, feigning nonchalance. I think he was quite taken with the idea of clicking his heels together and bowing stiffly before the monarch.

'*If* it's at Balmoral, which it won't be, then you'd have to take a crash course in royal etiquette, which you won't do, I'd have to get long white gloves and stick-on buck teeth, which I won't do, mum would have to babysit overnight, which she probably won't do, so the royal scullery maids would have to mind the kids, which they won't do, and Susannah would try to get off with Prince William, which . . .'

'Won't do?' supplied Stuart.

'Precisely.'

'Well well, who would have thought we'd be going back to Invermartin after last year?' Stuart said, yawning expansively again. 'I bet Brankin remembers *you*.' He grinned and I covered my eyes with my hand. 'Will we have to learn new dances, quadrilles and stuff? Esplanades? Ricochets? The Jolly Baguette?'

'Ha, you're ahead of me again, Watson!' I said, perking up and ruffling his hair. 'Too right we will! There'll be none of the old Gay Gordon and Dashing White Sergeant kiddie stuff at Esther's bash! She's drawing up a timetable of dance practices for the Committee, so that we don't let the side down on the night and squash all the corgis. But it'll be traditional Scottish country dances, so you can keep your Jolly Baguette to yourself.'

Stuart suddenly looked genuinely afraid. 'Now you're having a laugh. *Dance practices*? No way!'

''Fraid so. It's shape up, or sit it out, or so I'm instructed. Esther's planning to bring all her public school cronies out of the woodwork for the event, and she doesn't want us lot to show her up. Come to think of it, Claire Holmes and Sarah Barbour should be able to muster a

26

substantial nob element too, with Claire's Pony Club crowd and Sarah's job at Outram and Hill.'

'True,' mused Stuart. 'I've often wondered why Sarah became a land agent. She went to the same school as me, and she seemed hell-bent on changing the world back then. Very nice bum, if my memory serves me correctly.'

'I suspect she was taken on because her name reminded her bosses of their favourite outdoor clothing.'

'Mmm,' agreed Stuart.

'Or perhaps she has a cunning plan to revolutionise the world from the inside out – get to the heart of the Establishment and start tunnelling? God, that would be a first.'

Stuart closed his eyes and looked like he might nod off. Then he stretched so hugely that I could hear little crackling noises in his joints, and said through yet another gargantuan yawn, 'Do you think the White Sergeant would have been thought quite so Dashing if he'd been mixed-race? Or, say, Sudanese?'

I pondered that one. 'Hmmm. Probably every bit as Dashing, but there's no way he would have made Sergeant back then.'

We fell silent. Our toes writhed in front of us beneath our socks as though they were conducting the flames. Thomas grinned down at us from his school photograph on the mantelpiece. His dirty blond hair was cut in a squint fringe, and his resemblance to his daddy was comical: the direct gaze, the straight nose and the smile which involved his entire face, only in Thomas's case it included a big gummy gap which lent him a temporary lisp and a frustrating problem with his morning toast.

Emma's photograph was out of date. The big frilly baby who was baring her two teeth at a point just to the right of the photographer's lens (she was actually wondering why her mother was wearing a clown nose and trying to do a headstand while holding a cuddly toy in each hand) bore no resemblance whatsoever to the apple-cheeked toddler with attitude who was asleep upstairs in her toy-filled,Winnie-the-Pooh-themed room. She was one of those children whose features altered every day. Sometimes she looked like she belonged to us, and sometimes like she was just visiting.

And right in the centre, there was a third picture. Not a posed, scrubbed, grandparents' dream like the other two, but a slightly blurry Polaroid of a tiny, tiny boy, whose single day of life was captured in a solitary photograph taken by a nurse who could see into the future. Ben. Our middle child.

The next morning we shambled downstairs, a yawning tangled family mass of dressing gown and slipper. Thomas led the way eagerly, and I carried Emma, still half asleep, on my shoulder, our matching little clumps of bed-tangled hair at the back of our heads meshing softly together.

Every now and then Emma decides not to sleep very much, and unfortunately the previous night had been just such an occasion. Oh, she wasn't unwell – we'd taken her temperature and gently squeezed bits of her to see if they triggered any reaction, but they didn't – unless you count giggles, or whining entreaties to do a puppet show with Mr Rabbit and Mr Sheep. At one point, from the snugness of my bed, I'd been vaguely aware of hearing Stuart, crinkled and bleary, in her bedroom hissing, 'Look, munchkin, if I thought for one second that it would GUARANTEE you'd nod off I'd fly in the Muppets, the entire cast of *Sesame Street* and Barney the frigging purple Dinosaur right now but you and I both know perfectly well it wouldn't make any odds whatsoever so for heaven's sake just GO TO SLEEP!'

I stopped counting after I'd snuggled her up five times, and Stuart swore blind that he'd been up even more often than that with her, but, whatever, the harsh reality this morning was that it was her birthday whether she deserved it or not and she had to open her presents before Stuart went off to work. So if that meant prodding her awake and propping her up against some cushions to unwrap parcels, then so be it.

Thomas flung open the sitting-room door, where a large pile of pinkly wrapped presents lay on the rug in the middle of the room.

'Wow! Just look at those, poppet!' That was Stuart.

'Presents! Presents for the birthday girl! Who's a lucky thing!' That was me, but with the undercurrent proviso that if she'd wandered through to our room once more last night, then the whole pile would have been upside down in a skip by now.

'Co-ool!' added Thomas.

'VEEFABIX!' That would be the lucky birthday girl. So we abandoned the presents in favour of the kitchen for breakfast.

Fifteen minutes later, revived by assorted bowls of cereal and some strong coffee for the grown-ups, we shuffled back to the sitting room to try again.

'Come and see your *presents*, poppet! Who's a big grown-up girl then?'

'OK Em,' wheedled Stuart, 'which one first?' Emma was more interested in choosing her morning video, and Stuart was in danger of being late for work.

'Shall I open them?' Thomas asked, losing patience.

Emma didn't seem to have any objections so Thomas set to opening the parcels and waving the teddies, bath toys and bead sets (*bead sets*? For a two-year-old? And did they include instructions for the Heimlich manoeuvre?) in front of his sister, while she began to draw on her legs with a green felt-tip pen.

Stuart had to leave for work at eight thirty, giving him enough time to drop Thomas off at school on the way and leaving me with two and a half hours to conjure a birthday party from the mound of raw materials in the kitchen.

I completely see the point of *first* birthday parties. First birthday parties mark the occasion of the mother's return to seeing people socially, and not just at clinics, baby groups and the supermarket. You can invite whoever the hell you like, drink wine and sit around smugly, while any children who might be there (and they are not compulsory) eat, drink, and just kind of rootle around. Thomas's first birthday marked the first day I managed to have a shower before three o'clock in the afternoon for a whole year. Emma's was the day I made myself stop crying, and found the courage to put Ben's picture in its frame on the mantelpiece, between his big brother and his little sister.

Second birthday parties, however, are harder work altogether. Because the children aren't really aware of what's going on at second birthday parties, apart from experiencing a vague anxiety that their mothers are expecting them to behave differently from their usual, the main aim of second birthday parties is to try and prevent too many of the guests from getting upset. To this end my kitchen morphed into a shrine to comfort eating as I stuck Smarties on marshmallows, iced fairy cakes, cut up flapjack and chocolate crispie, emptied out industrial-size packets of crisps, washed grapes and spread fat peanut butter sandwiches.

'*Whooo-hoo!*' Mum arrived before I'd finished making the food, before I was dressed, before Emma was dressed, before I'd begun to tidy up and, frankly, a good hour before she'd said she was coming.

Always an ambitious dresser, this morning she'd got herself up in her favourite grass-green poncho, which was a Paisley-printed wool tableclothy affair, edged with short, matted black fringes. A long brown velvet skirt, brown Timberland boots, a black beret and her beloved jade boulder-drop earrings, the ones which made her earlobes look as though they were melting, completed the look, and as she breezed into my kitchen she surveyed the devastation and her dishevelled daughter with undisguised dismay.

'Gail, darling, have you been *ploughing* in here?'

Mum's always been a bit of an exotic around Loch Martin. I mean, she's local as local can be (her father, my grandfather, plumbed, re-plumbed and unblocked pretty much the whole village for forty years), but she's somehow cast from a rogue mould – she's my reminder that *fitting* in and *blending* in are two entirely separate things. She's also bloody hard to please.

'*Danny!*' Emma shrieked, hurling herself joyfully underneath the poncho.

'Morning!' she shouted. 'Where's my birthday girl? Op! *There* she is! Who's two, then? Who's clever? Who'll be using her *potty* now? *Course* you will! Not dressed yet, Gail?'

'Hi Mum,' I said apologetically, tightening my dressing-gown cord in shame. 'Thanks for the car seat, it's fantastic! Emma loves it. Coffee?'

'No thank you, I'm off to the dentist. Do you need a hand?'

'When's your appointment?'

'Ten minutes, but I'm sure I could easily change it.'

'No, don't be daft. I'm nearly there. It, erm, doesn't

31

really look like it, but beneath all this mess is a beautifully tidy house.'

'OK then. Bye!' She whirled round and Emma dropped out of the bottom of her clothes. 'Bye, Granny's best girl! Have a lovely party!'

'Um, any chance of some babysitting next week?' I whimpered at her retreating back. For some reason, I always prefer pulling out my fingernails with pliers than asking Mum to babysit. Or anyone, really. It's such a *horrific* imposition – taking someone away from their own fireside, their own telly and their own wine bottle so that they can sit in my house all evening, feeding the contents of the hospitality tray into the fire as they're on a secret diet. Then plundering the sultanas and flaked almonds in the baking cupboards and scoffing everything that won't be missed. Doesn't everybody do that?

'Should be all right.' Did I detect a faint *tone*? 'When?'

'Next Tuesday.' Oh well, I'd started now, so here goes ... 'In fact, the next *five* Tuesdays. And Saturday the twenty-sixth of June.' I started burbling out edited highlights of the ball and the dance practice itinerary as Mum climbed back into her car.

She nodded patiently. Or impatiently, I couldn't decide which. Then she said, 'Fine, either me or your dad'll do it.'

'I'll leave food out for you,' I sort of whined.

'Don't be daft, darling, I'm not a cat!'

''K then. Thanks. Bye. Thanks. Sorry. Thanks ...'

Yikes, only an hour to go. Spreading Minnie Mouse polythene tablecloths on the dining-room table, and then, after a moment's thought, on the floor as well, I glanced out of the window to see Theresa striding up my driveway, wearing a short tweed skirt, knee-high boots and a leather jacket. Her black hair was loose today, and it bounced around her shoulders like manic kids on swings. Tucked under her arm was Emma's present, done up with pink cellophane and tons of pink curly ribbon. As best friends go, she looked like a bad choice. I gazed down at my greying white dressing gown, with its coffee stains and its line of crusty snot along the shoulder, and slowly opened the door.

'Phwoar,' hooted Theresa when she saw me. 'Doing anything tonight, baby?'

'Oh, belt up and hoover my house,' I replied, as Theresa joined Emma on the sitting-room floor and handed over the present. Children swarmed round Theresa in the same way that cats do when they sense someone doesn't like them. Only I don't think it was so much that Theresa didn't *like* children, more that she felt she didn't quite know what to *do* with them, so she tended to just hover around in their presence until the children themselves were obliged to take charge of the situation, which they inevitably adored.

Inside the cellophane wrapping was a deep pink, crushed velvet hat, embroidered with hearts and butterflies, and lined with paler pink silk. Emma was thrilled, squealing with joy as she tried it on, then she pulled it off and began to fill it with beads from the bead set.

'Don't let her inhale any of those,' I said, dashing upstairs to get ready. By the time I returned Theresa had cleared up, hoovered the sitting room, put the last of the party food on the dining-room table, enchanted Emma even further by sellotaping the beads into a plastic tub to make a noisy shaker thing, and poured coffee.

'So who's coming today then?' Theresa asked, taking her cigarettes out of her bag then rolling her eyes and putting them back again. 'Let me guess, the entire toddler group plus your mother.'

'Pretty much,' I agreed, 'only Mum's already put in her guest appearance. *Wheeechooooooww!*' I mimed watching an object flash past, and cricked my neck. 'Ouch. Claire's bringing Rosie, Amber's bringing Jessica and Harvey, Val's bringing Rowan and Charity, Susannah's bringing Abigail and Isabella, and Sarah's working. Oh, and Esther's bringing Magnus. So that's, what, nine children including Emma, and seven adults?' I re-counted the party loot bags, which were stuffed with shop-bought trash, like whistles that didn't and puzzles that weren't and sweets that definitely were.

'Thought you didn't like Esther? Isn't she the bossy one with the funny voice?'

'Yes, and I don't, or at least I didn't, but I saw her at a committee meeting last night and everyone else was coming so I felt I couldn't really leave her out. Plus there's the fact that Magnus and Emma are going to have to go through nursery and school together, so I thought I should start making an effort now.'

'Ah.'

Theresa and I went way back. We'd met at university, and whereas I had worked for a few years with a software consultancy in London before returning home to get married and have children, she was single and had chosen to come and live in the Highlands so that she could combine freelance computer programming, which she did from her cottage just outside Inverness, with her love of hills and open spaces. Frequently she also combined it with partying all night and waking up with strangers, or taking shopping trips by herself to New York, or singing with folk groups. Whatever, every time words like 'committee' and 'school' came out of my mouth I felt foolish, as though I was her mother or something. I leeched her social life and lapped up the details eagerly like a *terribly* broad-minded auntie, while she hung out with my children and they loved her for it. And I loved her for it too. We checked that Emma was OK, then scuttled giggling out of the back door for a cigarette.

'Can I borrow you next Thursday night?' she asked, scrunching up her eyes through a blue cloud of smoke. I was peering round the corner at the back of the garage, keeping my eyes on the driveway for early arrivals.

'Thursday?' I repeated. 'Should be OK, I think. What's on?'

'My writers' group's having a bit of a do in Inverness Library. Couple of readings, lots of booze. What do you say? I could do with some moral support.'

'Moral support?' I echoed. 'I thought you said they were a nice bunch?'

'Oh, they are, in the main, but it's meant to be a sort of "bring-a-chum" evening, 'cause it's the last meeting of the session ...' She tailed off, embarrassed.

'Theresa, my poppet, you're having an end-of-term concert! How *exciting*! Have you been practising really hard?'

'Oh, shut up.'

'Sorry.'

'Will you come? I'd rather humiliate myself in front of you than humiliate myself in front of all of them by being the only Johnny No-Mates in the group.'

'I'd love to, you daft cow. Now could you just go in and make sure there's a loo roll in the toilet, please?'

I loved Theresa. I adored and admired her. Her beautiful face and body, her warmth, our shared confidences and good times, everything. I loved her verve, her ballsiness, but more than all of that I loved the streak of vulnerability, deep within her, which only I was allowed to see.

I suppose I should have realised that Val would bring

all four of her kids. Damn. Val and Janusz were educating their children at home, so while Thomas was getting stuck into topics like 'story' and 'choosing' at the thirty-seven pupil Loch Martin Primary, the little Grubers were taught real, live *stuff* like botany and astrology. In Gaelic. Only they weren't today, because they were at my house, clustered wanly round their mother and taking in their strange surroundings with round, sky-blue eyes.

Everyone else arrived in solemn procession shortly afterwards. Shy kids, pushy kids, shy mums, pushy mums. I threw all the coats and anoraks onto the utility-room floor, and put Emma's second wave of presents into a heap in the corner, for controlled opening later on.

The first thing the mothers did, in the time-honoured fashion, was to sit in a circle and play Pass the Parcel while their offspring attempted to sneak off to do something else. Most of the mums gamely rounded up their rebel children and wodged them between their knees so that they were forced to join in the FUN of playing the GAME, but it became clear that Esther's son Magnus was the only one who displayed a scrap of entrepreneurial acumen as he hung on to the parcel for dear life each time it came near him and refused to let it go. Claire, unburdened with child as her daughter Rosie had insisted on ignoring everyone and playing with the Lego instead, had to wrench it from his iron grip each time with a bright 'There we go! Got to pass it on, now, haven't we, sweetheart?' through clenched teeth. From my sanctuary in the bay window by the stereo (with my face turned away to ensure fairness), I tried to remember how many wrappings I'd put on the prize. Oh God, about twenty. Better step on it.

Rarely can there have been such a well-heeled contest for a box of Blo-pens. A veritable, what, arsenal? of toned bottoms was sitting, probably very uncomfortably, on my sitting-room rug, encased in designer jeans, suede skirts and expensively casual trousers. Esther's pale yellow pashmina blended beautifully with Claire's sage green one beside her, and Susannah's silk floral blouse was fastened at her slender wrists with daisy-shaped enamel cufflinks. Theresa had taken off the leather jacket to reveal (hang on, what was *she* doing in the game?) a cream broderie anglaise fitted bodice, and Amber, as ever, was in black cashmere and pearls. Val was on the sofa with her children squashed around her. They peered out from various openings in the rust-and-orange mohair jumper while she read aloud to them in Gaelic from the illustrated children's atlas she'd brought along.

The game seemed to go on for ever, punctuated only by Magnus's shrieks of fury as the determined Claire wrenched the parcel off him time and time again. Observing this from her comfort zone on the sofa, Esther remarked, 'It's because he's so bright for his age, he just can't see the point of a present with so many layers!' I fumed at her silently. *None* of us could see the point of the bloody game now, but fortunately at this point the last layer was reached and – oh! Theresa was declared the winner.

'Oh, fantastic!' she said to the staring losers as she unwrapped the Blo-pens and stashed them in her bag. 'I love drawing! And blowing!'

'Speech!' said Susannah, startling us all. 'Sorry!'

In all the frantic excitement, Emma had slipped unnoticed up to her bedroom, stripped down to her nappy and returned holding her beloved fairy costume, which Stuart had brought her back as a present when he returned from a court case in Edinburgh. Thomas had been given a rugby ball. So no danger of gender stereotyping in our household, then. Theresa, picking up on Emma's little plea for security in a weird situation, gathered her up and proceeded to dress her in the sparkly tights, white satin and net tutu, wings, wand and halo. She then rummaged in her bag and found lip-gloss and blusher, which she applied softly to Emma's enraptured face.

'Well,' I started, 'we seem to have lost a little, er, *cohesion* here, haven't we?' as we looked around for our children who were, to a man and woman, doing their own thing in different parts of the house. 'Shall we feed them now?'

I had found extra place settings at the table for Eden and Struan, and before long there were ten children (Charity being once again lost up the rust-and-orange mohair jumper on the sofa), messily munching and slurping, lost in their little sugar worlds. Calm and serenity returned as each mother stood over her child or children, like their own personal butler, trying and failing to make them eat the peanut butter sandwiches before the sweet stuff.

'Might've been a good idea to start off with savoury only,' remarked Esther, watching Magnus regurgitate five marshmallows back onto his plate after his world record food-cramming attempt misfired.

'Mmm, I'll do that next time,' I replied stiffly, handing round coffee. *Shame you won't be there.*

'What, no wine?' asked Theresa. I shrugged in a manner which was meant to convey apologetic solidarity, if such a thing can be achieved by something as two-dimensional as a shrug. I didn't know this crowd well enough to start pulling corks at eleven thirty in the morning.

The quiet munching continued. I watched as mummy after mummy furtively whipped chocolatey morsels off their children's plates and devoured them like polite lightning. Esther began to look a little preoccupied, retreating into herself and failing to intervene when Magnus appropriated an entire plateful of chocolate mini rolls for his own use. That job was left to me and I was rewarded with a glower and a fart.

All of a sudden the reason for Esther's preoccupied state became clear. Weary of not being the centre of attention for such a long spell, she picked up a plastic spoon and tapped it on the side of a paper cup. 'Could I just have everyone's attention for a tiny moment?' she asked with a simper. The children looked up in surprise for a nanosecond and then carried on eating, smearing and spilling. 'As most of the committee is here – *this time* – I just wanted to have a quick word about footwear for the ball. Now then, has everyone got pumps?'

'Breast pumps?' enquired Val.

'No, Val, dear. Dancing pumps! Proper ones! Everyone has to have them for doing Scottish country dancing properly, even the hubbies!'

'The *what*?' exclaimed Theresa, her eyes huge with mirth.

I decided there and then that the only way Esther or anyone would be able to deflect me from my beloved Jimmy Choo party stilettos would be at gunpoint, but said nothing, preferring instead to feast on the image in my brain of Stuart criss-crossing dancing-pump laces round and round his calves until his legs turned purple and dropped off.

'Well, there's plenty of time, I know, but it is going to be a mandatory part of the dress code for Balmoral, so you might want to think about getting some ordered. You'll want as much time as possible to practise in them, so I've got a couple of addresses of suppliers in my bag.'

'Esther,' I began, 'I think, well, some of us could

39

practise for a lifetime and never be any use dancing on an empty airstrip, let alone in front of the Queen, so don't you think—'

'Nonsense! We're only going to learn half a dozen or so of the simplest reels – once you've got the hang of the basic steps, under the expert tuition of Otto Mackintosh-Jones, your confidence will—'

'Otto who?' asked Amber.

'Mackintosh-Jones. He's frightfully nice. Ex-Gordonstoun. Army parents.'

'I *thought* so!' shrieked Amber. '*Dunny-brush*! He was in the same year as me! Good grief, I haven't seen him since we were at school! Oh, that's *right,* he was *sooo* light on his feet!' She squealed with laughter. 'Frightfully nice, though. Not married, I take it?'

Esther was put out. 'No. Well, not that I know of, anyway. And yes, he's an excellent dancer. Does a lot of teaching, so we'll all be in excellent hands.'

'Especially the *hubbies*, by the sound of it,' murmured Theresa.

'Why did you call him, what was it, Dunny-brush?' I asked, in a naive, spot-the-girl-who-never-went-to-boarding-school way.

'Oh, he was forever getting his head flushed down the pan for some misdemeanour or another. Got quite used to it, I suspect.'

'Oh. Right.'

Having unveiled her secret weapon to such derision, Esther came back fighting. 'Listen, that's not fair!' she practically shouted, with a quivering voice. 'I am *trying* to organise the event of a lifetime for all of us, and Otto is going to be giving up his free time to try and get us through this, and all I'm getting is the piss taken! How about some support?'

This was a little too much for me, given that it was my daughter's party, so I stood up and said, 'Cake?' just a mite threateningly, and stalked to the kitchen to light the candles on the world's pinkest cake. Esther had collected herself by the time I returned, and broke off from demonstrating the full curtsey to help sing 'Happy Birthday' to Emma, who was confused.

'Blow them out, sweetie!' I smiled, advancing towards her holding the flaming cake. She shrank back under the weight of the expectation that had been thrust upon her.

'Go on!' Then, in an inaudible-to-anyone-except-fairies growl, 'I'll give you a sweetie!'

This did the trick. But as she began advancing coyly towards the candles, Magnus decided to play Walter Raleigh by cutting in front of her, tripping her up with a Minnie Mouse tablecloth, and saving her the trouble of blowing out her candles by doing it himself.

'Oh, Magnus, you knew what to do, didn't you then, clever boy?' said Esther proudly, as I wondered whether to throttle him now, or later.

'Oh, for *FAP'S* sake!' exclaimed the fairy, hands on hips, before storming off to her room, leaving everyone to look at me pityingly.

'Hahaha, her first proper sentence!' I squeaked. 'That's quite good at two, isn't it? *Isn't it?*'

Chapter Three

Esther's royal rejection arrived the following day. I'd just finished off the post-party clear-up when her Range Rover pulled in at my gate and swaggered up the drive. Magnus sat, king-like, on a huge padded child seat in the back, sullenly clutching a beaten-up toy monkey and gazing out of the window at nothing. On seeing me at the door, Esther pulled a melodramatic frown and made an exaggerated thumbs-down sign.

'What's up?' I asked, as she got out and helped her reluctant child negotiate the vertiginous drop to ground level. 'Magnus not enjoy the party?'

'No no, it's not that! Well, yes, well, no! He had a lovely time. Didn't you, poppet?' Magnus folded his stout arms around his monkey and shook his head violently. 'It's not Magnus, Gail. It's the Queen. She's turned us down.' She reached up on to the passenger's seat and brought out a crested envelope, which she thrust into my hand with a snort. My body language threw itself into auto-sympathy before my brain caught up – furrowed brow, head to one side – the sort of gesture I'll probably make one day when Thomas tells me he's decided not to become a chartered accountant, or when Emma gets

42

chucked by some scumbag she thought she was in love with but hadn't checked with me first.

'Oh, Esther. What a shame! Why, for heaven's sake?' I quickly read the letter. '. . . regrets . . . other . . . engagements . . . good . . . wishes for a successful . . . *huh!* Flipping heck, Esther, that woman has *no* style! Doesn't recognise a grand day out when it's offered to her on a plate. Probably worried that we'd trample on her marigolds, or something.' *Would that do?*

She sniffed. It looked as if her faith in the monarchy and the entire British class system had been shaken to its foundations. But she was such a subdued version of the Esther I knew and feared that I asked her in for coffee.

Emma, who had recovered from her birthday strop (after all it *was* her party and she could cry if she wanted to), seemed to pick up on the air of despondency, because she silently caught Magnus's square little hand and pulled him into the sitting room, picked out a Tweenies video, put it in the machine, rewound it, and pressed the 'play' button. Then she accidentally spilled her box of raisins at his feet, whereupon he looked at her as though she were his long-lost fairy godmother, dropped to his knees in front of her and began to hoover them into his mouth.

'I think that's the junior equivalent of brandy and a bracing hug,' I said to Esther, as we watched them from over our coffee mugs at the kitchen table. I looked at her more closely. 'Would you like either of those things, by the way?'

She chewed her lip. 'No thanks, I'll settle for a digestive biscuit.' There was a silence. Well, there wasn't, actually, as the blare of the Tweenies theme tune starting up made all four of us jump. I shot through to the sitting room and turned it down. Emma glowered at me. I glowered back.

43

'I guess I knew it was a long shot,' Esther began when I sat down again, 'but somehow I didn't let that stop me from thinking that it was actually going to happen, you know?' I nodded. 'I mean, I can see now that the logistics would have been a nightmare, but, well . . . well . . . to be honest, Gail . . . Gail, *may* I be honest with you?' I nodded eagerly. 'It started out as a bit of a joke, really. Tony and I were having a discussion one evening; actually we were cooking up ways of outdoing last year's Toddle, and, well, you know how it is, we were alone together, and the suggestions got more and more outrageous, and we were having such a laugh, until Tony just, well, came right out with it! I got the shock of my life!'

Tony, Esther's husband, was reputed to be the most boring man in the world. 'Came out with *what*, exactly?' I asked, just in case there was the teeniest chance of some smut to share with Theresa.

'Asking the Queen, of course! He said something like, oh, how did he put it: "Esther honeykins," – that's his name for me – "at this rate you'll be holding a *ball* in the presence of the *Queen*!" It was *hilarious* – there we were, helpless with laughter about the very idea, and then something just came over me, and I just thought, well, why the bloody hell not? I mean, all this stuff about the royals being more approachable and accessible these days, it suddenly wasn't funny any more. In fact, Gail, it became obvious. *That* was what we were going to do. Simple as that. And it went from there, really. Only now I've told everyone about it and been knocked back, I feel a bit of a wally, to tell the truth.'

'Mmm,' I said helpfully. Poor old Esther. I did see where she was coming from, in fact, even though it was the sort of place I'd take the long route, the one with loads of traffic lights and roadworks, to avoid.

'Do you think everyone will be laughing at me? They will, won't they?'

'Yes' would have been an insensitive thing to have said just then, so I dodged the question and thought fast. 'People are basically lazy, Esther,' I began. 'The fact is, Esther, you *bothered*. None of the rest of us did. It's true that we were all very, er, surprised when you mentioned the Balmoral idea, but . . . but . . .' (Aaaargh! I'd said 'but' and couldn't follow it up! Code red! Code red!) Esther was watching me thoughtfully.

'But I could have pulled it off if only I'd been given the chance?' she offered.

'Precisely! Thank you! Of course you could have. And it would have been fantastic, too.' There had been no *need* to finish up with a fib, but I did anyway.

Esther seemed quite happy with that. *Bolstered,* even. Meanwhile Emma, who could watch telly for Scotland, hadn't taken her eyes off the box since the video started. Magnus had turned his attention to planting stickle bricks in my ivy. Oh well, ivies were unkillable. I knew this for certain as Emma had recently peed in that one. Or at least somebody had. Whatever, the sight of the two contrasting children in the sitting room, one slobbed out, the other being dubiously creative, seemed to demonstrate that I was a bad parent who let her child watch the box all day, and Esther was a good one who let hers express himself by doing whatever the hell he liked. With impunity. However much bloody mess he made. 'Magnus!' I bellowed. 'Stop that! *Sweetheart!*'

And so, with the preposterous notion of Balmoral dead and buried, the spectre of Invermartin House roused itself and settled, cackling, between us. I still didn't want to go back there, but I had begun to realise that none of the others seemed to share my misgivings about the place.

Maybe it was just me. Maybe I was prejudiced against people like Lord Jonathan Brankin through sheer jealousy, and therefore it was time to take a long hard look at myself. Maybe he was a kind person who genuinely wanted to help out the toddlers and assorted serfs of the village. Maybe I had been imagining his superciliousness last year. Maybe you can drown in maybes until someone pulls you out with a lifebelt of definitelies and as far as this whole event was concerned, I was a definitely-free zone.

'So it's Invermartin, then?' I asked, in an olive-branchy way.

'Unless you want to devil-worship round toadstools with Val,' replied Esther with a snort.

'Oh yes! Great! Let's do that, then!'

'What?' she jolted.

'Kidding. Sorry.' When would I learn that this woman was not of the same world as me? '*Of course* it's Invermartin again. I'm sure it'll be fine.'

'I'm on my way over there now, in fact,' said Esther, brightening, straightening and asserting all in one, terrifying, instant. 'I rang Joffy first thing this morning to let him know we weren't going to Balmoral, and he asked me straight over for coffee to make a start on the arrangements for holding the event at Invermartin. He couldn't have been nicer, Gail! People like that always manage to make you feel they've got all the time in the world for you, don't you find?'

'Can't honestly say I'd noticed, Esther.' That sounded rude. 'Erm, perhaps they do it so *subtly* that I never pick up on it?'

Ignoring this, Esther leaned forward and asked, in a wheedly voice, 'Gail, would you do me a *huge* favour?'

'Sure, I'll look after Magnus for you, no problem!' I

replied. The girl needed a break. 'He can watch TV with Emma. And me.' That last bit made me sound like more of a hands-on parent.

'No, it's not that. Would you come with me? Don't worry about the children, we can take them with us, Joffy adores little ones. Please, Gail? I would *really* appreciate your support.'

'What, right now?' I asked. ' Oh, sorry, I can't . . . I've got to . . .' Oh, heck. Got to what? I looked round. My kitchen, for once, was spotless. There was a casserole defrosting smugly beside the cooker, the party chaos was but a distant memory and I'd reached the bottom of the ironing basket, for the first time in weeks, at four o'clock this morning, having given up on persuading Emma to go to sleep and taken her downstairs so that she could doze off in front of a video. No, today it was a Stepford Wife kitchen, and no mistake. Stuart and the kids never knew from one day to the next whether I was going to whizz around from dawn till dusk creating harmony and cookies, or sit belching on the sofa complaining that there weren't enough hours in the day to get everything done, so why bother doing anything? I tried another tack.

'Esther, you know I'm not sure about Lord Brankin, so don't you think someone else might—'

'No! No, Gail, I really, really want you to get to know him better! He's *supah* underneath all that show, and he's so enthusiastic about the idea of the Toddle returning to Invermartin. In fact, Gail, I told him about you. About how you're the local girl who's so good at getting things done around here, and he really wants to meet you. Will you come? I'd *so* value your help. Please?'

'Did you remind him about my behaviour at the dance last year?'

'Oh, I didn't need to. He remembered.'

I bit my lip in shame. 'Ah. And?'

'Thought it was hilarious, ectually! Reminded him of his time in India, for some reason ... anyway, I need someone with loads of common sense, organisational skills and a ton of local knowledge, so you would be doing me, and the whole committee, the most *enormous* favour if you would at least consider ...'

'Fine!' Suddenly I *completely* saw her point. 'OK then! Let's go!'

'Don't you want to, er, freshen up a bit first?' Esther was trying not to stare at my battered red sweatshirt, jeans and clogs.

'Oops! Just about to say just that! Won't be a sec!' And I dashed upstairs excitedly, wondering what that strange, buzzing aura was that was floating round my head. I was sure I'd felt it before ... ah, yes, it was *flattery*! That strange, dangerous mix of manipulation and joy that comes from being *handled* by someone who needs something from you and lets you think you're in control of the situation. Last time I'd been aware of it was, oh, a couple of nights before when Stuart had wanted sex and I was knackered. He'd said something like, *'Well, I could do it by myself, I suppose, but there's nothing like the participation of a gorgeous woman to add that special something, so how about it?'* That had worked too.

Esther's voice followed me up the stairs, 'And could you bring down something clean for Emma to wear, too? Looks like a spot or two of Weetabix down her front.'

Invermartin estate lies a few miles to the north of the village of Loch Martin, and spans thousands of acres of picture-postcard, heathery Highlands. Ancient forests of twisted Scots pine and delicate birch shield trout lochs, noisy little streams and gung-ho waterfalls and above all that lot, the jagged tops of the Gorvaig Hills cluster round protectively, holding onto their snowy caps practically all year round. Furry and feathery creatures, the sorts that ought to be born with targets on their fronts, populate these hills, forests and skies, oblivious to the fact that if they just trotted, hopped or flew over to the next glen they'd fetch up in the Gorvaig Nature Reserve and be, *ipso facto*, protected. Although maybe they don't want to be protected. Maybe them stags, hares, pheasants and grouse hereabouts don't hold with no protection. Could be they reckon they can take care of their own womenfolk an' kin.

The silvery jewel in the Invermartin estate crown, however, is the four mile stretch of River Martin, which slices through the centre of the estate and meanders out into the sea via the sandy gateway that is Invermartin Beach. Being a favoured red-light route for horny salmon, the river is, inevitably, an A-list green welly and Land Rover magnet and so, during the fishing season, it attracts a constant supply of tweed people, thrilled to bits to fork out colossal sums of cash to stay in one of the four 'fishing houses' and spend entire days chest-deep in the river trying to get a fish to bite their hook, while their spouses and labradors pant in admiration from picnic rugs on the bank. It's the cash cow that funds the dream.

Esther drove like a madwoman along the single-track coast road that led to the entrance to the estate. 'Passing places are for wimps, don't you think?' she said breezily as postmen, forestry workers, dustbin lorries and buses were forced into the side of the road so that we could continue our progress unchecked. I waved sheepishly at them to say thanks as we barrelled past. 'Know these people, hmmm?' she asked, as we hurtled onwards.

'No, um, it's just that they're sort of, working, and we're, sort of, not, so I usually stop for them, so ...'

'For God's sake, this *is* work, Gail! If these people knew how much work we've got ahead of us to get this thing organised, for the benefit of their own community, they'd understand!'

Oh, heck. I was trapped in a big, posey car with Loch Martin's answer to Ivana Trump. I put my sunglasses on and spent the rest of the journey looking out of the side window pretending to be fluffily oblivious to the rules of the road.

We turned into the grounds of Invermartin estate, past the gingerbread lodge-house and the Strictly Private sign, and bumped along the potholed drive, which was lined with rhododendron bushes and framed overhead with mature specimen broadleaf trees, all carefully planted and nurtured for hundreds of years by generations of Brankins. Or at least, by the *staff* of generations of Brankins. It represented, I silently realised, a testament to the landowners' policy of keeping animals and ordinary mortals at bay in order to create a frozen-in-time haven for them to inhabit. I had always thought it beautiful, and tucked away the guilt and questions which came alongside.

We passed the little stone monument to eleven-year-old Eliza Brankin, who fell from her horse at that spot in the early nineteenth century, and was killed. It was a statue of a small girl holding a posy of flowers. I vividly remembered being brought here by bus with the rest of my classmates when I was about eleven, to draw the statue and hear the tale as part of our local history project. Of course the tragedy was pretty much lost on all of us back then, death being a concept none of us had ever concerned ourselves with, far less the death of someone in the last century. Now, though, I was taken by surprise by the sharp pang in my heart as I stared at the image of the long-departed Brankin family's beloved lost child.

The House heaved into view a little further on, a huge, granite, turreted symmetrical pile with massive oak front doors, greening slates on the roof and a jolly flagpole on top, which sported a ragged Union Jack. Shutters blanked out all of the first- and attic-floor windows, making the house look as though it was asleep, or at least dozing in the sunshine. I felt oddly nervous, and whispered to Esther, 'Lady Brankin's dead, isn't she?'

Esther was aghast. 'Dead? *Noooo*! They divorced years ago. She's farming ostrich in Puerto Rico!'

'Right. Children?'

'None. Tragic.'

Speaking of children, ours had both crashed out in the back, worn out by the heat of the car and the pressure of ignoring each other for such a long time. Esther opened the windows and we left them where they were and approached the front door.

'Shouldn't we be going round the back?' I hissed. 'Mightn't he set the dogs on us for being so presumptuous?' Esther gave me a killer of a look and rang the doorbell.

After a short while Lord Brankin opened the door to us, a huge smile on his face, and swooped down the steps to kiss Esther on both cheeks. He was tall, greying and military, around fifty or so, dressed in caramel corduroy trousers, a woollen waistcoat, striped shirt, and tartan slippers, and he was closely followed by a number of panting dogs – could have been four, could have been forty – who loped breathlessly past us to wag and sniff and squat on the lawn.

'Esther!' he exclaimed. 'How marvellous. Come in, come in! And this must be ... Mrs Macdonald! Hello! We've met before, I think.'

'It's Gail. Pleased to meet you. Um, again.' We shook

51

hands. Somewhere I recalled reading that it was naff to say 'pleased to meet you', but too late now. It was official – I was common.

'We've left the children sound asleep in the car, Joffy,' said Esther. 'Do you think we might . . .'

'Sit where you can keep an eye on them? Just about to suggest that, my dear! We'll go in the library.' He showed us into a large, wood-panelled room to the right of the entrance hall, which was lined with the sort of leather-bound books which I imagined nobody would have looked at for a hundred years. Probably stuffed with the copper-plate memoirs of a thousand minor toffs who travelled the high seas sticking pins in butterflies' heads and dissecting pygmies. I looked out of the huge bay window at Esther's Range Rover which held our, still definitely breathing, children, then my gaze travelled across the lawn, down the drive, and far out to sea. It was idyllic. 'There we go! I'll bring some coffee. Just milk, no sugar, no? That's what you young gels usually have!'

'Perfect!'

'Great, thank you.'

He left us to take in our surroundings. The sun warmed the room and its contents so that an ancient, musty smell of warm leather books, rugs and wood enveloped us. It was thick, and comforting, like being in someone's arms. Esther sat, looking completely relaxed. She seemed to somehow appear bigger, like she *belonged* within her space. Whereas, in spite of the warmth of the sunlit room, when I sat down on the squishy chintz sofa I crossed my legs and tensed my shoulders, ready to jump up again and apologise at a moment's notice.

We smiled awkwardly at each other, the room silent apart from the *lop, lop, lop,* noises coming from a fat old Labrador who was contentedly licking his balls on a rug

52

under a table in the corner. My gaze idled back out of the window, where after a few moments I made out a red pick-up truck approaching up the drive. It was laden with what looked like freshly cut logs, and it continued its bumpy progress round to the back of the house. I stood up to look more closely into the cab. The driver appeared familiar, somehow, but from that distance I couldn't quite place him.

'Something wrong?' asked Esther, a little sharply.

'No, nothing, just thought I saw someone I knew.'

'Well, sit down, then, for God's sake.'

Lord Brankin returned carrying three mugs of not quite hot enough instant coffee and a packet of rich tea biscuits, which he handed round clumsily before sitting down in the battered leather armchair opposite us.

'Bad show by the royals, if you ask me, Esther,' he began. 'But then, Balmoral's loss is my gain, what?' Esther chortled poshly. 'Now then,' he went on, 'how are we going to approach it this year – Toddle round the Daffodil Wood as before, then indoors for the ball? Or were you planning on hiring a marquee?' He certainly knew how to get straight to the point, old Joffers. God, but his coffee was foul.

'Well, that would be...' commenced Esther.

'Only, there's a slight problem with holding it indoors, as I shall have some hice guests to stay that weekend, so it may be a bit crowded, I'm afraid.'

'Oh! Quite! No problem at all!' brayed Esther, obviously choosing not to concern Joffy with the trifling detail of the colossal expense of marquee hire. 'Marquees are such *fun* in summertime, and with this glorious backdrop, a marquee will be just splendid! Don't you think, Gail?'

'But what about the toilet issue?' I replied. It wasn't exactly received chit-chat, but it *was* pertinent, and I was

53

inexplicably anxious to showcase my switched-on, thinking-local credentials at the earliest opportunity.

'Toilet tissue?' queried Brankin.

'Not tissue, *issue,*' I corrected. 'The issue of the toilets! Remember last year when the Portaloos toppled over?' Certainly Stuart would never forget it, having had to leap for his life to avoid getting engulfed in slurry when Esther's rugby club friends tried at one o'clock in the morning to lift them to a less muddy spot.

'Good point, my dear,' said Joffy, not unkindly. 'Why don't we adopt standard marquee procedures this year – girls in the hice, boys over the hedge – easy peasy!' I nodded, and made a mental note to forewarn all known al fresco thrill-seekers not to attempt a quickie too near the tent in case of unexpected showers. Or – then again – perhaps I wouldn't. We'd need all the laughs we could get.

'But Joffy, won't the hice be too far away?' asked Esther. 'Or is the marquee to be closer to it this year?'

'Hmm, you're right. Tell me, how far would a young lady be prepared to walk to spend a penny these days? In my party days gels'd go for miles...'

'Good question, Joffy – what do you think, Gail? How far would *you* go for a wee?'

They both looked at me earnestly. This was a most unpromising conversation. And that question was just, just *far* too hard.

'Oh, never mind, we'll check out the distance and if it's too far we can just hire Portaloos like last year, don't you think?' Esther went on, running out of patience. 'We'd probably have much more flexibility that way, what? Now, regular or deluxe?'

'Sorry?'

'Loos, Gail, loos.'

'What's the difference?'

'Towels, heating, sanitary disposal...'

'Excellent!' Joffy burst in, 'perheps you can sort that out later, what?' He looked most uncomfortable. I doubted whether the phrase 'sanitary disposal' had ever been uttered before in the library of Invermartin Hice. House.

'I must say,' he went on, 'it's terrific of you people to be taking on an event of this size; there are precious few formal balls these days, and most of these are monopolised by people from down south. Can't think when I was last at one, in fect, imagine that!' He looked a little wistful, and drummed his fingers on the arm of the leather chair, making a noise like a little cantering pony.

I could almost see the light bulb go on above Esther's head. 'Would, would *you* like to bring a party of friends to the ball this year?' she asked. Your house guests, perhaps? It would be delightful ... er, we'd be delighted ... you'd be delightful ...'

'Oh, Esther, my darling, I'd *love* to! Thank you so much, you *are* kind.' His whole, large-nosed face lit up with pleasure. I felt quite touched.

'We'd do you a special ticket rate, of course, given that you're the host,' went on Esther, before noticing Joffy's face cloud over. 'Oops, did I say that out loud? What I meant was, you needn't worry about paying for tickets, of course ...'

'But we'd love a prize for the grand raffle!' I put in, before Esther did the event out of any more revenue. 'Maybe a week's fishing?'

'A *week*?' he squealed. 'That's worth over two thousand pounds! A *day*, perhaps ...'

'Thank you so much. You *are* kind.' Ooo! I appeared to be finding my social feet. 'Perhaps you could be making one or two notes, Esther?' I suggested with a smile.

'OK,' said the by-now-flustered Esther, pulling out her checklist and attempting to compose herself. 'Now, yes, right, all we need to sort out now is the final positioning of the marquee, parking and access arrangements, and the Toddle route.'

'Everything, then,' I said unhelpfully.

'Yes, well, not to worry, Steven, my factor, can sort you out about all that.' Lord Brankin said, waving his hand regally. Honestly, no wonder he had all the time in the world for people if *other* people did all his work. But hold on, did he say ...

'Steven?' I puzzled aloud. 'Not Steven *Henderson*?' Recognition was dawning, and my ears were suddenly growing peculiarly hot.

'That's the chap! Comes from the village. I'll fetch him. He's just back from repairing some fencing at the forestry plantation. Know him, do you?'

'Erm, yes, we were at school together.' *Stevie Chip!* So *that's* who had driven past a few moments ago. Stevie Chip! Named after his father, who was named after *his* father, who had been a carpenter. Oh. My. God. I hadn't set eyes on him we'd left school – Stevie Chip! All in a jumble I wondered if he still looked the same, still sounded the same, even whether he was any less arrogant now than he was at age seventeen, when he bragged that he'd been out with every girl in our registration class. Well, 'out' being a relative term, of course. One liaison had lasted almost an entire lunch hour and took place from start to finish in the senior girls' toilets. Another went on for a full two weeks and two days, ending with a blazing row about lovebite positioning. *Aaaaargh*. That had been me. Great kisser, though.

Esther was looking at me in amusement. Oh, flipping, *no*! What little composure I had managed to muster was now slithering down the acceptability scale in direct proportion to the rise in temperature of my cheeks. One of the biggest hazards of returning to live in the place where you grew up is being unexpectedly confronted with the Stevie Chips of this world and having to deal with them like the adult you're meant to be. Whereas in London I could sit in wine bars and trade fantastically non-specific adolescent experiences with everyone else, here those adolescent experiences appeared to be opening the door, walking into Joffy Brankin's library and sitting down opposite me. But, hang on – *oh my! Didn't he turn out well!*

'Gail!' he exclaimed when he saw me, all of a sudden looking none too sure of himself. For once. 'Er, that your car?'

'Hi, Stevie. No, it's Esther's. Esther Smith, Stevie Chi— Steven Henderson.'

'How do you do?' enquired Esther coolly, looking in another direction, as one probably does when addressing the help.

'Pleased to meet you. Nice car!'

'Marvellous!' said Joffy exuberantly. 'Now, Steven, if you would be so kind ... ?'

'Oh, yes, no problem, er, Gail, would you, ah, care to step outside?'

'Why, do you want a fight?' I asked, dumb, dumb, dumbly. Lord Brankin and Esther looked at me in surprise. He really *had* turned out a treat, though, even if the moleskin plus fours were a bit much. His ultra-short dark brown hair and tanned skin, glistening slightly with outdoorsy good health, lent him the appearance of a rugby player who'd somehow come adrift from his ruck. Wow. Just as good-looking as before, only, well, more so. Stevie Chip!

He smiled and stood up. 'Not at the moment, thank you, but I believe I am to show you where to position certain things?'

And he didn't mean lovebites. Feeling more than a little shown up, red as a school paint pot and clumsy as hell, I followed him outside without saying any more. Esther stayed indoors to talk to Joffy about fishing. Stevie waited while I clambered into the back of the Range Rover to check the sleeping kids' vital signs, then we walked together down the semi-circular stone steps onto the rhododendron-fringed lawn.

'Marquee right over there?' he asked, pointing beyond the eastern edge of the lawn, almost to the horizon, where in the distance a flat field bordered the lush woodland.

'Fine. I didn't know you were the factor here, have you been here long?' Could I have found a more boring question if I'd tried? And why was I bothered?

'Factor? Is that what he's calling me now?' He laughed. 'Been here a couple of years, I think. Car parking in the lower field down there be all right?'

'Fine. Where were you working before? I haven't seen you around before. What have you been up to?' Gail the Interrogator closes in on her prey...

'Been in Australia for a few years, Glasgow for a few years before that, worked for dad for a few years before that . . . Toilet block?'

'We're not sure if we're having one.'

'Oh. Right. Course you're not. You lot *don't,* do you?' He was grinning mischievously.

'Cheeky git!' I shouted, swiping at his middle with my arm.

We laughed, and then looked at each other.

'Last time I saw you it was your wedding photo in the *Courier,* years ago,' he said.

'And very delightful I looked, too, just to save you the trouble of having to say it.'

'Weren't you wearing a *crown*?'

'I most certainly was not! My hair was up, and I had this antique headpiece ... it was rather a blurry photo, actually ...' I was flabbergasted that he remembered.

'You married?'

'Me? Nah. I was engaged for a bit, in Australia, but, no, still fiancée-free, as they say. Still on the lookout!'

'I guess the only unattached birds you see up here lay eggs and get shot,' I said. 'Sorry, that was rude.'

'Don't worry. I get by.'

I bet he did, as well. We ambled to the edge of the lawn and into the Daffodil Wood, to check out the path for the Toddle. The yellow carpet of flowers was dying in the late spring sunshine and the rhododendrons and azaleas were squeezing out their last bits of bloom for the season. A heavy scent of vegetation, following the overnight rain, filled my nostrils and made me dizzy.

The Toddle route was only a few hundred yards long. It followed an earthen path, which had been forged by centuries of fishers, fowlers and fresh-air seekers and their faithful hounds, and stretched down to the riverbank, where the huge trees gave way suddenly to the wide flash of slowly meandering river. We followed the route in silence, before stopping for a second on the tiny fishing platform at the water's edge, to admire the view.

'Better make sure none of the nippers takes a flying leap here,' Stevie said. 'I'll string some tape up along these posts to keep 'em out.'

'That's very kind of you,' I replied.

'Can't have 'em scaring the fish, can we?'

'Ha ha. Do you enjoy working here?'

'I do, actually, it's good. Brankin's not a bad guy to

work for, and I'm pretty much my own boss. As long as I keep the place under control, sort fences, deal with trees and logs, and run around after the fishing folk looking respectful, he doesn't bother me much.'

'Fair enough.'

'It's good to see you, Gail,' he said, in a different tone of voice.

'You too,' I replied.

'I, erm, heard from my folks about your baby, a few years back. Sorry.'

Flinching, I glanced at his face, which was gazing at the ground. 'Thanks. Me too.'

We completed the circular route and returned to the lawn, where Esther was sitting, with the very much awake Magnus and Emma on either side of her, looking murderous. There appeared to be a row in progress. A pile of macerated white flowers on Esther's lap indicated that she had tried to engage the children in a charming session of daisy chain making, which had obviously backfired.

'Come on, *spit them out*!' she was hissing at Magnus. '*Do as you're told*!'

'Hello!' I said brightly. 'Everything OK?'

'*Fine!*' she snarled, before putting her forearm around Magnus's neck, manoeuvring him flat onto the grass with a thud, prising his jaws apart and forcibly removing a wad of chewed daisy from the back of his throat. '*Bad boy*! I said *don't* eat the necklace! Shall we go, Gail?' She stood up, tucked Magnus under her arm and, ignoring Stevie, started marching towards her car.

'I haven't thanked Lord Brankin for the coffee,' I protested.

'He had to go and make some calls,' came the frosty reply.

'Oh.' I turned to Stevie. 'It's good to see you again.

Thanks for your time. You must have loads to do.'

'No problem. I'm knocking off now, anyway. See you around!'

He took off at a jog round to the back of the house. Emma badly needed a nappy change so I scanned the area for onlookers, pulled the changing bag from the car, laid her down and did the deed on the lawn directly in front of the house, much to Esther's mortification. I looked up at her. 'Would you prefer I changed her on the table in the billiard room?' I asked. 'Only I didn't think you'd want to sit in the car with the windows open all the way back to Loch Martin. Shan't be long!'

'Just bloody hurry up,' she growled.

We loaded everyone back into the car and set off in silence. Halfway back down the drive we heard the roar of an engine approaching behind us. Esther pulled over crossly, and a huge motorbike thundered past. The rider, kitted out from head to foot in black leather, gave us a cheerful, ultra-cool and not altogether unsexy biker's wave before vanishing into the distance.

There was a distinct feeling of returning to the real world as we reached the gates back at the entrance to the estate.

'Could you stop here for a second, please, Esther?' I asked.

'Forgotten something? Because it's really not good form to go back when Joffy's so busy . . .'

'No, it's not that. Won't be a sec.' I opened the door and got out of the car, breathed in the salty freshness of the coastal air, then deposited the old nappy in His Lordship's bin.

Chapter Four

'I didn't know you needed glasses!' I exclaimed, arriving at the door of Inverness Library, where a flushed-looking Theresa greeted me with a hug. Her hair was scraped into a tight ponytail which bobbed high on the back of her head, and zappy little black rectangular frames sat at an intellectual angle halfway down the bridge of her nose.

'Only for writers' group,' she whispered back. 'Clear glass – makes me look serious. Come and get a drink, you're going to need it.'

We entered the main reading room and wound our way through a small knot of assorted people, to a small table by the window where a bony woman of about fifty, with razor-cropped salt-and-pepper hair, was squirting hock from a wine box into polystyrene cups.

'Bonnie, this is my friend Gail,' Theresa announced, as we shook hands. 'Gail, this is Bonnie MacLeod, our tutor. Gail, Bonnie has actually had a book *published*!'

'Bonnie, have you *really*?' I gushed, sensing a Holy Grail moment in Theresa's estimation, while Bonnie made an aw shucks! gesture and handed me my warm white wine. 'What's it called?'

Bonnie came over all flappy. 'Oh, it's called *Kayla and*

the Wolverine, you may have heard of it in an adolescent education context?' she replied in an unexpected Geordie accent. 'It's about a young girl's journey through puberty, focusing on parallels in nature?'

I hadn't. My stupid smile grew wider in panic. 'Do you know,' I gushed even more deeply than before, 'I think I very well just might have done! How very exciting! Wasn't it the one where ... where ... that's right, it's ... oh my, but I mustn't monopolise you, you must get this sort of thing all the time! Oops! More people needing wine! Gangway, Theresa! Let's mingle! Bonnie! A pleasure!'

'I'm the one who's meant to be nervous!' laughed Theresa, as she steered me, in true Theresa-fashion, towards two middle-aged men who were standing a little apart from the otherwise mostly female crowd. They stopped talking as soon as they saw her approach, and rolled onto their backs to have their tummies scratched. Metaphorically, anyway.

'Gail, this is Ralph, and this is George.' We shook hands solemnly. Ralph had a lean, interesting face with slate-coloured eyes, and he wore a hairy tweed suit with an open-necked orange linen shirt underneath. His handshake was dry and papery. George was pretty much his physical opposite, well, apart from the gender, obviously – beard, pot belly, lumberjack shirt, low-slung jeans, plumbers' crack, clammy little paws, etc., but I saw at once that it was to George that Theresa seemed to be directing the bulk of her smoulder.

This was a bit of a typical ploy of T's, to pay flirty attention to someone, under the nose of the far more attractive person – I'd seen her do it several times over the past few years, usually with killer results. Not having expected tonight to be a hotbed of sexual intrigue, I studied Ralph a little more closely, while at the same time floundering for some chit-chat to fill the ensuing slightly awkward silence. Ralph was a good bit taller than the rest of us, and he looked down upon our circle without actually tilting his head, until I was aware of my scalp tingling under his scrutiny. And one of them, definitely, was wearing Eau Sauvage.

'So, you're both writers as well?' I finally asked, an octave or two higher than normal, taking a large swig of the thick wine and inwardly congratulating myself on yet another feat of conversational Polyfilla. George began rocking his head and joshing and mumbling stuff like *'Ooo-er, missus, not us, we just scribble stuff down! Just a hobby! Blimey, writers? Us? Amateurs, nothing more!'* in a kind of practised way, and Ralph just stood there looking enigmatic and wry. I decided that he probably counted himself just a pesky discovery or two away from rightful greatness, and looked forward to Theresa wiping the floor with him when it came to the readings. Both clutched bulging folders of loose-leaf paper and I could feel the onset of a long evening. The library was overheated and brightly lit, and I wondered how soon I'd be able to drag Theresa away to the pub for a proper drink and a gossip, but somehow she looked so alive and happy, stroking George's arm and greeting fellow group members with a raise of her cup, that I told myself to behave and try to enjoy her night.

'And you're a *Ralph*, then, rather than a *Raiph*?' I pressed on, sensing glumly from Ralph's demeanour that the encounter was heading for the rocks.

He looked down his nose at me (brilliantly demonstrating how it can be done), and sniffed, 'Correct,' before using the top of my head as a horizon from which to scan the rest of the room.

'Theresa here's our star, aren't you?' fawned George, looking at her chest lovingly. Ralph's expression twitched.

'Oh, hardly!' she replied, but her body language acknowledged the truth of the statement, and when Bonnie summoned us to take our seats she was off like a greyhound from a trap to take her place in the centre of the semicircle of writers.

Bonnie kicked off. 'Hello everyone, and thank you so much for coming along to our group to support your friends this evening! Now, has everyone got a drink?' *Not a real one*, I thought, draining the vile liquid and cracking the cup in the process. 'I suppose most of you know each other, but for those who don't, we have George, Myra, Elizabeth, Theresa and Ralph, who have all been working very hard this session on various aspects of the written word.' She was an expressive speaker, gesticulating with long slender arms at each phrase. *Thank you for coming! Working very hard!* 'Now, in my opinion Creative Writing is an organic, natural process, and to some extent that process should not be tampered with, but there are certain aspects which can always be learned, to make the end result work just that little bit better, wouldn't you agree?' She looked round at her class, most of whom nodded, but, judging by Ralph's face, he thought perhaps not. 'Each and every one of us here is a perfectionist to a greater or lesser extent with our work and our perception of it; and my task has simply been to bring out that perfection in an accessible way.'

Scratching my head, and wondering how the hell anyone could be a perfectionist to a *lesser* extent, I looked to Theresa for a sisterly snigger, but she was rapt, nodding in agreement at Bonnie's speech. Which seemed to be going on a bit. 'Each week,' she divulged, 'I have set a little assignment, dealing with various aspects of technique, and this week's, you'll all be pleased to hear, is simply, "brevity"!' A polite titter tickled the walls of the room. 'Brevity is not always a good thing, but each one of us needs to learn the discipline of condensing our creativity, while still retaining the essence of our art in the process. Now, I haven't heard anyone's pieces yet, so I'm looking forward to the readings as much as everyone else. The task I set the class, with "brevity" as the theme, was to tell a story in a hundred words or less!' Yippee! I could smell the Guinness in O'Flaherty's Irish Theme Bar already. 'And if we've got time at the end, then we can enjoy hearing some of the other work which the group has prepared for earlier sessions.' Oh, damn and buggery blast. 'OK, we seem to be missing a few people tonight – do we have Henry?'

'Working,' said George.

'Freda?'

'Too nervous, I think!' Myra bit her lip guiltily, as though divulging a secret, which she probably was.

'No friends, more like,' said Ralph nastily. Theresa sniggered and dug him in the ribs.

'And Jeremy will be late,' whispered Elizabeth. 'He can't come out until he's helped put his children to bed.' More sniggers. I sensed a group dynamic distilled from pure artistic poison, and began to think that this might be quite good fun, after all. In fact, I definitely had an 'oh, fuck it' moment coming on. Yup, there it was ... taking a deep breath, I stood up, ignored Bonnie, who looked a bit startled, and walked over to the drinks table, where I squirted myself another cup of syrupy alcoholic piss. Nobody else moved a muscle.

'Oh, so sorry, anyone else want more wine?' I asked, filling the silence. 'T?' She grinned and shook her head. A beat, and then about seven other audience members began to get to their feet and shuffle over to the wine box, where they formed an orderly, if a bit giggly, queue. Things had definitely started to brighten up in Inverness Library.

'Good on ya, lass,' whispered an old woman with a suspiciously red nose as she returned to her seat with two full cups of wine.

Bonnie resumed speaking after everyone had sat back down and had a slurp or two. 'OK, shall we start? Who would like to go first – don't be shy now!'

It was like watching a group of eight-year-old children being asked to sing a song. They looked shyly at each other and then at their feet, blushing and pointing, riffling their sheets of paper and looking beseechingly at Bonnie to pick someone else rather than them.

Luckily, Bonnie had her own agenda. 'OK, OK, why don't I get things going by reading mine, and then we'll go round the group in seating order, all right?'

She moved from the edge of the group to the centre, puffed out her chest like a Muscovy duck, and began to read from her notepad.

'*The young male sought truth, in the earth and in the air. His whiskers were his guide, his penis his radar. He snuffled spoor, seeking, sensing, sex and solace. The canyon opened out and his vulnerability magnified, hardened. But there was a compelling force which drove him on. The female did not want to be found, yet, found, she found herself, and in that finding, they found truth as one creature. Their coupling was fierce, frenzied, vicious, yet inevitable. Pain, pain, pain, the crank handle of the world, the mystery solved, continuation assured. They rest. They lick. They sleep.*'

She looked up at us and waved away our applause before any had come, so we applauded. I offered Theresa a puzzled look, which she ignored.

'OK, thank you for that,' exclaimed Bonnie, 'though I have to confess to a teensy weensy cheat here – I picked that text from the manuscript of my second adolescent educational novel – *Kahota the Young Cougar*!'

'Oh, Bonnie, you ratbag!' interjected Myra. 'There was us thinking you'd done your homework as well.'

'I know, I know, slap wristie-time! But I just felt that the piece contained all the things we'd been discussing last week – quest, conflict, resolution – all in one bite-sized chunk, as it were! And the rest of the book's just as good, I might add!'

Raucous laughter.

'OK then, who's next? George! Don't be shy, love, just do your best.'

George stood up and stroked his beard with his free hand. He cleared his throat noisily.

'Um, this isn't very good . . .' he began.

Bonnie interrupted. 'Now Georgie, what did I say? If you announce that something's not very good before you start reading, then it almost certainly *isn't*. Have some confidence, and *stop* doing that!'

Thus with his remaining confidence shot to pieces and hands all a-tremble, George began, in a low, soft voice:

'How sly, to hoodwink me so; leading me softly to a hidden place, on bare feet which moments before danced softly in long grass? But follow I do, chancing teasing and disaster, which for now are one and the same. Swiftly she turns towards me and we are in a glade, where sunlight rains lightly on her hair and gentle wisps of air whisper entreaties to risk all for a single kiss. I reach out to her, full of fear. Will she lend me a small fragment of my heart so that I can place it back into my promise?'

George found his shoes very interesting after he sat

down, and ignored the warm applause. I am impressed and mildly turned on. Realising that the absence of a neck, and the presence of a tattoo proclaiming *Raith Rovers Forever,* were no barriers to a romantic soul, I stared hard at Theresa to see whether her reaction was similar to mine, but she was whispering something to Ralph, who listened intently with a little sneer on his face.

'See, Georgie?' squealed Bonnie, 'you *were* listening! Conflict, mystery, *and* references to nature!' She turned to face us. 'I can't overstress to the class the essential of bringing nature into our work. It grounds everything we do – and, ahem, it sells rather well too! OK, Myra, your turn. Now Myra has been responsible for bringing a touch of homespun charm to our group – I hope you're not going to disappoint us this week, Myra!'

Myra took the floor. Homespun from blue perm to brogue, I crossed my fingers and willed her to start shouting out a pageful of swearwords and dirty sex.

'Who would have thought that so much happiness can be created by a simple rhubarb crumble? Fresh-picked from the garden, the crisp, pink stems cook down under their sweet topping into a dessert so delicious, it will melt even the hardest of hearts! And if you top it with home-made custard, the real thing, mind you, not the powder, then you truly have the food of the gods! Sometimes I sprinkle a little ground ginger onto the fruit and add a dash of orange juice instead of water, but whether you're entertaining or just making a warming pudding for the'

She sat down.

'Go on, please,' urged Bonnie. I leaned forward to hear more, interested despite myself in the ginger and orange juice twist, but Myra stayed put, looking anxious.

'Well, that was a hundred words,' she explained, 'so, erm, I scribbled out the rest ... oh dear, I knew this

wasn't going to be a good week! I thought that as long as
we did at least a hundred words then that was all you
wanted!'

Bonnie put her hand on her shoulder. 'It's all right,
Myra, that was lovely. Now, let's ...'

'I know!' Myra burst out. 'I'll do my Christmas tree
description! Remember my Christmas tree description?
When we all had to describe something memorable? I've
got it right here.' She started rummaging through her
folder, as Bonnie restrained her a second time.

'Maybe we'll finish up with the Christmas tree description later on, Myra? After everyone else has had a go?'
Myra looked a little crestfallen, and her folder slid off her
lap onto the floor, spilling loose-leaf paper around her
feet. 'OK, Elizabeth, your turn!' Now there was a
distinctly worried inflection in Bonnie's tone. 'How are
you tonight, Elizabeth, love?'

'Not too bad,' Elizabeth replied in a raspy voice, but
her appearance shrieked *'LIAR!!'* She was vaguely Gothic,
with wiry black hair, translucently pale skin, lots of black
eye make-up and silver crucifix earrings. About thirty or
so, she hugged herself inside a black woollen shawl, and
when she rose to her feet her hook-and-eye boots disappeared beneath a fringed black cotton skirt, and the thin
hand which popped out of the shawl clutched a tiny
notepad.

*'Alone at last, I stumble to the pan. It yawns to greet
my desperate mouth as my wet fingers force themselves
down my greedy throat. Then, too fast, comes the exquisite beginning. Tumbling out, filth and guilt and fear, more
and more, splattering and splashing, until I am left with
nothing but bile, dizziness, and a numb triumph. And the
stench! The sour, vile stink of my weakness assaults my
nostrils but cannot harm me. I am purged and free, and I*

70

have not been discovered. Only the sewer knows my secret, so it is halfway to the grave already.'

Well, she'd bloody well let the cat out of the bag now. Snorting with inappropriate laughter right in the centre of the thumping silence which greeted the end of Elizabeth's piece, I had to follow through with an odd sort of choking display to make it look as though my wine had gone down the wrong way.

A few people clapped, and Bonnie stood up again. 'Thank you, Elizabeth, for that, that, heart-rending' (*and gut-wrenching,* I thought) 'piece.' She turned to the audience. 'Elizabeth here has challenged us every week by tackling subjects which in some circles would be considered taboo, haven't you, pet?' Most of the audience shifted uncomfortably in their seats, and Elizabeth nodded. 'We are a broad church here at writers' group, and encourage freedom of expression, so, so, thank you, Elizabeth, and, erm, best of luck with everything!'

'I dunno what you mean – everything I write is pure fiction,' she rasped, outstaring Bonnie defiantly. 'I've got a friend who wants me to turn my self-harm essay into a screenplay, actually.'

'Really?'

'Yeah. He's applying for funding for it right now. Plan is to get something set up for next year's Glasgow Film Festival. There's a really good vibe about it.'

'Fantastic!' bluffed Bonnie. Elizabeth looked ready to tell us more, but Bonnie was having none of it. 'OK, Theresa, have you done your homework this week, love?'

'Yup, got it right here!' Theresa simpered, going a bit Vicar of Dibley on us. She stood up. As usual I gazed dispassionately at her long legs, flat tummy and miraculous bust and wondered again whether it mightn't be too late to find a plainer best friend. To my surprise I found myself nervous for her, and I clapped enthusiastically until she glowered at me to stop, and took a deep breath.

'She is all alone in an empty room. The grey walls press in on her. Deep down inside she knows she wants to go home. Suddenly she sees a light at the end of a tunnel and she feels as if a weight has been lifted from her shoulders. She feels a tangle of emotions as she moves towards that light. The atmosphere is electric and she owes it to herself to do the best she can. She is afraid of the future but she knows what she has to do. With one supreme effort she is free once more.'

She sat down to light applause, with the exception of George who clapped like mad and gave her a great big thumbs-up sign.

Now, was it just me, or was that not very good? Had I missed the irony? Did a subtle meaning fly right over my head and fall to its death at the back of the room?

'Thank you, Theresa, that was very nice,' said Bonnie kindly. 'Theresa's work has been improving steadily since her arrival here at writers' group, and we all love having her, don't we?'

Jeepers, creepers.

'OK, last up, we have Ralph. Ralph, pet, have you done the exercise I set, or do you have something else you'd like to share with us?' She turned back to the audience, this time looking a touch strained. 'Ralph doesn't do my exercises. Which is fine, of course!' she added hurriedly. I somehow doubted that. I bet she had a pin-encrusted Ralph doll in her fridge. 'Ralph?'

He stood up and turned to Bonnie. 'Well, Ms MacLeod, you'll be happy to know that I actually *have* done your exercise tonight!' There was a gasp from the group. Bonnie covered her face with her hands in melodramatic shock, as Ralph went on, 'But I've brought more of my conceptual novel for reading out later on, however.'

Right, that did it. Theresa was offering me no help or eye contact whatsoever, the wine was horrible, the chairs bumbone-throbbingly hard, and I'd well and truly done my bit. If Theresa wouldn't leave with me the moment Ralph sat down then I was going to have to resort to my Basil Fawlty faint.

'Ms MacLeod, I have prepared a piece as you, erm, taught us, but I think you'll find after listening to it that brevity, per se, as an aspirational device, falls down on one vital premise – that of *explanation*. What is literature without education? Why does the writer put pen to paper? Why, so that one can realise an expression of what others can only dream of expressing!'

'But . . .' Bonnie began.

'No disrespect, Ms MacLeod, your intentions were sound, of that I have no doubt, and out of, um, respect for you I have succeeded in performing your task by invoking a genre which embraces the concept of "brevity" out of necessity to its readership.'

Bonnie looked as though she'd heard enough, and waved him away with her hand. 'Go on then, Ralph, pet, knock yourself out!'

Ralph produced a typewritten sheet of paper with a flourish, set his face in an expression of feigned buffoonery where his eyebrows shot upwards to his scalp, and began:

Once there was a Big Fat Rabbit called Edward. He lived in a burrow with his mummy and daddy and his little sister Tulip. One day, Edward and Tulip wanted to go out for a scamper, but Edward had grown too fat to get out of his burrow. He got stuck in the hole. Mummy pushed, Daddy pushed and Tulip pushed, but it was no use. The birds and the reindeer pulled from outside, but that was no use either. Three days later, a farmer passed by, pulled

Edward out by his ears, and took him home to be jugged.'

He tucked his paper away and sat down, beaming.

'Well, thank you Ralph,' said Bonnie wearily.

Poor Bonnie – Ralph was taking the piss and all we could do was applaud like a roomful of cowed dummies.

'And thank you Winnie the Pooh and Peter Rabbit!' I shouted. 'That's plagiarism!'

Everyone turned to look at me, and a few giggled. Ralph looked down upon me, then calmly replied, 'Is not all writing plagiarism to some extent?'

We glared at one another. Ralph was now wearing an infuriating smirk. 'Maybe, but you don't notice with the good stuff!' flew out of my mouth. 'Theresa, I have to go now. Thanks everyone . . .'

I grabbed my jacket from the back of my chair and marched out into the warm evening, half exultant at my escape, and half terrified that Ralph would come after me for more intellectual mugging. But I kept walking.

Theresa caught up with me at the door of O'Flaherty's, where I was loitering cautiously, wondering whether to go in and order a gin and tonic on my own.

'You didn't need to leave as well,' I said apologetically.

''S'OK. I was done,' she answered. 'Ralph's conceptual novel left me behind a long time ago, so I'm not missing anything.'

I got the gins in, and we sat on plump leather armchairs, the depths of which took us both by surprise when we leaned back and simultaneously almost spilled our drinks down our fronts.

'That'd be a new one,' remarked Theresa, 'sucking gin out of each other's cleavages!'

'Mmm. Waste not, want not.'

'So, what did you think?' she asked, lighting a fag. 'The truth, now!'

Oo-er. The truth. That meant the real truth, not the ponced-up oozy version I could use with almost anyone else.

'I think you were really brave, to stand up in front of all those strangers and read out your work like that . . .'

'But?' she prompted.

'But? How did you know I had a but?'

'I can tell you're hiding a great big, wobbly but. Spit it out, Gail, I need to know.'

'OK, well, I was amazed that someone as perky, and witty, and, well, as fun as you had written something so . . .'

'Say it.'

'So, well, airy-fairy, I suppose.'

'Airy-fairy? Not wishy-washy, then?'

'Not wishy-washy, per se, but maybe a tad artsy-fartsy?'

She looked a little crestfallen. 'I'm *trying* to be artsy-fartsy, Gail! I *aspire* to artsy-fartsy!'

'Why, though? Why not just be yourself? It'd be far more interesting!'

'Because Ralph told me to.'

'*Ralph?* When? Where? Why?'

'The other week. In bed. Apparently I'm shallow.'

'Ah.' I couldn't think of anything to say.

'Say something,' Theresa urged.

'I can't believe you're shagging Ralph! He's so, so . . .'

'Full of shit?' she suggested.

'*Full of shit!*'

'I know, I know. At least, I know *now*. It was only a couple of times, after writers' group. It's been over for ages.'

'What was he like?' Well, I had to ask.

She thought for a moment. 'I found him quite sexy at

the start – I like a bit of a mean streak in a man, and, well, I certainly found it in Ralph. He'd been writing for years, and the way he'd go on and on in the group, putting Bonnie down and reading out his stuff like it was some sort of *gift* to the rest of us ... well, I was just really impressed by the fact that he's got a novel on the go.' She shrugged and twisted her mouth. 'And even though none of us could make head nor tail of it, he's just got such a *belief* in himself and his work that you feel it's your own fault if you don't get it – there's something very enviable about that, Gail.'

'So who made the first move?' His novel was the last thing on my mind.

'Both of us, really. I'd lure him back home for coffee – not that we ever got round to actually *having* coffee – we'd just jump straight into bed.'

'You make it sound so easy,' I said, wistfully.

'Practice, my dear, practice. Anyway, he'd leave at about eleven ...'

'Married, then?'

''Fraid so. But when we weren't in bed, he spend most of his time, well, when he wasn't talking about the conceptual novel, telling me how I should be approaching my writing, how I must *think, think, think* before writing a single word. To plot, and plan, and pace, and perfect, and, oh, what was the other word he used ...'

'Pleasure?' I offered. 'Pancake?'

She narrowed her eyes. 'Something like that.'

'Well, I think he's screwed you up.'

'Maybe you're right.'

'And if *Edward the Big Fat Rabbit*'s anything to go by, you've definitely been listening to the wrong man.' I finished my drink. Theresa jiggled her chest at the barman, who nodded and started pouring two more gins.

'We'll not be so smug the day *Edward the Big Fat Rabbit* earns him the Smarties Award for Children's Literature,' mused Theresa.

I giggled. '*If* that happens, then I shall personally give him a blow job in the middle of Inverness High Street.'

'Personally? You mean rather than getting someone else to do it by proxy?'

'Why, would you want the job?' I asked.

She shook her head. 'Nope. I'm all Ralphed out, thanks.'

'Eeuww.'

I looked at her through the fug of the pub, wondering what it felt like to have a fling with someone, and then, after it finished, to carry on your day-to-day routine with that person still on the scene. One of the great unknowns for me, I guess. How can you have a conversation with an ex-lover without thinking about the pair of you naked? Without wondering if others are thinking of you both thinking about each other naked? It's one of the perks of being married, I guess, that the whole naked bed-thing becomes blurred in the eyes of the outside world. It's like, 'We know you do it, you've got the kids to prove it, but given that you're *married,* society has pixellated my psyche.'

'How did you finish with him?' I asked.

'I didn't. He explored all my depths and then, well, moved on to shallower waters, I guess. I don't know whether I just stopped offering him coffee, or he stopped asking for it – we just reached a point when we were through with each other. Good riddance, as well; I was on the point of enrolling with the Open University.'

'Bloody hell. Why did you never mention him to me before?'

She looked at me guiltily. 'I ration my married men

77

when I'm with you, Gail. You'd be horrified.'

'Really? No I wouldn't! Well, unless you were doing Stuart, of course.'

She laughed. 'Nah, I know when someone's out of my league. Not that I'd—' she began, suddenly serious, as though she'd crossed a line.

'I know,' I said, because I did.

'Anyway, what did you make of the others?'

I thought hard. 'Well, let's see, Bonnie's possibly a touch full of herself, am I warm?' Theresa nodded. 'But Ralph had no right to be critical of her in front of everyone.'

'All in a night's work for him, I'm afraid.'

'Let's see, who else was there – blue-haired Myra the rhubarb woman is what I think I shall be like in thirty years' time unless I smarten up my act a bit, Elizabeth the vomiting Goth needs help, although God help the person who tries to give it to her, and George . . . George?' I thought about George. 'George was lovely, actually. Great writer. Is he attached?'

'Don't think so,' she replied, absently. 'All his pieces are full of romance – it's kind of nice. The other week our homework was about "Dreams", and he wrote this lovely poem called "Message in the Clouds" – after he was finished Ralph said in front of the whole class that he thought it was recherché.'

'Recherché? What's that?'

'It's a Ralphism for crap.'

'Well, he'll be Recherché Ralph in my mind from now on, and serves him right, too. Message in the Clouds? Clouds? Mac Clouds, by any chance? Do you think he's after your teacher? Isn't her name Bonnie MacLeod?'

Theresa jolted. 'Don't be daft, Sherlock. Bonnie's a card-carrying lesbian.'

'Is she?'

'Well, she looks like one.'

'Maybe Ralph was right – you *are* shallow.'

'Perhaps I'm just recherché.'

I yawned and looked at my watch. 'Are we heading for home now, or is it going to be another of those midnight taxi affairs?'

Theresa and the barman were exchanging flirty smiles. 'Oh, the latter, I think, don't you? How about some cocktails?'

Chapter Five

Despite his early enthusiasm about the ball, Stuart remained less than keen to attend Esther's dance practices. He'd been grumbling about them in a general way pretty much ever since we'd first discussed them, but now, as we were waiting for Mum to arrive to babysit so that we could attend the first one, he really began to get into his stride.

'Shouldn't the whole point of evenings out be to relax and have a good time? I mean, if God had intended us to go out and do tricks for our supper he would have made us all seals! Or, or prostitutes!'

'I know.'

'And what's the point of learning dances we're never going to do again?'

'I know.'

'And whose idea was it to agree to go to the ball anyway?'

'Yours.'

'Yeah, well, maybe so, but that's only because I knew that *you* really wanted to go, deep down, in the very core of your being, the place where ... where ...'

'Angels fear to tread?'

'No, definitely not there, let's see ...'

'The sun don't shine?'

'That's the one! Here's your mother.'

Dressed down in a pink velour jogging suit, green golf visor and white sneakers, Mum could just about be made out emerging from her car behind a knitting bag, a nearly completed patchwork quilt and – oh my God – a portable fan heater.

'Just found it a little chilly here last time!' she said when she saw my dismayed face. 'You know how warm I like it at home. Not to worry!'

'Sorry, Mum,' I mumbled. 'The fire's on, and I'll turn the heating up.' I looked pointedly at Stuart, who ducked off obediently to crank up the system. 'Emma's nearly asleep, Thomas is in bed waiting for a story, there's tea and coffee on the tray, biscuits, orange cake and fruit, so . . .'

'Yes, yes, you go off and have a lovely time. Dancing lessons, isn't it?'

'Unfortunately, yes,' Stuart called through from the kitchen, looking, and sounding, not a little like Eeyore. 'Against my better judgement, I have to say.'

'Why, Stuart, do you know how to do the dances already?' she asked sweetly.

'Well, no, but . . .'

'Then won't you enjoy learning something new? Not afraid of being *shown up,* are you?'

From the first day she met him Mum had found the knack of homing in on Stuart's tender parts and nipping one or two of them, whenever they encountered one another.

'No, Marjorie, I just don't enjoy the sensation of being pushed around by stroppy women, that's all.' Rejoining us Stuart looked distinctly huffy, so I steered him swiftly towards the door.

'Best never to try the quickstep with me, then, laddie!' she trilled as we closed the door quickly behind us, just as Thomas emerged at the top of the stairs. From outside I heard Emma shriek, *'Danny! Biscuit!'* from her cot. Stuart and I looked at one another, and scarpered.

'This is nice,' I said to Stuart as he drove us the short distance to Esther's house. 'Just the two of us, off out to play!'

'Hrrmmhhphh.'

'At least we're getting some time out of the house, away from the kids?'

'Mhhrrrrmmmph.'

At this point I began to lose it. 'Oh, for God's sake, will you happy up?'

'Must I?' he whined.

'Stuart, I am *so* not at home to Mr Grumpy this evening . . .'

He rolled his eyes. 'I hear you, Commander. OK, activating Operation Cheer-up, Beep, beep! Uh-oh, we have a problem Houston, Operation Cheer-up deactivated, I repeat, Operation Cheer-up deactivated . . .' He started to weave the car around the road. 'Control malfunction!'

'Pack it in!' I barked. 'We go, we dance, we leave! It's simple! Behave yourself.'

Straightening up the car, he stared very hard at the road ahead for a few minutes. Then gave me an evil, sideways leer. 'I've got a better idea. How about we skip the dance practice, have a pint at the Martin Arms then go for a walk? Maybe round off the evening with a wee shag on the football pitch? Nothing major?'

'Would that be your dream night out?' I asked, scrutinising his wistful features.

'Well, I have to say it wouldn't be half bad.'

We were approaching the public football ground as he spoke, where about a dozen assorted local males were having a kickabout.

'OK,' he admitted, 'maybe not there. The duck pond, then? We could commandeer a rowing boat and do it in that?'

'Do you think any of them would have electric blankets installed?' I pondered, betraying my age.

'Hmmm, doubt it. We seem to have mislaid some of our youthful *abandon* somewhere along the way, don't we? Remember France?'

I giggled. Our first holiday together was in Brittany, sharing Stuart's barely-two-man tent in a dusty campsite near La Baule. We'd pitched the tent after dark, clambered in and immediately, and very enthusiastically, become sweaty, paid-up members of the Under-Canvas Club. Then afterwards as we were drifting off to sleep, we distinctly heard someone in the next tent fart. Just a little parpy one, mind, not even a major trump, so if we'd heard *that* ...

Esther's drive was awash with shiny four-wheel drive vehicles, parked at showroomy angles around the Grubers' Dormobile. *'Here a jeep, there a jeep, everywhere a jeep jeep,'* sang Stuart as we approached the door.

'Just behave,' I ordered. 'We're *not* staying for coffee, and *don't* get pissed. Esther! Well done for getting us organised!' *Mwah!*

Inside Beige World, otherwise known as Esther and Tony's sitting room, clusters of people were sitting and standing around with their 'make-the-best-of-things, we're here now' faces on. Esther's husband Tony was standing in the middle of the room with Kevin Barbour, Iain Moffat, and Martin Holmes, Sarah, Amber and Claire's respective spouses, getting worked up over a discussion about the quickest route by car through Edinburgh to

Murrayfield Rugby Stadium. Val and Janusz were sitting, child-free, side by side on the sofa, staring at a type-written sheet of paper.

'Where's Charity?' I asked them in surprise, surveying the contours of the rust-and-orange mohair jumper to make sure she wasn't in there somewhere. They pointed conspiratorially over their heads behind the sofa. I peered over, and there she was, fast asleep in a wicker carrycot.

'Oh! Isn't she good? How do you manage it?' Blah, blah blah.

Sarah, Amber and Claire were sitting on the floor near the fireplace, also studying typewritten sheets of paper, while Esther bustled around putting jugs of orange squash and assorted glasses on the coffee table, which had been pushed to the edge of the room. Looked like it was going to be a riotous evening.

Centre stage, however, went to the pert, chino-encased bottom of, presumably, Otto Mackintosh-Jones, as he bent over Esther's CD player to organise the music. I wished Theresa were here, so that we could have hissed an evil commentary on the proceedings and provided a sub-layer of entertainment without the others being any the wiser – what else are friends for? Stuart plunged headlong into the Great Route Planning Debate with worrying gusto, and I joined the girls.

There's a leafy lane on the far edge of Loch Martin, which leads to Martinside Farm. About five years ago, Donnie Edwards, the farmer, allegedly bunged the Planning Department a large wad of tenners in exchange for planning consent for five, enormous, 'executive homes' in one of his fields, and thus grew up Martinside Rise, the most preposterously out-of-place clutch of McMansions ever seen outside Disneyland. There are turrets, conservatories, flying buttresses, pools, decks, summerhouses, swirly gates, triple garages, loc-bloc driveways, burglar alarms and garden statuary as far as the eye can see. Just a little further on you get to Donnie's cow barn where, aged fifteen, I vomited vodka and black-currant over Donnie's son Malcolm, who I was attempting to snog at the time. But anyway, into Martinside Rise had moved Amber and Iain, Claire and Martin and Kevin and Sarah (the builder of the development and his parents snaf-fled the other two), lured by Countryside Living Solutions, Jacuzzi baths and built-in waste disposal. They'd become inseparably great mates, particularly since their babies had started to arrive.

Claire handed me one of the sheets.

'What's this?' I asked, gazing at it and failing to recog-nise many of the words.

'Crib sheet,' said Amber, as though it were obvious.

'Right! Of course. And, er, that would be ... ?'

'Written instructions about how to do the dances, so that we can practise at home,' Claire explained.

I gawped at the sheet. It was like a foreign language. 'What the bloody hell's a Machine Without Horses?' I said, louder than I intended.

'It's a dance, sweetie,' replied the owner of the chino-clad bottom. 'I'm Otto. I'm here to help.' He sounded friendly.

'I'm Gail.' I replied. 'I think I'm going to need you.'

'Then, what are we *waiting* for?' He clapped his hands sharply to bring us all to order. 'Everyone? *Everyone*? Hi! Hiya! I'm Otto, for those of you who don't know me of old – Amber, for instance, *hello*, my darling! Tiss tiss!' Amber reciprocated with an extravagant air-mwah. 'I just wanted to say quickly that Esther has *very* kindly invited me here to help you out with your dancing for your *sen-sational* post-Toddle ball!' He was standing ramrod-straight with his chin thrust upwards, arms slightly splayed and palms outstretched, and he spoke slowly and smilingly, in the manner of a pantomime Peter Pan explaining that it's audience participation time. His blond curly hair, startlingly blue eyes and lithe frame actually added together to make him an arrestingly beautiful man. If you can blot out the 'tiss tiss' thing, that is, which I just couldn't.

Esther looked as though she might faint with bliss. 'Oh, Otto, nonsense! It's *us* who are completely indebted to you, aren't we, everyone?' She nodded vigorously round the room at us and we nodded vigorously back, chucking in a few 'absolutelys' for good luck.

'Now, now, Esther my angel, let's save the vote of thanks until we've cracked a few of these babies on this dance list, shall we? Hmm? So, let's make a start. Can I assume that everyone knows the basics? All manage a basic *pas-de-basque,* reel of three, and slip-step circle round and back?'

Silence. Most of the others nodded modestly, murmuring things like 'more or less', and 'just about'. Val, Janusz and I looked blank so Otto said 'allow me to demonstrate' and flung himself into the middle of the room, parting the crowd with a sweep of his arms. Then, pointing his pumps and bowing briefly to an imaginary partner (who judging by his eye-level was taller than him) he fixed a wide smile on his face and began to jump-step from side to side. Then he wove a neat figure-of-eight with his partner and another spectral figure, and finally he danced round in a huge circle and back, neatly corralling us all (apart from Val and Janusz who were still on the sofa) in the centre of the room.

'Oh!' I burst out, as recognition dawned. 'We can do that, can't we, Stuart? That's school stuff!' Stuart stood tall with the rugby boys. Was he pretending not to hear?

'It is indeed! Splendid!' Otto beamed at me. 'Okey dokey, let's see. We'll start with some basic dance steps, which you'll find occur time and time again in different dances. Believe me, once you've learned who your corners are and then mastered the basic poussette, grand chain and teapots, you should have *no* trouble getting to grips with nearly all of the dances on the crib sheet!'

The others, for reasons I failed to understand, seemed *not* to be stifling immature giggles, as I was. I had that 'other people's clubs' feeling where you're the outsider who finds it all hysterically funny because you're actually feeling left out and everyone else (with the clear exceptions of Val and Janusz) *totally* gets it and hopes you're not going to make things less nice for them by behaving like an oik.

Otto teed up a CD then turned back to us all, clapping his pale hands. 'So, if you'd like to grab your beloved, or somebody else's beloved, for that matter, and line up with the men on one side of the dance and ladies on the other, I'll show you how to do teapots!'

Everyone grabbed hold of his or her spouse except Amber who grabbed Stuart, leaving me on my own because Amber's husband Iain had gone to the toilet. For a moment Stuart glanced helplessly in my direction, before turning his attention to his pert little partner. Then on Iain's return, fair play to the man, he sized up the situation and gave gallantry his best shot by saying, 'Oh, great, I get to dance with you, Jane!'

'Gail.'

'Gail! Of course! Did I say Jane? Gail, *may* I have the pleasure?'

We joined the ranks and watched as Otto demonstrated teapots with the top two couples, Esther and Tony and Stuart and Amber. After two minutes even I understood that teapots involved two couples joining right spouts to form a wheel and going round in a circle, then offering left spouts and going round the other way. Iain's hands were warm and incredibly clammy. Perhaps he was suffering a panic attack after his *faux pas* over my name. More likely, he hadn't dried them properly after his visit to the little boys' room. I surreptitiously wiped my palms on my hips.

'Well, tip me over and pour me out, that was easy!' exclaimed Stuart. Amber shrieked with laughter and patted his chest. 'Oh, *you*!' she simpered. I gave him my best Paddington cold, hard stare.

'Well done everybody! Good work!' Otto's motivational skills were second to none, anyway. 'Now, let's poussette, shall we? Esther?'

He led the unprotesting, in fact the positively *coquettish* Esther to the middle of the room as the rest of us shrank back respectfully. Then, clasping her hands, they started leaping about like flea-bitten Rumpelstiltskins, switching direction with each move and ending up, it seemed, more or less back where they started. Val and Janusz's faces were pictures of polite bafflement as the panting couple turned to face us all.

'Poussette!' declared Otto. '*Voilà*! An exquisite little device for changing places with the couple to your left! Let's all try it!'

We tried it, over and over again. After ten collisions and ten thousand apologies it seemed, after a bit of practice, to be a basic parking manoeuvre, forward, turn, adjust, turn, reverse, turn, forward, turn, brake. Iain and I practised it slowly and cautiously, holding hands and staring at our feet, school-disco-fashion. Then we'd tried it at a leap with the music and miraculously, after what must have looked like a roomful of prancing lunatics trying to stamp on an infestation of mice, the end result was that we all changed places with the couples on our left.

Val was puzzled. 'Wouldn't the same result be achieved by saying "excuse me"?' she whispered to me.

'Probably, but it wouldn't be so much *sheer, bloody, fun,*' I hissed back, drying my hands again on the back of the sofa while pretending to check the baby. Stuart came over. 'Managing all right?' he whispered sheepishly. 'Sorry I didn't dance with you – couldn't exactly turn Amber down, *could I?*'

'Positively thriving!' I answered in my out-in-public voice. Stuart returned awkwardly to Amber. Be afraid, my lad, be *very* afraid.

'Well, I don't think you people need my help at all! That was *fantastic!*' proclaimed Otto. I wondered what heights of praise he reached when people actually *were* fantastic. 'Let's just walk through the grand chain and then we can break for some of Esther's delicious-looking, umm, *squash!*'

The grand chain involved the women walking round one way and the men the other, doing right and left handshakes in turn in a sort of hauling-in-a-rope action. This one was easy. I skipped around happily, imagining that I was tossing each person over my shoulder as they passed, splatting them against the wall like some live game of Space Invaders. It looked to me, having got this far, that almost everyone there had a fair idea of how to do this stuff. Esther, Amber, Sarah and Claire were gliding through the moves without any real difficulty at all. I supposed they got extra-curricular lessons in country dancing at their boarding schools, along with chit-chat and hair-flicking, while people like me struggled at the local high school with topics like pregnancy avoidance, drug awareness and blending into the background.

At the yummy scrummy orange squash break, it occurred to me that Susannah was missing from the group. This was strange, as she'd said she was definitely coming when we arranged the times at the meeting, particularly as she'd mentioned that she needed me to countersign some letters as soon as possible. I sidled over to Esther who was sounding off to Otto about some mutual friend.

'... said she'd joined Overeaters Anonymous; well, *honestly*, Otto, I just came straight out with it and said, "Darling, *is* there such a thing as an anonymous overeater?" You should have seen her face ... *yes*, Gail?'

'Sorry to interrupt, but I thought Susannah was coming?'

Esther looked around. 'Oh yes – she's not here, is she? Strange, you'd think she would have let me know ... oh well, that should even out the numbers for the next dance – be a sweetie and put your empty glass on the draining board, would you? And here's mine.'

One and a half hours of sweaty palms, wrong turnings and apologies of varying degrees of sincerity later, we had more or less got to grips with the Eightsome Reel, the Scottish Reform and the Inverness Country Dance. Otto became a bit frazzled as Val, Janusz and I, his special needs pupils, constantly got it wrong ('Val, darling, I said figure of *eight*? That appeared to be a figure of *nine*?'), but the sense of achievement all round was palpable as we trooped out into the late evening air and back to our cars, thanking Otto and Esther profusely in that over-effusive, thank-God-we're-going way that you do. Stuart went straight on to the offensive as soon as the doors were closed. 'Not too bothered that I had to dance with Amber first, were you?'

'Course not.' Damn. Anything I said now would sound

childish. Oh well, childish it was, then. 'But I didn't appreciate being abandoned like a leper only to be rescued by the Incredible Melting Man, who couldn't even get my name right.'

'Sorry. What did you make of Twinkletoes?'

'It's not Twinkletoes, it's Dunny-brush. Actually, I rather liked him. He was very patient with us, all things considered. Esther was a pain in the arse, though.'

I looked back at Esther's beige house. Val had rushed back in, having obviously forgotten something, and re-appeared a moment later carrying the still-sleeping Charity in her carrycot. Checking my watch, I noticed it wasn't yet ten o'clock. It was still quite light outside, although they sky was extravagantly pink.

'Could we stop at Susannah's house?' I asked. 'If she's in I can sign those letters for her.'

'So, no rowing boat for me tonight, then?'

'It shouldn't take a minute. But no, no rowing boat, my love.'

Stuart yawned. 'Ah, well. D'you think Susannah might have any beer on offer?'

I had been looking for an excuse to see inside Susannah's home for a long time. It had been an old church hall, which had been converted by Susannah and her husband into a fabulous-looking house and studio. I'd never met her husband, but I knew of him, as he ran Paul Grant Interiors, a horribly expensive curtain design and fabric shop in Inverness.

It was that sort of Peeping-Tom's-paradise time of night, when everyone's lights are on but nobody has closed their curtains yet. As Stuart drove through the village, I spied in windows to check out what the popu-lation of Loch Martin got up to of a Tuesday night. Judging by the number of them staring fixedly at the

91

corners of their sitting rooms, their faces eerily lit up in blue, watching TV seemed to be number-one pastime. Apart of course from those lucky ones who got covered with someone else's sweat and ritually humiliated in Esther Smith's beige front room.

The curtains were drawn at Susannah's. But, undeterred, and with a forthrightness of which Esther herself would have been proud, I noticed that the hall light was on so I marched up to the door and rang the bell. Stuart stayed in the car to wait for the go-ahead to come in. The curtain twitched and, after a pause that ought to have been long enough for me to take the hint and go back to the car, Susannah opened the door. I beamed at her in a '*surprise!*' sort of way, and then stopped; she looked absolutely dreadful.

'Hi Gail,' she said in a deadpan voice. Her eyes had all but disappeared in pillows of puffiness, her nose was bright red and her hair, normally so neat and shiny-smooth, hung around her face in thick greasy strands.

'Oh, Susannah, you look choked! No wonder you couldn't go to Esther's with a cold like that! Not that you missed anything .... .' A tear made its way from the slit that was once her eye down a well-worn track on her cheek. 'Ah. Right. What happened? Do you want me to go? Or stay?'

She broke down into sobs and fumbled up her sleeve for a paper hankie. 'It's nothing. I'm fine. Sorry.'

I went towards her and put a tentative arm around her. 'Susannah, what's up?'

'Paul's left me and I don't know what to do.' Blowing her nose loudly, she shook her head violently and tried to collect herself. 'Come in, I'll get those letters, they're on the desk somewhere ...'

'*What*?' I wasn't entirely sure I'd grasped the situation,

but I followed her in anyway, turning to shrug helplessly at Stuart, who clapped one hand to his forehead and thumped the steering wheel with the other.

The room was, as expected, gorgeous; a lofty, white-painted sanctuary with pitch pine stripped floors, filled with cream sofas, plants and paintings. Soft piano music seeped from a hidden CD player. If this was Susannah's version of turmoil I'd hate to see her when she was expecting company. She had her back to me, and was rummaging for the letters at her desk, which was the only dishevelled part of the room. Apart from her face, that is. I wasn't sure what to say.

'What beautiful curtains!' Not that, anyway, but out it came regardless.

'Paul's,' she choked, not turning round.

'Susannah, what happened? When did he go?'

'Two weeks ago.'

'*Two weeks*? And you've not told anyone? Susannah!' I remembered the committee meeting, and Emma's party, where she had come across as the very epitome of organisation, with her polished daughters, her handbag full of secretarial essentials and her enthusiasm for her art stall at the Toddle.

'It's only just sinking in,' she said quietly, returning with the letters and sitting down. 'My mother knows. She's delighted.'

'Pardon?'

'Well, maybe not delighted, as such, just not too bothered, really. She's had five husbands, you see, plus my father, whom she never married, so it's no big deal for her. And she never thought much of Paul anyway.' She started crying again. 'Sorry. Poor you, walking in on this mess!'

'Don't be daft. Where is he now, Susannah?'

'In Glasgow. With his girlfriend. She's ... pregnant. She's nineteen, she's a design student, and she's seven months pregnant. Which means, to save you doing the maths, that while I was going through hell giving birth to Isabella he was with *her*, Gail! Sometimes I can't bear it!' More tears. Poor, poor Susannah. She looked at me with what vision she had left under the puffy lids. 'I feel so *dumb*! He used to mention this Jasmine person who was spending last summer in the shop on work experience, but ... but ...'

'I take it that wasn't the only experience she was getting?'

'Correct. And now they're shacked up in a loft in the West End, Paul's selling the shop, I'll probably have to move out of here and the girls are going to have a horrible step-sibling!' She took a few huge breaths, and finally seemed to be all cried out.

'How are the girls?' I asked.

She managed a damp little smile. 'Well, Isabella's oblivious, of course, poor lamb, and Abigail's great, actually!'

'Great?' I repeated, uncertainly.

'Yup, great! I think Mummy and I have done rather too good a job on her, to be honest. She thinks her life is going to be one enormous carnival of train rides, new babies to play with, holidays, shopping trips and extra attention.'

'I guess if you put like that it sounds like an OK deal,' I mused, half to myself.

'I know. Still, at least the excitement she's feeling should help acclimatise her to the new arrangements. Loads of families break up, don't they?' She squinted up at me for affirmation, which I supplied by nodding vigorously. 'I just never thought mine would be one of them. I so wanted to prove Mummy wrong, Gail, and I've failed miserably with my first attempt!'

'No you haven't, Susannah.' I said fervently. Had she? If you take into consideration the folly of getting hitched to the sort of miserable slimeball who'll screw around while you're in labour with his child, then yes, she had. But then, she wasn't to know, was she? None of us know. We can't legislate for arseholes, as I'm sure somebody must have once said. 'Have you met this, this *Jasmine* child?'

She winced. 'No, but I've seen her. She's Belgian. Or Dutch, or something, who knows. Her parents are furious, apparently.'

'Hmm, that's a toughie. Is there any chance of sorting it out – of you two getting back together? Jasmine going back home?' I asked, not at all sure, once again, if it was the right thing to say.

She smiled and shook her head. 'Absolutely, definitely, and utterly not. He's gone. He says he's in love with her, that he couldn't help himself, all that crap. I've just got to come to terms with it and then get over it. I've started painting again, actually. It's really helping me to get my head together.'

'That's terrific!' I looked round the walls at the soft floral watercolours. 'These all yours?'

'Most of them.'

'They're lovely. I suppose now you'll have a back room filled with abstract horror images of mutilated males, as part of your therapy?'

She actually laughed! '*Excellent* idea!' Then she went on, 'He was really messy around the house, you know,' in a voice which hinted that maybe, in time, she would be OK. 'Would you like a cup of tea?'

'That'd be lovely ... hang on, I should be making you

a cup ... Oh!' Suddenly I remembered my own husband. 'Oh, lord, Susannah, Stuart's waiting in the car – I haven't even left a window open, or fresh water, or anything – I'll need to run. Is there anything I can do to help?'

'You could bring him in, or would he chew the furniture? No, thanks, Gail, you've cheered me up, though, and that's no mean achievement. Here are the letters, envelopes and stamps. Would you mind posting them after you've signed them? Esther gave me the list of people to write to – even told me what to write – so if there are any you're not sure about, could you give her a shout rather than me?'

'Of course I will. Take care, Susannah. I'm so sorry.'

'Don't be. 'Night.'

'G'night.'

Fortunately Stuart had fallen asleep to the predictable strains of Classic FM. He woke with a start as I opened the car door and got in.

'Hnnnrrhh?'

'Hi sweetie. Sorry, I was ages. You OK?' I told him briefly what had happened. He shook his head, and tutted sympathetically.

'Tell her to make an appointment to see me in the office as soon as she can. We'll nail his bollocks to her easel. Now, where to next, ma'am? Duck pond?'

'Take me to the secret place with the thirteen-tog duvet and the instant hot chocolate, Jenkins,' I ordered sternly.

Mum was watching TV when we got in.

'Couldn't get on with my patchwork in this light. Or my knitting. How did it go?'

'Sorry. It was fine,' I replied. 'We've mastered the Eightsome Reel, the ... er ... something else, and one other dance.'

'And I can do teapots,' added Stuart.

'Not for me, thanks, I had coffee earlier, and I must get back. Gail, dear, where did you get that orange cake recipe?'

'Oh, I think it's from Nigella Lawson's book. Did you like it?'

'It was very nice. I've got a wonderful *Good Housekeeping* recipe for orange cake at home – I'll let you have it next time you're round. It's as light as a feather!'

'Thank you. That would be great,' I said, feeling, once again, seven years old with shoddy homework. 'How were the kids?'

'Oh, yes, I didn't tell you, did I? Thomas lost another tooth!'

'What, *another* one?' exclaimed Stuart. 'From the top?'

'No, the bottom. First bottom tooth! Poor wee lamb, he was very brave. There was a bit of blood on his pillow so I've changed his bed and put the dirty linen in the machine. He had some water to drink, and he's gone off to sleep just fine.'

'I didn't even know another one was loose,' I mumbled guiltily. I had taken an unnatural interest in the process of the loss of his first two teeth, holding his head to 'check' them at regular intervals, when really I just wanted to touch them and give them a wobble. The process stirred deep, childhood memories in me of losing my own teeth, the fragile mix of pain and curiosity, the metallic tang of blood, and the ultimate, indescribable 'tock!' as the tooth, terrifyingly, came away. I wanted to rush upstairs and give him a belated cuddle.

'Just as well you told us,' I said. 'Is the tooth safely under his pillow?' She nodded in a don't-teach-your-granny-to-suck-eggs way.

'Can't have the Tooth Fairy going on strike for the

night,' added Stuart. 'He'll be a wealthy young man if he keeps losing them at this rate. I wonder what he does with the cash, anyway?'

'Oh, he told me that, all right,' said Mum, as I grimaced in realisation of what she had found out from my son's innocent lips. 'He takes it to Woolworth's and spends it on sweeties! Goodnight, Fred and Ginger!'

Chapter Six

The cleaning lady swayed down the main school corridor behind her dustbin-sized floor polisher. Had Stevie Chip been walking alone towards her it would have looked as if she was sashaying towards him to entice him into a dance, but I was there too, clutching the arm of his blazer so possessively that the tips of my fingernails were throbbing.

The polishing pads of the meandering machine buffed the dark red linoleum tiles into a lethal gleam, but, owing to their circular shape, the shine never quite made it into the corners, so thick crescents of grime blacked out every crevice. I guess if the corridors weren't clean, then at least they were streamlined.

Our timing was all wrong as we tried to negotiate our way past her. We shied to the left just as she switched direction and polished to her right, and then we all re-adjusted at the same time, sidestepping the other way and nearly colliding again. I giggled.

'Sorry', said Stevie, pulling me to the other side.

'Sorry,' said the cleaning lady, following suit and blocking our path yet again.

'Sorry!' I spluttered, as for a fourth time we failed in a passing manoeuvre to the left.

'Oh, just fuckin' move,' she murmured, revving the polisher and driving one of its pads over my foot as she forced her way past.

'Ouch!' I squealed, though it hadn't hurt in the least. Stevie whipped round and jabbed a finger at her back.

'You've no right to say that to us!' he shouted, 'and you better be more careful with that machine in future!' She ignored him, so he yelled, 'I'm reporting you – you'll get the sack for that!'

'Aye, aye,' her low voice drifted over her shoulder, 'you do that, son.'

'He will, too!' I yelled back, grabbing hold of his arm again and giving the overalled figure a spiteful glare through my spidery blue mascara.

Stevie shrugged and shook his head nonchalantly, and we continued our swagger through the school. He prised my hand off his blazer sleeve and threw the freed arm casually round my shoulders, raking his hair with his other hand and studiously ignoring the attention we were receiving from onlookers.

From my vantage point, peering out from under the yoke that was his arm, life just didn't get any more dandy than this. There I was, out in public, out in *school,* with Stevie Chip! Helloo!! Yoo-hoo!! Bullies, Bimbos, Gigglers, Gossips, Tarts and Teachers! Come ye hither, one and all, and witness the heights of acceptance and cool to which swotty Gail Buchanan has ascended! I basked in the knowledge that I would never be thought of as square again. As of now I was officially out there – one of the 'sort of girls who had boyfriends'! Oh, but I planned to hold it together, schoolwork-wise – even if Stevie and I were to get engaged, or anything, I'd still want my independence and my own career! I'd taken to practising my married signature, in secret, on odd scraps of paper –

'Gail Henderson' sounded just fine, 'Gail Chip' less so, so I vowed to myself that I'd begin, um, chipping away at the popularity of the nickname as of today onwards. A nickname that's only just entered its third generation should be easy enough to dislodge, shouldn't it?

'Where are we going?' I asked, casually, like.

'A little walk,' he replied, pinching my chin gently with his spare hand. We kept up a pretty fast pace, speedy enough for most people who got in our way to swiftly get out of it, but not so fast that we went all out of step like a slow handclap gone wrong. Down the stairs we strode, past the junior cloakrooms full of chattering tinies, past the deserted senior cloakrooms (everyone'd be out having a fag behind Chemistry), the senior girls' toilets (always full of crying noises), the senior boys' toilets (always stinky), the notice board, the music department – but I was hardly aware of walking at all; it was as though I was cruising through the school on celestial roller skates, down more steps towards the yellow fire exit, and then, just when I thought Stevie was going to break the emergency glass and whisk me out into the sunshine with a flourish, he ducked sharply left, pulling me with him, through the swing door which led into the drama department corridor.

The drama corridor had mint-painted breezeblock walls, lined with pinboards which were bare apart from some sheets of fire regulations, a smattering of graffiti and scores of drawing pins which impaled tiny corners of coloured paper to the wall, relics of art department posters advertising curriculum-approved productions of depressing am-dram. The only light available to the corridor came from the little windows above the two doors into the classrooms on either side, so a murky, neglected atmosphere pervaded, probably because due to cutbacks the drama department only functioned for one term each year.

'Where are we going now?' I whispered, oscillating between fear and wild excitement.

Saying nothing in reply, possibly because by now it was bloody obvious, Stevie propelled me forcefully, and rather thrillingly, towards the end of the corridor, where chipped grey double doors led into the defunct drama studio.

The noise from my chunky black school shoes on the floor was deafening as we approached the doors, and Stevie nudged me in the ribs.

'Shh! D'you want an audience?'

I giggled again. I giggled all the time, back then. 'Well, we're in the right department, I suppose ...'

'Very funny. In here.'

To my amazement, the doors were unlocked and Stevie, glancing furtively over his shoulder, stepped into the dark, pulling me with him. My heart was thumping as the doors swung closed and then, enveloped in stuffy blackness, Stevie immediately pulled me by the shoulders towards him and started hungrily kissing my face.

Distracting though his kisses were, I knew I had to get my bearings a bit, just in case this was all a horrible hoax and any second now the lights would come up and the whole school would be revealed shouting 'Surprise!' blowing tooters and bursting into spontaneous applause. I wrenched my head back, gasping.

'Hang on, Stevie, I need to put the light on for a minute. Where's the switch?'

'You like the lights on, Miss Buchanan? I'm impressed,' Stevie teased.

'No! I just have to see where I am before we ... we ...'

'Go on,' said Stevie.

'That's right, before we *go on*,' I flustered.

Keeping a tight hold of me, Stevie moved back a few

paces to the doors and fumbled for the switches. There seemed to be about eight of them, and he flicked on them all until the dust-specked studio was fluorescently revealed, empty but for its chairs stacked against the wall, its sections of chipboard stage propped up against each other, its bulging black bin liners futilely awaiting collection, its stage lighting that never worked, its blacked-out windows and its shockingly under-resourced resource cupboards. All were entirely nonplussed by our arrival.

'Um,' I said.

'What?' asked Stevie.

'It's big, isn't it?'

He smiled at me. 'Ye-es, it's big. It's also warm, empty and undiscovered, and we've only got twenty more minutes of lunch hour to make the most of it! Sooo ... ' He kissed the tip of my nose. 'Can I put the lights off now, or would you like me to set up the stage for you and we can do it on that?'

The last thing I wanted to do was to betray my nerves but I was so close to saying 'Do what?' in an anxious voice that I ended up just nodding and saying nothing at all, trying to come across as mature and compliant by smiling and licking my lips, while panicking like mad underneath. In fact, my next, unscripted move was to put my arms round his neck and start kissing him, the first time ever, if my memory serves me right (and it didn't have all that many files to check through), that I had been the one to initiate a kiss.

Stevie and I had been together for just over two weeks. He had finally got round to me after dumping Kerry Patience at an eighteenth birthday party just before the Easter holidays. I'd begun to think that he'd never be interested in me, and decided that my Snob Hill credentials would deter him from giving me a go, which was a shame, as I fancied him like mad and was forever having *Officer and a Gentleman* fantasies of him marching into assembly and carrying me off, first to the hollow behind the chemistry block, and then to a pre-arranged wedding in Vegas, conducted by Elvis Presley or similar. But my fantasies, although a safe haven for all sorts of sexual experimentation, were no place for any red-blooded male to be hanging out when he could just as well be right here in the flesh while he was about it.

So, despite thinking I didn't stand a chance, I'd been making a big effort to lure Stevie (or anyone, to be perfectly honest), over the previous few months – to try and bump myself up the queue, as it were. I'd taken to arriving at school early and ducking into the senior girls' toilets to put on extra make-up, replace my little gold ear studs with dangling silver crosses, and spritz myself with inexpensive body sprays with names like 'Hot Tiger Musk', or, 'One Whiff of This and I'm Definitely Shagged'. I put mousse on my hair to give it a bit more of a just-out-of-bed look than my usual shiny bob, and worked on my giggle a bit to try to appear impressionable and more fun. OK, to appear a bit easier.

It wasn't that Stevie was your standard useless Loch Martin High layabout, though – far from it. He was more, well, the nearest thing we had to a high school Jock (not counting Jock Armstrong, lab technician) of the *Grease* variety – he managed, through good looks and an in- herited gift of the blarney, to be practically all things to all women, which was a rare and precious commodity for us talent-starved senior girls of Loch Martin High. He was popular with the staff as well, charming to the female teachers and good-humouredly co-operative with the males. Sometimes it was almost as though his presence in a classroom had a calming influence on the rest of us –

God help anyone wanting to analyse that, but if visions of lions and their prides are hoving into view, then maybe it's best to leave it at that.

I guess the faintly paradoxical thing about Stevie was that he was a *nice* guy – I mean the cleaning lady abuse was quite out of character; normally he'd have made a joke about it and she'd have gone away smiling and wishing all the boys in this dump were like that nice young lad ... I'd once watched him wade into a fight where a first year boy was having his football boots tossed from bully to lout – the wee boy was crying and darting about and not standing a chance, while other assorted cretins dropped their schoolbags and ran to join in, until the odds were about twenty to one. Stevie, taller than most of them but still outnumbered, caught one of the boots, then systematically cuffed boy after boy about the head until he reached the one who held the second, grabbing him by the collar and frogmarching him over to hand it back. The thing about that one was that when I had praised him gushingly about it later, all he'd said was, 'Nah, I didn't really do anything, the kid had the situation well under control.' No wonder, really, that I'd already picked out names for our children (Tiegan, Ashleigh and Bryce).

Anyway, after he'd dumped Kerry we'd all marked out Fiona Porter as next in line, as we'd seen her sitting on his lap in the senior common room the following day. So I was well and truly caught off-guard when a couple of evenings later, at home, Mum, in the middle of dyeing her hair aubergine, bustled through from the hall with a polythene bag on her head and said to me:

'That's Steven Henderson on the phone for you Gail – Bob and Margaret's boy.' I froze for a second while my brain digested the information. Mum was a little flushed, and simpered, 'Do you know, he thought that I was *you*, would you believe! He said I've got *such* a young-sounding voice! Can you imagine! Gail? *Telephone*?'

Dad shook his head and rolled his eyes behind his newspaper while I jumped up, at last, to take the call.

'Hi Stevie.' I took some deep breaths and tried to keep my voice quite calm and low; protecting myself in case he was only ringing up to get Fiona Porter's number.

'Hi Gail, how are you doing?'

'Fine, thanks. You?'

'Great, yeah, thanks. Gail ...'

'Yes?'

'Would you like to come and see the Bond film with me on Friday?'

I tried to play it cool, really, honestly, I did. I tried for about a second and a half.

'James Bond? Oh wow! I love James Bond!' I didn't. 'Yes please!'

'Great.'

'Thanks!'

'If we got the seven o'clock bus,' he continued, 'we'd have time for a burger or something before the second screening?'

'Great! Thanks!' Then I had an ill-timed rush of over-helpfulness. 'Or I'm sure Dad wouldn't mind running us up ... ' *Eeek!! Pull back! Pull back!* 'No! Hang on! What am I saying! Of course he couldn't! The bus will be fine.' See what happens when you try and date pampered darlings like Gail Buchanan, Chip?

'Great. See you.'

'See you. Thanks!'

And that was it, really. We started snogging outside the burger bar (on the way *in*), and then we snogged a whole lot more both during and after the film, so much so that my lips were swollen and inflamed the next day, and the skin cracked up and fell off them the day after that. But once I'd healed up, we irritated the hell out of my friends and everyone else by snogging (not to mention nuzzling, stroking, giggling at nothing, the usual stuff) pretty much at every opportunity over the following days and evenings, moving on, in private, of course, to more and more investigative groping, until that particular lunch hour which found us alone, with our twenty minutes to spare, in the near-darkness of the drama studio.

After I drew away from the kissing I'd initiated I heard myself whispering, 'Where shall we go?'

Our eyes were growing accustomed to the dark as Stevie took my arm and led me across to the opposite corner of the room, to a small space behind the stacked-up pieces of stage. There, on the ground, was a mound which looked to be an assortment of beanbags, velvet curtains and bits of costume.

'How about here?' he asked in a low voice. I don't really know how I felt exactly, apart from an overwhelming feeling of excitement and curiosity as Stevie pulled me down onto a velvet stage curtain, lay on top of me and started kissing me more intensely than he ever had before.

It was lovely. I moaned and wriggled and held him as tightly as I could, imitating women I'd seen in the movies, clutching at his shoulder blades, stroking his hair, moaning, turning my head from side to side, and rubbing my hands over his hips. He, meanwhile, was rubbing everything he could get hold of and very soon I was breathless with terrified desire, pushing him away and pulling him close all at the same time.

As his kisses moved down to my neck and collarbones, he deftly unbuttoned my blouse, slipped his hand inside my bra and began massaging and probing my breasts, while his mouth formed a necklace of kisses at my throat. But just then, all of a sudden I was aware of a hot, nipping sensation just below my right ear – it was as if Stevie had been sucking at my flesh and it *really* hurt, so I cried out, pushed his head away sharply and put my hand up to touch the sore bit, which felt tender and inflamed.

'Sorry,' he mumbled, before starting again with my mouth. 'Getting carried away. You're incredible!'

Well, in the face of such flattery I made a concerted effort to get back to business. Right, what had I not done yet?

'Hey, Gail, steady on!' Stevie gasped as I decided to make an enthusiastic lunge at his trousers.

'But you said we've only got twenty minutes!' I giggled, wriggling a bit more and half-unzipping his fly. God knows what I was trying to do. I'm not sure when I would have stopped, or even *if* I would have stopped, if Stevie hadn't rolled off me at that moment and lain still on a green velvet curtain, breathing heavily and covering his eyes with his hand. I propped myself up on my side, unsure what to do next. Stevie's head was only just discernible in the gloom, facing the other way, and after a moment he spoke in a low voice to the wall:

'Do you want it?' This time his voice sounded completely different, husky and urgent.

'Want what?' I asked, being a bit slow in the realisation department and quite keen to get on with the kissing, given that there were probably only about ten minutes …

'Sex,' he said, turning round, as though it were obvious, 'because I've got, you know, a packet of … you know …'

'What? *Sex?*' I almost shouted, 'Noo!' before realising that this wasn't exactly the best way for a gal to keep her man. I mean, call me naive, but the idea of actually having *sex* with Stevie hadn't really come into my head, although I was vaguely aware that the messages I was giving out shrieked quite plainly otherwise. 'No, I mean, yes! Yes, of course, *sometime,* but not here, not in school! Oh Stevie, did you mean now? I'd need to change! Someone might come in!'

'No one ever comes in,' he said, a bit fiercely, sitting upright but still not looking at me. 'That's why I come here! Look, forget it, Gail. It doesn't matter.'

'Sorry.' I was burning with humiliation and a prickly realisation that I was a Failure as a Girlfriend, so it took a moment to process what he'd said. When I did, I was unsure whether to make things worse by speaking up, or to prolong the awkward silence by saying nothing, but as neither of us seemed to have anything else to discuss, and because the last thing I wanted was for him to get up and abandon me, I put my hand on his shoulder and asked:

'So, is this where you bring everyone you go out with?'

He shrugged. 'Pretty much.'

'Ah.'

'Apart from the ones who've left school.'

'Oh. Right. Of course,' I said, extremely huffily.

'Look, Gail,' he began, turning to face me and sounding exasperated. 'Have you got a problem with that? It's a great place! It's private and atmospheric, and it's the only place in the whole school where we can get some guaranteed peace! Where else could we go?'

He was right, of course, but there was something about being the latest incumbent in Stevie's nest of guaranteed peace that made me sit up as well.

'Well, yes, OK, but it's sort of weird, you know, being taken to your, your, *place,* if you know what I mean. It's like being the latest in a long line ...' Which was precisely what I was.

109

'But you're special, Gail! You know you are! This is, er, special . . .'

'Really?'

'Sure.'

You could almost hear little crashing noises as we couldn't look at one another, the spell broke and humdrum reality bit. Stevie sighed and got up, fumbling for the light switches. As I stood up shakily to follow him the drama studio burst into a blaze of unsexy fluorescent brilliance and there was a silence, which I felt compelled to fill.

'Could we try this again, maybe, you know, on neutral ground?'

'It's not a bloody football match, Gail,' Stevie snapped. 'And your make-up's smudged. You look like a panda.'

'Thanks a bunch.'

'No offence.'

'Well, offence taken. Look, I'm going to go now, it must be about time for the bell.'

We could hear the distant sound of lunch-hour voices coming from the concrete schoolyard outside. I followed him out of the studio, and he peered from the drama corridor into the main part of the school until the coast was clear and we could rejoin the school day.

'I'm going in here,' I said shakily, nodding towards the door of the senior girls' toilets. 'This panda's got her fur to fix. See you.' I attempted a dignified shoulder against the stubborn door. Stevie touched my arm, seeming desperate to be somewhere else.

'Are you finishing with me?' he enquired of his right shoe.

I couldn't think what to say. What is the word that sounds like 'yes', but means 'no'? The word that sounds like 'of course, you bloody idiot', but means 'sweat a bit and beg me later, loser'? Why haven't the females of the species invented a 'holding' word they can use to keep their men on tenterhooks while they consider their options? Stevie had to content himself with a mascara-smudged, tear-rimmed look, a hopeless shrug, and the aromatic swish of the toilet doors in his face.

Luckily I had the toilets to myself. There were five cubicles, although only three had doors, and I gingerly checked to make sure they were definitely empty. The wire waste-paper basket overflowed with used purple paper towels and assorted other rubbish and above it, to the right of the slimy wash hand basins (cold water only) was a small scratched mirror. *Stevie Chip is a Pure Ride* had been scrawled on it with some sort of sharp implement just a few months before.

When I summoned up the nerve to look at myself, it wasn't the electric blue smudged circles around my red eyes which caught my attention. Nor was it the swollen, blotting-paper lips I seemed to be prone to after a major snogging session with Stevie. Rather, it was the angry, New Zealand-shaped love bite, which shone out from the opening in my white blouse, all purple and yellow with inflamed red edges. I clutched at it and burst into tears.

Mum'll kill me! I thought. No, fuck it, I'll kill myself. That bastard's taken me to his den and *branded* me, and I'm buggered if I'm going to give him the satisfaction of seeing me in polo necks for the next two weeks!

I went into one of the cubicles and grabbed a handful of toilet roll from the dispenser which was hanging off the wall. Then, still snivelling, I returned to the mirror to begin the clear-up operation on my face. It was going to take some time – my 'Electra' blue mascara was water-proof and would have been ideal for the most leisurely of Channel-swimmers, judging by the way it refused to budge from my sore face.

So, that seemed to be it. I had completely blown my relationship with Stevie, and it was all my fault – how could it not be? All I'd needed to do was to pull my knickers down and lie back; surely I could have managed that? I slapped more and more disintegrating blobs of gritty local authority toilet roll on my lacerated eye sockets, wondering if *'inability to perform sexually'* would be an acceptable ailment to write in the sick register in order to procure the rest of the afternoon off.

And he'd brought condoms! That was so *sweet*! Even if I hadn't let him have sex with me at least I should have offered to give him a blow job! But what *was* a blow job? See? I'd have had to ask! You can't be asking your boyfriend what a blow job is when he's probably used to getting them all the time! I was in a completely no-win situation! Unless of course I'd pulled my knickers down ... so the argument comes back full circle and it's definitely my fault again.

Or was it? If he'd only given me a bit more time maybe we could have, well, done *something* approximating ... you know. And he'd hurt me! I didn't sink my teeth into any part of *his* body, well, not so's to leave a mark, anyway. So then what does he do? Tells me I look like shit. Goes all impatient and frustrated. Doesn't give me any help. Takes me to his bloody shag-pad and assumes ...

He was probably back in the senior common room by now, I fumed to myself, trading 'nudge-nudge' remarks to his cronies as they quizzed him about his prolonged disappearance with prim little Gail Buchanan.

I looked back over at the graffiti, then searched in my blazer pocket for my pen. After a moment's thought, I inserted the words 'twenty-second' between 'pure' and 'ride', and went storming off in search of the man himself.

I had expected to have to wade through a roomful of his satellites in order to get to him, but instead I found him alone, leaning against a radiator outside the entrance to the common room. He saw me approach, and then looked down at his feet.

'Sorry about the panda thing,' he mumbled.

'I don't care about the panda thing, but I do care about *this*,' I said, trying to keep my voice from trembling as I opened the collar of my shirt to reveal the love bite in all its Technicolor glory. 'What's this all about? Am I twelve? Are you twelve? Did you need to show everyone that we'd been ... *together*?' My voice cracked on the last word. '*And it bloody hurts*!'

A few heads popped round the door of the common room to see what was going on, and forgot to pop back again. Stevie glared at them, to no effect.

'Gail, can we go somewhere else?' he pleaded, trying to take my arm. I shook him away. 'Don't touch me! Haven't you done *enough*?' You have to remember that *Dallas* and *Dynasty* and the like were pretty big back then and couples said this sort of thing to each other all the time.

Anyway, that, and the audience, triggered a change in Stevie's mood and he growled at me, 'It's only a fucking love bite, Gail, it doesn't mean anything ...'

This was perfect, absolutely perfect. For a confused, emotional girl not sure whether she was in the process of splitting up or patching up with her boyfriend, and in front of a growing crowd who couldn't believe their luck, openings like that just didn't come any easier for the delivery of a killer line, regardless of whether it's what she intends to say or not.

'You're right there, Stevie, it doesn't mean anything. You make me sick! We're, we're, *finished*!'

*

So anyway, it wasn't Stevie Chip who relieved me of my virginity. That actually happened the following year during my first week at university. I'd been at the Freshers' Week bouncy castle disco, trying to avoid Duncan and Graham, two former schoolfriends who were clinging together for security in a corner, because I was with fledgling new friends called Candida, Hussein and Lucas and was busy trying to reinvent myself as Interesting, Kooky and Worth Getting To Know.

Alcohol-wise I'd left my vodka and blackcurrant-drinking days behind in Loch Martin, having moved on to the infinitely more sophisticated tipple of half a pint of cider with a chaser of Blue Bols and lemonade.

Needless to say I was plastered after an hour and a half, and Candida, Hussein and Lucas, panicked by the thought of bright blue projectile vomit splattering all over the bouncy castle being attributed to one of their group, disappeared.

It was Duncan and Graham who came to my rescue, picking me up as I slid to the floor, helping me outside into the fresh air, flagging down a taxi and easing me into it, instructing the driver to return me to my hall of residence, while I mumbled incoherently how much I loved them from the far corner of the back seat. Unfortunately neither boy thought to rescue my bag – they were probably still inexperienced enough with girls to assume that everyone carried their cash in their hip pockets – and so, because I couldn't pay the driver, because he propositioned me not-too-rudely, because sex *had* in fact been somewhere on my Freshers' Week must-try list, and because it's really bad manners to order something and not be able to pay for it, I somehow let him screw me in the back of his cab.

Chapter Seven

Sometimes it's great to have the sort of husband who believes that parenting is a piece of piss. I mean, Stuart is no stranger to the nether ends of both of our children – he has staggered up in the middle of the night with the best of them, yawned his way through endless repetitive stories, mopped up puke and snot and anything else that needed mopping up when I wasn't within stumbling-over-it-first range, cooked eggy meals, refereed splashy baths and become cross-eyed with bewilderment over more episodes of *Teletubbies* and *Booh-Baahs* than most ordinary mortals of his generation, least of all the male ones.

Oh sure, he has his tetchy moments, like when he's doing the daddy bit but really wants to be doing something else, or when the children don't want to play the games he wants to play, or if he feels his modern-man efforts aren't being fully appreciated, but, in general, he thinks he's amazing and that I have a pretty cushy time of it.

For the most part I haven't done a great deal to dispel this belief of his. I reckon there's more to be gained by giving an overall impression of coping, rather than constantly wailing that life's not fair and demanding my metaphorical ball back because, for one thing, pretending that parenting's easy makes Stuart less likely to protest if he has to cope with the children without me. Being naturally competitive (the result of having parents who wouldn't buy him a bike until he beat them both at Scrabble), on the few occasions when he has to take charge of them for any length of time, he generally takes his responsibilities on the chin.

Like today, for example. Some idiot in the Government's Think Tank for Bloody Silly Notions decided to call today 'Take Your Daughter to Work Day'. This person presumably envisaged legions of bright young girls, perched on the edges of the nation's desks *à la* Kirsty Young, asking sparky questions, charming all the others in the office and generally gaining revelatory insights into their parent's Meaningful Other Life.

Only it wasn't quite so in our household, as I cheerfully packed Emma's changing bag, lunch, toys and favourite blanket into the boot of Stuart's car, kissed them and waved them off for their day of government-approved bonding in the litigation department of Matheson and Morrison. Thomas was there too, en route for school, grinning toothlessly from the front seat and waving the spanking new pound coin which the increasingly impoverished Tooth Fairy had fortunately remembered to leave him.

Stuart had started off by thinking that taking Emma to work was a fantastic idea. I think he was anticipating the brownie points to be gained from the females on the staff by cruising through an entire day in the office with his two-year-old baby playing cutely at his feet, while he raked his fingers sexily through his hair and churned out hard-hitting yet still compassionate legalese in the style of the men in *Ally McBeal*. Also, having recently been made partner, he was viewing today as a chance to introduce a softer, more caring image to management, just as I'd told him he had to. However lastly, and most plausibly of all, he was going to Edinburgh at the weekend to sit in pubs with some old university friend or other, so he had to make some fairly hefty donations into the give-Gail-a-break-from-the-kids piggy bank before he left.

However, his bravado was wobbling as he left, which wasn't a pretty sight.

'Will you come and pick her up if things get difficult?' He tried to ask this nonchalantly, like he didn't really mind what my answer would be. I kissed his furrowed brow.

'Not a chance! Byee!' I waved until the car was out of sight, then skipped back into the house to clear up the breakfast carnage.

By the time Theresa called in an hour later, I was lying on the sofa with a mug of coffee in one hand and the TV remote in the other, switching between 'My Husband Wants to be my Sister' on one chat show and 'Hey, You Don't Know It, but Today's Your Wedding Day!' on another. She made her own coffee and sat down.

'What's the best chat show you've ever seen?' she asked, as, on screen, 'Donald' emerged from backstage as 'Dorothy', wearing a brown pleated skirt, floral blouse with a bow at the neck, brown tights and peep-toe sandals. His long black wig looked like one of Cher's cast-offs.

'Easy,' I answered, as Dorothy embraced his tearful wife. "Obese and Mad For It", without a doubt. There was this guy, who was so fat that he couldn't get out of bed – they had to put cameras in his bedroom – and he was telling the camera that he'd had sex with about a thousand women, and then his so-called girlfriend came in, and she was this lap-dancer with tattooed tits, and she just went ahead and climbed aboard to demonstrate how they did it!'

'Fantastic!' said Theresa, looking thoughtful. 'Sick, but fantastic.'

'I mean, it was the one question that absolutely every-one wanted to know, you know, *How the hell do you manage it*? And they just went right ahead and demon-strated! It was incredible! Total telly gratification. Should've won a Bafta.'

'Perhaps it did. Did she have to go down there with a snorkel and head torch?' Theresa was thinking hard. 'Or did she use some of those hairdressers' clips to keep his gut out of the way while she located his . . . oh God, what must *it* look like? Did they show you?'

'Sadly not. I don't think she could have found it before the end of the show. She just took her top off and sort of knelt on top of him – there was no way she could have straddled him, the woman would have had to be a contor-tionist – and started writhing her tiny butt around.'

'As you do,' said Theresa. 'Did she keep her pants on?'

'Course she did! And some stupid micro-skirty thing. It was the Ricki Lake show, or something like that, there's a limit to how porny you can get on those things.'

'*Is* there? Actually, I've never slept with someone who was, like, enormously fat.'

'Would you want to?' I asked.

'In a funny sort of way, yes, actually. So that I could put a tick in the "lardy sex" box on my Life Checklist. Just imagine those acres and acres of soft, splungy flesh to roll around on, huge folds of tumbling tummy to wrap around you like some sort of great, warm, live shawl . . .'

'Singing "I Feel Pretty"!' I giggled.

Theresa joined in tunelessly: '*And I pity, any girl who's with some fit bastard to-night!*'

Theresa's Life Checklist made scary reading. She once auditioned for *Stars in Their Eyes* as Chrissie Hynde, but despite wearing the tightest black leather trousers the world had ever seen and propositioning the casting man she didn't get picked. She was hospitalised when her tongue abscessed after she let a boyfriend pierce it with a darning needle and an ice cube, and years ago she busked her way around South America alone with no money and a five-stringed guitar. Actually I doubted that one, although I'd never openly challenged her about it. Her parents had loads of money, and most of the postcards she sent me had things like 'Hotel Splendido' printed along the bottom.

I sometimes wondered why she had settled here, rather than, well – *anywhere* seemed more exotic than here to me these days, as I looked out from my nappy-soaked window on the world.

'So what about you, then?' I asked. The guy on the wedding chat show was looking none too sure about being surprised into tying the knot with his girlfriend of fourteen years by whom he had eight kids.

'What *about* me?'

'Best chat show. Come on, your turn.'

'Oh, I hardly ever watch them.'

'Liar. We all say that.'

'OK . . . umm . . . well, I'm not sure about the best one, but I definitely remember one of the worst. That was when they got this old woman in who hadn't seen her brother for sixty years, and they spent about half an hour saying stuff like, "And Doris, you thought you'd never hear anything about him again, didn't you love?" and she got more and more shiny-eyed and excited, until just at the end, the presenter said, 'Well, Doris, sadly Frank passed away ten years ago but here's his spotty, slouching grandson Wayne, all the way from Swindon, hoping to prise some sort of inheritance out of his new-found elderly great-auntie and get his big ugly face on telly for ten seconds . . .' Do you know, Gail, it was the first time I ever threw something at the telly?'

'Mmm. Quite right. What did you throw?'

'A custard cream. It was all I had without getting up.'

'You big scary revolutionary.'

'Don't I know it.' She raised her fist.

I reached over to the coffee table and picked up the pile of correspondence Susannah had asked me to sign. Dozens of near-identical begging letters, Esther's brainchildren, to local businesses, trying to scrounge prizes for her sodding grand raffle. I began to read through them.

'Have a listen to some of these,' I said, sitting upright as the force of Esther's nerve hit me. '"Dear Sir, We in the Loch Martin toddler group are holding our charity Toddle and ball on Saturday the twenty-sixth of June" ... blah ... "grateful if" ... blah ... "show support" ... blah ... "by donating a day's painting and decorating of the prize-winner's choice!"'

'How would one decorate a prize-winner's choice?' asked Theresa, yawning. 'What does the next one say?'

'"... a small dinner service, or an item or two of crystal" – flipping heck, Peggy at the ironmonger's will love that.'

'Maybe she'll run to a bag of nails instead. Or perhaps Esther will screw some screws out of them. Next?'

'"... a portable colour television from Jock the TV repair man"!'

'What, not a widescreen plasma job, then?' Theresa queried.

'Nope. Strange – Esther probably thought that was showing restraint, asking for a portable rather than some big digital job.'

'Or maybe she assumed that the people at the ball would appreciate a discreet little portable TV for their third guest bedroom. Next?'

'"... a round of golf at Royal Dornoch followed by lunch at Skibo Castle." Aha, now that's a prize!'

'That's much more like it,' agreed Theresa.

'Shame we hate golf. Such a wanky game.'

'True. But we could just have two lunches instead. Next?'

'They just go on and on – sacks of potatoes from Martinside Farm, vouchers from the butcher, vouchers from the florist, vouchers from the kitchen shop, vouchers from the leisure centre, vouchers from the chemist ... good grief, even vouchers from the undertaker!'

'Well, you never know the minute, I suppose,' said Theresa, lighting a cigarette. 'Is she going to ask the doctor to donate a complimentary cervical smear?'

'Or a choice between that and a full testicular examination? Let's see now ... oh my God, here's a letter to Stuart asking for a voucher for two hundred pounds' worth of legal services, though. How embarrassing! Why couldn't she just ask me about that direct?'

'Maybe that would have been too easy. Or maybe she's scared of you?'

'Nah, she's not. She's just weird. Or at least, incredibly thick-skinned. Anyway, you'll have to sit beside her at the ball. I shall be relying on you to provide me with a string of Estherisms to sustain me in my old ... oh!' I tailed off and clapped my hand to my mouth. 'You *are* coming, aren't you?' I suddenly remembered that I hadn't actually invited her. And if I hadn't, then nobody else would have, either. She'd been abroad the previous year, and I somehow hadn't entered her into the equation this time.

Theresa blew a jet of smoke dismissively out of the side of her mouth and smiled at me. 'I wondered whether I was going to get asked along, actually.'

'Oh, Theresa, I'm so sorry! Millions of sorries! Grovelly embarrassed sorries! I assumed from the start that you'd be there! You being Punch and all that and

121

there being no show etcetera! You *will* come, won't you?'
Catching sight of her amused face, which was wearing its
come along now, child, I know you better than that look,
I stopped and bit my lip. 'OK, Mother Superior,' I began
over again, 'let me think how to put this. I suppose,
subconsciously, I must have wanted *you* to ask *me* for
tickets. I knew you'd have been laughing at us all from
day one, organising a posh-frock affair like this, and I
didn't want to give you the satisfaction of turning me
down because then I'd feel even more of a boring pleb for
being involved in it at all. That's why.' I folded my arms
in a mock sulk, and for some reason felt tears pricking the
backs of my eyes. 'I hate the fact that the effing post-
Toddle effing ball is the best my life has to offer you.
You're always doing *fun* stuff!'

'I see,' replied Theresa eventually. 'And why on earth
would I think that putting on an enormous frock and being
bossed round a tent by a ringmaster called Dunny-brush
was boring?'

'Hmm, if you put it like that ...'

'And what's more, if you're saying now that I'd have
the chance to get my will drawn up *and* win a coffin in the
raffle, then it's sounding like the most surreal evening
known to woman! Who in their right minds would turn
down a chance to go to that?'

'I suppose you've got a point,' I agreed, cheering up.

'But I'm obviously not in my right mind, because I
won't be going, thank you very much all the same.'

She seemed to mean it, as well. 'Oh.' I said. 'OK then.
Can I ask why not?'

'Nobody to go with.' She shrugged, as I opened my
mouth to squeal in disbelief.

'Get away with you!' I spluttered at last.

Looking away, she replied, 'It's no big deal, Gail, but,

well, it's going to be a deeply *couplesy* do, isn't it? Even the tickets are being sold in pairs, and I really don't want to go on my own and be sitting on the sidelines having all the wives eyeing me up as some kind of potential husband-seducer. Not that any of them are worth ... sorry, apart from Stuart, that is, not that any of them ...'

'You can stop there, thank you, you've made your point.' Typical! Most women going to a party on their own would be anxious about being a wallflower, and having people take pity on them! Not Theresa, though. 'Poor old you!' I said in mock tenderness. 'You're right! It'd be horrible for you, being the only *femme fatale* in the place while the rest of us peel off our Marigolds and frump around the dance floor watching our breast pads fly out of the tops of our frocks like UFOs – God, is that what it's like to be gorgeous?'

'What is this, Misunderstanding Day?' Theresa retorted. 'I just don't have anyone to go with, that's all, and I'm not going on my own. OK? Now I'm embarrassed. Can we talk about something else?'

We both gazed glassily at the same spot above the fireplace, somewhere between the three kids' photographs and the little hole in the plaster where Stuart had fired his air rifle (long story). 'No, Theresa, we can't. If you want to come, then you're coming. Can't you rustle somebody up from somewhere? Under your bed? Down the back of your sofa?'

She thought for a while. 'No, not really, to be honest.'

'But you know *squillions* of men!' I said in exasperation. 'I rely on you to be the nymphomaniac of my acquaintance so that I don't have to be it. Come on, what about Eddie? Fraser? Mick? Brad Pitt?'

She shook her head. 'Nope, no go. Most of them are, erm, *unavailable*, at least from the point of view of being seen with me in public, and I *think* you know what I mean,

123

do you not?' She squirmed in a not entirely unpleasured way and I nodded disapprovingly. 'And, well, the ones that *are* free just aren't the types to, well, you know ... *play ball* at that kind of thing.'

'What do you mean, *play ball*? It doesn't matter if they can't dance, Theresa – trust me, I should know.'

'No, it's not that. It's all the other stuff, Gail. The, well, the *niceties*.'

'Niceties?'

'Niceties,' she confirmed. 'And the chit-chat.'

'Chit-chat?'

'Chit-chat. Not to mention the hobnobbing.'

'Hobnobbing?'

'Hobnobbing.'

We were trying not to giggle. 'Were you by any chance about to mention kowtowing?' I asked.

'Kowtowing?' smirked Theresa.

'Kowtowing.'

'No, but I *was* just about to mention *quaffing*.'

'Quaffing?' We were giving in to convulsions of laughter.

'Quaffing.'

'Isn't quaffing a bit la-di-dah? I yelped.

'La-di-dah?' roared Theresa.

'La-di-dah,' I repeated, spilling my coffee.

'Only for hoi polloi like us!' squeaked Theresa, wiping away a tear.

'Hoi pol ... Oh, for heaven's sake, enough already!'

Theresa sat up and composed herself. 'But you get my drift, anyway, Gail – there's nobody I know who's both available and trustworthy to take to a ball, really there isn't. I'd be much happier to give it a miss, thanks all the same.'

But she was too late; I had already begun plotting. Or, more precisely, I had begun picking up on an idea that had been slowly germinating in my mind since the day after my visit to Invermartin with Esther. I was allowing my mind to roam over firm thighs in green moleskin, up and beyond a broad chest heaving with exertion beneath a lumberjack shirt, and along tanned arms wiping sweat from glistening brows, as their owner wielded his enormous mallet to drive thick fence posts into dark, yielding earth – bang! Bang! Bang!

'I know someone you could go with,' I said, matter-of-factly, as though I'd only just thought of it.

'Dunny-brush, you mean?' Theresa enquired, 'only I think I'd prefer to take him shopping than to a ball, by the sound of him.'

'No, not Dunny-brush, for God's sake – give me *some* credit. A guy I went out with for a while at school called Steven Henderson. Works as an estate factor for Joffers Brankin. I ran into him for the first time in ages the other day when I was up there with Esther. He's really cute, actually. Biker. But with short hair. Been to Australia.'

'What makes you think he'd want to go?' Theresa asked, interested despite herself.

'Dunno, but I could always ask. Might impress his boss. What do you think?'

She was definitely wrestling with herself. 'Nah. Don't bother, Gail. Thanks. I'm not so desperate that I'd let myself be set up with a stranger just to go to a dance in a tent.' She didn't sound at all convinced. Not convinced at all. I decided to play it underhand and mean.

'Fair enough,' I said in a way I hoped sounded like the end of the matter. 'I suppose he was a bit of a wild card anyway. That is, if his past's anything to go by.'

'Oh yes?' That *unmistakable* metaphorical pricking up of ears. Careful, now, I nearly had her. *Eeeasy does it.*

'Yes. So don't worry. Forget it. It would have been a real

long shot. He's got a bit of a reputation as a Jack-the-lad anyway. Probably got a woman tucked away somewhere anyhow. Lucky cow. He can kiss like you've never—'

'Phone the bastard.' Theresa never could resist a challenge.

'Attagirl. "Faint heart never won fair laddie," as my old wet nurse used to say.' I reached for the phone and phone book, and dialled Invermartin House. Joffy answered.

'Brankin speaking,' Joffy announced, with that plummy authority that jerks you into wanting to say, 'Oops, sorry, wrong number,' then slam the phone down and curl up in a ball in your airing cupboard.

'Oh, hello, it's Gail Macdonald here, I was . . .'

'Gail! Lovely to hear from you, my dear! Marvellous day, what? How's that lovely little girl of yours, has she woken up yet?' It's funny, but I was starting to realise what Esther meant: he really did give the impression of having all the time in the world for you. Doesn't half put one off one's stride.

'She's great, thanks. Actually, I'm sorry to bother you, but I was hoping to get hold of Steven. Do you have a home or mobile phone number for him? I was hoping to . . . er . . . speak to him about fencing. I mean, um, *parking*.'

'Well, you're in luck, because he's just popped into the room to check some figures with me. Here he is.'

Not expecting such an instant result, I came over all peculiar, like I was about to be introduced to Robbie Williams. I was aware of a whooshing sensation as all the spare blood in my body shot to my cheeks, as though it was trying to burst out and get a good look at the cause of all this unnecessary-ness.

'Gail? Hi. How's things?' Ooooohh.

'Great, thanks, you?' Strange how riveting a girl can

become when she's trying to impress.

'Not bad. What can I do for you?' The little tease.

'Well, it's not for me, exactly, more for a friend.' This was already turning into a *déjà vu* conversation of the type not used by me since Stevie and I were in geography together about six hundred years ago. 'I was wondering, well, would you like to come along to the ball?'

There was a short pause. 'What, and leave your husband to babysit?'

'Sadly no . . .' Did I really say *'sadly no'* just then? Out loud? Eeek! 'Nooo! Not with me, with my friend Theresa. She needs a partner and you're available. I mean that in the sense of you being handy. As in you being on the premises already and maybe not minding. Can I start again please?' Theresa was gurgling hysterically into one of my sofa cushions. 'What I mean is, Stevie, the ball's going to be a real laugh, and I've got this gorgeous friend who's also a real laugh, and I wondered whether you'd do her a big favour . . . *Ouch!* Sorry, she kicks, too, and be her partner for the night?'

'How gorgeous do you mean, exactly?' he asked in a low voice that sounded as if it was smiling.

'What, on a scale of one to ten, you mean?' Theresa twigged, and leapt up to brandish ten outstretched fingers two inches in front of my face.

'Ten, apparently. Although personally I'd put her at more of an eight and a half. Just to put some distance between her and the *true* tens.'

'Like yourself?'

'Precisely.'

'Ah. Right.'

There was an awkward silence, which of course I felt compelled to fill.

'This is an awkward silence.'

There was more awkward silence, which of course I

127

also felt compelled to fill.

'Are you thinking about it, or have you nodded off?' Unorthodox in terms of persuasion, admittedly, but there you go.

'That would be very nice.'

'What, nodding off?' God, how unfunny and unflirty was that?

'No, going to the dance with, what was her name?'

'Theresa. Theresa Robertson. She's really nice, dark and petite and a really good laugh.' I made violent thumbs up gestures to Theresa who pretended to shoot herself.

'Theresa Theresa Robertson. Is that one of those double-barrelled names, then?'

'Oh ha ha. You'll need to meet her – can you make it to the next dance practice on Tuesday evening? In fact, why don't you come and have supper at my house beforehand so that you could meet each other properly?'

'Fine.'

'Are you sure?' I couldn't believe it had been that easy. 'Stevie, you didn't burst out laughing at the concept of a dance practice! What's *wrong* with you?'

He laughed. 'I've been at Invermartin long enough to have picked up a nicety or two, Gail.'

'Nicety!' I squealed over the receiver at the prostrate Theresa. 'He's got niceties! Sorry, Stevie, I'll explain when we see you. About half-past six? We'll need to eat early to get to the practice in time. Do you know my house?'

'Yes, I know it.' He knew my house! He knew my house!

'OK, see you then. Bye!'

'Bye, and thanks for the invite.'

I replaced the receiver, grabbed a cushion and hopped round the room like a scalded rabbit. 'He's coming! I can't believe it! Theresa, you lucky old witch! Can we share him? Please?'

Theresa had got up and was looking stern. 'What was all this petite and dark stuff, then? Were you offering him a dance partner or a bloody Thai prostitute for the evening?'

'Believe me, once you meet him you'll wish you were the latter, my dear. He's coming! Yahoo! Male totty at the ball! Result!'

'Tell you what,' Theresa interrupted, 'why don't *you* partner Stevie and I'll entertain Stuart for the night? Sounds like you wouldn't be in the least bit averse ...'

'Don't be daft. He's just a bit gorgeous, that's all.'

'And you say you went out with him? Tell me more!'

'Well, it was only for a few weeks. He managed to work his way round every single girl in our geography class, even Janine Rae who's a lesbian now, and, well, it wasn't half bad, even though I had to disguise the teeth marks on my neck for a few days so that my parents didn't make him marry me or anything ...'

'Gail, why have you gone so red?'

'Stop it! I'm just flustered, that's all! I'm not in the least bit interested in, in ...'

'Having another go?'

'Correct. Not interested *In The Least*. There.'

'Hmm. Methinks the lady doth protest too much.'

'Well, youthinks wrong,' I lied.

Just at that moment the phone rang and prevented me having to talk myself any further into the shit. 'Probably Stevie wondering whether I ze American dollar take,' Theresa muttered. She was wrong, it was Susannah.

'Gail? Hi. It's me. Sorry.'

'Susannah, how are you now?'

'Oh, fine thanks. Much better. Gail, thank you for listening the other night. I'm so sorry you walked in on me in such a state, but it was nice to have someone to unload everything onto. I just hope I didn't bother you too much?'

'Course not. I shouldn't have arrived without ringing you first, but I'm glad I did. Any time. So what can I do for you?'

'Oh, nothing really. Just wondering if you were, er, at home today, that's all, er, because I was hoping to pick up those letters.'

'Sure, no problem. They're almost done. But I thought you wanted me to post them? Whatever, I can drop them off—'

'No!' she shrieked, sounding like I'd just offered to murder one of her children. 'No! I'll pick them up. Sorry, but the place is a tip and I'm, um, out and about today anyway and it's no bother as I'll be passing later on anyway and you might not catch me if you came here. I'll get them sometime this afternoon, if that's OK?'

'Well, if you like.' A bout of noisy children's squealing started up in the background on Susannah's end of the line. 'Sounds like you've got your hands full this morning – how are the girls?' I asked.

'Fine! Fine. Fine. Sorry, better go. See you at your place later, OK? Bye!' And the phone went dead immediately. I replaced my own receiver thoughtfully. The beginnings of a shiver were making their way northwards from the base of my spine. I sat down on the sofa, and Theresa looked at me quizzically.

'Something up?' she asked. I sat back further and hugged a cushion.

'Not sure,' I said slowly. 'That was Susannah, phoning to make sure I'd be at home all afternoon.'

'Ri-iight?' Theresa prompted.

'There was a child making a noise in the background,' I went on, plunging my chin into the top of the cushion.

'Ye-ees?'

'I'm certain it was my Emma.'

130

Chapter Eight

Don't ask me why I didn't mention my suspicions when Stuart came home at six that evening. He staggered in with Emma under one arm and his briefcase under the other, looking exhausted and also very peculiar with a large rectangular sticker on his forehead saying Do Not Remove. I stared at it for a few moments.

'Tell me that has only just found its way onto your head,' I said, as recognition dawned and my hand moved to my mouth.

He dropped Emma and the briefcase gratefully on the sofa and winced as he peeled it off. 'This? No, I've had it on all day; Emma was playing with it in the car and slapped it on as I carried her into the office. I think she saw it as an ownership-of-Daddy badge so I left it on – seemed to make her giggle. Made a lot of the office giggle, actually. Where'd it come from, anyway?'

'It's the hygiene strip from my new swimming costume.'

'Ah. Right. OK. Shit.'

'How many people saw it?'

'About a hundred million.'

'And not one of them saw fit to enlighten you?'

'Nope. Most of them just looked at it and laughed.' Crestfallen, Stuart resembled a small child who'd been entertaining like mad all day and instead of getting showered with praise, being informed that he had a bogey dangling from his nose.

'And it never occurred to you that having something stuck to your forehead couldn't have been *that* good a joke?'

'Oh, bugger it, it doesn't matter.' He sat down and raked his hair like it really, really *did* matter.

'You look like you've just taken your seat on an aeroplane and the guy next to you says "How do you do, the name's Rushdie!"' I quipped. He scowled at me. 'How was Emma?' I went on, as she clambered on to her food-encrusted kitchen chair and started munching the star-shaped cheese sandwiches I'd cut for her. 'Tough day at the office, sweetie?' I soothed, stroking her soft hair.

'Joosh!' came the sandwichy little reply, so I obediently went to pull some apple juice from the fridge.

'You'll be demanding your paper and slippers next, munchkin. *THOMAS! TEEEEEA TIME!*' Thomas ambled downstairs, engrossed as usual in Pokémon Yellow on his Game Boy. I prised it out of his grip and he gave me a dirty look. 'No toys at the table,' I reminded him, stashing it out of sight behind my hundred and eighteen celebrity recipe books.

'Hiya sunshine!' called out Stuart.

'It's not a toy, it's a Game Boy,' he replied huffily, deservedly ignoring his father. 'It's not an Action Man or a bit of Lego, is it? *Well* then.' He shook his head in a 'see-what-I-have-to-put-up-with' way and started eating his grapes and car-shaped sandwiches.

'She was fine,' came Stuart's voice from the sofa. We were experts in the parental art of retrieving the threads of long-lost conversations after the intervening requirements of our offspring had been dealt with. 'Didn't see much of her, to be honest, she spent most of the day with Daphne in the secretaries' room being fed biscuits.' And right on cue, the star-shaped sandwiches hit the floor as Emma cleared her plate and her throat to yell 'Ife Cweam!' at the top of her voice.

'So it would appear,' I sighed in a righteous way, picking the food off the floor. 'You mean you palmed her off on those poor women all day? But that wasn't supposed to be the idea, was it?'

'Not all day, but some of it. She was bored stiff playing with the paper and stuff in my office. As a matter of fact, when I did catch up with her she spoke a whole lot more sense than most of the other tossers I'd been spending the day dealing with. It was non-bloody-stop. *Je-sus*.' Stuart's language was always a bit City-boy when he got in from work, but he was usually fine once I got him settled. 'Remember the guy who shagged the dog?'

I did. 'Didn't he just *allegedly* shag the dog? Wasn't he claiming the dog led him on? Or was that part of a bad joke I heard somewhere?'

'Oh, he shagged the dog all right. Police picked him up last night in Peter Mackenzie's sheep field. Wellies on, the lot. He's been carted off for psychiatric—'

'Daddy, what happened to the shaggy dog?' asked Thomas matter-of-factly. 'Did it die?' Stuart and I looked at one another in panic, reminded that Thomas was turning into an actual human being who listened to stuff.

'No, Thomas, it didn't die, it's fine,' said Stuart quickly. 'How was school?'

'Can't remember.'

'Not even one thing?'

'Nope. Well, I had lunch.'

'Terrific! What did you have?'

'Can't remember.'

'*Marvellous!* Gail, why do we pay those astronomical school fees, remind me?'

'We don't, Stuart, we don't. Seems the poor memory's hereditary, anyway. What else happened at the office?'

'Oh, not a lot, really. It was pretty dull for Emma, although I honestly did try to keep her amused.' He pointed meaningfully at the angry red stripe on his forehead and shrugged, as if no further proof were needed, and then went on, 'She's done a little crayon fresco on my wall which is really rather good. But although I sometimes have my suspicions about the mental age of some of my colleagues, the office really isn't a place for a two-year-old to spend an entire day. Is it, babe?' He pulled the ice cream from the freezer and kissed the top of Emma's tired head. I looked at him carefully, watching for alterations to his behaviour; some sort of sign that he wasn't being truthful. It was a strangely enervating experience. I'd never done it before.

'So, you were stuck in the office for like, the *whole* day?' Holding my breath. There was a pause while Stuart concentrated on forming perfect pink ice cream balls and plopping them into two bowls. He didn't look up at me, but then, I supposed, he was busy.

'Yup! There we go! Emma's spoon! Thomas's spoon! *Thank you*, delightful Daddy!'

'Thank you, delightful Daddy,' droned Thomas obediently.

I pressed on. 'Emma as well?' He finally looked up at me, in a strange way.

''Course, apart from when I sent her off down the High Street for a burger and twenty fags. What do you think?'

*

Later, when the children finally dropped off to sleep and we'd finished dinner, we bundled ourselves onto the sofa and snuggled up, as usual. I'd lit the fire, even though it was mild outside, and after about ten minutes we had to push the sofa back a bit to escape from the heat.

'Drink?' asked Stuart.

'Go on, then, just a little one.'

He got up and went through to the dining room, returning with two clinky crystal tumblers of malt whisky on ice.

'Do you think we should get a cat?' he asked absently, after he'd settled down beside me again.

I looked at him in surprise. 'A *cat*? What do we need one of those things for?'

'Dunno, really. I used to like cats, when I was a kid. We had this old, smelly one . . .'

'Brucie?'

'Oh, that's right, I told you about him, didn't I? Anyway, I guess he wasn't always old and smelly, but I don't remember him any other way. He used to wake me up in the morning by head-butting my cheek and stroking my face with his paw. It was sort of nice.'

'*Was* it?' I said, incredulously. 'I would have jumped out of my skin if I'd woken up to find a big hairy face two inches from mine . . . oh, but I suppose I do that every day these days, don't I? Did Brucie *snore* as well, by any chance?'

'No, but he had a flaky skin condition.'

'How horrible,' I said, shuddering.

'I'm not convincing you at all, am I?'

'Well,' I pondered, 'I suppose a cat would be preferable to a dog, but . . . nope, sorry my love, try as I might I just can't get my head past that whole arsehole/kitchen worktop connection. And who'd be the one who'd have to fish the poo out of its litter tray, might I ask?'

'You wouldn't need to, it could poo outside!'

'What, in the flower beds? Sandpit? On the lawn?'

'Well ... hmm, I see I'm not very good at this persuasion malarkey.'

'Anway, if it went outside it'd get squashed on the road,' I continued, easing my argument home. 'We'd have to peel it off the tarmac like gum before the kids saw it. It's bad enough trying to keep the children in one piece, never mind an animal as well.'

Stuart waved a 'stop' gesture with his hand. 'Fair enough, I shall climb down gracefully. No cat.'

'What happened to Brucie anyway?' I asked.

'He got squashed on the road.'

'Ah.'

'We buried him in a Sainsbury's bag at the bottom of the garden. Do you want the telly on?'

'Nah, I checked the paper and it's all crap.'

We eyed the sleeping telly accusingly, before simultaneously taking large gulps of fiery malt whisky. The golden liquid roared and stung all the way down but its honest, peaty butt-kick felt just right at that moment – no nonsense, just an oak-aged, Highland escape route from the trials of the day. Exhaling sharply through my mouth and wiping watering eyes, my hazy gaze fell next on Ben's picture and, tracing the top of my glass with my finger, I felt the familiar dark, hollow pit of grief begin to well up from the depths of my insides. I took a few deep breaths; I was too worn out to cry tonight. *Come on, girl, this isn't fair to Stuart!*

'Didn't really need the fire tonight, did we?' Stuart murmured. Our faces were ablaze from the whisky and the heat.

'Habit,' I replied. 'Plus I find it comforting. The grate's so empty without it. Sort of ... disappointed ...' *Shaky voice ... oh, God ...*

'Hmm, I know. And with Ben's photo above it – I guess the fire's sort of like a candle in his memory, isn't it? Gail? Oh, love!'

I broke down into gulping sobs. Stuart rescued my glass and held me tightly. 'Where's my baby, Stuart?' I wailed. '*Why* did he have to die?'

' 'I don't know, I don't know,' he whispered, rocking me, ever so gently, to and fro, to and fro, until I felt his own tears begin to plop onto the top of my head.

'I'd give *anything* for it not to have happened! Anything!'

Stuart gripped me more tightly. 'I know, shhh, I know. There was nothing anyone could do, though, was there? We used to take comfort from that, didn't we? He just wasn't well enough ...' He tailed off and loosened his grip on me, sniffing and wiping his eyes. 'Although sometimes I can't help feeling that the only person who did nothing to try and help save him was me.'

'You?' I repeated, looking up at him in watery astonishment.

'Yes, me!' he repeated angrily. 'You were so weak after the birth, trying to feed him and everything, the doctors were rushing about doing all their resuscitation and stuff, and the only plank left doing bugger all was me!' His voice was hard with an edge I hadn't heard before. 'I should have made them find a ... a *helicopter* or something, to take him somewhere they could have operated on him! He didn't stand a chance where he was! But I just left it up to them and did nothing – I let you both down!'

He turned his head away and wiped his cheek on his shoulder, before rubbing his eyes, staring straight ahead and, finally, crumpling into miserable tears again.

Shocked, and frightened, I stroked his hair. 'Stuart, you

didn't – it wasn't your fault, it was nobody's fault! You know how many people we've spoken to, all the stuff we've read . . .'

'I just can't help thinking we might have done more, that's all. He was so precious, and so small, he was *relying* on us!'

'And we were there for him, weren't we? We were there every single minute. Both of us. And he's always right here with us, even now. And he always will be.'

He nodded and pulled away and I handed him the box of tissues, after grabbing one for myself first. After a mighty tear-wiping and nose-blowing session, the tissues hit the fire with a hiss and we finished our drinks shakily, commencing yet another episode of pulling ourselves together for the other one's sake.

'He would have been starting school this autumn, wouldn't he?' Stuart said quietly.

'I know,' I replied. 'I think about that all the time. I just don't know how I'm going to be able to bear it when I drop Thomas back on the first day after the holidays, and see all the little new ones Ben's age . . . in their little new shoes, knowing that Ben should be one of them . . . oh, Stuart! Don't let me cry again – it's too sore!'

'I'll come to the school with you,' he said.

'That would be nice, I'd like that.'

We managed damp smiles. 'Come on,' I said softly, 'let's go to bed. I'm going to hunt out a fur mitten to stroke your cheek with, just the way Brucie did.'

Esther cornered me at the puzzle table at toddler group the following morning, as Emma and I were engrossed in completing our elephant jigsaw.

'Tail!' exclaimed Emma.

'Trunk!' I countered.

'Rabbit!' she decided.

'No, sweetie, *elephant*. Nelly the Elephant.' What a good parent may have said at this point was something like, 'Yes, it *could* be a rabbit, couldn't it? It's the same colour as a rabbit, isn't it? Grey! Emma say it! Gre-e-ey! Shall we do a rabbit puzzle next?' or something equally politically correct and up-in-the-clouds dandy, but something inside always prompts me to nip inaccuracies in the bud. For their own damn good. Emma scowled at me and pulled the puzzle to bits as I heard the thunder of approaching footsteps. Nelly herself was on her way.

'Gail, we need to have another meeting. Right away.' Esther hurled herself into the space between Emma and me, threw Magnus into one of the other minuscule chairs and thrust a bucket of Lego into his podgy arms. Which, strictly, ought to have been left at the Lego table, really. I mean, just what sort of a precedent does it set when Esther, of all people, does that sort of thing? Before you know it we'll be condoning glue at the drawing table. Paints at the snack table. Infant toys in the grip of senior toddlers. Tractors in the soft play area. It would be anarchy and the fast-track route to hell, so it would.

'Hello Esther. Something up?' Magnus grabbed a piece of the elephant puzzle. Emma grabbed it back and started sucking it. Esther planted her elbows on the table and thrust her not altogether small chin into her hands. My parental experience diagnosed the onset of a fairly major sulk.

'*Everything's* up, Gail. Joffy's bringing a party of twenty-six, the marquee hire is going to cost more than we've got in our funds, we're going to need a bar licence which we haven't got yet, I can't find anyone to make our sashes, nobody's sorted out the catering arrangements, the band's not confirmed yet and there's a delay with the

139

raffle tickets. The whole thing's going pear-shaped and nobody here seems to give a shit.' She flicked a disgusted glance round the hall at the other mothers who had the nerve not to be wailing and beating their breasts, or even trembling fearfully. In a way I ought to have been touched that she had approached me first to sound off to but one little word from somewhere in the centre of her tirade seemed to be fogging up my head.

'What . . . sashes?' I asked slowly.

She looked at me in surprise. 'Didn't I say? The committee will all be wearing tartan sashes to mark themselves out as committee members. Sorry, Gail, sometimes I forget that you're new to this sort of thing. The organising committees of Highland balls always wear tartan sashes, and I'm trying to find a seamstress . . .'

'I'm not wearing a sash, Esther! I don't really think I'm a sashy kind of gal, to be honest.'

She rolled her eyes. I was clearly more trashy than sashy. 'Oh, come on, Gail. *Course* you'll wear one! I'll lend you my silver citrine brooch to fasten it, how about that?'

'We'll look like a school netball team,' I grumbled.

Esther ignored this and bounded off to tell the other people on the committee to stay behind for an emergency meeting. Not ask, mind you, *tell*. Claire, Amber and Sarah, to a woman, flicked their hair and reached into their bags for their mobiles, presumably to tell their au pairs to get the lunch on. Susannah went to fetch a cloth and wipe down a table on which to spread out her stationery. I watched her closely as she cupped her pale, newly ringless left hand to gather up the crumbs corralled by the cloth which she wielded in her right. She didn't *look* like a woman who'd been meeting with my husband behind my back. She'd even said hello to me on the way in! Perhaps she was hard as nails, though, devoid of conscience, extracting dirty thrills from suspending her secret right under my nose? I just couldn't quite bring myself to believe it, somehow. Val (who, strictly, wasn't on the committee at all but who probably viewed herself in a sort of talisman capacity) disappeared outside and returned with Eden, Struan, some jotters and assorted small rocks and fossils. Looked like they had been having geology in the Dormobile. Those other mothers who were not Esther's Chosen Ones quickly took the hint and left early, depositing their rubbish in the big green bin on their way out.

We perched in a circle on tiny infant chairs. Esther found an adult-sized one, so that the effect was a bit like Snow White and the Seven Dwarfs. I sat between her and Amber, who was next to Sarah and Claire. On Esther's other side was Susannah, perched behind her clean little table, ruling a margin down the side of her pad.

'Val, would you watch the kids?' instructed Esther, just as Val was about to pull up a chair. 'Try and keep them quiet so that we can get on, yup?'

If Val was miffed she didn't show it. She smiled at Esther, tenderly placed the unnaturally well-behaved Charity in her carrycot on the floor, slipped into the kitchen and returned carrying a plate of biscuits. Sarah tutted, and pursed her lips, but said nothing.

'Not for Rosie, thanks Val, or she won't eat her lunch,' worried Claire.

'And, um, Val? Excuse me? Harvey's wheat thing, yah?' warned Amber, looking ready to knock Val's block off if she went within twenty yards of Harvey with a Hobnob.

Magnus and Emma on the other hand sensed a biscuit opportunity and dashed round Val's skirt to get their hands on the biggest ones.

'OK, girls, crisis time,' Esther began. 'The whole thing's turning into a bloody shambling arse-up and I don't know why I bothered trying to organise it in the first place.' We tensed for her to continue, like a class of children settling in for a lengthy telling-off. But to our surprise she didn't; instead she folded her arms and sort of pouted – not that I'm exactly sure what a pout's meant to look like – but in any event, it seemed she had thrown down some sort of gauntlet.

'Wobbler, Esther?' asked Amber, calmly fingering her pearls. 'It can't be that bad, surely?' Esther gave her a withering look.

'Could you perhaps give us a list of the items we need to sort out so that we can, well, sort them out and then get home?' suggested Sarah briskly, like the working mother with precious little time to piss around on committee minutiae that she was.

Esther still said nothing; she just sat there, overbreathing and *boiling* with unsaid stuff. By now Val had cornered everyone's children on the other side of the room and had given each of them a piece of rock to feel. '*Ammonite,*' whispered Eden tenderly to Magnus. '*Ammonite.*'

'Amamite,' he repeated, stroking the fossil's inviting, contoured nooks and crannies. The other children were similarly absorbed, touching and stroking.

'Been slipping them Ritalin, Val?' I called out in admiration. She turned and softly shook her head. Honestly, in my house things like that are missiles, not fossils. Where's the Committee of People who Pick Saints when you need 'em? Val would be home and hosed.

'You want a list?' Esther growled. 'OK then, I'll give you a list. *One,* the marquee's too bloody expensive. *Two,* Joffy's is bringing twenty-six non-paying guests. *Three,*

142

we don't have a band. *Four,* nobody's heard from the caterers—'

'Hang on Esther,' interrupted Susannah. 'Am I to minute Lord Brankin as *Joffy,* or is it *Lord Brankin*? Only I'm not sure if Joffy ...'

'Call him whatever the hell you like, Susannah,' she replied stonily. 'Call him a great big liberty-taking git if you like. I don't care.'

'Joffy's got fewer letters,' suggested Amber.

'And we'll all know who you mean,' affirmed Claire.

'Personally I'd plump for Lord Brankin, or, at a push, *His Lordship*,' said Sarah, thoughtfully. 'I mean, social rules are a bore, admittedly, but they do serve—'

'For God's sake, can we get on?' Esther almost shouted in exasperation. '*Five,* there's nobody to make the sashes. *Six,* we need a bar licence, and *seven,* the raffle tickets haven't arrived yet. Got all that, Susannah?'

'You're kidding,' said Amber. 'No sashes?'

'Oh God! Nightmare!' groaned Claire.

'We'll look such idiots without sashes!' exclaimed Sarah, who seemed to have turned a slightly paler shade of porcelain than her usual pale porcelain. They all stroked their shoulders contemplatively, probably wondering whether it was too late to get their designers to rustle up a different style of ball dress, this time allowing for the *absence* of a sash.

'I know, I know,' agreed Esther. 'It's hideous. There must be hundreds of seamstresses out there who'd do them for us, but I just can't find any for love nor money. I've even trawled the Yellow Pages, can you imagine? One idiot woman clearly didn't have the first clue what I was talking about – sorry, Gail, no offence, another said she was too busy and couldn't possibly fit us in, and a third told me she's just doing curtains these days! Anyone else got a dressmaker they could lean on?'

Three glossy heads looked troubled. 'Not in this country, unfortunately,' apologised Amber. 'God, what a disaster!'

'Mine'll be too busy just now – he's doing the outfits for the Corrs to wear at the Brits,' said Claire, almost to herself. 'I can't even get him to pull out the stops for me for Ascot. Such a nuisance, when one's designer becomes well known.'

'Mmm,' I agreed, tapping for a moment into Planet Whoo-Whoo.

'And mine's totally off the rails just now,' Sarah complained. 'I'm having to buy absolutely everything off-the-peg these days. I feel like an absolute bag lady!' She gazed disgustedly at her long, butter-yellow suede skirt and crisp, white linen shirt, shaking her head and turning her whopping diamond solitaire pendant round the right way.

'I'll make them for you,' said Val, looking up from her armfuls of blissed-out children on the other side of the room. 'I can sew.'

'Sorry?' spluttered Esther.

'It's no problem,' Val went on. 'I make most of the children's clothes at home on my mother's old Singer sewing machine. I mean, it'll be just a basic long scarf, won't it?'

'Long scarf?' squealed Amber. 'I can't see my *couturier* calling it a *long scarf*, somehow!'

'It's sweet of you, Val,' Sarah began, 'but I think that *proper* sashes are more like a sort of, well, deconstructed, elongated, erm, *bandeau* thingy, actually. I doubt you could possibly just *run them up* at home!' She shook her head at the notion.

'Sarah's right, I'm afraid,' added Claire kindly, standing up. 'Sashes are cut on the cross, for a start, so that they move with the body!' She swayed her shoulders in a slow shimmy. 'With a little *knot* action on the edge of the hip!' Va-voom! *Out* went those hips. 'Some *ruching* going on at the shoulder, yah?' I glanced at the others. Susannah appeared to be as perplexed as me, Esther was clutching her forehead and Amber and Sarah were nodding knowledgeably.

'You're dead right, you know,' said Esther suddenly.

''Fraid so,' sighed Claire, sitting down and flicking her hair.

'Not you, Claire! *Val!* It *is* just a bloody long scarf, isn't it?'

'Sounds suspiciously like one to me,' I agreed.

'Sorry, but me too,' put in Susannah.

'Thanks Val, if you could run them up that would really save the day! I'll drop the tartan silk off at your house tonight, and we can discuss the measurements. God, what a relief! That's wonderful!' The others didn't look sure, but had the sense to worry in silence. 'OK, that's great! Anything else, or is that it?' Esther beamed round at us.

'Um, how about the other six, obviously *minor*, items on the agenda?' I prompted. 'No marquee? No band? No food? No raffle tickets? No money?'

'Oh yes, of course,' said Esther quickly, picking up the reins and regaining control. 'Which one will we start with? The money, perhaps.' Sarah, Amber and Claire all checked their watches at the same time.

'What happened to all those thousands we made last year?' asked Sarah.

'Most of it went to Children in Need after we bought the new play equipment for our lot,' Esther replied.

'Couldn't we ask for some of it back to cover the cost of the marquee?' suggested Amber brightly.

'I imagine it's been frittered away on Aids medication and clean drinking water by now,' I couldn't stop myself from saying.

'Sorry, but I think I may be able to help here?' Susannah put in, reaching into her bag and producing a sheaf of letters. 'Let's see now. Ah yes, here we are! The marquee company have agreed a thirty per cent discount because it's a charitable function, and they're quite happy to wait for payment until *after* the ball, Plum Duff Caterers confirmed their booking yesterday, and the Archie Patience Ceilidh Band confirmed theirs the day before. Oh, and the raffle tickets arrived this morning – I've got them with me to share out. Sorry I didn't say anything earlier, but I think that should help a bit, shouldn't it?' Susannah's cheeks had turned a little pink as she looked down and fingered the edges of her letters of confirmation. Esther, on the other hand, unaccustomed to having the rug pulled from under her, seemed almost indignant at what she'd just heard. She rounded on Susannah, nostrils undoubtedly flaring.

'Susannah! Why ... why was I not told?' she demanded.

'I ... I've only just found out properly myself,' Susannah stammered. 'I had to get *written* confirmation for the minutes ...'

'*Fuck* written confirmation! I'm up to my eyes in worry for this blasted event and nobody even thinks to tell me what's going on! Christ!' We all exchanged glances.

'Well done, Susannah,' came a soft voice from across the room. It was Val, gently rocking a frazzled Magnus to sleep. Susannah smiled back at her gratefully.

'VAL!' Esther shrieked when she caught sight of her. 'DON'T let him sleep! For God's sake, he'll be up half the night!' And she bounded over, picked up Magnus's lolling body and started shaking it.

'Great! OK, can we go now?' asked Claire. 'I've left
Pepita minding a cassoulet – she'll never cope.'

'They're hopeless on their own, aren't they?' agreed
Amber.

'Hang on, hang on,' warned Esther, balancing her semi-
comatose son on a toy tractor and sending it across the room
with a push. 'There's still the question of the bar licence,
and Joffy's regiment of guests to deal with, so stay right
where you are, if you please? First up, the bar licence. Right
then. Here goes.' She took a deep breath. 'Tony and I think
that it's far too much to expect people who aren't pro-
fessionals in such things to deal with stuff like bar licence
applications, and we don't want people rolling about drunk
all over the place like last year' (she only gave the merest
glance in my direction) 'so we thought if we just have *soft*
drinks on the night, then it'll be a lot less hassle for everyone, and then we can really concentrate on the dancing,
which is what it's all about, anyway . . .'

'You have *got* to be kidding,' I said in horror, voicing
what seemed to be the reaction of everyone else in the
room as I pictured us all wearing preposterous long frocks
and drinking beakers of Ribena through bendy straws.
'Are you a recovering alcoholic, or something, Esther?
Soft drinks!'

She met my gaze with a kind of martyred one of her
own. 'Well, yes, Gail, I suppose I am.'

The stunned silence which greeted her admission was
only punctuated by the thud of Magnus sliding gently off
his tractor into the ball pit, where he curled up, and closed
his eyes for his longed-for nap.

'Ah. I'm really sorry, Esther. I didn't know.'

'Oh, God,' added Claire, 'same as my stepmother!
Esther, is there anything we can do to help? My step-

mother knows a terrific clinic in Harley Street, long way off, of course, but she travels everywhere by train since her licence was taken away . . .'

'Don't be ridiculous,' Esther barked back. 'It's my business, and I'm dealing with it in my own way. No pissing about with counselling, just Tony, self-help books, and a bit of discipline.' Scary beads of sweat were beginning to show. 'Erm, thanks, though.' Despite the show of bravado she seemed diminished, somehow, by the admission; her frame was smaller, her shoulders not exactly hunched, but definitely less military, and the way she chewed her lip suggested more than a touch of anguish. I guess if it had been anyone other than Esther one or other of us would have put our arms around her, but the very idea seemed as nuts as trying to hug a tiger with a thorn in its paw.

'Poor you, Esther,' Amber ventured, fingering her pearls. 'Perhaps, under the circumstances, no alcohol . . .'

'And I'm sorry too, Esther,' cut in Susannah, almost in a whisper, 'but I'm afraid Plum's done it already.'

'Plum?'

'Plum Duff, the caterer.'

'Plum Duff is a *person*?' I couldn't believe it.

'Oh yes,' said Susannah. 'I made sure it was in her contract to obtain the bar licence for us. Seemed obvious at the time, given that she's organising the drinks as well as the food. Sorry Esther. I didn't know about your, er, affliction . . .'

'Tell you what!' burst in Claire excitedly. 'Why not instruct Plum to lay on loads of *delicious* fruit punches as well as booze? My stepmother can't tell the difference between a Bloody Mary and a Virgin Mary on a good night, for instance – they both seem to get her squiffy!'

Susannah looked uncomfortable. 'I've spoken to Plum about that already, and she's digging out some recipes. Sorry.' Thus ended Claire's contribution to proceedings, and Esther shot Susannah a look which was fit to melt her eyeballs.

'Is that it *now*?' asked Amber. 'Oh yes, gosh, Joffy and the Freeloading Multitudes. There's a tricky one. Esther?'

But Esther seemed to have temporarily shrunk back into her own troubled little world. Her arms were folded and she was gazing at the ceiling, lost in thought. It might have been a trick of the fluorescent strip lighting but I think there were tears in her eyes. She obviously wasn't in a fit state to address Amber's question and so, ignoring the whiff of ulterior motive which was creeping selfishly into my head along with a rather wanton image of a steamy pick-up truck, I came to her rescue by saying, 'Oh, don't you worry, Amber. Just leave Joffy to me.'

I drove Emma home so that I could give her lunch and a nappy change, and freshen myself up before driving to Invermartin to speak to Joffy. This 'freshening-up' operation involved changing into a short skirt, putting on some make-up and perfume, fixing my hair, and brushing my teeth – well, a girl never knows when she can be let down by a furry mouth, does she? Then I strapped Emma into the car, climbed in myself, and we set off towards Invermartin. That the ticket issue could far more swiftly have been dealt with by simply picking up the phone was obvious and therefore not to be thought about, save for convincing myself that the delicate matter of wringing money out of the Brankin wallet (which according to local lore was tighter than a fish's arse) simply had to be dealt with face-to-face.

Each time I glanced in the rear-view mirror I caught sight of Emma's trusting little face, bent in concentration as she made confetti of Thomas's *Beano* comic. Strange to think that only a few days ago there had been nothing more and nothing less than *us,* the Macdonald family, albeit with an incurable ache right at our heart where Ben ought to have been. He ought to be here, in the car with us! I often tried to visualise what he would look like by now; I'd think of Emma and Thomas's faces and sort of mix them up to try to form a third, but my brain just wouldn't complete the process. Some things are too much to ask.

And where was that family now? Well, for a start I was dressed up to the nines, heading for Invermartin in the hope of catching a glimpse of a guy I knew at school and couldn't get out of my head. Stuart was possibly seeing Susannah on the quiet. I was *certain* that the shrieking in the background on Susannah's end of the phone line had been Emma. Of course, I reasoned to myself, Stuart could have gone to her house to discuss her divorce proceedings. But then he would have told me about that, surely? Stuart told me everything that went on in the office, especially if it concerned people I knew, which it often did given that I knew most of the local population. Neither of us remotely considered it a breach of confidentiality – Stuart and I were kind of, well, *one person*, really. And why would Susannah have rung me up about something as banal as Esther's raffle letters when Stuart was in the house with her, if it wasn't to make sure I wasn't likely to pop in?

I gripped the steering wheel tighter, and began to drive like Esther, foot down, no prisoners. Is this how marriages go wrong? First whiff of a potentially unfaithful spouse and, instead of becoming hysterical with grief, you treat it as a free pass to do some fooling around of your own? Like a sort of matrimonial 'Get Out of Jail Free' card? Use it up and get back to the game? God, too much analysis. I put a CD in the machine, turned the volume up and tried to make myself focus on what I was going to say to Joffy about paying for his tickets. Besides, I didn't want to analyse my way into having to turn back and use the phone after all.

Chapter Nine

Spud Ritchie's fish suppers are getting smaller, I grumbled to myself as Emma and I drove out of the village and along the main road, heading towards the junction that would take us to Invermartin estate. It used to be that you could get all the way down to the MOT garage on the Inverness road before you reached the scrunched-up newspapers and greasy polystyrene trays strewn all over the verge and the road. Now they were showing up a good mile or so earlier, just past the 30 mph signs at the edge of the village; cold and spent, their crumpled tits and headlines flashing wearily at us as we passed.

When I was little we'd have a Spud Ritchie fish supper most Saturday nights as a treat. Mum would stay at home warming plates and setting the table, for there was to be no bare-knuckle guzzling in our house, oh no sir, while Dad and I drove into the village discussing what to have. Mum usually had scampi, Dad the fish, and I was a devotee of the smoked sausage supper. Dad would park the car outside Tourist Information, give me the money – five pounds more than covered it, and I'd queue up and order. Mum once ordered chicken, but when Spud had asked, 'Leg or breast?' I was too embarrassed to say 'breast' out loud so I asked for leg, knowing, correctly, that Mum wouldn't be happy. Brown chicken meat was for soup. Pies, at a push. Anyway, as well as the hot, vinegary parcel, I'd emerge with three Crunchies and a bottle of ice cream soda, and Dad and I would speed back to our house at the very topmost top end of Snob Hill to munch our food contentedly round the kitchen table, before going through to the fireside and spending the rest of the evening in front of the box. And because there was no school the next day, I got to stay up late.

Couldn't recall ever catching sight of a youthful Joffy Brankin in Spud's queue, even though I knew that Joffy had spent his childhood at Invermartin. Scempi? Don't think so. What did life's Joffies do for treats?

Stately homes cry out for clichés. Hell, stately homes *are* clichés. Anyway, pulling up at the front of the big fat cliché that was Invermartin House, my tyres scrunched on the gravel, the building loomed down imposingly and my hand shook as I rang the big brass bell. See?

Woofings and yappings from within greeted the noise of the bell, as stately dogs alerted their master to the presence of potential riff-raff. Then a long wait. Probably busily buggering the bellboy, I thought, realising not for the first time that I was in a stinking mood, brought on partly by anxiety about being at Invermartin in the first place and partly by the force of the headache which had been shrouding me all day. I left Emma strapped in the car, peering sideways at me like the Queen on her way to church. There was no sign of Stevie. I'd scanned as much of the grounds as possible on the way up the drive, but to no avail; there wasn't even so much as a glimpse of a pick-up truck or motorbike.

Joffy eventually opened the door, tall and straight, like

a maypole around which what seemed to be about fifteen assorted dogs twisted and whirled.

'Bed, dogs!' he commanded, pointing sternly into the house, and they obediently pushed off, muttering amongst themselves. 'Gail! What a pleasant surprise! Come in! I was just about to have some coffee, would you care to join me?'

'No!' I barked, *far* too quickly, jolted by the memory of his pale, tepid coffee from the last time. 'Not for me, thank you, I only wanted to have a quick word, and Emma's in the car . . .'

'Bring her in, bring her in, why don't you? I've got a box of wooden bricks somewhere she can play with.' He beamed at Emma, who was staring back at him with inquisitive clarity. And as I turned to look round at her little unafraid face, all of a sudden something inside me became calm. I mean, I was her *mum*, for God's sake, so if I couldn't be upfront about something as utterly frivolous as party tickets then what hope was there for me standing up for her in future?

'Lord Brankin, I—'

'Joffy! Joffy! Please, Gail.' Oh, Ambassador, you're spoiling me . . .

'Joffy, you might not want me to darken your door ever again after I've told you what I'm here about,' I began. *Or call you Joffy, either.*

His face clouded. He was actually a very good-looking man, in an angular, chiselled way – what an *inconvenient* time to notice! 'Sounds ominous,' he said with newscasterly gravitas, stooping slightly and stroking his chin. 'Do go on.'

I plunged in. 'Twenty-six people is a hell of a lot to bring to the ball, Joffy, and Esther thinks . . . well, no, actually, I agree with her, that the event may well run at a loss if we don't ask you to pay for your tickets after all. Sorry. That's it.' Phew, done it. Any moment now he'd set that pack of dogs on me. He was looking straight at me, with a definite glint in his clear eyes ... murderous or amused? Outraged or impressed? From where I was standing, four steps below him and silently cursing his three-foot-plus height advantage, it was hard to tell. I attempted to think of something else to say, to take the edge off what all of a sudden seemed like a slightly unfair demand for cash, soften it up a bit, hurl in some chit-chat and possibly a nicety or two, but 'Seen Stevie today?' was all that sprang into my head so for once I said nothing and waited for him to speak. Would he perhaps chuck me under the chin and call me a plucky little wench? Hopefully not because then I'd have to say, 'Oh sir, you are a saucy one an' no mistake,' and he'd have to say, 'Up into the hay loft this instant or it'll be the worse for you,' and I'd have to say, 'Lawks m'lord, that's the third time today an' what with my chores to do and all,' and he'd say ...

'Fine! No problem at all!'

'Sorry?'

'Absolutely fine, Gail, my dear. In fect, I've been dealing directly with your delightful friend Susannah, only a few minutes before you arrived, sorting out the money side of things.'

'*Susannah* rang you up?' Bloody hell, talk about High Priestess of the Dark Horses.

'No, not at all, I phoned her, ectually. The chaps in my party were all horrified that you weren't intending to charge us for tickets for a ball in aid of the little ones – felt a tad shifty about it myself, to be honest – so I rang Esther up to offer to pay my whack.'

'Ah. Great.' Pass me my smelling salts. 'But, hang on,

I know you said *Susannah* a moment ago, but didn't you mean *Esther*?'

'Mmm. No, I didn't. Let me explain. I rang Esther first, but she didn't quite sound, er, how shall I put it, quite *herself,* for some reason. Bit short with one, in fect. Anyway, she gave me Susannah's number and told me in no uncertain terms that *she* seemed to be running the show now. Anyway, Susannah was frightfully nice when I got hold of her.'

'I bet she was,' I hissed. 'Did she ask for written confirmation that you'd cough up?'

He either failed to spot or chose to ignore the sarcasm. 'Not at all, of course not! But it's sorted out anyway.'

Emma banged on the window, wanting out. 'That's, erm, great,' I faltered. 'Wonderful. Thanks. Anyway, look, Emma's getting restless so I'd better be off. I'm so sorry for bothering you about this ...'

'Don't be, I'd have done the same thing myself. I must say I'm impressed that you came all the way up here to speak me in person, when you could have given me a ring. Always best to do things face to face, what?' I gave a funny little squeaky laugh and fumbled for the car door handle. Joffy beat me to it and opened the door.

'Thank you,' I said, clambering in.

'Not at all, my dear. Pretty gels are always welcome at Invermartin, that's my motto!' Ooh! I started the car and wound down the window to treat him to my best sideways look, and perhaps a nonchalant wave. 'Especially when they bring their mothers!' he shouted as I began to pull away, his nose pressed against laughing Emma's window, eyes crossed and cheeks blown up like a hamster.

In the days leading up to Stevie's arrival for supper, I began to look at my house through different eyes.

155

Although I still loved its chocolate-box cuteness, its leaded windows and its meandering garden, gravid with roses, my pride in its perfection found itself simmering down into a light unease that the place ought, in fact, to belong to two ancient and whiskery maiden aunts. I mean, what had I been thinking of, twining clematis round the door? What, in heaven's name, was the point of that giant terracotta urn in the herbaceous border? For storing dinosaur ashes? And why, would someone please enlighten me, did I have that snotty red tin letter box attached to the gate? It was like, *'Ooh, Mr Postie Working Person, pray don't sully my doorstep with your horrid proletarian presence . . .'*

Inside was the same story. With the anticipation of Stevie Chip seeing inside my house clawing scales from my eyes with the viciousness of one of our old classroom bullies, I realised that the inside of my home was nothing short of a car crash of 'styling solutions', dumbly copied from a cornucopia of lifestyle magazines. A sort of *Ideal Antiques* meets *Good Periods*. I devoured every homes and interiors publication on the market, the glossier the better, stockpiling snippets of style to import to unsuspecting Loch Martin in order to impress the pants off everyone who came through the door. Hints and tips. Tints and hips. And then, like an addict needing to be purged of the shameful traces of her addiction, I'd foist them onto Stuart, who would drop them in the waiting room at Matheson and Morrison, from where they'd be promptly nicked.

Take the dining room, for example. As if it hadn't suddenly become worrying enough to have a *dining room* in the first place, it began to occur to me that the room had been papered and curtained and wall-lighted and carpeted with such po-faced determination that it looked exactly like a businesspersons' hotel on some anonymous ring road, lacking only a cigarette machine in the corner and thin piano muzak squeezing out of wall-mounted speakers. And the only stuff which populated the room, including the table and chairs, had been wedding presents, most of which I either disliked or couldn't see the point of. I mean, the silver plated swirly candlesticks in the middle of the table always obscured the view of whoever was sitting opposite and had to be removed as soon as everyone had sat down, and the bone china serving dishes with lids which sat squatly on the sideboard – *see, I even had a sideboard!* – were never used because they were just so eminently, disgustingly smashable. It crossed my mind just to smash them and be done with it but unfortunately the people who'd given them to us were still alive and living locally, so I hung onto them, treating them like squat little anti-disapproval devices.

My kitchen, all butchers' block and hanging colandery stuff, was in the Shaker style. Fake Shaker. I was a dirty little Shaker Faker. Usually it was an eye-wateringly untidy hovel, but on the rare occasions when I cleaned it up it was the very epitome of middle-class design-within-a-budget lifestyle solutiony thingy. Which was not exactly the sort of impression I would have chosen to create for the appearance of Stevie Chip in its midst – ideally I'd have had something far funkier, something looser, free-standing, *bohemian* – (*Stevie! Drink? Joint? Spot of yoga?*) but well, there you go. However I did stop yearning for an Aga, right there and then.

The sitting room, though, was dominated by my red velvet sofa. My huge, plumptious, squishy-squashy, red, red, RED velvet sofa. It was the reddest, velvetest thing in the whole wide world, and yet ever since its arrival, instead of celebrating its redness and its velvetness with a holiday and a tickertape parade, I'd been toning down the rest of the room as if to apologise for it, like you would a farting dog. Walls of Heritage White. Neutral throws. Eau-de-Nil pouffe (I'd *have* to hide that – *'Oh, Stevie, dooo take a pew on my eau-de-Nil pouffe . . .'*). Candles. Lots of wood – the oak floor with its designer rug and the Gwyneth Paltrow-pale coffee table. To say nothing of the entire wall of respectable books. The really good reading was in my bedroom and on a shelf by the upstairs loo.

I loved my sofa. It was the sexiest piece of furniture I had ever laid eyes on, and over the last few days I'd come to realise that all the neutral stuff I'd been flinging on and around it were nothing short of attempts to cover its modesty. When I first saw it, the year I got married, giving out hot and sultry come-hither vibes in the corner of a chi-chi Glasgow design store called Pseud!, I had wanted to go over and lie naked upon it, face down, and imagine delicious things being done to me at the behest of a faceless lover driven wild with lust by the soft, red welcome beneath him . . .

'Pants are falling down,' I quietly scolded my blushing couch as I straightened its neutral throw.

Theresa arrived early as instructed to help put the children to bed. At least, Theresa's breasts arrived early, with the rest of Theresa following a short interval later. Now Theresa *is* petite, as I had so enticingly described to Stevie on the phone, but her breasts are whopping and spring effortlessly from her tops like Roger Rabbit's eyes the first time he laid eyes on the pulchritudinous Jessica. Child-rearing has depressed mine to roughly the profile of ski jumps (the sixty- *and* the ninety-metre), which need to be coaxed into something approaching va-va-voom by my va-va-valiant Wonderbras.

'For God's sake, Theresa, give the boy a chance!' I exclaimed scratchily, taking in the contours of her tighter-than-tight lilac top, over which a purple crocheted cardigan had been thrown, possibly for modesty, though it failed miserably if that was the idea. It seemed to peer anxiously from around her armpits, quivering, 'There's no way I'll get round them, guv ...'

She laughed and looked down happily. 'Oh, this old thing? I'm sure from the sound of him Stevie'll be able to handle it.'

'Handle *them*, don't you mean?' She put her hand on her thrust-out hip and gave me a trailer-trash pout. Damn! How I wish I could do that! 'Emma's in her cot but could do with a story and a cuddle, and Thomas is playing with his sticker book – I told him he could keep his light on for another half an hour.'

She fished in her bag and pulled out a packet of Action Man jumbo felt pens for Thomas and a pink tiara for Emma, hitched up her chest, maliciously, in front of me, and hurried upstairs before I could think of anything else to say.

Stuart came in, rumpled, as I was still staring at the stairs, listening to the squeals of joy from the bedrooms as Theresa appeared with the presents. He came over and hugged me warmly from behind, enfolding me with jacket and chin and cheek and stubble and warmth and, and *perfume*? I whirled round and planted my nose in his neck, inhaling. And again. In, out, in, out, what the fuck's this pong about?

'What is it?' he asked, taken aback by the unusual welcome. 'I know I'm a bit sweaty ...'

'Oh, nothing, I just thought I could smell something, that's all'

'What?' He drew back abruptly and looked at me.

'Erm, aftershave. You wearing it today?'

'Nope, I never wear it to work, you know that. Remember that day I put some on and Iris from filing told me my office smelt like a tart's boudoir?'

'Like she'd know,' I said, hugging him again, cautiously this time.

'Besides,' he went on, 'I'm amazed you can smell anything above the fug of Theresa's perfume. I take it she's here somewhere?'

Ah. Of course. Theresa's perfume. That was it. It was strange, to have leapt to a conclusion, and then to be left feeling foolish and not to be able to share the whole thing with Stuart. Not to just ramble on as we did about everything else, listening, grunting, sympathising, sounding off and generally rumbling through the process of marital communication without forethought. It seems that you need to be on your toes if you choose to mistrust.

'Yup, she's upstairs showering the kids with gifts. You've got a few minutes to get changed, Stevie'll be here in . . . what's up?' He had turned white. Then he crouched down slowly, clenching his hair with his fists until he was wobbling in a sort of huge foetal position.

'Oh. Sodding. Shit. It's bloody *Come Dancing* night, isn't it? Gail, nooo! Rangers are playing Man United live tonight! Gail! *Gail!* I've booked the sofa!' He reached over to his briefcase and opened it to reveal, pathetically, eight cans of beer. Then he briefly straightened up before slumping melodramatically onto the sofa with his head in his hands. Hmm. This was most unfortunate. Trying not to panic, I judged that a firm response was my only hope, so I slid astride him, gently took hold of both of his wrists and leaned into him so that the tip of my nose found his.

'Now listen to me, laddie,' I began, 'we have got FRIENDS for DINNER, and then we are going OUT. We

160

cannot just cancel for the FOOTIE. We are GROWN-UPS. You KNEW about tonight because I TOLD you. It's been written on the year planner for NEARLY A WEEK. Had you told me about the footie earlier we could have DONE SOMETHING ABOUT IT. But we CAN'T. So go upstairs and GET CHANGED. PLEASE. And if you make any comments about Theresa's top you are in BIG TROUBLE. We can VIDEO the footie and WATCH IT LATER. OK?' I gripped his wrists tighter and wriggled a bit. Quite often when I took a tone with him like this I'd have ended up being dragged upstairs for a thorough sorting out, but this crisis went beyond that, clearly, as Stewart bit his lip and looked ceilingwards. Besides, we had company. Finally he nodded, then stood up so abruptly that I slid off his lap, landing on my bottom on the sofa. The roughness of that simple action was so unlike him that for a moment I felt the beginnings of tears at the back of my eyes as I watched him lumber sullenly upstairs to change. In fact I was so rattled I barely even noticed the doorbell, and it was a few seconds before I jumped about two feet in the air and rushed to let Stevie in.

He did that thing of having his back to the door and pivoting round casually when I opened it. We looked at each other for a few seconds without saying anything. For a millisecond I wanted to lunge at him and kiss him. And I didn't mean the 'Stevie! How nice!' sort of *mwah* kiss either. We Highlanders don't just kiss willy-nilly. Well, only at New Year. Oh God. Something weird was happening to my insides. It didn't help that he seemed a little flustered as well.

'Hi! You made it!' I managed. He brandished a gorgeous bunch of flowers at me – taut lilies and inviting pink roses. I fumbled the handover and they fell onto the step between us. 'Oh no! Sorry!'

'It's OK, my fault,' he said, picking them up and handing them to me. 'At least it wasn't a bottle. How are you doing?'

'Fine! Come in, come in. Stuart and Theresa are upstairs.' He raised an eyebrow – another high-scoring trick I remembered of old – and grinned. 'I mean, Stuart's getting changed and Theresa's doing bedtime stories. For the children.'

'Right. Got you.'

He followed me in to the kitchen, where I began fumbling for a vase. I was pricklingly aware that my bottom was being checked out. What the *hell* was going on? Why did I feel so raw, so exposed? He took off his jacket and slung it over the back of a chair. His white open-necked shirt and dark blue cotton trousers looked crisp, and fresh, and . . . oh, for heaven's sake.

'Nice house,' he said, looking round.

'Thanks. Bine or weer? I mean, wine or beer? Or something else?'

'Beer, please. Better watch it, though, I'm driving.' He came over, took the flowers from me and began to unwrap them, standing squarely within the boundaries of my personal space. Still prickling, but now tingling as well, I slid out of range to go and fetch the beer, then immediately wished I'd stayed where I was. I might even have thrust my face into his neck and begun licking, but maybe it was just as well I moved, as at that moment Stuart emerged from upstairs, also crisp and fresh in an open-necked white shirt and dark blue cotton trousers. Following my introductions they exchanged amiable blokey handshakes, and Stuart, muffling his disgruntlement about the footie and ever the social smoothie, quipped:

'Gail's told me lots about you, but she didn't mention your excellent dress sense! Rangers man?'

'Too right!' Stevie replied. 'If I can't watch the game at least I can wear the colours!'

And they were off. Grumbling good-humouredly about the unfairness of life which meant a man couldn't watch the footie where there were women around to thwart them at every turn. They could have been reading from the Great British Lads' Script of Life, the way they shrugged and shook their heads and swigged their beer. Actually, I hadn't told Stuart 'so much about' Stevie. I'd kept him pretty much to myself, only sketching in the vaguest facts about asking a guy I was at school with to partner Theresa at the ball. Stuart, playing his part, didn't ask more, maybe afraid that asking probing questions about someone who was ostensibly no more than dance-partner fodder would brand himself a Great Big Girl.

The menu had been planned with care, so as to project that Nigella-esque display of throwing together a fantastic meal in about six minutes flat, drizzled with olive oil and fragrant with lemongrass and coriander. And it worked to a certain extent, if you gloss over the fact that the whole exercise in simplicity had taken four solid days in the planning and execution. Because I'd worked out that we only had just over an hour from the start of the evening to Mum's arrival to babysit, I'd just made pasta with home-made sauce and salad, to be followed by a rich and sticky chocolate cake to eat with coffee. For which simplicity I had done a forty-mile round trip to the Italian deli in Inverness for fresh pasta and Parmesan, secured three different kinds of mineral water and eight different beers and lagers from the supermarket, phoned in an extra wine delivery, harangued a mail-order chocolate company until they'd given in and sent their most expensive, seventy-per-cent proof chocolate up by courier, bought a coffee-bean grinder and a new set of beer tumblers, overhauled my nails, eyebrows, hair, shoes and underwear, and visited the dental hygienist for a quick scale and polish.

Theresa's entrance was heralded by a *boing-giddy-boing-giddy-boing* as she bounced downstairs. She was giggling uncontrollably, and appeared not to notice the identikit males whose evenings had just been brightened considerably by her pneumatic arrival.

'You'll never believe what Thomas said,' she spluttered at me, propping herself against the cooker and giggling.

'He wasn't asking who his real daddy is again, was he?' I replied as Stuart rolled his eyes.

'He told me he's got to pray for the cars and lorries at school! You know, in the Lord's Prayer, "For Thine is the kingdom, the cars and the lorries, amen!"'

Stuart and I had chuckled over this one for weeks, not to mention his earnest, 'Our Father, Pitcharting heaven, Harold be thy name ...', but, chuffed by the promising start to the evening, we roared with overloud, God-this-is-a-*fantastic* night! laughter. It was only then that she appeared to notice Stevie, and before I had a chance to commence introductions she walked over to him and stopped less than a foot in front of his face.

'Hiya!' she chirped, looking at him confidently. 'You must be my partner in crime? I'm Theresa – nice to meet you!'

'Likewise,' Stevie answered, offering his hand while, I suspected, trying not to let his eye contact slide south. 'Always happy to help out in a crisis.'

They smiled as they appraised one another, and, with Stuart and me looking on, a short silence ensued. Oops, my cue.

'How heroic,' I said, in a clipped little voice which took even me by surprise. 'Drink, T?'

'Red, please Gail.'

Stuart spoke. 'That's a nice top, Theresa. Just as well the kids didn't, urm, you know, dribble on it or anything ... what I mean is ... ' He tailed off, looked at me and shrugged in defeat. I glowered back.

'Thanks,' Theresa replied, keeping her gaze on Stevie.

'Did you come on your bike, Stevie?' I asked, then immediately wanted to giggle in a *Carry On* film kind of way.

'Course not, I took the pick-up.' He stopped, then realised we all thought he was going to say more. 'Um, it's nice to be able to offer people a lift home, for one thing.'

'I'd have been fine on the bike,' purred Theresa, running her free hand down the side of her thigh. Stevie laughed uncertainly, Stuart coughed and I banged plates about.

'Let's eat.' I barked. 'We haven't got all night.'

You know when you buy a pair of trousers, and they're fantastic? Then, at a later date, you spot an ass-kickingly sexy top which you just know for certain will make you weep with the sheer perfection of it all when you team it up with said trousers? So you rush home, rip your clothes off, climb into the trousers, wriggle into the top, shimmy over to the full-length mirror, *feast* your eyes, and ... oh bugger. It's just not quite right. *Well,* that's how it seemed to be with Stevie and Theresa. I mean, Stevie is un-questionably one must-have pair of trousers, and Theresa is a seriously sparkly top, but together, at the full-length mirror that was my dining-room table, they were, well, somehow more Gauche than Gucci. If I'd been antici-pating a big, drooling, saliva-fest as they got acquainted with each other to the exclusion of everyone else and all that sort of stuff, then it soon became obvious that it wasn't going to happen. Although they did manage to complete a bronze-level dinner-table starter conversation, Module A, Foundation Unit One, with a full complement of 'reallys?' and 'that must have been interestings', not to

165

mention 'I could never have done thats', 'did yous?', and more 'mmms' than a bound-and-gagged chocolate-taster.

Stevie and Stuart got on famously though, mining the rich seams of football and rugby for a while, and then moving on for the second time to the puzzling topic of how they got themselves roped into attending dance practices at the homes of peculiar control freaks.

It was me Stevie ignored, if anything, apart from to compliment the pasta (*'Oh, this old standby – it just took minutes!'*), and, later, to say something nice about the chocolate cake *('The cake? Bit of a cop-out but it was quick!')*, praise which I quietly gathered up and claimed as my own, even though he had addressed it to his plate rather than to my face. Theresa lowered the tone (hurray!) by answering, 'No thanks, I'll be completely fatarsed,' to my offer of more cake, at which Stuart – *my* bloody Stuart – offered to do some test-squeezes to put her mind at rest, but, for pity's sake, that was it on the flirting front.

Mum was unable to ring the doorbell this time, encumbered as she was by the fan heater, her sewing and an anglepoise lamp. Stevie got up when she appeared in the doorway, wiping his mouth on his napkin and moving forward to help her with her stuff.

'Hi Mrs Buchanan, how are you doing? Can I give you a hand with that?'

'You can do petit point?' Mum replied sweetly, removing her black mac to reveal what seemed to be the national dress of Iran but was actually her favourite mail-order 'lounge shift', in powder blue. 'I'm impressed. Just take the heater, if you don't mind.'

'Her little joke,' I growled. 'Hi Mum, thanks for coming.'

'Hello, darling. Stuart. My, my, Theresa, we're all to the fore tonight, aren't we? Would you like to borrow my jumper? It's actually quite chilly out there, you know.'

'I'll be fine, thanks, Mrs B, all the leaping around we're going to do is bound to keep me warm.'

Mum turned her attention back to Stevie. 'So, Steven, Gail told me you were coming tonight! When did you get back from, oh, where was it, Canada?'

'Australia. Four years ago, now, I think.'

'*Four?* Really? I don't think I've seen you since, oh, would it be round about the time you wrote off your father's car and damaged your . . . your . . .' She jerked her head meaningfully in the direction of his crotch.

'Can't quite remember, Mrs Buchanan. Do you want this through here?'

Stuart interrupted: 'Just leave the dishes, Marjorie, I'll sort them out when we get back.'

'Oh Stuart, you're such a *catch*!' exclaimed Theresa, poking him in the ribs.

'Don't you worry, Stuart, I'm not washing anything up tonight. Now off you go to your lesson. Good to see you again, Steven. Have fun, bairns!'

When we arrived at Esther's, the men were revolting. Tony, Janusz and the others were huddled round the portable television mounted on the kitchen wall, joshingly engrossed in the footie. Stuart and Stevie exchanged happy looks and pushed into the throng.

'Still nil–nil,' advised Tony, his eyes not leaving the screen, 'but Rangers have had all the possession and a goal disallowed. Ref's a joke. Fanta or Irn-Bru?'

Clinging to Dunny-brush's arm, Esther was bristling with umbrage. Then it seemed that she could contain herself no longer, as she marched over to the huddle of chaps, forgetting to let go of the startled Dunny-brush, wriggled to the front and switched the set off.

'Can we just remember why we're here, thank you?' she instructed. 'Now, places, please, for Shiftin' Bobbins.'

'Esther, do tell us you made that title up,' Val giggled, conjuring Charity from under her jumper.

Esther ignored this and Dunny-brush stroked her arm, turning to the muttering crowd. 'Well, Esther, my love, let's see if everyone can shift bobbins as well as you can shift footie fans! Good evening everyone! Ready for more red-hot ceilidh action? Let's do it!'

'Wooh!' Theresa whooped, probably thinking for a second she was back in one of her body-pump classes.

The grumbling males shrugged their partners onto their arms and went through to the beige sitting room. Esther thrust her face in front of Stevie.

'It's Steven, isn't it? Just listen to Otto and try to follow the others. OK!'

Stevie, in the true-blue, baddie-thwarting tradition of turning preconceived ideas on their heads and stamping on them, was a fantastic dancer. The bugger had done this before. It wasn't that he pranced around like Nureyev or anything, he just followed Dunny-brush's instructions so effortlessly, leaving himself loads of scope to be attentive to Theresa, who struggled a bit with her teapots and her skip-change-of-steps. In fact, her comment of: 'Isn't this the sort of thing you'd do in dressage, Claire?' didn't go down very well at all with most of the rest of the room, but Stevie laughed softly and said, 'Easy, girl,' in a dirty way I wished I hadn't heard. Stuart, partnering me for a change, had a better night than previously and was soon letting slip the occasional *'Hooch!'* which had me quite embarrassed but which Dunny-brush and those in the know acknowledged as a kind of shorthand for *'Cracked it, by Jove!'*

Even Val and Janusz, whose bewilderment the last time

168

had been even greater than mine, didn't get lost too often and were soon smilingly wafting through the steps, until Eden, Struan and Rowan, dressed in pyjamas and encased in sleeping bags, jumped into the room from outside, looking for something to drink.

Esther was not amused. 'They've been out there all this time? For God's sake, what if your van had blown up when they were in there on their own?' she barked at Janusz.

'Oh, don't worry, it hasn't got nearly enough petrol in it for that,' he replied earnestly, smiling at his sleepy brood. They were each handed a glass of milk and then Esther made them shuffle into her dining room, snarling at them not to touch anything and to go to sleep on the floor.

'Let's all break for a drink,' suggested Tony, glancing at Esther to make sure he was allowed to take such a major decision. I watched as Stevie kept his hand draped around Theresa's shoulders while we trooped through to the kitchen for our juice. I could see furtive male glances being shot between the television set and Esther, followed by little sighs of anguish.

'Just going to check the score, OK Esther?' Stevie broke away from Theresa and switched the set on. The men looked admiringly at Stevie and crowded round the little screen once more, letting out a tribal '*Nnneeeuuurrggghhh*' followed by a well-brought-up, hissed, '*''Cksake'* when they saw that Rangers were two goals down. Esther, seeing that there were only a few minutes to go, corralled us women-folk around the kitchen table.

'Listen, girls, crisis meeting tomorrow, at Susannah's house, ten o'clock, right?'

'Crisis?' repeated Claire, startled. 'Not . . . the *sashes* . . .' Her hand shot to her shoulder and she looked across at Val in panic.

'Nope, they're done,' said Val simply.

'No, no, not the sodding sashes,' raged Esther. 'It's, just, just, *everything bloody else*! There's hardly any time left to go, and the organisation seems to have been taken *completely* out of my hands. Nobody's arse has a clue what anybody's elbow is up to, so yesterday I confronted Susannah about it and decided to take the mountain to Mohammed and call a meeting of no-confidence motion of quorum to remove from office by-election committee chairperson ... buggery ... quorumy, *thingy*. At her house. For a change. OK?'

'Oh, Esther,' I said, 'Susannah's not really in the mood for this sort of thing just now ...'

'And I suppose you think I am?' retorted Esther. 'Susannah's all fluster and apologies, but behind the scenes she's charging on with arrangements and bookings, without telling a living soul what she's up to! Yesterday she owned up that she's already been up at Invermartin sorting out how to connect power cables from the house to the marquee, for God's sake!'

There was a cheer as Rangers scored. The run of the game had switched and Rangers were dominating the midfield. There were fifteen minutes of normal time left for an equaliser. Or even a winner. If they got it, then it would mean Europe next season, with all the euphoric, jubilationy, open-topped bus, boys-done-good glory that went with it. The men were clutching the edges of Esther's worktop and straining their necks upwards towards the little screen like a nestful of hungry thrushes. It would have taken a totally insensitive megalomaniac with a hide like a rhinoceros to realise that there would be no more dancing for the duration, so, needless to say, Esther had to be put in the picture by tactful Amber and Claire, who drew her away, pleading to be shown round the beige house. This was Tony's cue to do an exaggerated tiptoe through to switch on the big telly in the sitting room, where, to a resounding cheer from Stuart, Janusz, Martin, Iain, Kevin and Theresa, he turned on the Big Match. Even Dunny-brush tripped excitedly through and found a cushion to sit on, from where he could get a really good view of the action. Val picked up Charity and swept through to tend to her children who were struggling to get to sleep on the beige rug underneath Esther's mahogany-veneered oval dining table. I watched her gather her children around her into a big, cosy heap in a corner, and, with Charity plugged in for milk, she found at least two free hands to stroke tired heads and then, warmly rocking, began to sing them a Gaelic lullaby.

Back in the kitchen Sarah had whipped out her mobile and her Palm Pilot and began making some calls. Lots of 'yup, yup, sure, sure, OK, yups' began to fill the air and, feeling like an eavesdropper upon the corridors of power but unsure where else to put myself, I slipped outside.

The evening was soft and lilac and kind, and as I took deep breaths of grass-scented air some of my edginess began to subside. Calm, calm, calm. I walked across the newly cut, semi-circular lawn and sat down on a low wall which separated the grass from a raised bed full of regimented white flowers, determinedly planted in ascending order of height and resembling a herbaceous school photograph. A sudden roar, and whoops from indoors heralded an equaliser, and I smiled at the chaps' delight.

I *so* wanted Theresa and Stevie to get together, marry and have children. I *so* wanted Theresa and Stevie to have a terrific relationship and be great buddies. I *so* wanted Theresa and Stevie to enjoy each other's company. I *so* wanted Theresa and Stevie to tolerate each other until the ball was over. I so wanted Stevie and Theresa not to get together. *I so wanted Stevie*.

Hmmm.

Knowing that I was thinking like the lustful sixteen-year-old I was when I'd first had the hots for Stevie didn't help much. Telling myself that I was a happily married mother of two beautiful children, bereft of a precious third, provided an essential reality check. And watching Stevie quietly come out of the front door and cross the lawn towards me brought me right back to square one.

'Hi,' I said.

'Bit too exciting in there,' he said, nodding towards the sitting-room window, where the beige curtains had been drawn, and sitting beside me on the wall.

'So you thought you'd seek out something boring?' I shot back, trying to be smart but sounding instead like a sarky adolescent. 'Where's Theresa?'

'Inside, in front of the box. Explaining the off-side rule to Dunny-brush.'

'Ah.'

'She's nice.'

'Course she is. I told you she was, didn't I?'

'I guess you did.' We were both swinging our legs and gazing at the patches of lawn just beyond our feet.

'Where did you learn to dance?' I asked. 'We didn't do this sort of weird stuff at school, as I recall?'

He grinned. 'Nope. 'We did a bit of other weird stuff, though, didn't we?'

Stevie Chip had always known how to make girls blush, and he was doing it to me now. I silently thanked the fading sunlight for disguising my cheeks, and whacked his arm.

'Don't avoid the question, if you please,' I said as sternly as I could.

'At university, Gail, in the Scottish Country Dancing Club.'

172

'Oh!'

Stevie smiled at the surprise in my voice. It hadn't occurred to me that he might have gone to university, somehow, and now I felt horrible. It wasn't that I cared whether he'd gone to college or not, it was the fact that I'd made the assumption that he *hadn't*. He put his arm round my shoulders and gave me a squeeze. A lovely one. For a moment I leaned fractionally in towards him, before reluctantly lifting his arm off and returning it to his side.

'Why dancing?' I faltered. 'You weren't interested ...'

'Because the club was organised by a girl called Becky Holland, who looked a bit like Elizabeth Hurley, only ...'

'Less plastic?' I supplied sweetly.

'Something like that.'

'Did it pay off?' I asked in a nasty voice.

'How do you mean?'

'Did you get off with her?'

He laughed and turned his whole body round so that it was facing me, stooping slightly so that he could peer under my hair directly into my eyes. 'Yes, Gail, as a matter of fact, I did get off with her! Can you credit it? What was I thinking? Oh, my, God! I got off with a girl at uni! How weird is that?'

'OK, OK, sorry.'

I looked away and we were quiet for a minute or two. Then I said: 'Is it OK, you know, roping you into all this stuff?'

'Sure, why not?'

'Well, you don't think it's a bit ... well ... *snobby*? I mean, a stupid sponsored Toddle and ball, you know, poncing around, expensive tickets and stupid rules and long dresses, it's not ... well, y'know—'

'Gail,' he interrupted, sounding serious, 'when I was in Australia I learned a couple of things about people. Or maybe I just grew up a bit. I mean, when I arrived there I was just, well, *me*. Myself. All anyone had to go on when they met me was face value. And it was the same with me about them. There was no history, no family, and no hassles. I discovered snobbery in the weirdest places, but never where I expected it. And just because you're all getting yourselves into a lather trying to organise an event in a certain way doesn't take away from the fact that you're a nice bunch of people attempting to raise money for the kids, does it?'

'But Esther . . .' I faltered.

'Is insecure. That's all.'

He'd moved closer so that our upper arms were touching from shoulder to elbow. I kept my eyes fixed on the *fascinating* daisy just to the left of my right foot. And we both jumped when another ear-splitting roar burst out from Esther's house, signalling a Rangers winner and everlasting joy. We looked at each other and grinned, then got up to go back into the house, just as Theresa and Stuart came out to find us.

'Three–two!' yelled Theresa. 'They did it!'

'We know!' we responded in unison. Stuart grabbed me for a hug and Stevie, rather self-consciously, went and stood beside Theresa.

'Where were you?' Stuart asked.

'Talking about school,' I replied.

'And the Toddle,' added Stevie. 'I was just telling Gail that there's a meeting with the community police officer at Invermartin to check the route on Thursday, and she'll need to be there to double-check I've put the markers in the right places. That OK then, Gail?' He looked straight at me, confidently, defying me to bottle out. I looked back and pretended a weary sigh.

'Oh, I suppose so.'

Chapter Ten

'Daniel's granny died yesterday,' Thomas announced solemnly, as I drove him to school the next morning.

'Oh dear,' I drifted back.

'That means he's only got one granny to go, doesn't it?'

'That's right, well done.'

'Will you be dead one day?' he persisted, jolting me back into real time.

'Of course not, sweetheart, that's a sad thing to think, isn't it? Try to think of nice things, like sunshine. Or toys.'

'My little brother died, didn't he?'

'Yes, poppet, he did.'

'Are there toys for him in heaven?'

'Loads and loads.'

'Will Emma die too?'

'No, of course not.'

'How do you know?'

'Mummies know everything. Here we are, then!' I pulled into the school's car park, crowded with revving-engined cars disgorging children and their various schoolbags, teddies and footballs into the private community that was their playground. 'Have a lovely day at school, big man, and make sure you have the hot meal at canteen, not the sandwich, won't you?' I opened the car door and he was off, with my 'It's macaroooniii . . .' trailing unheard into the buzz.

I watched him running, all arms and legs, flapping anorak and bouncing schoolbag, across the playground towards his knot of friends, who were standing in the muddiest patch of playground they could find, earnestly trading Pokémon cards.

It was funny how little the school had changed since my day. Presumably since my dad's day, too. Although, come to think of it, there was one major difference: when I was a pupil I'd always had to look *upwards* at things: teachers, windowsills, coat hooks, blackboards, cupboards – they all existed in the grown-up airspace above my head, while I toiled my way through primary school in that unique children's low level environment, full of chalk-dust, important rules, secrets, order, and confusion.

Now, looking the place squarely in the eye, the only tangible changes were the addition of three lumpen grey Portakabins to house the larger numbers of pupils, extra parking for ever-larger cars, and, inside the building, the shrunken appearance of the desks and chairs which, when I occasionally went in and sat down beside Thomas to look at his work, brought back physical pangs of my own childhood which by happenstance I'd replicated for my own children.

Driving off towards Esther's crisis meeting at Susannah's, with Emma co-piloting in the back, my mind raced with thoughts of the previous night. I'd hardly slept, as I ricocheted from excited panic about Thursday's trip to see Stevie at Invermartin to tumbling conjecture about Stuart and Susannah. I knew there wasn't much hard evidence about the two of them, but I still couldn't make my suspicions go away. Apart from a vague suspicion that Stuart had something on his mind he wasn't telling me, and the perfume thingy, I remained utterly convinced that Emma had been there, in the background, that day Susannah had made that pointless phone call to me about paperwork. I knew it, but I didn't know what to do about it. I could ask Stuart straight out at any time, but I guess the only reason I could give myself for not having done so was that, in a marriage so hitherto stable, any *accusations* of infidelity would be almost as bad as the real thing. Once the trust goes, so too the marriage. Well, the trust was going. Then again, maybe I was subconsciously keeping the wedding band loose for my own none-too-decent purposes.

But, for example, Stuart had spent the previous weekend in Edinburgh, catching up with a rugby club friend from university. On his return, he wasn't exactly bursting with information about how the weekend had gone, but judging by his pale face and Garbo-esque desire to be on his own, I'd initially just assumed that he was trying to conceal a massive hangover.

'I'm afraid I didn't get to the shops in Edinburgh,' he'd said, feebly, as he handed me a bunch of carnations which looked suspiciously like they'd come from the petrol station in the centre of the village. Then he pulled some tubes of Smarties out of his jacket pocket and lobbed them awkwardly onto the kitchen with the speed of Yosemite Sam trying to offload some sticks of dynamite before they blew up in his face.

I'd glowered at the tightly closed scarlet buds, throttled on their forced stems. It was a bit pathetic, I know, but I couldn't hide my disappointment, nor that strange feeling of unease which had been creeping in a lot from left-field. It was out of character for Stuart to buy me crap flowers and it really pissed me off.

'Oh, darling, you shouldn't have – chocolates? And filling station flowers – how I *love* filling-station flowers!

From the man who just doesn't have a minute!'

Stuart looked miserable. 'The Smarties are for the children, Gail.'

'I know,' I'd muttered.

And the flowers Stevie had brought the night before, fresh and personally chosen from Amanda Bain's florist's shop in Church Street, mocked us from the windowsill.

Entering Susannah's sitting room, I decided it was designed with comfort only a secondary intention, after the primary objective of inducing inferiority complexes in visitors was fulfilled. Apart from the paintings and the creamy cleanliness, I think it was something to do with the profusion of big, sculptural plants which emanated green vitality from every pore, or whatever it is that leaves breathe through.

Furtively, I massaged the edge of a huge, waxy Swiss cheese leaf to check if it was real. Then, realising that Susannah had been watching, I snapped my hand away and felt compelled to fill the ensuing silence.

'Just *had* to make sure they're real – I've never seen such healthy plants! Well, apart from fake ones. Do you water them often?' I flashed royal-visit eyes and Susannah smiled, kindly, as she took my coat.

'Only when they need it. I can't bear artificial plants. Or anything fake, for that matter. Being surrounded by dishonesty. It's not healthy, somehow ... oh, I don't know. Sorry – ignore me, I often talk rubbish!'

She resumed flustering and I looked at her closely. Fake? Dishonesty? Hello? Sounds familiar? Maybe she was about to come clean and tell me she was lifting Stuart from under my very nose and installing him, like a live Damien Hirst, in her immaculate home? Oh, God.

'So how are you?' I asked, noticing that there was no trace of her former desolation either on her face or anywhere else in the gorgeous room. She just looked her usual, waify, groomed little fair self.

'Me? Oh, I'm fine, thanks! Just great!'

'Sure?' I persisted.

'Completely, thanks. Everything's just fine. In fact, I'm starting to think the whole thing's been for the best, actually. The girls are happy, I'm happy, and well, I think, um, sorry, I'll put the kettle on!'

'Uh, good for you!' I chirped. Wonder what had perked *her* up so dramatically?

Emma and I were the first to arrive, but before I'd managed to get her out of her anorak, Emma sidestepped Susannah and disappeared behind one of the sofas, emerging triumphantly with a fat armful of dolls. 'Babies!' she announced, before charging across the room, opening a side door and marching into Susannah's conservatory, rumbling three-year-old Abigail who was hanging onto baby Isabella's baby walker, with said Isabella, beaming and oblivious to her peril, snugly strapped in as the contraption barrelled at breakneck speed around the gleaming parquet. Emma's appearance put a stop to that, though. Abigail hopped off the machine, sent it and its infant contents careering across the room with a hefty push, and began pulling dolls from Emma's grasp. The two girls sank to the floor and straight away embarked on that self-absorbed, semi-interaction process that passes in tiny-kid-world for 'playing together'.

Now, my wee Emma is not a shy child. In fact, if asked to come up with twenty adjectives for my daughter (not, admittedly, something that's likely to happen), I'd have gone straight to the *Thesaurus* or whatever cunning book deals with that sort of stuff, and fished out the twenty words most approximating the exact opposite of 'shy'. For instance, the sight of her, aged just over one-and-a-half, squealing, '*Come on! COME ON!!*' and dragging her nervous and much bigger brother into Santa's grotto in Inverness shopping centre the previous December, is the sort of thing Stuart is likely to trot out at the poor child's wedding. She likes to climb onto the laps of those whom she meets. Her doctor. Checkout operators. The minister. She dances on tables, experiments with face-pulling and programmes other people's video recorders. She is a confident child.

But this behaviour went beyond confidence. There was something so odd about how she'd gone directly to the toys and then straight to where she knew Abigail would be. Something about how she didn't look over her shoulder to double-check I was still there. Something about managing the door handle. This was *familiarity*, I realised, with a horrible lurch in the pit of my stomach.

Fuck it. 'Have you seen Stuart or anyone about a divorce?' I called through to the kitchen, suddenly desperate to know the answer and throwing caution to the wind. I heard the sound of the kettle being thumped down onto the worktop and she was back through in a flash.

'Stuart? Nooo! Of course not! Why would I see Stuart?' She stumbled over to the sofa and started plumping up some already perfectly plump silk cushions.

'Um, because he's a lawyer? And because I suggested his name to you because you've got a divorce to sort out, and, um, well, I just thought . . .'

'Paul's handling all that. And Mummy.'

'Mummy?'

'I'm just not interested, Gail. Mummy's a pro at all the settlement stuff, she's done it tons of times before, and, well, I just don't want to give him the satisfaction of watching me ask for things for me and the girls. I'm stepping out of the whole thing. One day Mummy's just going to turn up here with a divorce paper to sign and I'll sign it. Then – freedom!'

180

This could hardly have been more of a contrast to the distraught little heap I'd walked in on the other week. Time, or something, had really worked its magic, that was for sure.

'So, what about Paul, you're just going to ignore him?'

She sighed. 'No, Gail, I'm not *even* going to ignore him. He's an irrelevance. He'll be able to see the girls more or less when he wants, and Mummy will sort out the money side of things. She's got a great female solicitor in Edinburgh who can do this sort of thing in her sleep, as can Mummy, so I'm just getting on with my life. That's that. Sorry.'

'Don't be.'

The doorbell rang and Val appeared, clutching Charity, who was wearing battered orange pyjamas. Susannah and I craned our heads past her in anticipation of the other three children following her in, but they didn't appear.

'Janusz is making a bender with the others in the woods.' Looking at our blank faces, she elaborated, 'You know, a bender? A shelter of bent branches? Morning!' She slid Charity off her hip to plop onto the sofa. 'I've brought raspberry buckwheat muffins!'

Claire and Amber arrived together, having left their children with their au pairs. Claire had brought warm flapjacks and Amber a jar of home-made rowan jelly. I decided to leave my packet of twelve KitKats in my bag and say nothing at all about them. When Susannah came through from the kitchen with freshly ground coffee and hot scones with zingy lemon curd, the atmosphere of the room switched from comfortable chattiness to tummy-sucking uncertainty – it became a shrine to the Great God Calorie, as though the Fat Wizard from the Ministry of Chubby had popped his head round the door and waved his lardy wand. Suddenly tense, the room pondered What To Have.

Claire and Amber twittered and shuddered at the array of temptation before them and agreed, there and then, that as soon as they were done at Susannah's they'd go straight to Fit Farm, the most expensive new gym Inverness could muster, to work their tiny little butts into a Lycra-lather.

'Dig in – I won't as I've had a huge breakfast,' Susannah implored, stroking her concave tummy and pouring coffee. She probably meant an *entire* slice of toast. Claire and Amber discussed what to do, eventually agreeing to halve a flapjack and share it, while Val munched happily like a normal person and I automatically went for the lowest calorie item available – one scone, no butter, no lemon curd. Emma and Abigail careened into the room and were rewarded with their very own plastic plate of bakery items, cut up small by solicitous Susannah. Duplicitous Susannah? Mistressicitous Susannah?

'Where's Esther?' Amber asked. 'She's the one who called the meeting, isn't she?'

We were answered by a small squeal of brakes, followed by some ominous snarlings from Susannah's drive. *'Come on! Just leave it alone and bloody get out! Move it!'*

The door flew open and Esther clattered in, carrying a huge pad of white paper and some marker pens and dragging a sullen and miserable Magnus in her wake. She glowered at us all before slamming the door behind her, picking up Magnus by the armpits, marching him over to the open conservatory door and dropping him between the cake-eating girls.

'Right,' she began, wheeling round to the rest of us and putting her hands on her hips. 'Counshel of war. Tall and Boddle to sort out before we all lose the plot. Is that coffee?'

Then, to our horror, she took a few uncertain steps forward and practically fell into the only vacant seat, beside Val and baby Charity, where she sat back and closed her eyes, rubbing her temples.

I glanced round at the others. Amber was stifling

giggles, trying to catch Claire's eye so they could share the moment. Claire, however, looked horrified; her eyes were bugging out of her head as years of breeding dropped away and she simply stared, open-mouthed. Val hugged Charity closer to her and tentatively touched Esther gently on the shoulder, while Susannah had adopted an unreadable expression as she poured a large mug of coffee.

'Hello Esther,' she said coolly. 'I think you should probably drink this.'

Esther opened her eyes and reached for the mug. 'Cheers,' she mumbled, taking a noisy slurp. 'Aaaah. Bloody good coffee. Is that flapjack? Scones? My my, ladies, having a baking bee, were we? Delishish.' She helped herself to a flapjack and took a huge bite. 'Right, shall we get going? I've just brought this pad along as a visual aid. Susannah? Minutes, if you pleeeease?' She waved a queenly hand at Susannah who sniffed and stalked out of the room.

'Esther, love, are you OK?' asked Val, stroking Esther's shoulder. 'You look a bit, well . . .'

'Emotional,' I said. Well, she did.

'Bollocksh!' Shards of flapjack shot across the room. 'Just as soon as we sort out the fucking ball and fucking Toddle I'll be fucking tickety-boo, OK?'

This was too much for Susannah, who had returned with her stationery collection. 'Esther, you're pissed! How could you have driven over here in that state? What about Magnus?'

'I am NOT pissed! It's eleven o'clock in the fucking morning!' It was quarter past ten. She gulped at her coffee and wiped her mouth with her sleeve. 'Rightio, agenda.' She propped her pad against the back of the sofa and wrote STRAGETIES in large capital letters along the top.

'Erm, think you've got a mistake in there,' ventured Claire. Esther whipped round to glower at her then checked her pad.

'Oh yes. Thanks, Claire,' she replied ungraciously before amending the heading to STRAGETIE'S. Then, continuing down the page, she scrawled:

1. Apologies
2. The Ball
3. The Toddle
4. A.O.C.B.

Quite stunningly simple, really. Then she sank back into the sofa and closed her eyes again. Over to someone else.

What shall we do with the drunken Esther? Well, you either over- or underdo it, I guess. You can flap like the Funky Chicken, call the police, administer aspirin and arrange for Magnus to be taken into care, or else you can be frightfully British, cover for her and pretend this sort of eccentricity happens all the time. Which is precisely what we did. I suppose if she truly was trying to sort out her problem like she'd told us at the previous meeting, then didn't she really need just a dust-down, and a leg-up back onto the wagon?

'Ok,' I said bracingly, 'shall we get going?' I was trying to quell the sensation inside which was suspiciously close to pity for Esther, while realising that I didn't want to be there one moment longer than was absolutely necessary. 'First up, Apologies. Anyone?'

'Sorry I didn't bring some fucking pancakes!' snorted Esther, convulsing into private hilarity. Everyone tutted and shook their heads, apart from Val who reached for the coffee jug and refilled Esther's cup.

'Well, Sarah's working, so you could put that in?' suggested Claire.

'Good idea,' agreed Amber. 'Definitely Sarah.'

'Yes, but did she actually contact anyone to send apologies?' queried Susannah, 'because I really can't put someone in "apologies" unless they've actually *tendered* apologies to another committee member. Sorry, but that's the way it is.'

'But we all know she's at work!' protested Claire.

'Poor little thing,' added Amber.

'Yes, but I can't minute an apology that hasn't been formally tendered. Sorry.'

A short stand-off ensued as Claire looked expectantly from the pad to Susannah's face and back again, while Susannah laid her pen down and folded her arms.

'Wait a minute!' said Claire, waving her arms around, 'come to think of it, she DID ask me to pass on her apologies, I'm sure she did! Last night at Esther's, I'm certain she said something along the lines of, um, "So sorry I won't make it tomorrow, but I shall be at work!" Yes, that was definitely it! And then, as she was going out the door, she definitely said something like, um, "Do make sure you tender my apologies, won't you!" So silly of me to have forgotten, hahahaha!'

'Absolutely,' said Amber stoutly. 'I heard the whole thing, too. Tender apologies from Sarah!'

'Will that do you, Anne Robinson, or would you prefer them in Latin?' growled Esther.

'There's no need to be snippy,' said Susannah snippily, as she began writing.

'Right then, the ball,' I said, anxious to move matters along. 'Esther?'

This was the opening Esther had been looking for. She sat up as straight as she could and sort of leered.

'Why are you asking me? I don't know what the hell's happening. As far as I can see it, Susannah's got the whole thing sewn up! Which really pisses me off because it was MY idea, but nobody seems to give a shit about that!'

'Esther!' I cried, 'that is so unfair!'

'No it'sh not.'

'Yes it is!' I retorted, contemplating the merits of an *is! isn't! is! isn't!* ping-pong with a stroppy lush, and ploughing on. 'We all know it was your idea, don't we?' Claire and Amber nodded like crazy. Susannah looked furious. Val murmured an almost inaudible, 'Not half.' 'I think it's safe to say that none of us would have dreamed up such an, erm, ambitious event! There's no way it would have got off the ground if it hadn't been for you!'

'And now I've been schlapped in the face!' she continued. (*'She needs to be slapped in the face,'* growled a tiny voice – could that be Susannah?) 'I'm not being consulted about anything!' She jabbed a finger at Susannah. *'She's* done it all!'

'I can't believe we're arguing about this!' I yelled. 'Aren't we all wanting this to be a success? Don't committees depend on different types of people to do different things?' Nobody said or did anything so I searched my head and ploughed on. 'Esther, you're obviously an ideas woman, aren't you? The world needs people like you to come up with stuff which makes life more interesting for the rest of us, OK? Whereas Susannah is a doer – she realises she can do something and just goes out and ...' I was tailing off as I realised where my theorising was taking me. ' ... well, just does it. It wouldn't have occurred to her to check with you because she probably didn't give a thought to the fact that she may be hurting other people ...'

'You're right, of course,' said Val. 'Personally, I'm a Pisces, and that means ...'

'Excuse me, but I am still in the room?' said Susannah. 'I can't believe I'm being accused of hurting people's feelings when all I've done is make a few bookings! What else does a secretary do, for heaven's sake?'

'Some of them say nothing and just write things down,'

said Esther, who looked to be sobering up and returning to being plain old bolshie.

'You're not being accused of anything, Susannah,' I lied. 'Now let's sort this out once and for all. The ball. Esther?'

'Oh, all right. We've sold a hundred and forty tickets, including the cash Susannah wrung out of Lord Brankin's lot. The band, caterers, bar and raffle are organised, and the marquee, parking and loos are arranged. The sashes are done, thank God, or thank Val, I should say, so that means we've got all the rest to do and there's hardly any time left! It's a bloody nightmare. That's why I needed an extra meeting.'

'Quite right, Esther,' soothed Amber. 'So, er, what exactly do we still have to do?'

Esther gave her a withering look. 'Hadn't you realised? *Dance programmes*, for God's sake! Dance programmes, and, and flowers! *All* the flowers!' She lolled back again and sent thousands of flapjack crumbs into the crevices of Susannah's sofa, which pleased me not a little.

'Erm, that's it?' asked Claire tentatively. Esther didn't reply.

'Esther dear,' began Val, 'I know it'd be asking a lot, but do you think it'd be really cheeky if we asked you to collaborate with the band and lovely Otto on a dance programme? I truly feel that's the only viable way out of this horrendous dilemma, doesn't everyone else?' She looked round the room with her soft eyes and I swear I caught a little wink in my direction.

'It'd practically save our lives!' overdid Amber.

'And I could really quietly type it up for you,' whispered Susannah.

'Fine. I'll do it. But I'll type the bloody thing myself, thank you.'

'Fantastic!' I said. 'So it's just the huge issue of the flowers, is it?'

Esther's demeanour had altered completely. She sat up and surveyed us all in triumph. 'Nobody thought of flowers, did they? Organise your way out of that one, Susannah!'

'Well ...' she stammered, suddenly looking like a kid caught with her hand in the cookie jar.

'Susannah, you haven't!' I said in mock horror.

'I'm so sorry,' she began, 'but I did have an idea about that one.' Esther clasped her head in her hands. 'It's just that, well, sorry, but I've learned a bit about flowers from doing my paintings, and when I was, erm, up at Invermartin sorting out the tickets and wiring and stuff, I sort of half-arranged that I could do some table arrangements with flowers gathered from the estate – Lord Brankin was really happy about the idea ... but of course, if you want to do something different ... oh gosh ... sorry, I'm beginning to see what you mean, Gail! I'm a control freak!'

'Get that woman into therapy!' squealed Amber. 'Where's Oprah when you need her?'

'What's Oprah?' asked Val.

'Let me guess, Val, you don't have TV, do you?' said Claire.

'No, why, is Oprah a drug, or something?'

'Something like that.'

'Well, bugger me,' said Esther. 'Susannah, you are a higher breed of species than the rest of us, that's for sure. Tell me, what am I having for dinner tonight?'

'OK then, is that settled?' I was hitting my stride as unofficial chair and anxious to get home and plan what to wear to meet Stevie on Thursday. 'So, just the Toddle. Has everyone been sticking to their toddler training programme – workouts, high-carb diets, endurance stuff?'

'Only the high-carb diet bit, I'm afraid,' said Susannah, as we looked towards the conservatory where most of the bakery items were being polished off. 'But I have bought her some Barbie sports wellies, does that count?'

'Totally. Esther, would you be kind enough to take us through what still needs to be done here?'

Esther tried to sit up straight yet again and gathered herself for another leadership attempt. 'Rightio, the Toddle. Well, we need a meeting time and place, don't we?'

'Ten o'clock at the top of the Daffodil Path,' answered Susannah, writing furiously in her minute book. There was a nine-months' pregnant pause while we all glanced nervously at Esther, then Susannah looked up sheepishly and added, 'I'm sure I heard someone *else* suggesting that at some point over the last few weeks?'

Esther cleared her throat. 'Well, I thought we should start a little earlier as we'll need all our time to get ready for the ball at night, won't we?'

'Talk for yourself!' I spluttered. 'Who needs an entire day to get ready for a party?'

Claire and Amber shifted uncomfortably in their seats. 'Well, we do, actually, and Sarah too. We've booked Lorenzo's for the whole afternoon, but it's going to be a real rush, fitting in all the treatments, plus hair and make-up.' Lorenzo's is Inverness's flagship hair and beauty emporium, the sort of place where women spend hours and hundreds of pounds on hair and beauty treatments, then muss it all up by having to double-kiss and hug the entire staff on the way out.

'Wow, I thought it was just a ball, not the flipping Oscars,' I said petulantly. 'So, maybe a nine thirty start, Esther? By the time everyone's faffed around and been to the toilet, we're unlikely to get going before ten anyway.'

'OK. Susannah, make sure everyone knows the start time. Next up, sponsor forms – did everyone get one?'

'Most of the Highlands got one, as far as I can see,

Esther,' said Claire. 'I've sponsored myself and about five others already.'

'Me too,' agreed Amber.

'Excellent. Now, we need someone to collect in the forms and the sponsor money at the end. Susannah, you can do that, you made up the forms.'

'Sorry, Esther, but as you keep reminding me I'm the secretary, I'm not prepared to do the job of the treasurer. Hang on while I minute that.' She picked up her ruler and made a new heading.

'Suit yourself. Who is treasurer anyway?'

'Sarah,' chorused Amber and Claire.

'Well, make sure she knows that's her job, you two. Next up, publicity. Have we organised telly and press for this year?'

'I tried, Esther,' I fibbed, 'but it seems we're not big enough news this year. Just the local paper and the possibility of Inverness Radio sending a newscar. Unfortunately the Toddle clashes with a Council Tax Awareness Workshop at the Town Hall, so the newscar's only going to divert to us if nobody shows up at the Town Hall.' Esther looked crestfallen.

'But that's quite likely, isn't it?' said Claire.

'I did manage to fix it with the paper to come along to the ball, and take a picture of all the organisers with Lord Brankin!' chirped Susannah.

'When did you do that?' I said, miffed. The paper was MY pigeon. Suddenly I had an inkling of how Esther must be feeling – which in itself was an uncomfortable thought.

'Oh, gosh, I can't think. A while ago.'

'And Joffy knows?' asked Esther.

'Erm, yes, Joff— Lord Brankin knows. Sorry.'

'Oh well, fair enough. Sashes ho, ladies! We're going to be in the paper!'

'So, is that it?' I asked hopefully.

'Think so,' replied Esther. 'Oh yes, the route, has that been sorted out? Weren't you organising that with that factor chap? What was his name again? Simon?'

'Stevie. And yes.' My face suddenly seemed very, very hot. 'It's a short, simple route round the Daffodil Wood, which takes us on a circular path past the river. It won't take all that long. I'm, er, going up there on Thursday to meet the community police officer to check safety.'

'That's interesting,' said Esther, who was soberer by now. 'They've never done that before. I'd better come with you.'

Shock. Horror. Disbelief.

'No! No need! You'll have masses to do with your, your, dance programme and everything, and I'll be fine on my own.'

'Oh well, just make sure Simon's there too so he can sort you out.'

'It's Stevie.' And he just might.

Emma, Abigail and Magnus truffled in for more cakes and the room suddenly filled with that unmistakable warm, eggy whiff which meant only one thing.

'Ooh, think you're the guilty party, Emma love. Susannah, could I borrow your nappy changing facilities, please?'

''Course, they're in my en-suite bathroom. Through that door, first on the right.'

Joyously, Susannah's bedroom was a mess. Clothes lay everywhere, *Heat* magazines mingled with tights and toys on the floor, the curtains were still closed and the huge sleigh-bed was unmade. Her bathroom was no different, with make-up, towels, hair products and cotton-wool balls everywhere. The tiled atmosphere was damp and lived-in, a lot like my own bathroom, in fact. I searched out the changing mat under a red discarded bathrobe, upended protesting Emma and changed her nappy.

'More cake!' she squealed when we were done.

'No, we're going home. Hard luck, madam.' I turned on the tap and gazed at my reflection in the splattered mirror. Definitely a bit pink and guilty-looking, as I thought how I'd shrugged off the chance of a chaperone for my meeting with Stevie and the police officer. Baaad girl. I could wear my jeans and crushed velvet shirt. Or the raspberry cashmere V-neck which was just a shade too tight . . .

I finished washing my hands and watched the soapy water swirl down the sink, and then I noticed something which, for a few moments, didn't make any sense at all.

Around the top of the sink was a definite, wavy ring of shaving stubble. I hadn't noticed it at first, probably because the bathroom was such a general mess and anyway, I'm so used to seeing it at home because it never occurs to Stuart to wipe down the basin after his morning shave – it's one of my sore points.

But Paul had walked out on her *weeks* ago – surely, despite the bathroom chaos, that couldn't be his residue? Susannah obviously had a well-hidden messy side, but a downright *mucky* one? I didn't think so. She seemed to have washed that man right out of her life and that had to include wiping his stubble from her personal bathroom sink, didn't it? Could she have a private and very unusual personal facial hair problem? Or – and this was gradually dawning on me as the only plausible option – *could she recently have had a man staying the night?*

But then, I reasoned, Stuart hadn't been away anywhere, apart from his rugby weekend. And I couldn't exactly phone his friend to check he'd actually gone, could I? Then it occurred to me: I didn't even *know* his friend. Or where he lived – he was just a name from his past. Stuart could have been absolutely anywhere last weekend and I'd have been none the wiser.

I dried my hands and, on autopilot, followed the skipping Emma back to the sitting room where everyone except Esther had left. She had a face like thunder and was looking for Magnus, who clearly didn't want to leave and was hiding. I noticed him behind a parlour palm but didn't have the heart to blow his cover.

'Gail, make sure you ring me to report what the community police officer has to say, won't you? Sure you don't need me to come with you? *MAGNUS!! COME HERE THIS MINUTE! THIS IS YOUR LAST CHANCE BEFORE MUMMY GETS REEEALLY CROSS!!*'

'Quite sure, thanks, Esther.'

Magnus, with more experience than the rest of us of what Mummy's like when she gets reeeally cross, crawled out from the parlour palm and was hoisted by his collar to his feet and practically dragged out to the car. Esther rummaged furiously in her bag for her keys.

'Esther,' I called. 'Get into my car. Let me give you a lift home so that I can consult you about the Toddle route on the way.'

To my surprise, she stopped rummaging, looked at me with an expression that may even have been gratitude and heaved Magnus over to my car. I unlocked the door for them and then turned back to Susannah.

'Susannah, can I ask you something?'

'Of course,' she replied, looking a bit puzzled. Or worried, perhaps?

'Have you started seeing someone, by any chance?' She jerked her head towards me and looked for a moment like I'd hit her with a rock.

'I don't know what you mean. Sorry,' she replied, turned, and ran back inside.

Chapter Eleven

Stuart wasn't much up for talking that night. He was busy preparing for a complicated child abandonment case, where a mother had dropped her child off at playgroup one morning and then, without telling anyone, caught a flight to Ibiza for a week. It wasn't that there wasn't a father on the scene because there was; but the case was a money thing – the father had had to take time off work to sort the childcare situation out, resulting in 'intolerable pressure' on his business and mental health. So the husband was suing the wife for divorce and emotional damages, largely, as far as I could make out, because she had rich parents and he had a horny secretary. Stuart's legal involvement was that when the wife returned from Ibiza, refreshed, profoundly apologetic and ready to pick up the reins again, she learned that her husband had spent the week of her absence putting 'intolerable extra pressure' upon said secretary (long hours, dinners, hotels etc.), to the extent that the secretary had decided to sue him for compensation. And the wife, upon learning of this, completing the three-ringed circus, threw her hat into the ring with a counter-claim for custody and a hefty monthly allowance.

Representing the secretary posed all sorts of stresses for

Stuart, who secretly thought that she was lucky to have had the overtime, and in any event, this sort of multiple action always played havoc with his single-mindedly male organisational skills.

'Gail,' he'd called through, 'when you take off to Ibiza without warning, will you at least leave out an activities timetable for Thomas and Emma?'

'Course I will, my sweet,' I replied. 'And some bolstering casseroles in the freezer.'

So, again, I got to the end of another day without broaching the Susannah 'issue', instead heading upstairs on my own and leaving Stuart downstairs with his files, his Dictaphone and his conscience. I had a long bath, did my eyebrows, gave myself a manicure, waxed my legs and bikini line, flossed my teeth, deep-conditioned my hair and told myself it was all just general maintenance when it quite patently wasn't. It was preparation.

I was beginning to admit to myself that there was something horrifyingly exhilarating about the thought of Stuart with someone else, something fundamentally challenging, and, well, downright *interesting*. Although on another level it tore me to pieces, there was a tiny little bit of me that was intrigued by this extra dimension to our relationship. If only we could have brought everything out into the open! *'Gail, I'll be a bit late tomorrow, got to stop off at Susannah's for a bit or she'll kill me!' 'Oh, OK then, sweetie, I'll just nip up to Invermartin and shag Stevie . . . more coffee?'*

But at the same time I missed the unguardedness of our relationship. We'd always been a kind of chaotic team, where the first thing which came into either of our heads was the thing that we spoke about. What would a relationships expert make of us just now, if there happened to be one conveniently hovering above our heads? Observe us for

195

a couple of hours, then sit us down and say, 'OK, Gail, I can tell from your actions that you're having fantasies about someone with biceps, no? And you think your husband's cheating on you and you have Betty Boop tattooed on your arse. That'll be fifty quid please.' 'Uncanny,' I'd say. 'And Stuart?' 'Ah, Stuart. He is pondering whether or not to have a beer while wondering if the secretary in his court case has bigger knockers than you. That's another fifty quid, thanks.'

When I dropped Emma off at Mum and Dad's on Thursday morning, I felt an overwhelming urge to sit down, eat a chocolate biscuit and tell them all about it. Then Mum would decide what to do, I'd go and do it, and everything would be all right again, just like the old days.

But as it turned out, while I did eat the chocolate biscuit (two, in fact), the opportunity didn't present itself. Emma was whirling round and round between the fridge and the rest of the house, as my parents operated an 'access-all-areas' policy with their grandchildren which certainly wasn't in place in my day, so conversation was limited to exchanges like: 'You'll have to get that girl's hair cut,' and 'Aren't those shoes getting a bit small for her?' though once it veered towards the ticklish when Mum suggested, 'Why don't you just take her to Invermartin with you – a run around in the fresh air would do her the world of good,' to which I mumbled about wanting to give my full attention to the community police officer, and shot out of the door before we could discuss it further. And before any comment could be passed about my particularly well-done hair, nice make-up and new tan leather boots.

It was a cloudy day with a chilly wind, but at least it wasn't raining. Rain definitely wasn't part of my imagined scenario, though countless other things were. I drove out of Loch Martin, past a few mums and buggies heading off for toddler group – shit! I had completely forgotten that today was toddler group day! I thought of phoning Mum up on my mobile and suggesting that she might want to take Emma along, before remembering that she'd said something about making a fairy princess castle with her in the sandpit. *Sandpit* – another thing I'd never had. In fact the two of them were heading solemnly outside, clutching orange and green buckets and spades as I left, so it was probably best to leave things be as they had serious business to attend to.

Unlike me. I sighed and started thinking about Ben. My mind was never far away from him, but particularly so when I was driving; it was my private wallow-time. It may have had something to do with having three seats in the back of the car, or the thought of journeys he'd never take, or maybe it said something about what I did with the rest of my day, filling it with distractions so that I couldn't go quietly – or noisily – insane with grief.

Ben was born, four weeks early, after an uneventful pregnancy. Stuart was there at the birth, and although I was groggy and knackered, I still remember our glee as he was handed to me, red, slippery – and silent. The first thing I remember saying was, 'I can't believe Thomas is a big brother!' before giving him up to a nurse for the usual checks. That was the only time I held him as an 'ordinary' baby while he was alive.

At some point just after his birth he'd had a huge bleed into his brain, and he was rushed off to the Intensive Care Unit where the doctors fought for four hours to locate the source of the bleeding and stabilise him. However, despite all sorts of interventions and resuscitations, he'd died that evening in our arms, hooked up to all sorts of tubes and machines, which, with anguished hearts and a physical pain that went beyond description, we tearfully allowed to be switched off.

The early days afterwards were a blur of tears, visitors, sore breasts and funeral arrangements. I think Stuart and I only managed to survive it because of Thomas, then aged two, who, contrary to everyone's expectations, didn't seem to relate to the loss of his brother, and bounded around trying his utmost to get his parents back to normal so that he could begin having a bit of fun again. Mum and Dad had been amazing, coping with their own sorrow by being there for us in every way, answering the phone and the door, bringing food and sorting out clothes and flowers, taking Thomas away when he was rowdy and we couldn't cope, and later on, before we realised we needed him with us, quietly bringing him back.

After the funeral, when we'd sung 'Jesus Loves Me' and tried to believe it, Stuart and I lowered the small white coffin into the grave beside my grandparents, asked the stonemason to carve *'Forever in our hearts'* on the head-stone, then went quietly to pieces for a while; going through the motions of living and wondering if we'd ever stop being on the threshold of tears or else actually crying all the time. We learned to graciously deflect well-meaning platitudes which stung more than anything, like 'You'll have another one soon,' or, 'You'll get over it in time,' rather than letting fly at the well-wisher and clawing their eyes out, screaming, *'NO! NO! NO!'*

But yes, we did have another one, fiery Emma who dried up most of our tears and brought the sun back out, but no, we didn't get over it in time – we just learned to live around it.

'Glad you could make it,' said Stevie as he walked over to meet me in the beech-rimmed clearing at the entrance to the Daffodil Wood.

'Didn't have much choice, did I?' I replied. 'That was a bit of a devious trick you pulled at Esther's, wasn't it, putting me on the spot like that?' I was ridiculously nervous, trying to hide it with a mini show of aggression.

'I know. Sorry. Good laugh, though. Your face was a vision!'

'Cheers. But honestly, Stevie, if you'd only mentioned the police visit earlier, it would have made things a lot less awkward, you know.' Then I reminded myself that he was giving up his own time to help us out and added as an afterthought: 'Though it's good of you to give up so much of your time for us all. Is the policeman here yet?' I looked around. There was no sign of any other vehicles, no noises of approaching panda cars on the drive, no signs of Loch Martin's finest checking the route for ... well, for *what*, exactly? Just what was it about a sponsored Toddle that merited bloody police intervention? I whipped round to look at Stevie, who was looking as guilty as hell.

Realisation dawned. God, I was so slow sometimes. 'Tell me you're kidding,' I said menacingly. 'Stevie, there had better be a real, live, police person in this woods in the next five minutes or else you are in one hell of a lot of trouble.'

He wrung his hands in a show of contrition. 'Sorry, Gail, there's no policeman. I made it up.'

'You utter and complete—'

'I just wanted to see you on your own for a bit.'

'Bastard!'

'Sorry.'

I stared at him. 'Stevie! I don't believe you! I nearly brought Emma! And *Esther* nearly came too, for God's sake! What would you have done then?'

He looked a bit taken aback by that one. 'Oops, sorry again. Calculated risk, I suppose. I would've had to bluff my way out of that one. Hmmm, yes, that would have been dodgy. Still, here we are, though! It worked!'

'You're a devious sod.'

'That I know, Mrs Macdonald.'

We stood awkwardly for what seemed like about ten hours but must only have been thirty seconds or so. The daffodils were well past their best, but remnants of their vivid yellow hopefulness still carpeted the woods. Giant daisies were taking their place, and from the treetops a million warbly little birds laughed down at us. *'Cuckold! Cuckold! Cheap! Cheap! Herewego! Herewego! Trolloptrolloptrollop! Stuartstuartstuart!'*

'Well, what now?' I said, feigning a nonchalance which my thudding heart certainly couldn't live up to.

'Do you want to walk for a bit?'

I hesitated. 'Well, seeing as we're here we *could* just check the route, I suppose. I'll have to be able to report to Esther about *something* when I get back. If you've got time, that is.'

That was a silly one; he'd invented the whole scam to get me up here – I should have been flattered. Heck, I *was* flattered. But this was a bit intense, though, striking off into the undergrowth with a big handsome bloke who'd brought me here on false pretences and for whom I quite evidently had the hots. My best imaginings of this morning had seen us snatching a few moments together either just before or just after the – fictitious – community police officer's inspection, maybe a bit of flirting, some discussion of our previous relationship, possibly a big fat apology from Stevie for the lovebite all those years ago, who knew? But now, the whole idea of a police visit to check a sponsored Toddle route seemed so ridiculous that I couldn't believe I'd fallen for it. I mean, yes, the retrospectoscope is a marvellous instrument, but how much more hip would I have appeared to him if I'd rumbled his scam from the outset – and we could maybe even have plotted something together? No, what I mean is, I could have nipped it in the bud ...

Whatever, lovebites aside, this time he had me for a different type of sucker.

We started walking down the path through the Daffodil Woods to the river. The sun was trying to squeeze out, and every so often flashes of brilliant light rushed through the trees at us before ducking back round the slate-grey clouds.

'It's funny, isn't it,' Stevie said, 'us living so close to each other and our paths not crossing for such a long time.'

'Yes, isn't it?' I replied. 'You obviously don't spend much time at the swings or the school car park then. Or Tesco.'

'Aha, so *those* are the Loch Martin talent hotspots then! Dammit! I wish I'd known years ago.'

'Still the flirt, Stevie.'

'Only with the good-looking women.'

'I rest my case.'

An incurable personal-space invader, Stevie's arm brushed mine constantly, but as we continued our walk we didn't talk any more. My mind was racing – suppose he tried anything on? Suppose he *didn't*?

Before long we reached the riverside, already marked off with yards of thick red tape which was securely tied to sturdy stakes. My mind wandered back to my original vision of Stevie at Invermartin with his trusty mallet but fortunately a flabby old cliché-aversion muscle kicked in before I started to say, 'Wow, did you hammer these in all by yourself? You must be sooo stwong ...'

The River Martin is a wide slick of icy-coldness, some-

201

times blue, sometimes brown, which rises in the hills immediately behind the estate, bursting down the steep sides in tumbling streams of varying degrees of impressiveness, streams which curtsey to one another and then link arms to form one of the best, and prettiest, private fishing grounds in the country. The patch of bank we were standing on was grassy and inviting so we sat down wordlessly, our legs dangling off a small ledge which gave onto an area of gravel right at the water's edge. A frog suddenly jumped just below my boots and I leapt about three feet and yelped in alarm.

'Whoa, you were lucky, that was a poisonous one!' said Stevie, putting his arm round my shoulders and squeezing protectively.

'Really?'

'Nope.'

I swiped at him crossly with my hand. He laughed and dropped his arm, and I stared out at the river, while the frog harrumphed and went about his business.

'Stevie, what are we doing here?' I asked eventually, turning towards him and finding he was looking at me, a fact I had already known. His green eyes had a disturbing liquidity about them and his face showed an unaccustomed vulnerability that was in turns alarming and unbelievably sexy.

'Don't know, really. Are you sorry you came?'

'I'm sorry you made a mug out of me with the police thing, that's for sure.'

'Ah.'

'But ... but no, I'm not sorry I came.'

He leaned towards me, slid his arm across my shoulder, stroking the hairline at the nape of my neck as he did so, and kissed me. Ever so gently. Just lips, mine and his, lingering together for a few, soft breaths while my hands clutched his upper arms and the rest of my body just sort of drifted with the flow of the river.

Who pulled away first? Oh, I don't know. We both did, or didn't, or did. Stevie kept his arm around my shoulders and tried to gently pull me closer towards him again, but I shook myself free and stared down at the water, which was still flowing idly despite the goings-on on its bank; though the moment, along with the frog, seemed to have gone.

It was lovely, that kiss. Exciting and perfect. Not too hard, nor too wet, and just enough insistent pressure to make me realise I wanted more; my mouth was holding an imprint of his which was like a small, tingly magnetic field. So, responding to an impulse that had nothing whatsoever to do with my head, I turned and looked up at him, put my arms round his neck and we kissed again, but this time it was different, more searching and urgent and far, far longer-lasting.

Much later, it was *definitely* me who pulled away this time, no doubt about it. Panic was setting in, and Stevie wasn't letting up so I had to plant the palms of my hands on his chest and do a sort of netball chest-pass manoeuvre in an attempt to prise our bodies apart.

I was struck by how utterly useless words can be at times like those – not that I'd experienced any times like these before. Extramarital snogging, not counting my Robbie Williams poster on the kitchen wall, was definitely a new one. I was buggered if I was going to whisper anything like 'we can't', or 'we mustn't', or 'we shouldn't', because for one thing they were horrible clichés and for another we just *had*. Then I saw why I'd found it difficult to prise him away; somehow while we were kissing Stevie had manoeuvred me onto my back on the riverbank, and he had been lying on top of me.

'Stevie . . .'

'Uh-huh?'

He rolled away and I sat up and looked away from him, breathless and shocked as I realised how much I wanted him. Part of me wanted to jump up and run hell-for-leather back to the safety of my car, another part wanted to push him to the ground, straddle him, tear his shirt off and shag him senseless right there and then, but the remaining part, the worried, married and incredibly bloody boring part, won the day, as I hugged my knees and mumbled: 'I think we should stop now.'

'Do you?' Stevie said softly. 'Really? Because I don't.'

'Well, I didn't think we'd be . . . at least I've never . . . God, Stevie, I'm petrified!'

'Don't be,' he replied, taking my hand and kissing my fingers.

'And we're outside!' I added unnecessarily. Stevie's eyes rolled up to inspect the cloud-filled sky.

'Well, bugger me, so we are.'

'Someone might come,' I said, then, noticing his raised eyebrow, added, 'Someone *else*, Steven.'

He pointed further along the riverbank. 'See that?' he said, indicating a small, wooden shed about a hundred yards further down the riverbank, shaped like a miniature sports pavilion with a tiny veranda overlooking the water.

'It's a fishing hut,' I replied, grateful for the diversion.

'Ten out of ten, Watson. It's a fishing hut.'

'And?'

'It's a fishing hut for which I hold the only key, actually. Right here.' He patted the breast pocket of his jacket. 'And can you guess what we might find if we were to enter said fishing hut?'

'Um, a Harrier jump jet? Giraffe?'

'A *sofa*, Gail! A big, squashy sofa, and not only that,

some of the best malt whiskies that Brankin and co have to offer. How about it?'

My legs were trembling as he pulled me to my feet, and hand-in-hand we stumblingly followed the wiggly fishing path downstream to the hut. Choppy thoughts rushed through my head – *but it's a bit cold ... what if somebody sees us ... Emma ... Thomas ... Stuart ... Stuart ... my bottom's bigger than it was in our schooldays... wish I could have a shower first ... bit early in the day for whisky ...*

By the time we reached the hut Stevie was breathing heavily and as he pulled me up the steps onto the veranda and fumbled in his pocket for the key I eased my hand out of his and turned to look anxiously out over the river. There was nobody else in sight; only a herd of unconcerned brown and white cattle on the opposite bank, bunched up, for some reason, in a single muddy corner of their field. My everyday response to this would be to point and say; 'Look, lovely moo-cows!', and this only amplified the realisation that everyday responses were not what was called for here. I turned back to Stevie as he wrenched open the door and, grinning, pulled me inside.

It was musty and gloomy inside, and smelt of old wellies, ancient tweed and decaying wicker baskets; which figured as these were the main items festooned on hooks around the four walls of the tiny hut. A chipboard worktop on the right held a little primus stove, a dented old aluminium kettle, some mugs, a crumpled bag of granulated sugar, Mellow Birds coffee powder, some dirty teaspoons and a rusty Peek Frean's biscuit tin. Oh, and taking up almost all of the available floor space, a saggy, grimy velvet sofa in a shade of red which once may have rivalled mine but which, I realised as Stevie pulled me roughly down onto it and started kissing me ravenously, wasn't half as comfy.

Lying full-length on top of him, I kissed him back enthusiastically, shocked and exhilarated by the sensation of being so close, so *desired* by this new/old person. He was still a great kisser, his mouth a tantalising combination of insistence and teasing, never quite suffocating but never quite letting up either, making me believe he never wanted to stop and that we could just go on lying there, kissing until, well, until those cows went home.

He wasn't a moaner, either, no 'primal grunts' as Theresa calls them, the nasal noises some men make which Theresa insists are designed to bully you into realising it's time to step things up a bit or else risk being left behind. No, we just kissed, until, raising my head for a moment to tuck some annoying stray hairs behind my ears, I became aware that my blouse was undone and that Stevie's hands were making their way around my bare back towards my bra catch.

'Stevie, stop,' I gasped, 'please.' I sat up and pulled the edges of my blouse together, feeling my face burning hot with a mixture of embarrassment and extreme horniness.

'What's up?' he asked. 'You were fine a moment ago.' He pulled himself upright and I saw that his shirt was unbuttoned as well. Oh God, yes, wait, I did that. Whoops. I looked away.

'Stevie, I'm so sorry, but . . .'

'But what?' His voice was gentle, but with a slight raspiness which made the wanton half of me just want to climb back on top of him and finish the job, right there and then.

'I can't.'

'Can't?'

'You know. Do it. Just now. Oh, God, not again!'

'Didn't seem that way to me,' he said, sitting up and

ruffling his hair in an exasperated way.

'I know. I want to, and I'm really sorry for, well, going this far, I mean, it's not fair, I know that, and I'm sorry, for going this far when I can't, well ...'

'Why not? There's nothing to be afraid of, is there?' Stevie's obvious dejection made him seem tender, and somehow vulnerable. God, I hate letting people down.

'You're not the problem, Stevie, I am. It's, it's the home thing.' I didn't want to mention Stuart, Emma or Thomas's names aloud, as though saying their names would bring them right into the hut with us, and taint them with my deception.

He sighed. 'Fair enough. But you know I really like you, Gail, don't you?'

'Yes, and I like you too.' There was an awkward silence, which I felt compelled to fill. 'I'm sorry, but I think, no, well, I've realised that I don't want to jeopardise my home life, Stevie. I can't risk losing my children.' *Or Stuart? Could I risk losing him?* 'I'm sorry.'

He remained quiet for a few moments, then looked into my eyes. 'Gail, I don't *want* to jeopardise your home life. I'd never want you to leave your husband and your kids, if that's what you think. I *like* you. I like your life. And I really like my life, too. I don't want it messed around with families and complications and great big husbands. I just want to, well, see you sometimes, that's all. I *want* you, Gail.'

'Ah.'

'Does that sound really, well, bastardy?'

'No, course not. A bit dastardly, perhaps, but definitely not bastardy.' It sounded absolutely lovely, I realised. If only life was a straight line and complications were things that only happened to hapless people in fiction. 'But it would never work.' Dammit, first cliché!

'Why not?'

'These things never do, do they? People get, well, too involved, for starters.' *And who'd babysit?*

'*We* needn't, though, Gail, there's too much big stuff at stake for that! Come on, it'd be fun! I won't mess with your life, I can promise you that, and you won't mess with mine – we've both got too much to lose. We can just enjoy the moment – have a laugh, and . . . stuff.'

'Stuff?'

'Yes, stuff! You know - *sex*. Lots of it, with no strings. What do you think?'

What did I think? I knew what I ought to think, that I should pull out a fan to swat him with and then flounce home to insist my husband challenge him to a duel for besmirching my good name by treating me like a common trollop, or something. But then, I pondered, here I was, being offered, practically on a plate, a guaranteed no-strings – *affair*? – with someone who'd never blow the whistle? What did I think? What did I think?

'I think I'd have to think about it.' Oh dear, poor old Stevie. This wasn't the first time I'd put the brakes on just as things were heating up. A sidelong glance at his face showed he was thinking the same thing but he smiled and squeezed my shoulder.

'OK then.'

We straightened ourselves out and left the hut more or less as we'd found it, but for the thin film of condensation on the cracked window panes. I wondered if he'd take my hand, or put his arm round me, but he didn't, and given that I sensed the beginnings of an awkward silence, I searched the back rooms of my head for something to say – almost always a bad idea.

'What about Theresa?' *See? Wrong thing again!*

'Sorry?'

'Um, Theresa? Weren't you two . . .'

'Going to the ball together?'

'Well . . .' My cheeks burned.

'Yes, we are. Is that still OK with you, boss?'

Cheeky git. I found, somewhere back in my mental scullery, a lovely and mature riposte: 'When did you stop the lovebiting thing?'

'What makes you think I have?'

'Well, there aren't any wounds on my neck this time, for a start.'

'Looks like my vampire days are behind me, then.' We started walking back up the path.

'Maturity finally catching up with you?'

'Something like that. Or perhaps it's the chronic shortage of virgins round here these days.'

'No thanks to you, methinks.'

When I got back to Mum's the world hadn't suddenly turned purple, I hadn't grown an extra head and my flustered face, pink from rushing around was eclipsed by Dad and Emma, who were wearing dressing gowns and standing on the sofa dancing along with Mowgli and Baloo to 'The Bare Necessities' on the video. Mum had bought a book on crystal healing and was sitting at the dining-room table pressing a piece of amethyst to her forehead.

'How did it go?' she asked, which was a damn cheek and none of her business. Oh, hang on, yes it was.

'Fine! Just great! Um, the police didn't come, so we just went over the Toddle route. No problem.'

'Must be a long route,' she murmured, 'the time it took you.' How's Steven?'

'He's fine, Mum. And, erm, we had coffee and a chat as well.'

Mum rescued the crystal from her forehead and continued,

209

'Mmm. And how's Stuart?'

I winced. 'Oh, he's the usual. Caught up in some daft custody case which should never have come to court. No change there.'

'Mmm,' she said again, rummaging in a hessian bag for another semi-precious lump of rock.

'What?' I challenged. 'Mmm what?'

'You've got that screwed-up face.'

I looked at her. 'What screwed-up face?'

'That screwed-up face people put on when they talk about someone they're angry or fed up with.'

'What are you on about?' She was definitely making me nervous.

'I'm sure you don't realise you're doing it, dear,' she explained. 'It's just a tiny wrinkling of the face; I've seen it many times, on many friends, but never on *you* before. What's going on, Gail?'

If ever I needed a little prod to tell me that I was on severely dangerous ground, then that surely must have been it. I just managed to glower at Mum and mutter something about Mystic bloody Meg before I scooped Emma up and carried her, wailing furiously, into the car. Then, with Dad still strutting his stuff on the sofa, I drove erratically home, where I crept outside to light a cigarette, crouching in a dark corner with the slugs.

Chapter Twelve

There's a bookshop in Inverness with a café upstairs, the sort of place that serves you healthy chocolate bars filled with cherries and toenails, and blueberry muffins so large that merely holding one gives you a poignant flashback to what life felt like when you were a small child. Plus, you have the smug knowledge when you're up there that you're eating your cake in a clever, bookish, purposeful environment, rather than one whose sole purpose is to supply you with cake, which, as any female knows, halves the calories instantly by halving the guilt.

It was Friday morning, which meant Mum had Emma, Thomas was at school and Stuart was going to the pub straight after work so there was no immediate pressure, of the home-making variety, upon me. The children would be happy enough with sausages, or boiled eggs and Marmite soldiers for tea, and Stuart would probably swagger in at about half-past nine, trying not to look pissed and brandishing takeaway prawn tikka masala, having overdone his end-of-the-week swift one with the lads from the office.

I'd taken to spending large amounts of my free time there whenever I was in town on my own, and today was no exception. As a source of self-indulgent time alone it's unbeatable; you can choose a new book at your leisure, then get stuck straight into it over a coffee upstairs, without the inconvenience of having to drive home first.

I love reading. Reading a novel is a bit like sex, for me. Generally speaking my taste, both in books and in bed, tends towards the 'conservatively varied', with emphasis on comfort rather than discovery. I'm always on the lookout for something light-hearted yet meaty, but I'm not all that comfortable if I veer too abnormally from a well-trusted path. When I pick up a new book to read the first question is: Am I in the mood for this? Is it going to be worth the investment of time and effort? Sometimes it takes a bit of persuasion to get going, and I have panic attacks – maybe I could just stop now, forget it, and try again another time? But usually I decide that, having made up my mind to make a start, it would be churlish not to keep going.

After the first few pages, hopefully, I'm committed to seeing it through, and I can begin to settle down and loosen up a bit. I like to take my time, to get properly into it, get under the skin of the characters, even go back over bits that I feel haven't been properly savoured earlier (Stuart loves that). Then somewhere in the middle section, if all the conditions have been right earlier on, a personal Rubicon is suddenly crossed and I take on a completely different persona, reading faster, more intensely, gripped and abandoned both at the same time, shrugging off distractions and forgetting about everything to do with the outside world, until the crashing, bitter-sweet joy of reaching the end, whereupon I hurl the book aside, breathless, blinking in the sunlight and wondering how on earth the spent, snoozing tome beside me had been capable of such an incredible feat.

Anyway, browsing the Romantic Fiction section I was

212

struck by my literary promiscuity as realisation dawned that I'd read most of the titles on offer, so I drifted off towards the chilly rear of the shop and the uncharted waters of Biography and Self-Help. There were far fewer shopping bags littering this part of the shop, which probably said more about its patrons than anything else. Celebrity upon celebrity shimmered down at me from the Biography and Autobiography shelves: Titchmarsh, Jonsson, Halliwell, Hastings, Faldo, Widdecombe, Beckham, Winslet, Connolly and more, urging me to read the stuff that the newspapers and gossip magazines (another weakness) had already printed months ago, along with the rest of the books' contents which weren't interesting enough to go in the papers. No, I decided, I wouldn't be purchasing a biography today, thanks all the same.

Self-Help, though, now there was a department which I was hardly in a position to snub these days, was I? Trouble was, I loathed self-help books, having overdosed on them years ago, in London – and discovering to my cost that the only topic on which there is NOT a self-help manual available is that of How to Give Up Self-Help Books. How many versions of *'so you see folks, all I needed to do was reclaim control of my [insert appropriate noun here] . . .'* could there possibly be in the world? Every self-help book I had ever read, on any topic from raising kids to becoming a better person, seemed to have only One Good Idea, which they'd spend five chapters hinting at, one chapter revealing, then ten chapters repeating, flabbed out with gushing examples concerning people with young sons called Bill.

But as I was about to turn away my eye fell upon a shiny hardback entitled *How to Cheat and Get Away With It*, written by a shrewish-looking Canadian woman called

Barbara Jean Sunbeam who, my conscience hissed, was reaching through the cover and shouting 'YOU THERE!' Glancing furtively over my shoulder, I picked it up and leafed through the chapter headings. 'Tame your Inner Fidelity!' 'Cheating as a Lifestyle Choice!' 'Have your Cake – Eat It – Then Have Hers!' 'Bluffing and Fluffing!' 'Divided Loyalties – Twice the Fun!' 'Ten Things We Keep to Ourselves!' and 'How to Cheat for the Rest of Your Life!'

I shuddered, knowing that here was a book that I was probably meant to own but for obvious reasons never could. Surely the very fact of having it in the house would blow your cover anyway, and so wasn't it basically a mammoth exercise in shooting yourself in the foot? Judging by the testimonies on the cover – *Canada's No.1 Million Seller! Reading this gave me it all* [Madonna]*!* perhaps not. Or maybe there were a million Canadian women out there who had clever hidey-holes in their closets?

I replaced the book on the shelf, and swear that Barbara Jean 'tsked' as I hurried away.

Safely back in the ample bosom of Romantic Fiction, I snatched a copy of the newest title which was piled high on a table and being plugged like mad by the store – *Pizzazz!* – slapped it on the counter to pay for it, and made my way upstairs to the café.

Soon I was gratefully slurping scalding cappuccino, dabbing at my chocolate-crusted foam moustache with a serviette, and settling down with my new novel. Checking the clock I calculated that I could afford about twenty-five minutes' uninterrupted reading time, and still have time to race round the supermarket *and* visit Sandy Maclennan, the Loch Martin butcher, for sausages on the way home.

'May I?' said a voice far, far above my head, a few

minutes later. I looked up from my book to find a vaguely familiar figure, holding a cup and saucer, sliding into the armchair opposite, without waiting for an answer.

'Oh!' I exclaimed, 'I know you, don't I – Clive?'

'Ralph,' he corrected curtly, taking a sip of his espresso and settling back to stare at me disconcertingly.

'Ah ...' My cheeks began to heat up, and in the ensuing awkward silence I began to plan how best to phrase my apology for shouting accusing insults at him at Theresa's writers' group, after his Big Fat Rabbit story. I decided to start with a spot of sucking up.

'How's the conceptual novel coming along?' I asked.

'Reasonably.'

'So, tell me then, Ralph, what's *conceptual* about it?'

He sighed and rubbed his nose with his index finger, as though he'd been asked that very question by one pleb too many today already. 'Well, to put it simply...'

'I'd appreciate that!' I quipped, to no response.

'It demonstrates the essential futility of the human being by showcasing emotions and relationships via *ideas* rather than via individuals.'

'So, what, you mean there are no people in it?' I d'oh'ed.

'In a nutshell, yes,' he said slowly, 'but the fundamental ...'

'What, no snogging then? No car chases?' I didn't intend to sound snippy, although I *was* aware that my precious reading and coffee-drinking time was seeping away down the Drain of Ralph, so I must have sub-consciously wanted to wrap him up and get back to it before he turned into even more of an über-bore.

'I don't think it's the sort of thing you'd underst— appreciate,' he said. 'What are *you* reading, anyway?' He jerked his head towards my novel, and I closed it to look at the cover, dazzling both of us with the shiny gold lettering which was revealed on the front.

'Um, it's called *Pizzazz!*' I said. Then, flipping it over to read from the back, I went on, 'It's a gritty reality tale of an orphaned supermodel who's being blackmailed by this movie star who's going slowly blind and who's really her brother but neither of them knows it, and then there's this missing horse—'

'I get the picture,' Ralph cut in. 'A real challenge, then?'

I glanced up at his smug, pinched face and twitched in irritation and embarrassment. 'No, not really, but I don't necessarily *like* to be challenged when I'm trying to relax.' Then, realising quite by accident that what I'd said could be construed as yet another insult lobbed Ralph's way, I quickly added, 'With books, I mean! I didn't mean you!'

'Are you sure about that?' Ralph's eyes narrowed until he looked like a snake.

'Yes!' *No!*

'In my opinion these things are an utter waste of money,' he said disdainfully, wrinkling his nose at my book as though it was a piece of cat-sick. 'Sheer, formulaic trash.'

'Fair enough,' I replied, 'you're entitled to think what you like – it's just as well we're all different, isn't it?'

He raised his eyebrows and had another sip of espresso. He was wearing an open-necked checked shirt and grey canvas trousers, and a silver signet ring glinted on the little finger of his right hand. Men like him never wore wedding rings. He'd propped a tattered brown briefcase against his chair, but aside from that the only things he seemed to have to entertain himself with were his espresso, and me. The slate eyes never left my face for a second, until, bored by the effort of trying not to get any more irritated, I got more irritated. And somewhere along the line my resolve to apologise for my outburst at writers' group had evaporated like the steam off my cappuccino.

'There are some newspapers over there, if you'd like something to read,' I attempted, bravely keeping a grip on civility.

'It's Gail, isn't it?'

'That's right.'

'Theresa's friend?'

'Right again.'

'Well, Gail, you really showed yourself up a bit with your little outburst the other week, didn't you?' he asked in a slow, even voice.

'Well,' I began, closing my book for a second time, 'I regret rushing out of the room so fast, but I really did have to go, and . . .'

'Oh, the rushing out was to be expected after you'd made such a fool of yourself. You *totally* missed the point which I was trying to make regarding Bonnie's so-called "brevity concept"! By focusing on the character content of my piece you only served to highlight the culture of character-led dependence which my novel is seeking to redress! Now if, like the others, you'd been listening to the chapters I've been reading out over the last few weeks, this would *clearly* have been all too apparent, but no, you saw an ideal opportunity to get some attention for yourself, didn't you?'

The irritation was beginning to give way to slight fear – my God, how on earth could Theresa have gone to bed with this man? 'Ralph, does it matter now?' I said in a high voice. 'I'm sure you have a point, but the fact is that you were taking the mickey out of your teacher! Anyone could see that, and it wasn't fair, was it?' *And you shamelessly copied Winnie the Pooh! Just how not on is that?*

217

'Bonnie's no teacher! She's a plant-eating crochet basket case!' Ralph spat.

'So why do you keep going to her classes, then?'

That got him. He sat back in his chair, and I began to quickly gather my stuff together to get the hell out of there.

'Look . . .' he began.

That did it. 'I hate people who start sentences with *"look"*,' I shot back crossly, searching for my car keys. 'It's so bloody arrogant!'

'Do you want to come with me to a hotel room?'

'WHAT??' Somebody, somewhere, dropped their cup. I'm sure it was my fault. 'Shhh,' Ralph went on. 'It's OK! I can handle it, and I can *definitely* handle you, my girl.' He licked his lips and appraised me slowly, from head to toe, while internal bits of me began to curl up and hide.

I got to my feet, terrified and shaking like a leaf. People had started to stare as I made for the steps. 'You're a sick bastard!' I hissed, and turned and fled.

'YOU WON'T THINK THAT AFTER I'VE SCREWED YOU IN HALF!' Ralph called down from the balcony, as I broke into a run. 'RUSHING OFF AGAIN? GAIL? *GAIL?*'

I didn't stop until I'd reached the safety of my car. It took a couple of goes to get the key in the ignition but once I did, I threw the gearstick into the wrong gear, then tried to move off without releasing the handbrake. *Pizzazz!* had got dropped on the ground at some point during my flight but I knew, as the screaming car bounced away like Edward the Big Fat Rabbit, that I'd rather never know what became of that missing horse than retrace my steps to try and retrieve it. I indicated left and headed for Theresa's.

*

Theresa's cottage was so cute that it had once been featured in a double glazing commercial, for which she'd been paid in windows. White-painted stone under a slate roof with a chimney at either end, it had an overgrown garden which hid neglected specimen shrubs and the odd cannabis plant. It lay at the end of a short single-track road and was completely hidden from the main road by a rigid forestry plantation; and although it was only ten minutes from Inverness, as you approached it you got the misleading but welcome impression of being in the middle of nowhere.

She'd bought the cottage by lucky chance a few years back, before property prices had gone through the roof. It had been built a hundred and fifty years ago as the stalker's cottage for the mighty Ness estate, but had been rented out for years, and the year Theresa took on the tenancy on a six-month contract coincided with the estate's decision to downsize their heritable property portfolio (that's how they put it anyway; truth was they needed a big lump of cash, and fast, to sort out a tax nightmare), and so Theresa was offered the place on a first-refusal basis. She knew she'd have been mad not to go for it, and anyway, she said, living in a place called Stalker's Cottage was a real turn-on ...

'I should call the police,' I said to her, as I sat in her kitchen drinking a tumbler of port fifteen minutes later, all thoughts of the supermarket and the butcher's long forgotten. 'The man's a psycho!'

Theresa had listened sympathetically while I blurted out everything that had happened. I'd never disturbed her at home unannounced during the day before, treating her 'working woman' status with the reverence and sanctity I felt it deserved. So today, when I'd beeped the horn at her gate and marched straight inside without waiting for her to come to the door, she must have known that I was really rattled about something or other, because she'd switched her computer off instantly, and poured me a drink.

'He's not a psycho, he's just an arse,' diagnosed Theresa.

'But I was petrified!' I reminded her.

'I know, I know, but if you think about it, you weren't in any actual danger, were you?' she reminded me gently.

'How was I supposed to have known that? Should I have *checked* with him? He seemed bloody dangerous to me!'

'The only danger you'd find yourself in with Ralph is that he'd bore you to death with his conceptual novel. The man should be locked up for that shedload of crap he's so proud of.'

'I seem to recall you saying that you were really impressed with it,' I reminded her.

'Not with it, with *him,* and his stupid self-belief! I've wised up a lot since then, Gail. D'you know, last time he read out a chapter I counted the word "clearly" in it twenty-seven times, and yet the whole thing's about as clear as custard. It's like he's trying to hammer the words into our skulls, using a big sledgehammer with "clearly" embossed along the sides . . .'

'Whatever,' I muttered. 'I'm afraid I don't give a shit about his crappy book, and I repeat, I was scared.'

Theresa had sprawled herself over a turquoise floor cushion, but she straightened up a bit at my words. 'OK, let's get this straight. He called you a fool, then propositioned you—'

'*Threateningly,*' I cut in. 'In fact, I think *"challenged me to a shag"* would be a better way of putting it. It was like he wanted to drag me off somewhere to teach me a lesson . . .'

'Sounds OK when you put it like that!' Theresa giggled. 'Shame it was Ralph, though. Trust me, he wouldn't have kept you for long. What else happened?'

'Well, he made fun of *Pizzazz*, the novel I was reading . . .'

'Darling, I'd have made fun of a novel called *Pizzazz* too, if I'd been there! What else?'

I sighed. 'Nothing else, I guess.'

She gestured towards my empty glass. 'Do you want a refill? Or coffee?'

'I'd better not. I'll have to get back and pick Emma up in a few minutes. Theresa, can I ask you a personal question?'

'So long as it isn't that old one about which vegetables I prefer as sex toys,' she replied, playing with a strand of hair and gazing out of the window, down the hill towards the forestry plantation.

'OK. Theresa, you get asked out all the time, don't you?'

'I suppose, now and again – why?' she asked. 'Actually, I don't mind that one, come to think of it. It's aubergines.'

'Ouch. Well, do you get used to it? I mean, all those men, looking at you in, well, in *that* sort of way, isn't it . . .'

'Fun?' she offered.

'No! That's my point! Isn't it kind of, oh, God, I can't say it. Sorry.'

'Say it, schtoopid,' Theresa urged. 'Worst that can happen is I throw you out – come on!'

'*Demeaning?*' I forced out through a very clenched face. 'I'm not used to being viewed like that by men, I just don't have a flirty bone in my body...'

'That's what you think,' said Theresa. 'Although I have

to say that flirting's nothing to do with bones.'

'No, it's true! What Ralph said in the bookshop has left me feeling like shit! Like, like that's all he saw me as being fit for, somehow.'

'Oh, come on, Gail! I think you're pushing it a bit now,' Theresa protested. 'Turning yourself into a victim because Ralph demanded to get into your knickers isn't the same as being chatted up by men, available or otherwise. Sadly it's mostly otherwise with me lately, but that still doesn't stop it being exciting! And no, it's not demeaning – you just had a bad experience, that's all. I mean, for heaven's sake, *Ralph* ...' She tailed off, lost for words.

'I get your drift,' I said. 'Were you going to say more?'

'Well, it depends who it is, obviously, but I guess my view would have to be that tapping into basic attraction instincts is one of the most powerful things we can do, isn't it?' Then she clapped her hand over her mouth melodramatically. 'Oh! But then, I guess you're so far out of the loop you'll have forgotten all that, won't you, Mrs Wife? You've traded chat-up for chit-chat! You *sold out*, honey!'

That's what she thought. 'Guilty,' I said.

'Anyway,' she continued, 'what you were saying about not being used to men viewing you as something they want to have sex with ...'

'Did I say that? Oh yes, I suppose I did!'

'You've just forgotten what the signals are. Men do it all the time – they can't help themselves, poor things!'

'What, so you mean I'm not unattractive, I've just got, what, rusty radar?'

'Yup, that and a delicious husband – that must take the edge off your appetite, so to speak – how is the lovely Stuart?'

'Fine, thanks. I'll pass on your best.'

'If you think you're up to it!' I finally made a move to get going. 'Feeling better now?' she asked, rubbing my back.

'Yes thanks, a bit. The only thing I feel now is a mild urge to hunt Ralph down and cut his bollocks off with a blunt bread knife. Thanks for listening, T.'

'Any time. I think the main problem was that you tickled the ears of the dog that doesn't like having his ears tickled,' she sighed.

'Excuse me?' I said. 'Are we back to Ralph here?'

'Yup. He can't bear criticism,' Theresa explained. 'I should have told you after the writers' evening – it's like a red rag to a bull. Bonnie gave up trying to teach him anything ages ago; he just made her life a misery if she did, arguing back, taking the piss, oh, loads of stuff.'

'But he's got no right!'

'I know. Personally I think his wife gives him a hard time at home, so it's probably payback time whenever he goes out . . .'

'Theresa!' I gasped. 'You can't go blaming the wife, that's outrageous!'

She backed off instantly. 'OK, OK, sorry!'

'I mean, had you considered that maybe she only gives him a hard time because he's a philandering dickhead?'

Her face clouded, and she was silent for a few moments, before saying, 'Hmm, I hadn't looked at it that way round, I suppose. Fair enough.'

We looked at each other across the chasm of our different experiences, hugged, and then I left.

Chapter Thirteen

There was only a week to go.

I had a guilty conscience that felt as obvious to the outside world as ringworm on my forehead, a potentially philandering husband, a suspicious mother, a ball to go to which had been hijacked by my husband's query-lover, an untidy house and a sore throat. On the other side of the coin, I had a permanent, body-shuddering ache built from fear, excitement and lust, which coloured my every waking moment and made each day a filmset of imagined illicit possibility. It also made me several pounds lighter and I felt sexier than I ever had before.

So, in the circumstances, I took the only course of action possible, which was to catch the early Edinburgh train and go dress-shopping with Theresa.

Stuart had reluctantly taken the day off work to look after the children, mollified by my promise to bring him back some decent socks, so I waved goodbye to them all early in the morning, while Stuart was racking his brains to answer Thomas's enquiry about who you need permission from to go to the Moon, and Emma was watching children's TV wearing nothing but my oven glove, which was on her head.

My jeans, skinny white polo neck and shopping-friendly deck shoes paled in comparison with Theresa's cranberry minidress and knee-length boots, but at least I had the edge when it came to provisions, as I conjured a bottle of wine and peanuts out of my bag about an hour after we were settled on the train. It was quarter to eight in the morning. Theresa looked impressed.

'I need it,' I muttered, pulling the cork and pouring two plastic cupfuls, handing one to her and taking a large swig from the other. 'Bottoms up.'

'And up yours,' Theresa replied with a Gallic shrug, tearing the top off the peanuts with her teeth and pouring a landslide of them into her mouth, simultaneously garbling, 'who needs coffee and croissants when there's wine to be drunk?'

The ticket inspector crept up on us unawares, pursing his lips with an '*I assume you two aren't going to be any trouble*' sort of air which he probably learned on a course, but given that the train was almost empty and Theresa's cleavage was directly underneath him, he didn't actually say anything.

'It's not what you think,' Theresa told him charmingly, while leaning forwards and touching his arm. 'You see, we're intensive care nurses, just off night shift, aren't we, Sister Clodagh?' She gave me a naughty look and I nodded, fixing my eyes on my lap. 'Absolute hell, it was,' she continued, 'nearly lost about a dozen of 'em! This is just an after-work drink for us, isn't that so, Sister?'

'Mmm,' I managed. 'Inverness's angels, that's us!'

'That's very interesting, Gail,' replied the inspector, as my head shot upwards to examine him more closely. Oh, shit. It was Lachlan Broomfield, a harmless sort of bloke who'd been a few years above me at school. 'Didn't know you'd taken up nursing; you certainly hadn't when I ran

225

into your dad the other day.' He feigned puzzlement. 'Or changed your name, for that matter. How are you, anyway?'

I shielded my eyes in shame as he chortled at my expense. 'Oh, fine, thanks, Lach. Drink?' Gah, rumbled. Theresa shovelled more peanuts into her mouth to stop her giggles from turning into an explosion. Her chest jiggled merrily – any moment now she'd choke and Lachlan and I would be showered with nutty fallout.

'No thanks, my shift's just started, unlike you and Miss Nightingale, here.' Theresa giggled some more. 'Take care now, ladies – see you, Gail!' And off he went to punch more tickets and, without a shadow of a doubt, to tell the whole world and his dog how he came across Gail Buchanan pretending to be a nurse while getting pissed on the early Edinburgh train.

Rule One. If you absolutely must return to live in the town where you grew up, do NOT, even for one second, contemplate reinventing yourself. You Will Definitely Fail.

The truth was I'd had an ulterior motive for producing the bottle at the crack of dawn. Theresa had been un-usually quiet about Stevie since they'd met and I knew that a long train journey would be the ideal opportunity to tease information out of her, so I hoped the wine would soften her up into telling me what the state of play was between them. Oh, I knew they got on well enough, that he gave her a lift home after the dance practices even though it was out of his way, and that they both had a similar capacity for flirting, which blurred my intuition somewhat, but her uncharacteristic reticence in discussing him, coupled with Stevie's delicious pursuit of me, made their relationship anyone's guess.

I'd been bursting to unload everything onto someone,

and as Stuart and Mum were obviously not in the running as confidantes, Theresa simply had to be the one. So, once we'd finished the bottle, I took a deep breath and asked her outright. 'How's it going with Stevie?'

'Fine.'

'Shagged him yet?' My heart pounded.

'I couldn't possibly say.'

'What, you mean you can't remember?'

'I mean I couldn't possibly say.'

'That's not like you, T!'

'No, it's not, is it? God, that wine was a bad idea! I'm nodding off.' She yawned expansively and closed her eyes. 'Sorry Gail, got to go ni'night for a bit.'

And that was that.

By the time the train pulled into Edinburgh Waverley Station we had both fallen asleep, woken up, guzzled paper pails of scalding coffee and straightened up our hair and make-up. In fact, I thought as I checked my reflection in the train window and Theresa wrote down her telephone number for Lachlan, we looked pretty damn good for a couple of chicks down from the sticks. Theresa always looked eye-catching, though, turning heads wherever she went; using her confident, *is she or isn't she?* bouncy walk to maximum effect. *But I've got more depth*, I reminded myself. And a slightly larger arse.

'Right then,' I said with determination, as we marched towards Jenners. 'Dress code. According to Esther, we need to find full-length gowns, but not too long so that we trip when we put our pumps on, with plenty of room for our legs to move, long sleeves or else shawls to cover our shoulders while we're eating, and, oh, what was the other thing ... oh yes! Nothing that clashes with the sashes.'

Theresa snorted. 'Esther told you *what*, Gail?'

'Well, she only gave us a few pointers ...' I faltered.

'Legroom, did you say? I thought we were here to buy dresses, not a bloody car!'

'OK, but ...' But nothing.

'And what's she on about, clashing with sashes? I suppose boys don't make pashes at girls whose sashes clashes?'

'Something like that,' I giggled. 'But come on, mate, we'd better co-operate ...' I suddenly couldn't for the life of me see why.

'Why, exactly?'

'I suddenly can't for the life of me see why.'

'Attagirl,' Theresa approved. 'If that bonkers mare thinks I'm going to spend a fortune just to end up looking like a toilet-roll cosy she's even more deranged than I gave her credit for. Hasn't she heard of Lycra? Does she live in the twenty-first century? Has she got a Mr Darcy thing going on? Or, or a wooden leg she needs to hide, maybe?'

As we approached Jenners I savoured the peculiarly Edinburgh scents of hot dogs and hyacinths which filled the air from the gardens below us, and let the sounds of busking bagpipers and bad-ass city traffic fill my achy head. That wine on the train had been a mistake; I felt like asking the winos on the park bench beside the Scott Monument to budge up a bit so that I could join them for a kip. But I was overwhelmed with a need to prod Theresa a bit more; for some reason I felt like it was now or never.

'What sort of dress do you think Stevie would like to see you in?' I asked, lightly, staring straight ahead.

'Stevie?' she repeated as though the name were unfamiliar to her, as we entered the heat of Jenners' ballgown department. 'Who knows? No dress at all, probably. Don't suppose he's bothered. I'm just going to the ball for the laugh, Gail and ... oh ... my ... God! I imagine laughs will be pretty hard to come by if we're trussed up like tartan wedding cakes.'

Row upon row of voluminous silk tartan ballgowns greeted us. And as we moved through rail upon rail of big jostling dresses, straining to get the upper hand over one another as though they were already filled by big-armed women queuing for a buffet, it occurred to me that they weren't exactly the sort of thing Stevie would take one look at and instantly want to tear off. I peered round at the back of one of them, half-expecting to find a big metal wind-up key.

Clutching Theresa's arm, I hissed: 'What was that you were saying about Lycra?'

'I'm saying we need to find something with a bit more Lycra and a lot less acreage. Or at the very least a good-going split up the leg – anything to give us legroom that won't make us look like we've fallen off the top of a Christmas tree. Come on, through this way.'

Convinced I heard a couple of those dresses whispering about us, we hurried past into the designer room, where things immediately began looking up. It was crammed with enticing drapey dresses, zipped into clear plastic covers, which shimmered and simmered in a 'beg for it, you bastard' sort of way – I felt the onset of real progress. Theresa locked like a cruise missile onto an emerald green sheath dress with the longest split I'd seen outside *Hello!* magazine, unzipped it and moaned with pleasure.

An assistant came over. 'Darling, isn't it?' she said without the least trace of irony.

'Does it have matching pants?' I asked. 'Looks like it'd need them.'

'Bit much?' Theresa murmured, not caring what either of us replied.

'Well, no legroom issues, that's for sure. Try it on.'

The assistant, who wore a gold plastic badge with

'Sandra – Senior Sales Adviser' on it, stashed it in an opulent, brightly lit changing room while we rummaged, in a high-class designer room way, through the others. After rejecting everything else in the room as being too big, too frumpy, too busy, too restricting, or just too expensive, I eventually picked out a sequinned, burnt orange twenties-style flapper dress with maribou feathers around the shoulders, and an asymmetric hemline. It was bustin' with promise, and I marched excitedly past an unsure-looking Theresa into the fitting room next to hers, where I tore off all of my clothes and wriggled into it. It zipped cunningly up the side, and in my excitement at feeling a size eight zip glide up my robust size nine body, I only gave myself the briefest of shimmies in the mirror before swishing out to parade in front of Theresa. Both she and Sandra stood looking at me, chewing their lips for a very, very long time.

'Well?' I prompted, turning this way and that, then, after a pause, the other.

Theresa finally shook her head. 'You look like you've been Tangoed.'

Sandra nodded in agreement. I glared at her. 'Aren't you supposed to tell me I look wonderful?' I said accusingly.

'Hen, naebody's gonnae tell you that in that get-up,' she deadpanned. 'You need somethin' wi' a bit less fuss.'

'Yup. Something that doesn't look like you've been caught up in a horrendous house-fire,' agreed Theresa.

I skulked back into the changing room and peeled the orange off, where it collapsed to the carpet in a sequinned rush. Meanwhile, Theresa was next door, trying on the slinky green number. We came out at the same time, me in my jeans, clutching the orange mistake, Theresa looking – predictably – unbelievable.

That green dress had come home. It clung to Theresa's body, hugging her waist and hips and flowing, *gracefully,* there was no possible other word for it, to the floor. And as she glided towards the huge mirror a few feet away, I was mesmerised by the tantalising glimpses it gave of her great legs. As for the top half, the simple, Grecian cut of the shoulders showed off her toned arms, and the neckline plunged in a sharp V almost to her middle, giving her an Oscar-night cleavage, held in place by some sort of gravity-defying undergarment and finished off with a small, diamanté cross just below her breasts. I gawped. Sandra folded her arms in satisfaction. Theresa smiled, slowly, and ran her hands sexily down her hips.

'I'll take it,' she said.

'You'll take it, all right,' I replied.

'She'll take it!' beamed Sandra, hurrying away to get busy with tissue paper. *But could Stevie take it?* I wondered.

The dress cost six hundred pounds, and Theresa handed over her credit card without flinching. I guess it was just one of those things which was so utterly right that it went from being unthinkable to being essential, like toothpaste or sunscreen. I watched the transaction, the studied matter-of-factness of the assistant as she handed Theresa the docket for signing, and smiled as Theresa scrawled her signature and thrust it back to Sandra like it was a little time bomb.

'That's a lot of money for a party in a tent, T,' I said with a smile. She ignored me pointedly before taking the red rope handles of the glossy bag from Sandra and offering opulent thanks, like it had all been Sandra's doing.

'Well, that was easy!' she squeaked as we made for the exit. 'Nothing else in here suit you?'

I glanced over my shoulder at the roomful of style.

'Naah, not really. Blimey, though, you're going to knock 'em dead in that! It's fabulous, daahling! It won't just be Willows they'll be Stripping at Invermartin on ball night!' I sounded far more cheerful than I felt. Oh, I was thrilled for her, sure – seeing your friend transformed and delighted by a jaw-dropping piece of clothing is a lovely experience, but mixed in was a combination of jealousy and anguish, based partly on the simple fact that I hadn't managed to find a dress for myself in the smartest designer room in the city, but mainly on the thought that if once I possessed the thought of having a gorgeous man dangling on the end of a string wondering whether he was going to be fortunate enough to be allowed to sleep with me, then it was about to be blown out of the water once and for all as soon as Stevie got to grips with beautiful, available Theresa in her Green Goddess glory, in the hands-on environment of the Invermartin post-Toddle ball. It was like being on a long car journey pondering whether to stop to buy a Mars Bar, and if so would it be now, or perhaps a little further on, and making the dilemma last for miles and miles, before deciding to go for it and then realising you haven't got your purse on you.

'Okey-dokey, now to get you fixed up,' Theresa announced, linking her spare arm through mine and pulling me along Princes Street. 'There's a gorgeous little designer boutique down the other end, or we could work our way along George Street – even look in on John Lewis if we draw a blank everywhere else. We *must* get you sorted before lunch so that we can buy evening bags and some shag-me shoes before we go home.' She was looking at me with concern, and her arm moved up to round my shoulders and gave me a squeeze. 'You all right?'

'Me?' I replied, forcing a grin. 'Oh, I'm fine. Just not sure how to compete with your beautiful dress, that's all.'

It was the truth, or at least some of it.

'Rubbish!' she retorted. 'Who's competing? Come on, just because I was first to find the only half-decent frock in that arsey place doesn't mean there aren't rails and rails of fab things out there whose sole purpose is to knock Stuart's pants off.' Her suede boots clattered a purposeful tattoo on the pavement, while my soft shoes whispered alongside like an echo. 'Or are they boxers? Calvins? Thongs? Nothing at alls?'

'Whatever. Sorry, T, I'm thrilled for you, honestly, but I get the distinct feeling we've peaked for the day. And they're boxers.'

'Thought so.'

Judging by the High Street store windows, it wasn't the ideal time of year to go dress-shopping. Far from the displays of tulle and glitter of Christmastime, with their banners egging us on to *Be a Christmas Cracker!* or suchlike, they were crammed with beach towels, bikinis, denim miniskirts and blouses knotted at the belly button. Some were thoughtfully anticipating the onset of autumn, with macs and polo necks making early, pastel appearances, but none of them looked like anyone went out in the evening at all – except perhaps those who progressed from the beach straight to the barbecue without having to go home and change, a feat which, in the bracing climate of Loch Martin, was achievable maybe once a year if you were lucky. But at least the streets were easier to negotiate than they were during the Christmas rush, where, apart from their increased numbers, shoppers' individual widths increased at least twofold by the addition of thick coats and fans of shopping bags in each hand.

Topshop's window was much like all the others (*Sizzle on the Beach!*), with small, lemon and lime garments draped over deckchairs, but just as we were almost past,

Theresa and I simultaneously spotted a long, slim black dress, with tiny straps of red ribbon and a belt of the same red ribbon placed low on the waist, half hidden in the corner, looking a bit like it was spying on the fun being had by the others out front, or perhaps waiting apologetically to be moved to its proper spot further back in the store. I kind of knew how it felt.

'Something a bit like that would be nice,' I said as we passed by without breaking stride.

Theresa agreed. 'Mmm. Let's see if we can find a decent version of that then, shall we?'

Theresa's highest hopes were pinned on a favourite boutique of hers, with the unpromising name of The Wee Dress Shop, run for the past fifteen years by a no-nonsense woman called Bunty Maguire and tucked away in a cobbled street behind Charlotte Square. According to Theresa, The Wee Dress Shop was the Holy Grail of Edinburgh's frock-hunters in the know, a secret treasure trove of just-the-job evening wear, a veritable glamour G-spot, and as she pulled me inside its discreet little blue door an overhead bell tinkled and a fug of spicy pot-pourri hit my nose. I nearly went over on my ankle with the shock of stepping on so thick a carpet and a gravelly voice rasped, 'Theresa King, if that's a Jenners' designer room bag in your hand you can put a pound in my swear box right now!'

Bunty Maguire was a short, plump woman in her fifties, who wore lots of vivid red lipstick, and behind black-rimmed rectangular glasses which were attached to a gold chain her eyes were almost obliterated by heavy black eyeliner and clagged-up mascara. Her bobbed hair was cut geometrically into a razor-sharp slope, lacquered mercilessly into rigidity and dyed so utterly black that it almost appeared blue in the elegant lighting of her shop. She wore a clingy beige wool shift dress flecked with black, and the black chiffon scarf at her neck, long jet beads, black tights and patent shoes gave her the appearance of an expensively-singed chicken leg. She and Theresa embraced without actually touching, before Theresa launched headlong into a pack of lies about how she hadn't really meant to buy a dress in Jenners; that we'd only dashed in for a second as it was close to the railway station and the assistant had sort of forced it on her, and she wasn't at all sure about it and it was probably a big mistake, but when Bunty suggested, 'Why don't you return it, then?' Theresa shot back, 'No bloody way!' and they both roared with laughter.

'Bunty, this is Gail, my best friend, also known as Cinders, and we need to find her a ball dress. Gail, meet Bunty, your Fairy Godmother!'

'A pleasure, Gail,' Bunty said warmly, appraising me with one professional sweep of her black eyes. 'Let's see now, size eight to ten? Nothing too fussy?'

'Correct on both counts, I suppose,' I replied. 'But you're the second person today to say I'm not to go for anything fussy . . .'

'Sandra in Jenners?' smiled Bunty.

'Well, yes,' I stammered, wondering if I'd strayed into a competitive dress-selling minefield. 'But why can't I have fussy if I want fussy? I quite *like* the idea of fussy! What is it about me that screams, *Get this woman a plain frock*?' I was horrified to find that my voice was trembling.

Bunty walked over to me and took both of my hands. 'Because you're lovely, that's why, m'dear. You've got the bonniest wee face I've seen through this door for a long while, and we're not going to have it at war with a dress that's full of detail. We'll leave those ones on the rail for the people who need them. Now, you go and sit yourself down over there.' She pointed to a gold chenille sofa, which was wedged between two glass display cabinets filled with chain belts, clutch bags and feathery hair ornaments. 'Theresa, my love, nip through the back and put the kettle on, and I'll see what we've got here for Gail to try on. Off you go!'

Theresa saluted gaily and disappeared. I sat down on the sofa and then, surprising myself, but not necessarily Bunty, burst into tears. Bunty produced a box of tissues (how many women broke down in designer dress shops in the course of the average working day, I wondered), patted my shoulder and then began rifling through her stock.

By the time Theresa returned with three mugs of tea, I'd pulled myself together apart from a few residual sniffs and splutters. Bunty waved away my apologies and Theresa, when she sat beside me, was full of concern.

'Hey, missus, what happened to you?' She handed me a steaming mug and rubbed my arm.

I blew my nose. 'Sorry, it's nothing. Must have been the early morning wine. I can't believe I'm getting in a state about buying a dress! It's never happened before ... I just need to get out more!' I finished, so adding another half-truth to the day's tally. But Theresa seemed convinced, and after a few noisy slurps of tea I was ready to see what Bunty had picked out.

'Right, m'dear, let's see what you think of these.' She brought the dresses over one at a time. The first was a classic ballgown of the Scottish variety, a cherry velvet strapless bodice with a full, silk tartan skirt. It was soft and richly-coloured and far nicer than the ones we'd swished past in Jenners, but as I'd already decided to veer away from the bouffant look, I said, 'Ooh, it's lovely, but

I really had something straighter in mind, if that's OK?'

'Our great friend Esther would simply love that though, wouldn't she?' remarked Theresa.

'Well, you just tell your friend Esther it's here if she wants it,' Bunty called over her shoulder as she went to fetch number two. It was a narrow georgette column with a halter neck and chiffon 'wings' which draped from the shoulder and would have flown wonderfully while dancing – but unfortunately it was a similar shade of green to Theresa's.

'We'd be like a pair of leprechauns,' Theresa whispered, looking genuinely afraid.

Deciding for once that honesty was the best policy I said to Bunty, 'Do you know, I love it, but Theresa's dress is green and, well ...'

'You don't want to be like a pair of leprechauns?' said Bunty. 'Quite right. Shame, though, it would have suited you, Gail.' She stroked it and put it away. I turned to Theresa and mouthed, 'You *bitch*,' and she hissed back, 'I *know*.'

'You don't have it in any other colours, by any chance?' I asked in desperation.

'This is The Wee Dress Shop, not Benetton, m'dear – sorry,' Bunty replied, with a patient smile.

Her last offering was a mid-blue, bias-cut straight dress with an overdress of pale blue chiffon and diamanté spaghetti straps. Like the others, it was beautifully made, but my heart sank at the prospect of wearing it. I'd never worn anything in pale blue, and this dress seemed more in the executive bridesmaid capacity than the sophisticated ball bracket. I didn't even let myself think of the fact that pale blue was the colour of the blanket we'd wrapped Ben in after he died ...

'Wonderful! Can I try it on?'

Well, Bunty had been so kind. I entered the commodious changing room and, shaking my head at the puffy pink face which stared back at me from the huge gilt mirror, stripped off and dropped the dress over my head. I felt like I was putting on a nightie and getting ready for bed. And when I saw that it cost three hundred and eighty-five pounds, I realised that Bunty could be as nice as she liked, there was no way I was going to buy it.

Stepping out of the changing room, Bunty and Theresa's faces said it all.

'I'm sorry, Bunty,' I said, 'but it's not quite right.' Bunty nodded and Theresa shook her head but they both meant the same thing. 'I don't suppose you've got anything in black?'

'Not in your size, m'dear. Only ...' she reached into the rail behind me and pulled out a black crêpe de Chine gown with one sequinned shoulder strap, a sequinned bodice and finely gathered straight skirt. 'This! It's a twelve and it'd drown you, but I could have it altered in time for your ball – try it on!'

So I did, and although it reminded me of a Princess Diana rip-off, and although it didn't fit properly and although the one-shoulder look made me feel butch and lop-sided, I shuffled out of the changing room, avoided Theresa's eyes and said I'd take it. A snip at two hundred and fifty pounds; I held it in at the waist and twirled uncertainly while listening to Theresa saying, 'That might be really nice if it was altered!' and Bunty remarking, 'Bit fussier than we intended but you get away with it with that bonnie face of yours!'

I stood on a gold brocade stool, wobbling on the in-house stilettos which were four sizes larger than my feet, while Bunty pulled and pinned and tucked it to approximate the shape of my body. Then I got dressed and we left the dress to be altered, with fond farewells all round and Bunty's insistence that I didn't need to pay anything until after her seamstress had been in on Tuesday.

Theresa had arranged to meet a banker called Walter for lunch, which for some reason she thought would take about three hours, so we parted at twelve thirty and arranged to meet up later in a designer shoe shop.

'Hope you manage to find some really fabulous socks, darling!' she gushed, hitching her top and turning towards the Caledonian Hotel. I set off back down Princes Street to buy a magazine and find somewhere anonymous for a sandwich and a coffee. The pavements were much more crowded than they had been an hour previously, and a light rain had started to fall, so I dodged umbrellas and quickened my step. It wasn't even a conscious action which took me into Topshop, where the black dress, still standing demurely at the edge of the window, seemed to say, 'What kept you?'.

After scouring the entire shop to ask permission to remove it from the dummy and try it on, I queued for ages before entering a tiny box with saloon doors, where it took a fair amount of agility to undress and climb into it.

I knew that I didn't really need to go through the rigmarole – it was made for me. I actually caught my breath as I craned my neck to catch a glimpse of it from behind, loving how it moulded itself into the small of my back and smoothed out over my bottom, before veering in again to glide down my legs to the ground. The deep split at the back was visible only when I moved, and the little red ribbon round my waist hung, *provocatively!* loose and low.

Queuing again at the checkout, I glanced at the price tag. Thirty-nine pounds ninety-nine. Last time I'd gone clothes shopping I'd spent more than that on tights –

Theresa would be horrified. But I felt calm and settled. It was lovely. Hell, *I* was lovely, apparently, and maybe, just maybe, Stevie would dance with me, and maybe one of those little ribbon straps would fall from my shoulder ... and maybe Stuart would like it too.

The sales assistant (Leona) took the dress and prised out the blood-filled security capsule, before scanning the price tag. 'That's a nice wee frock, that,' she said as she slid it into a bag. 'That's twenty-eight pounds, please.'

'Sorry?'

'Twenty-eight pounds – there's thirty per cent off evening wear just now, didn't you see the sign?' She pointed behind me to a banner – *Midsummer Madness!* – as I handed over my card.

I left the store feeling giddy. I'd just bought a beautiful dress which was just over a tenth of the price of the less-than-beautiful dress I'd agreed to only minutes before. That left me with several things to do before catching up with Theresa in the shoe shop. Firstly, I went into a lingerie shop and spent a large chunk of the saving I'd just made on a gorgeous black strapless bra edged in handmade lace, matching tiny knickers and two pairs of black silk tights. Then I powered along to John Lewis and, in a surge of maternal and wifely concern, picked out an armful of socks for the entire family. After that I went into W.H. Smith and bought my magazine and a single postcard with a Scottie dog on it. And lastly, in an exhibition of cowardice which will haunt me for years to come, I sat in the restaurant at the back of BHS and wrote a note to Bunty at The Wee Dress Shop, explaining how after Theresa and I had left her shop I'd slipped on the pavement and broken my wrist, and so wouldn't be going to the ball after all.

Chapter Fourteen

Emma's trousers gave birth to the previous day's nappy as I dressed her on the morning of the Toddle and ball. The final dance practices had been and gone, with Esther and Otto finally pronouncing us all more or less fit to go on parade on the big night, and Stevie and Theresa, as far as I could make out, continuing their stilted, polite acquaintance and not giving anything away. Stevie had been keeping out of my way, and I his, apart from some *extremely* meaningful looks passing between us when no one was looking during the practices, not to mention the lingering of hands whenever we encountered each other during dances. The word *frisson* has been specially invented for the feelings which accompany such moments, I think. Sheer onomatopoetry in motion.

Around us in Emma's bedroom lay the predominantly pink clutter which pertains to the two-year-old female child, clutter which had long outgrown all conceivable hiding places, although a good look at the Winnie-the-Pooh-themed-every-bloody-thing on the walls, curtains, lampshades, rug and bedspread demonstrated that somewhere, sometime, someone's decorative intentions had been good.

The soft toys, which numbered around seventy-eight

thousand, were supposed to live in an old wicker log basket under the window, but they had a habit of frothing over the edge and migrating to every corner of the room, where they'd rub shoulders with socks, lift-the-flap books, plastic ponies with tinsel manes and stupid educational activity toys. I'd given up keeping the kids' rooms tidy months ago – having had my soul destroyed on a daily basis by their instant unravelling of my back-breaking efforts, these days I restricted my movements to essential low-grade decontamination and clothing management.

The only non-childlike article in the room was a framed photograph of Stuart's dad, which Emma had taken a shine to, calling the smiling, grey-haired image 'Rumpa' and kissing it goodnight whenever she remembered, usually in the mornings. Stuart's dad died of cancer just before Stuart went to university, so I'd never met him, but their physical resemblance was striking, and by all accounts he was quite a man.

His funeral instructions, for instance, had been clearly written down and were carried out solemnly and to the letter. After he was cremated, his ashes were poured into a specially-made egg-timer, as he'd always said how interesting it would be to see how long he lasted before he ran out. Stuart's mother moved south to live near her two sisters in Kent shortly after his death, from whence she reported that he wasn't quite long enough for a properly cooked soft yolk, but she used him every now and again to warm up the odd croissant in her Aga.

Thomas had football training on Saturday mornings, which both he and Stuart took very seriously indeed, so it was agreed that I'd do the sponsored Toddle thing with Emma, the boys would do the footie, and then we'd all meet up at the Mountain View Café in Loch Martin for lunch. I parcelled Emma up in the purple puffa anorak which made her look like a lagged hot-water tank, a green bobble hat and pink wellies – for although it was June and the sky was piercingly blue, there was a nasty nip in the air. 'Got to keep those athlete's muscles warm and supple, poppet!' I said, as by way of afterthought I added a red fleece scarf and matching mittens. Then it was just a case of sorting out changing bags, camera, sponsor forms (fourteen sponsors, all offering varying ludicrous amounts, all forged by me using different pens and handwriting styles), and we were ready to head for Invermartin.

After buckling Emma into the car, I darted back inside for a last, nervous pee, and an appearance check in the hall mirror. OK, yes, Brandi at the Clinique counter had been quite right yesterday, their new tinted moisturiser *did* give a lovely, healthy glow in natural daylight. And the fibre-free mascara had been well worth the money – no spider-eyes for me today! Just as well, they would have looked silly up against the barely there 'nude as heck' lip gloss which was only a few quid more and which qualified me for the free anti-ageing toolkit in its own leatherette pochette.

Well, yes ma'am, the reflection which was shaking its head right back at me wasn't looking too damn bad at all. Heading back towards the door, my hands briefly clutched hot, tintedly moisturised cheeks and my knuckles brushed against the impulsively bought earrings which had lain accusingly at the bottom of my handbag overnight and nearly went straight into the bin this morning – large, Loch-Martin-High-be-praised, silver hoops.

It was the overhead gantry with FINISH in large yellow letters which struck me as funniest when we arrived at the top of the Invermartin Daffodil Wood, a few minutes after half-past nine. Or on second thoughts maybe it was the giant digital clock rigged up to the scaffolding to the side

... no, scrub that, it was the Land Rover with the huge antennae and 'Official Race Car' plastered all over it, parked butchly under a monkey puzzle tree. Faced with all that, the sight of Esther wearing a fluorescent bib and baseball cap, holding a walkie-talkie in one hand and a megaphone in the other while trying to string ribbon across the finishing line, was nothing special. She spotted me parking the car and came bounding over.

'Ah, Gail, I'm putting you on rear-guard duty – make sure you stay at the back and nobody gets lost. Copy?' Tony, sporting a red tracksuit and identical baseball cap to Esther's, bustled up behind her with a clipboard and pen, looking focused and ready to tick some ass.

'Copy,' I repeated solemnly. Tick. 'My word, Esther, this looks absolutely—'

'Yes it jolly well does, doesn't it?' she cut in. 'Susannah Grant's not the only one who can manage an event round here, you know. Got your sponsor form?'

'Yup, right here.' Tick. I handed the form over, secretly enjoying the jibe at Susannah, however trifling.

'Route map?'

'Nope, it's at home. Thought I'd just about find my way round the half-mile . . .'

Esther clapped her hand to her head and nearly brained herself with her megaphone. 'Ouch! Tony – spare map for Gail.' He conjured one up from the pouch in his jogging top and ticked another box. 'Health and Safety, Gail, Health and Safety!' Then Tony handed Emma a number to stick on to her Toddle clothes – fourteen – ticked once more, and I was free.

I went to join Val, who was unloading kids from the back of her van. Defiantly, she'd dressed them all up as fairies and elves anyway, despite having her cosmic chanting procession thingy vetoed. Even little Charity, who was

244

bawling, for once, hadn't escaped being costumed, which was a shame as her green felt pointed hat, complete with felt stalk sticking out of the top, combined with her dark red face to make her look like a big wailing strawberry.

'Isn't this amazing?' I said as we watched the growing crowd of parents, children, gun dogs, and grandparents gather close to the start of the route. Esther was embracing a reporter and a photographer from the local paper, and Tony was still ticking. 'Where on earth did Esther get her hands on that gantry and Land Rover and stuff? And *why*?'

Val shrugged. 'Apparently it belongs to the insurance company Tony works for – Esther told me he travelled to Wigan specially to borrow it all. Can you believe it?' I could. It dawned on me subliminally that the logo on the gantry, the Land Rover and Esther and Tony's baseball caps must be that of the Lancashire Mutual Friendly Society. I guess they'd have also been responsible for the isotonic sports drinks which were lined up on a table just past the finish line too, judging by the logos on the side of the bottles. I looked around further to see whether they'd supplied any of those tinfoil capes as well, maybe a motor-cycle for a cameraman to track the leaders . . .

'Been allocated a job yet?' I asked.

Val nodded towards a rucksack in the back of the van. 'But of course, Tony ticked me off with one, as it were. Got to look after Magnus, and give them all a banana halfway round. You?'

'Rear-gunner. I think I'm meant to shoot anyone who falls more than ten yards behind.'

Val spread a rug on the grass and we sat down. In one swift movement she whizzed Charity up her top for a feed, zipped Eden into her tinfoil wings, filled Rowan's brown felt quiver with home-made arrows, and sent Struan off to find ten different types of wild flower. They were such a peaceful bunch of people, I thought, gazing at them going about their little ways, until I was jolted by the sight of Emma hurtling towards me, squealing with glee and dragging in her wake someone's half-throttled miniature dachshund on a yellow lead.

I leaped to my feet to grab my child, just as the dog's owner, who, from her features and clothing could only be Claire Holmes's mother, appeared, rushing down the drive in evident panic.

'Isolde! Isolde! Are you all right, my precious?' She scooped up the panting little dog, whose ends sagged where they protruded from under her arm.

'I'm terribly sorry!' I began, mortified. 'I wasn't—'

'Will you *please* keep that child under control? Isolde is very sensitive!' She stalked off before I had decided whether to apologise some more or launch into a showy telling-off of Emma, so I didn't bother doing either. I just shrugged and sat down again beside Val, who smiled and stroked my shoulder.

'Are you all right?' she asked.

'Fine, thanks. I suppose I should have been keeping a better eye on Emma, though.'

'Don't worry,' she replied. 'It's a day for the children, isn't it? The lady should have been keeping a better eye on her pooch.'

I hadn't actually thought about it in that way. 'That's a lovely way of looking at it! You're quite right! Sorry, Emma, my love!' Val smiled, and squooshed Charity over to her other boob. 'Don't you find it hard, all this, this keeping up?' I said, twisting a buttercup around my fingers and watching the crowd of nicely dressed mummies, daddies, grannies and nannies limber up near the start of the route.

'How do you mean?' she asked.

'It's just so tiring sometimes, behaving in a way you know will go down well with everyone ... oh, I dunno.' I shrugged and scanned the landscape until I located Emma, who'd shot off again and was sitting with Amber and her children.

'Why not just be yourself?' Val asked simply, and I could not, for the life of me, come up with a response, apart from realising that that was precisely the advice that I'd given Theresa that night at her writers' group. *'Don't practise before you preach!'* as an old school bully had once yelled viciously at me even though neither of us had a scooby doo what it meant – I smiled at the once-painful memory and decided that her moronic phrase could have a home here, with me now. It was just as well we spied Esther raising the megaphone to her mouth before I had to start explaining that little lot to Val.

'Uh-oh, we're off.'

'GOOD MORNING CHILDREN, MUMS AND DADS, GRANNIES AND GRANDPAS AND GENTLEMEN OF THE PRESS! WELCOME TO THE WORLD-FAMOUS LOCH MARTIN SPONSORED TODDLE! NOW IF YOU COULD ALL JUST LINE YOUR LITTLE ONES UP AT THE START, THE PHOTOGRAPHER WILL GET A COUPLE OF SHOTS FOR TUESDAY'S PAPER!'

I guess there were about sixty people there in total, if you counted the children, and after an outdoor riffle of applause the participants began to migrate slowly towards the start. Too slowly, unfortunately, for Esther.

'FOR GOD'S SAKE WILL YOU LOT MOVE IT? WE'LL BE HERE ALL DAY! SOME OF US HAVE A BALL TO GO TO TONIGHT!'

I picked Emma up and ran to the starting line, worrying that Esther may have perhaps partaken of a little Dutch courage before setting out this morning. The photographer bunched us up ruthlessly into a narrower and narrower group until the ones in the middle began to bulge out towards the front and some of those stranded at the back gave up and went off to play. The reporter rolled up his sleeves and started asking some of the children their names. Hang on, what did that tattoo say on his arm? *Raith Rovers Forever*?

'George!' I called out, waving like an idiot. 'It's Gail – Theresa's friend?'

He smiled back delightedly. 'I know – saw you earlier! Theresa not here as well, then?'

'No way – she's probably washing her hair – catch you later?'

He gave me a thumbs-up and returned to coaxing names out of infants. Then Esther, Tony and Magnus (who wore a tiny Barbour jacket, green wellies and a scaled-down deerstalker), positioned themselves right at the front, unfurled a banner proclaiming *Lancashire Mutual – Proud Sponsors of the Loch Martin Toddlers!*, a flashbulb went off, and the Toddle began.

'GOOD LUCK EVERYBODY!!!' screeched Esther, as Amber blew a whistle to start off those who hadn't started off already.

Tony ticked a box. 'Well done, Amber, off you go, now,' he said in an oily voice, retrieving his whistle and watching her backside as she hurried to track down Jessica and Harvey, who had taken an early lead. Esther rushed off to confiscate the tricycle which Claire's daughter Rosie was using illegally, Val's children skipped and danced and twirled in their costumes like lifelong forest creatures, and Emma and I took our places at the back.

Tony's voice hit me from behind: 'Are you sure everyone's under way?'

'Totally,' I lied over my shoulder.

Tick.

It was much warmer now, and the air became thick with small items of peeled-off outerwear being tossed at assorted parents and grandparents. Esther and Tony stayed behind to guard the equipment and brief the press, and Magnus, a few yards in front, clutched Val's hand and determinedly tried to pull her towards the front of the group.

But all in all it was a happy huddle; pleased to be on its way and savouring, in the case of the adults, at least, the gorgeous surroundings of one of the prettiest little forests for miles. Progress was inevitably snail-like, as children found endless little nooks to explore, and interesting things to pick up. I spotted little Jordan Reid getting an embarrassed row from his mother for picking up a handful of rabbit droppings and asking what they were, and another child, Chloë Foster, trying to connect her new-found 'wand' with her baby brother's eye, but in the main, everyone seemed to be having A Nice Time.

Nice, but not Fast enough for Emma, who hated being stuck at the back and kept racing ahead, stopping sharply, and stamping her feet. My out-in-public-explanation-for-everyone-else's-benefit of 'Emma, poppet, come back sweetie! Mummy has to stay at the back to keep all the children safe!' was ignored by everyone except Val, who turned round and hollered, 'Gail, mightn't there be some synergy in Emma coming with me? After all, Magnus is pulling like a rodeo bullock, and do you know, I really do feel a bout of skipping coming on!' And with that, she began to prance towards the front of the procession, with Charity slung around her back, while Emma, Magnus, Eden, Struan and Rowan clapped and followed like the rats of Hamelin.

Loitering at the back, I found myself thinking of Stevie – hardly surprising as I was located squarely within his neck of the woods, once more dressed to kill, and only a stone's throw from the fishing hut.

The situation was getting out of hand. My brain felt like it had its own little combine harvester inside it, travelling ruthlessly up and down and turning whatever logic and reason I once possessed into a useless pulp. I knew I had to decide, and soon, between two courses of action:

1. Would I agree to a trial affair with Stevie, in other words to meet up with a man I really liked, laughed a lot with and fancied the pants off, whenever we got the chance, for no-strings sex? Would I take the chance to experience what it was like to be with someone else, when that someone was an old friend who understood my situation and standpoint and would never blow my cover? Would I seize the chance to try out one of those things which I so envied about Theresa's life – the thrill of a new entanglement? Would I surrender to Stevie's invitation in the knowledge that such circumstances surely would never, *could never*, come my way again?
2. Or not.

I think I saw him before he saw me, although he must have known I'd be there at some point. We'd reached the halfway point, at the riverbank, the place Stevie had roped off for us. Val was diligently handing out bananas, and Stevie was declining her offer of one. The others seemed to want to continue the walk rather than stop by the river to eat, and Stevie, amidst admiring sidelong glances from not a few of the mums, solemnly applauded our progress. He caught my eye, or at least he decided to catch my eye, as I drew level.

'Thanks for coming to steward the dangerous bit,' I said, as the silver hoops banged against my neck.

'Like I said, lot of valuable fish,' he replied, then he nodded towards the others. 'You're letting them beat you.'

250

'I'm meant to. Bringing up the rear so's nobody gets left behind.'

'And a very nice rear . . .'

'Yes, yes, thanks very much.' I wasn't in the mood for innuendo. But the river gurgled on regardless, as did the procession of toddlers, for that matter, and within a few moments we were left alone together. He reached out to me and tucked some stray hair behind my ear, exposing the earrings, in all their senior school glory, even more. But he didn't say anything, and nor did he move any closer. Ages, weeks, years passed – a good thirty seconds, at least. He was messing with my head. The combine harvester had detoured south.

'You're messing with my head,' I said tetchily.

'Sorry.'

I glanced down the path where the last remnants of Toddle had well and truly disappeared round a couple of corners. It was decision time, it had to be. I walked up to him, pulled his face gently – but firmly, oh yes, firmly – towards mine, and kissed him. Don't ask. Don't know. Just did.

It didn't cross my mind that someone might double back from the Toddle group, or that a latecomer might heave into view from behind. All I knew was that at that precise moment I wanted to kiss him, to taste his lips and feel his arms and shoulders – the decision was going to have to make itself, because I was feeling about as impartial as Cyprus at the Eurovision Song Contest.

'I'd better get back to the others,' I said when I drew away.

Stevie nodded, and half-smiled. 'Will you come back later?' he asked, keeping hold of my right hand and looking at me imploringly.

'Later?' I repeated, looking back down the path. *How could I? Emma's just down there!*

Was that a decision? It was moving bloody fast if it was. I

251

grabbed it before it disappeared, like a butterfly. 'I'm not going to have an affair with you,' I whispered, and then I kissed him again. 'I'm sorry.' Turning away, I began to walk in the direction of the others, before someone sent a search party out for the search party. 'See you at the ball.'

'Now who's messing with whose head?' came the quiet reply, but I kept on walking.

Esther, Tony, a few dads and grandparents and Lord Jonathan Brankin were there to greet our triumphant return. I could just make out George, being monopolised by Tony, who looked as though he was trying to get him to accept some baseball caps. There was no sign of the local radio car. Maybe the Council Tax Awareness Day at the Hall was really rockin'. Some people had spread out picnic rugs in the clearing beside the entrance to the path, but the creak of wicker hampers, pop of champagne corks and rustle of Kettle Chip packets was blown to the four winds by Esther's running megaphone commentary on the finishers.

'AND NEXT UP IT'S YOUNG EMMA MACDON- ALD, NUMBER FOURTEEN, WELL DONE SWEETHEART, COME AND HAVE A POWER SNACK COURTESY OF LANCASHIRE MUTUAL, OOP! IT'S MY MAGNUS NEXT – GOT SOME GRASS ON YOUR TROUSERS, I SEE – TONY, GO AND SORT HIM OUT, THEN WE'VE GOT LOVELY ABIGAIL GRANT, NUMBER ONE, GOOD FINISH, LITTLE ONE, GO GET YOUR JUICE COURTESY OF . . .'

I arrived within sight of the finish just in time to see Amber, still flawless in black cashmere and pearls, sail smilingly over to Esther, tap her on the shoulder and say, in a well-bred low voice which the megaphone picked up to perfection: 'ESTHER, MY PET, IF YOU DON'T SWITCH THAT BLOODY THING OFF I'M GOING TO SHOVE IT UP YOUR ARSE,' before returning to her springer spaniels and her Range Rover picnic.

George broke free from Tony when he saw me, and hurried over.

'This your wee one, then?' he asked, crouching down to Emma's eye level. 'Well, missy, didn't you do well? What a long way you walked!' Emma beamed and reached her arms out towards him. George bent down obligingly and Emma kissed him wetly on the cheek.

'Aww, thank you missy, that was lovely!' he said, smiling at her and patting her head.

''Fraid she's a bit forward!' I laughed, as Emma scuttled of to join Val's children. 'It's nice to see you again, George, I'd been hoping for a chance to say how much I enjoyed your piece the other week at the library. It was lovely.'

He turned pink. 'Oh, you know, I'm just playing at this creative writing thing. Facts and news stories – no problem, but *storytelling* ...' He shook his head, as though he'd been asked to explain the human genome project. 'Theresa, though, now there's a writer!'

'Are you sure?' I couldn't help asking, looking at him closely. Judging by his wistful face, he was.

Ah, well, maybe it was just me.

Later, in the floral warmth of the Mountain View Café, we exchanged stories about our mornings. Stuart was having an Ambitious Parent Moment, as Thomas had spent the morning at football training being praised for his corner kicks.

'You know, there's definitely a touch of Beckham there, Gail, I saw it! The way he used his head, lined up the shots, thought about his placement before taking the kicks ... and he did it over and over again, until he got it right! Didn't you, big man?' Thomas nodded through his mouthful of burger. And I was kissing someone else this morning. 'Must make enquiries about summer camp train-

253

ing. The stuff they do at school's not nearly enough to nurture a real prospect ... do you think we could contact Rangers, or Man U, to see if they run schemes? We could base our summer holidays round it. What do you say?'

'Let's do it.'

'How was the Toddle?'

I kissed Stevie in the middle of it. 'Great! Wasn't it, Em?' Emma, in her new Lancashire Mutual baseball cap, nodded and returned to her plate of chips and ketchup. 'Esther thinks that once the sponsor money is all in, the Toddle alone should have raised a couple of grand!'

Stuart was still mentally at Hampden Park on Cup Final day but good manners eased out a follow-up. 'Any pipers this year? Herds of buffalo? Majorettes?'

'Nope, it was much more low-key, thank God.' If you discount your wife's snogging incident, that is. 'Well, apart from Tony Smith's efforts to make it look like the London Marathon.'

'Mmm.'

'And I've got a complimentary voucher for ten per cent off Accidental Death Cover, courtesy of Lancashire Mutual! Isn't that brilliant?'

'Mmm. Do we have time to nip to Inverness to get Thomas some better football boots?'

I managed to persuade Stuart to take both children to town so that I could go round to Mary-Bell's salon for a cut and blow-dry. Mary-Bell Ritchie and I had been in the same year at Loch Martin High, although she left after fourth year to do hairdressing and beauty therapy at Inverness Tech. Her father, Spud from the fish and chip shop, bought and equipped the salon for her when she qualified, as a birthday present, and it had gone from strength to strength ever since, with a large staff of attitude-endowed local girls dressed in black with belly-button rings. Mary-Bell wasn't the sort of hairdresser who'd ask you what you were doing for your summer holidays – usually she'd got that information way beforehand from some source or other, so we always enjoyed a conversational saunter around our old friends and acquaintances instead.

'So,' she began as she got to work with the scissors, 'You're going all posh tonight, I hear! A ball, no less!'

I cringed. 'Oh, it's not really posh. Not really a ball, actually. They're just calling it that. Can't think why. It's only a dance in a tent! Bit pretentious if you ask me, but . . .'

Mary-Bell laughed at me. 'It's OK, Gail! You're allowed to go to a ball!'

'Yes, I know, but . . .'

'I went to a grand ball for the Stylist of the Year finals in the Ritz in London last year – I'm not exactly ball-starved, myself!' She resumed snipping.

'Oh well then, your ball's definitely bigger than mine!' I replied, feeling tons better.

'Well, you've got lovely weather for it, that's the main thing. What are you wearing?'

I told her proudly about my Topshop dress and then she told me that she'd got her dress for the stylists' ball in Prada in Sloane Street and I did another memo to self never to make assumptions about anything or anyone as long as I lived. Then I gave my ego a little turbo-charge by describing the handmade silk underwear and my Jimmy Choos (Mary-Bell had four pairs), and was just beginning to feel warmly at home among my kinfolk when Mary-Bell, still snipping, said casually, 'Hear you've been seeing a bit of Stevie Chip?'

'*What?*' It's just as well I was sitting down.

'God, Gail, what a colour you've gone! After all those years! Come on, he wasn't *that* good – I should know, I had him in third year! That den of his in the drama studio – remember it?'

'Wh . . . what makes you think I've been seeing him?'

'Not *seeing* him, Gail – come on, I know you better than that! He comes in here to get his hair cut and told me he was helping you out with the arrangements. Nice guy, don't you think? Still cute.'

Burn, burn, tingle, tingle.

'Suppose so,' I started. 'It *was* a bit weird seeing him again after all this time – I'd had no idea he was working up at Invermartin.' Sweet, flipping heck, could the whole world feel me trembling?

'And he's partnering a friend of yours tonight, Theresa, isn't it?'

'That's right. I set them up. Not sure if it was a good idea or not – I don't even know if they're getting on all that well, actually.'

'Oh, don't you worry about them, Gail,' Mary-Bell said in a preoccupied voice as she dragged locks of my hair painfully downwards, to make sure they were even on both sides. 'Stevie likes her fine! Told me he'd definitely give her a go after he's . . . oh, now, what did he say?' I was all ears. Terrified, damp, haircut ears. 'Sorted out some unfinished business! That's it!'

'He said what?' I squeaked.

'Yes, I'm sure that's what he told me – but he refused to go into any more detail. Don't look so shocked, Gail, I'm sure your pal can handle herself, from what you've told me about her. Personally I think it's something to do with that lassie he was engaged to in Australia. I know he was really cut up about her – that's why he tucked himself away at Invermartin, if you ask me. Mind you, that was a long time ago now – you'd think Stevie Chip, of all people, would have moved on to pastures new! You want some product on that?'

Chapter Fifteen

Unfinished business. *Unfinished business!* How classy is that?

Maybe a bit classier than *finished* business, but definitely not nearly as classy as not having turned into business in the first place. Whatever Stevie meant by that remark he'd made to Mary-Bell, and I was pretty bloody certain that it was me he was on about, it brought the reality of our situation home to me with a sharpness that took my breath away: *we would have been found out.* Maybe not for a while, but there was no doubt in my mind that Stevie's easy-going openness towards everyone, coupled with my Wales-sized guilty conscience, was a confidentiality-match made in hell. To say nothing of the fact that Mum was plainly on to me as well – I'd just chosen not to admit it earlier.

I escorted my hairdo home, and was relieved to find that Stuart and the children hadn't yet got back from Inverness. The house was musty and unnaturally quiet, but the kitchen was a breakfast bombsite, with abandoned cereal bowls littering the table, their half-eaten contents hardened into concrete, dried outlines of milk puddles on the table, lidless jam jars with knives poking out of their tops, crumbs everywhere, and a used teabag on the floor. I jumped about two feet when a myopic sparrow, perhaps mistaking me for a juicy worm because that was how low I was feeling, flew into the kitchen window-pane with a crunch and catapulted himself backwards onto the lawn, before tottering to his feet and flying off, looking this way and that to make sure he hadn't been seen.

A burst of housepride descended from somewhere and I began to clear the kitchen table until I realised, first, that I was blatantly putting off the evil moment, and, second, that I'd better step on it before Stuart came home. Trembling, I walked over to the phone and dialled Invermartin. After a few, terrifying rings Joffy, once again, answered.

'Hilleaur?' he enquired.

'Ah, Lord Brankin, please may I speak to Stevie? I need to ask him something. About tonight.'

'Is that lovely Gail Macdonald? Mother of lovely Emma Macdonald?'

'Urm, yes. Joffy, I'm really sorry but it's a bit urgent, erm ... I'm on my way out, and it's about tonight, and I only need a quick word, and something's burning on the cooker ...' Could I squeeze any more fibs in, perhaps, if I tried a bit harder?

A pause. Then, 'Hold on, my dear.'

I listened in agony as his steps faded along what sounded like a flagstone corridor, and wished I'd gone to the toilet before picking up the phone. After a wait of two, maybe three minutes, Stevie came to the phone.

'Gail?'

'Is Joffy still there?'

'No, he's gone to take the dogs out. What is it?'

'I need to get a couple of things sorted out before the ball.'

'Oh yes?'

'Stevie, you know what I said this morning?'

Another pause. 'The head-messing stuff?'

'Yes.'

'Uh-huh?'

'I meant it, Stevie. I've got to put a stop to all this, now, before the ball.'

'Ah.' I tried to stay calm as I listened to him take a few deep breaths. 'Am I allowed to ask why?'

Sometimes the right words never come. Sometimes they come to you just after the moment when you ought to have used them has passed. Very occasionally, they're right there for you, like best friends. And most of the time, they are a best attempt of all of the above, like a verbal revolving door of good intentions. Realising this didn't help one bit.

'Do you know, Stevie, as soon as I decided to make this call I've been rehearsing what to say.'

'Uh-huh?'

'I mean, at first I decided I'd have to say sorry. For leading you on, yet again, and then, well . . .'

'I understand.'

'Thanks. And then, after a bit, I decided I wanted to say thank you. Just for, well, giving me a good time, if you'll pardon the expression.'

'You're welcome, I guess. But . . .'

'I'm not finished yet. Then after a bit, I decided to settle for a nice, simple "goodbye". But Stevie, do you know what?'

'Yes, Gail, I'm listening.'

'I'm going to say this and after I've said it you'll still be that nice guy I grew up with who knows my folks and I'll still be me with the same life, OK?'

That confused him, I could tell. Baffled myself a bit, to be honest.

'Go on.'

'Stevie, what we did, or nearly did, isn't worth any of those big words, is it? If either of us used any of them then they'd be spoiled for other good stuff, wouldn't they?'

He sighed. 'If you say so, ma'am. So, what's left? What do we say?'

Ah. I hadn't got any contingencies looked out, actually. 'Oh, I don't know. We, we just had an "oh my God" episode, I guess.' I'd decided not to challenge him with the 'unfinished business' thing. Pots, and kettles, and all that. 'Will that do? Stevie?'

'OK, Gail, fine. Oh my God to you too, and I'll see you later.' He put the phone down.

'Oh my God, Stuart, what now?' I whispered to the silent line.

Stuart zipped me into my dress.

'Well?' I prompted, slithering round to face him and doing a little writhe. The little Topshop dress was singing with delight as it skimmed my body. With my new underwear, Jimmy Choos, and shiny haircut, I felt amazing, despite my anxieties about seeing Stevie again, to say nothing of the small remaining issue of Stuart and Susannah.

'You look gorgeous. Take it off again this instant.' I could tell his heart wasn't in it, though – he didn't even meet my eyes. Time was he'd have pulled that old zip right down again and not given me any choice about being late for wherever it was we were going. He'd say things like, *'Aha, I knew I'd ordered room service!'*, or he'd follow me into the shower and lather me all over with my expensive Christmas soap - his urgency used to drive me potty in all sorts of different ways – but mostly good ones. Tonight, though, his mind was elsewhere and I was hardly mentally equipped to do much about it.

'You're not so bad yourself, sir,' I replied, curtsying and fluttering an imaginary fan, even though he wasn't watching me; he'd turned to pick up his clothes brush and was worrying a few specks of scurf on his shoulders, his mouth set in a tight line. I tested out my long-frock walking skills, wiggling over to the window and scanning the garden below, full of shrubs and pots and discarded little tractors and pails. It was still lovely outside - the early evening was tranquil and a light breeze lifted the leaves to wave us off, like Cinders and Buttons, to the ball.

'Funny going out done up to the nines when it's still so light outside,' I said, absently, as my breath fugged the pane.

'Mmm. How do I look?'

I turned round and looked at him, standing rigidly upright in his Macdonald tartan kilt, black Prince Charlie jacket, wing-collar shirt and white bow tie. He stood wide-eyed and outstretched-palmed, in that dumb pose all men use when they're being scrutinised. I was technically very lucky to have such a good-looking, successful husband but given the current situation that didn't amount to a heap of crap.

'Fine. Great. She'll love you in that.' I added that last bit under my breath as I turned back to look out of the window, whilst the taxi pulled up outside and beeped its horn at us.

'Sorry?'

'Oh, nothing.'

'Got the mobile in case your mother calls?'

'Yup,' I replied, 'but she won't. Personal pride thing.' I'd dropped Thomas and Emma off at Mum and Dad's for their sleepover soon after Stuart returned with them from Inverness, together with the travel cot, a potty, nappies, toys, books, the baby listener, a new bottle of Calpol, a buggy, pyjamas, two changes of clothing, anoraks, a skateboard and a bunch of flowers. Then, driving off, I'd bought and devoured a Jumbo Snickers. Mum had decided that she was going to use the occasion to start potty-training Emma, and again, as with Stuart, I was hardly in any position to object. She could have told me that she was going to pierce their nipples and that would have to have been fine too, such was the weight of my anxiety. Being a dirty philandering tart is so disempowering!

'Know what, we should have asked Theresa and Stevie round for a drink first,' Stuart mused as he wiped a speck of dust from his shoes, 'then we could have shared the cab.'

'No way!' I shot back, before getting a grip on myself. 'Erm, Theresa was going to be a bit pushed for time, so we agreed just to meet up at Invermartin.' That was about a quarter true. What had actually happened was that I'd rung Theresa and said, 'You're going to be pushed for time, aren't you, so why don't we not bother meeting for drinks beforehand and we'll just see you at Invermartin?' She'd been a bit taken aback, but luckily hadn't argued. I couldn't have coped with the four of us being so, well, *undiluted,* even for a short time. Anyway, Stuart was satisfied by the explanation, so that was what mattered.

Flinging on my long black coat, I had a last look in the mirror and for a secret, don't-tell-anyone, delicious moment, decided I looked really lovely. Like a tiny Angelina Jolie, all eyes and lips and fantastic clothes. I picked up my rose silk evening bag, the one that squishes and slides and slips like an old-fashioned quilt, imagined I was Catherine Zeta Jones, or possibly Angelina again, running the gauntlet of the paparazzi and clambered into the taxi, leaving Stuart to put the lights out and lock the door. The taxi driver swung round in his seat as I eased the seat belt over my fabulous self.

'Well well, if it's not Ed Buchanan's wee lassie!' he cried, flashing yellow teeth in my direction. 'I've not seen you since years!'

Smashing of slippers, chiming of twelve and emergence of pumpkins.

I stood in the ladies' cloakroom queue behind an enormous, chiffon-wreathed woman who was waiting to check in a full-length mink coat and a pair of wellington boots as though it were the most natural thing in the world. The crowded area was an olfactory minestrone of expensive perfume and cosmetics. The mink welly woman was chatting noisily to her companion who was three ahead of her in the queue, something about whose barn they'd be borrowing this summer for their Norfolk holiday.

'Roly's got a super barn in Burnham Market, but the Zieglers' barn's just got so much more space!'

Sympathetic nods. 'I thought we'd be using the Ashcrofts' barn at Overy Staithe but it's full, which is annoying, so we may well have to end up using the Metcalfe-Smiths' barn after all ... ah well, *c'est la vie*! Happy reeling, darling!'

I checked in my coat and wriggled into the main part of the marquee to find Stuart, who'd managed to pick up two glasses of champagne. After a giant swig which narrowly avoided reappearing down my nose, I took in the scene, which was rapidly filling up with coiffed people in kilts and posh frocks.

Twelve white linen-draped tables formed a horseshoe around the dance floor, each displaying Susannah's gorgeous posies of wild flowers and a card with the name of the party which was expected to occupy it. Loch Martin Rotary Club. Inverness Yacht Club. Highland Rugby Society. Mr and Mrs Jolyon Westbrook and Guests – Amber's parents had put together an upmarket party of grannies and grampas. Lord Jonathan Brankin and Guests. Outram and Hill, Land Agents – Sarah's lot. Gorvaig Golf Club. Mrs William Fraser and Guests - Shona Fraser was a toddler group mum who had sensibly kept clear of the organising shenanigans but who nonetheless heroically drummed up a table of Loch Martin, non-committee parents. Inverness Solicitors – Assorted. Highland Dental Society – they'd have nice teeth. The Honourable Lavinia Crickett and Guests – that must be a joke, surely? And finally, the Committee and Guests.

At the far end of the marquee, Plum Duff and her staff, wittily dressed in chefs' whites over black and white tartan trousers and matching bandannas, were fussing over the buffet and the drinks table. As arranged by Susannah, large glass bowls filled with fruit punch lined up in colourful stripes with rows of champagne and wine bottles. The plan was to eat first, and commence the dancing after a short interval. I had a knot in my stomach and couldn't see, for once, how I'd manage to eat any food, but it seemed to be easing off with the help of the champagne – I drained my glass – elegantly – and swiped a second from a passing waiter with a tray.

To our right lay a little platform where the five-piece Archie Patience Ceilidh Band, wearing tartan tuxedos and black bow ties, were warming up their instruments. The right-hand corner of the stage displayed a rectangular tub filled with flowering shrubs which Esther had extorted from the tiny Loch Martin Garden Centre, and, on the left, an enormous amplifier supported five pints of lager.

'Ah. No trombones,' murmured Stuart. 'I so hoped there'd be trombones.'

'Didn't know you liked trombones,' I said absently.

'I don't, really. I just like the word,' he said. '*Trombones*. Here's your dance card, by the way.

Apparently we have to fill them up with who we plan to dance with all evening.' He handed me a folded piece of purple card with the names of the dances on them, and a tiny pencil attached to it with ribbon.

'What, every single one? What about the element of surprise?' I looked down the list. Thanks to Esther (now there's a thing to say!) I recognised almost every one – the Duke and Duchess of Edinburgh, the Inverness Country Dance, the Machine Without Horses, Postie's Jig, and so on down to the Duke of Perth at the bottom. But as for how to *do* them ... well, blame the champagne or whatever, but my mind had gone utterly blank.

'Help, I can't remember a single one of those bloody things!'

Stuart looked smug, and stroked his hairy sporran. 'Fear not, for help is at hand!' Opening the clasp of the sporran, he pulled out a crumpled (and warm) copy of Otto's crib sheet.

'Mmm, what else have you got tucked in there to help a girl out?' I asked, before catching sight of Esther, looking ... *stupendous* in a massive, cleavage-busting puff-ball of gold lamé, lassoing Sarah Barbour with a thick yellow tartan sash. Oh, shit, I'd forgotten about the sashes. My heart sank, and I clutched at my shoulder mournfully. Adieu to beautiful me, hello to Goal Attack conformist frumpy person.

Sure enough, over she sailed. 'Gail! Don't you look sweet!' *Mwah!* (there was no obvious smell of booze, which had to be a good sign). 'Here's your sash, isn't it divine? Now we all know what Val's for! Well, apart from being a big walking breast, that is!'

'Val's my friend and I don't appreciate that, Esther.'

'Oh, Gail, you are funny! Here's the brooch to fasten it – enjoy, and don't screw up the dancing in those shoes, will you? Time to make our way to our table and prepare for the first dance. Where we go, the rest will surely follow!'

Stuart bleated softly as we made our way to our seats, passing a table covered with a tartan travelling rug and groaning with the raffle prizes Esther had screwed out of the natives. Behind that, two easels displayed Susannah's watercolours, the ones Esther planned to auction off during the interval. Several people had gathered to admire them. One showed a delicate basket of sweet peas, and I had to grudgingly admit that it was beautifully done. The other, though, was far more striking. It was a cluster of young women, all dressed in pastel-coloured Victorian ballgowns, in some kind of drawing room. They were fussing over one particular young woman, who was seated in the centre of the picture, looking enigmatic and wearing an old-fashioned theatrical mask. Stuart was looking at it too.

'That one's called *"Who would have thought it?"'* he commented.

I whipped round to glare at him. 'And how the *hell* would you know that?'

I swear he jumped.

'I had a closer look as you were hanging up your coat. See, there's a little label attached to the frame.'

'Susannah may not be coming tonight,' I said nastily as we sat down, scanning his face for reaction. He fumbled in his hairy sporran for his handkerchief and busied himself blowing his nose. 'What with Paul deserting her, and all. This'd be the last thing she needs.'

'Oh, maybe she'll put in an appearance later, um, to see her paintings being auctioned, or something.'

Now why would he say that? He didn't know her, right? 'Stuart,' I hissed, gripping his arm tightly. 'What's going on with you two?' The table was filling up but I couldn't let that one pass.

266

'Not *now*!' he snapped. 'We'll talk about it later, OK?'

Amber was stunning in a tight red velvet gown – the black cashmere had the night off but the pearls were resolutely still there, a fact noticed by Esther, who hollered, 'Amber, my love, are these things *riveted* to your neck?' This was presumably revenge for the mega-phone/Toddle/arse incident but Amber sensibly let the comment roll over her, and she and Iain seated themselves opposite Stuart and me. We exchanged air-*mwahs*, with Stuart and me covering our real faces with Oscar-winning happy ones.

Esther and Tony sat closest to the band. Tony was swaggering a bit in a white dinner jacket, looking more like a tipsy pimp than Frank Sinatra, whom I suspected he was trying to emulate.

Val's dress had been hand-knitted out of spider's web and hemp. Actually, it hadn't, but it could have been – it was pure linen in potato-sack brown, gathered up into an old-fashioned gown which draped around her soft body. This, along with an orange mohair shawl and loose, wispy hair adorned with fresh daisies, gave her an aura of Druidic regality, probably exactly what she was aiming for. Janusz wore an embroidered waistcoat and matching skullcap, gathered maroon silk pantaloons and shoes with pointy toes. They clasped their hands together and bowed at us before sitting down, to a big round of appreciative applause.

'Kids?' I mouthed across the table.

'In the van,' she hissed back.

Sarah and Kevin Barbour were presiding over the Outram and Hill table on the other side of the room, and Claire, wearing a seventies-styled crêpe de Chine printed kaftan (which ingeniously toned with her sash) and some whopping diamonds, introduced us to Tiggy and Rufus, large, amiable friends of hers from the Pony Club, who joined our table.

267

Otto Mackintosh-Jones frisked over, wearing an orange tartan kilt which showed off the thinnest legs in the room (and that included the smooth-haired fillies imported from London who graced Joffy's table, devouring Marlboro Lights), and escorting a very pretty young woman in a blue strapless gown. He kissed everyone extravagantly.

'Darlings!' he beamed. 'Isn't this fun! Allow me to introduce Sheila, my wife. Sheila – *everyone*!'

'Hello, *everyone*!' repeated Sheila. 'I've heard so much about you all!'

'More than we can say about you, Sheila! Stuart Macdonald, how do you do?' He introduced us all. Amber, Claire and I had the good grace to look ashamed of ourselves.

I leaned over to Amber and whispered, 'Thought you said he was gay?'

'I think you'll find I said "light on his feet",' she hissed back primly, before adding, thoughtfully, 'my bet is he's gay in every respect except sexual orientation,' and returning to her drink.

Susannah hadn't turned up, which didn't surprise me, but neither, so far, had Stevie and Theresa. After a confusing few minutes while we exchanged dance cards and agreed on a more or less strict rota of partners for the evening, Archie Patience stepped up to the mike.

'Laydeesangennellmenn, good evening! Welcome to the Loch Martin Ball! Dinner is served!'

There was a riffle of applause and Esther was off like a bullet to be first in the queue. Tony followed, but only after muttering, 'Surely it should have been "*My lords*, ladies and gentlemen"?' In fact Joffy himself didn't seem to have arrived either – probably waiting for some kind of red-carpet-and-drumroll introduction like the year before.

We ploughed our way through an enormous buffet of

cold salmon and beef, salads and wine, followed by chocolate roulade and fruit salad. Oh, the conversation flowed easily enough, Otto, on my left, was marvellous company, as were Amber and Iain opposite, but Stuart, on edge and off his food too, practically ignored me, chit-chatting with Claire and Martin Holmes and the pony people, checking his watch and constantly shooting glances towards the exit. And Stevie and Theresa still hadn't shown up.

It was only after the coffee was drunk, tables cleared and the dancing about to get under way that I thought I caught a glimpse of something which made my blood run cold. I noticed the teeniest swish of the curtain that screened the exit and behind it, for the merest fraction of a second, I swore I caught a glimpse of Susannah's face. Whether Stuart saw it too or not, I couldn't say, but all of a sudden, having ignored me for the best part of an hour and a half, he turned and put his arm across my shoulders.

'Gail, I've got to go out for a moment – get some fresh air before the dancing starts. Back in a minute!' He kissed my cheek and before I had a chance to say anything (not that any words would have come out, anyway), he was gone.

'Gail, my poppet, what's the matter?' Otto took hold of my hand, which was shaking.

'Nothing, thanks, I'm fine.'

'Oh, no you aren't,' he said gently. 'What is it?'

'Stuart's up to something. Outside. With Susannah Grant. My world is in the process of coming to an end. Otherwise, I'm fine.'

'Laydeesangennellmenn, first dance, please!' boomed Archie. 'TAKE your partners for the Inverness Country Dance!' The band launched into some warm-up bars of bouncy music, and people began to get to their feet.

'Sweetheart, go after them!' implored Otto. 'Find out what the hell they're doing and sort it out!' I looked at

269

him, and a tear which felt as big as a butter bean fell down my cheek and sploshed onto my lap. 'Go on!'

To an ear-splitting *heeeuch!* the dance got under way. I'd been due to dance this one with Stuart anyway so apart from the people whose toes I trod on in my haste to get out of the tent, I didn't cause too much disruption by pushing my way outside.

It was beginning to get dark, but the air was still and balmy as I hobbled in my Jimmy Choos around the tent in search of Stuart. But, apart from the waiting staff clustered in a knot smoking cigarettes and swigging from the necks of pilfered champagne bottles, there was nobody around. The music from inside the tent thumped into the night air as I scanned the field, the car park and the bumpy road to Invermartin House. Nothing. A man in a dinner suit emerged from behind a rhododendron, zipping up his fly, but a quick check from a safe distance ascertained that he'd been there alone. I didn't know what to do. Then, as I peered into the woods at the far edge of the field, I noticed for the first time that there was a little path leading off through the trees, so, having nowhere else to go (Invermartin House was too far away – he'd have needed to hot-wire the electricity cable to his backside to get there that quickly), I tore off my sash and wobbled across the field towards it.

This was nuts. Where the heck was he? Or, *they*? God, it was eerie in the woods. The heavy ceiling of foliage made it seem almost pitch dark at first, and it was a minute or two before my eyesight adjusted. Fortunately the path was firm and smooth underfoot, and I settled into a brisk, tottering pace, trying to compose myself and wondering whether I was going off my rocker.

After what seemed like miles but was probably only a hundred yards or so, I rounded a sharp corner and almost yelled in terror as the silhouette of a stone figure appeared right in front of me, blocking the path. With a start I realised that it was the statue of little Eliza Brankin, Joffy's eleven-year-old ancestor who'd been killed in a riding accident at this spot generations ago. I'd had no idea that the path led this way – in fact I was quite close to the road. But my shock at stumbling across the statue was nothing compared to the sudden sight of the two people who were standing close together beneath it. It was Stuart and Susannah.

'Gail!' gasped Stuart, running over. 'You shouldn't have followed!'

'So it seems,' I replied, suddenly feeling my legs turn to jelly. Then, 'I need to sit down.' I half-staggered over to the statue and sat down on a kerbstone at its foot, where I began crying uncontrollably. Stuart engulfed me in his arms and rocked me. I didn't have the strength to push him away.

'Gail, it's most definitely not what you think!' he said, his voice high-pitched and desperate.

I vaguely heard Susannah add in the background, 'What? Oh, heavens, noooo! It's not that! Sorry!'

I looked up at her. 'Don't you *dare* say anything!' Summoning up strength from somewhere, I shook Stuart off and stood up, glowering down at him. 'I *know* you've been seeing her! I heard Emma in the background when she called the house! You've stayed the night! You weren't in Edinburgh at all, *were you*?'

He looked aghast. He and Susannah exchanged looks which may have been horror or may not, then Susannah tiptoed over and said softly, 'I'll leave you alone to sort this one out,' before melting away down the path. She wore a long, dark velvet cape and for a moment I wondered what century we were in, as she wafted away.

But at that moment I didn't care if she stayed or not.

'Gail, Gail, I am NOT having an affair with Susannah! Bloody hell, how could you think such a thing? I can't believe it!'

'But you've been seeing her behind my back! I can prove it!'

'You don't need to prove anything, Gail! Yes! I have been seeing Susannah without telling you! For *this*!'

I noticed for the first time that he had a little velvet box in his hand, which he now thrust in front of my bleary face. Then he fished out his hankie and handed it to me. Wiping my face and giving my nose a robust blow, I stared at it. 'What is it?'

'Open it and see.' He pressed it into my hand. 'God, I didn't envisage giving it to you like this! Gail, how can you *believe* I'd have an *affair*!'

Maybe because *I* sort of had one? I opened the box. Inside, nestled in a tussle of shredded tissue paper, was a fat, heart-shaped locket of antique gold, completely plain apart from its tiny hinge and clasp, attached to a slender chain. Looking up at Stuart, and even though it was so dark, I saw tears glistening in his eyes.

'Open it,' he said.

Trembling, I unlatched the clasp. Inside, through the near-darkness, I saw a miniature portrait. Not some miscellaneous Victorian nobleperson – not even Stuart, or Thomas, or Emma. It was quite simply the most beautiful image I had ever seen, of a tiny, baby boy. It was Ben. And on the opposite side from the painting was engraved the single word, 'Forever'.

'Oh! It's . . . it's . . .' There were no words. We held each other tightly and cried, and cried.

Chapter Sixteen

'I commissioned Susannah to do it after I saw some of her stuff in Inverness Art Gallery,' said Stuart much, much later as we walked, arm-in-arm, back to the ball. I didn't even realise at first that it was your *friend* Susannah from Loch Martin, but once I realised it was her, the idea just grew and grew. She was brilliant – do you know that the paintbrush she used was so tiny it only had five bristles?'

'One for each member of the family,' I murmured.

'Mmm,' agreed Stuart.

'How did you get the photo to her? I can't believe I didn't notice it was gone from the mantelpiece!'

Stuart let go of me, stopped walking and stood for a moment, staring into the depths of the woods. He didn't seem to know what to do with his hands. 'I didn't need that one. I've had a copy of that photo in my desk drawer at work ever since ... ever since we got it.'

His voice was cracking again. Such a tiny revelation, yet, well, probably one of those sentences which will stay with me for the rest of my life. How much attention had been paid to Stuart when Ben died? Even in the depths of my misery I think I was aware that the majority of the sympathy and support came my way rather than jointly to both of us. Stuart had had to make do with a lot of pats on his shoulder – I was probably busy sobbing on the other one. I slid my arm back around his waist and gave him a squeeze. We walked again, holding each other tightly.

'Anyway,' he went on, 'Susannah asked me to go round to her house a few times, to look at the work in progress. She was desperately insecure about it; she *so* wanted you to like it. I was constantly having to reassure her – I knew from the first visit that it was going to be really special. I just don't think she's got much faith in her own ability, for some reason.'

I stopped again and peered through the growing gloom at the little portrait. How had Susannah managed it? She hadn't just copied the photo, she'd somehow, via skill, or trial and error, or sheer fortunate happenstance, instilled a little essence of our whole family into that tiny face. I saw Thomas's expression. I saw Emma's mouth. I saw Stuart's fingers in the little hand that clutched the top of the white shawl.

'It *is* special. Desperately special, Stuart. Just like you.' He looked at me and we both smiled. 'Do you know,' I continued, 'I'd even got it into my head that you never went to Edinburgh at all the other week! It was the stubble . . .'

'The stubble?'

'Yes! The stubble!'

'Pray tell me about the stubble, Gail?'

'It was at Susannah's . . .' But I tailed off as soon as I began. All of a sudden this wasn't the night for airing my suspicions. Realising that I was on the verge of joking to Stuart that Susannah's stubbly wash-hand basin had convinced me of his infidelity didn't make me feel too proud of myself. 'Please may I not? I'm so sorry – oh, Stuart, that sounds so inadequate!' He little knew.

'Where else but Edinburgh would I have found the perfect locket to put the portrait in? Loch Martin Post Office? Anyway, to go on with my story, Susannah and I got our wires crossed about when I was going to give it to you. I said at the start that it'd be nice to have it for the ball, but only because I fancied sliding up behind you in our bedroom and placing it round your neck – you know, like in every movie we've ever seen?'

'Mmm. Good plan.'

'But unfortunately Susannah got it into her head that she didn't need to have it ready until the ball itself, and her anxiety was starting to do my nut, so I decided not to bother putting her right, and so she didn't finally finish it until a couple of hours ago. Then she wanted me to go "somewhere really private" so that I could see it first, and before I could even say, "Madam, have we met?" I was being dragged off into the woods! God, no wonder you were suspicious!'

'Well, I'm still thinking about challenging her to a duel ... *ouch*!' There aren't many soft forest paths in Knightsbridge and the confused old Jimmy Choos finally wobbled over, taking me helplessly down with them. I made a grab for Stuart, missed, and slid helplessly down the side of his kilt.

A nice, warm, fresh cowpat for my bottom to go *splat!* into would have completed the picture, and serve me bloody well right, too, but luckily Mother Nature's practical joke department was on its fag break and I landed instead on a carpet of dock leaves and fir cones to the gentle strains of my lovely husband killing himself with laughter.

Piggybacks are always the best revenge, though, and after hitching my dress classily up around my waist and climbing aboard, Stuart carried me gallantly out of the woods, unloading me at the door of the Portaloos so that I could attempt a repair job on my wrecked face and sponge the mud off my shoes.

'Do you want to go back in there?' Stuart asked when I emerged, nodding towards the marquee, from where sounds of raucous partying were beginning to emanate. 'We could just nip home, if you like. 'S'up to you – you look exhausted.'

I pondered the suggestion. If we called a cab right now, I could be in a hot bubble bath, with a cold gin and tonic and two aspirin on the side, in under sixty minutes. There'd be no kids to get us up through the night and we'd score at least ten hours' sleep. Nobody would see my shiny red face and we'd avoid the really hard dances, the ones Esther had scheduled for near the end when we'd all warmed up. I wouldn't have to see Susannah until I'd properly sorted out just what I was going to say to her. But on the other hand, if Stevie had any plans at all to show up, I wouldn't see him, either.

'Nah, let's stick it out, shall we?' I said eventually, keeping my voice light. 'There's still the raffle, after all, isn't there? Not to mention the challenge of the Machine Without Horses?'

We re-entered the marquee and were almost thrown backwards by the wall of noise and thick, sweaty heat which greeted us. People had really loosened up, with shiny, exercised faces and shrieky women everywhere. Two ladies in identical silver beaded Monsoon ballgowns were having that shouty, huggy, we-don't-care encounter on the edge of the dance floor, betraying their mortification and leaving me wondering whether or not to tip them off about Bunty at The Wee Dress Shop for next year.

'Hey, you two, you haven't half buggered up our dance cards!' bellowed Esther when she saw us. 'What the hell

276

have you been up to, or shouldn't I ask?' She nudged me painfully in the ribs.

'If I told you I'm afraid I'd have to shoot you,' deadpanned Stuart, making Esther look slightly worried for the first time since one of Joffy's dogs had made a lunge for her crotch, all those weeks ago during our first trip to Invermartin House.

She recovered herself soon enough, though. 'Har! You're such a card, erm, erm . . .'

'Stuart.'

'Stuart! Of course! Got your name right here!' She checked her dance card. 'Stuart! What do you know! You're dancing with me next, you lucky devil! Chop-chop! Shift your ass – we're Shiftin' Bobbins! Hope you've been brushing up!'

Tony Smith oiled up to Sheila Mackintosh-Jones, tapped his dance card, and claimed her for the dance with condescending largesse, as though she were a *Big Issue* vendor and he'd just told her to keep the change.

'And I've got you, my sweet,' whispered Otto, appearing from nowhere and taking my hand. 'Everything OK?'

'Perfectly, thanks, Otto.'

I stole a look at the crib sheet, was none the wiser on the Shiftin' Bobbins front, and we lined up in long ranks stretching from one end of the marquee to another. Further down from me a line of women of uncertain age with high-maintenance, reptilian skin tut-tutted at our inability to get organised quickly, but we got there eventually and with a 'Da-rraaa!' from the Archie Patience Band, the dance got under way.

Otto was a dream partner. There was no need to tell him that I was struggling – he'd place his hand firmly in the small of my back and, using his fingertips, 'steer' me in the direction I was meant to go next, like a ventriloquist

277

manipulating a great big dummy with sore feet – which, of course, I *totally* was. He did this while maintaining eye contact and a dreamy look of sheer bliss throughout, like he'd been fortunate enough to land Ginger Rogers as his partner. With friends like these, who needs Esther? I told him snippets of what had happened in the woods each time I skipped past his ear, which did nothing for my concentration, but I felt he was owed that much.

'Golly, Gail, I'm filling up!' he said with a sniffle as the dance came to and end and I realised that, thanks to Otto's technical brilliance, I hadn't killed anyone. The dancers swept back to the sides like salt blown from a table, and Otto took me back to my seat with the tenderness of a policeman returning a lost child.

A snarled 'fingyouverrymuch!' from Archie Patience heralded the interval. And there was still no sign of Theresa and Stevie. I stared at the two empty places at our table and was suddenly fuming; angry and embarrassed that they'd obviously got together and decided that the poxy Loch Martin mumsy, poncy, parenty ball was beneath them – they were probably sitting in the pub right now, congratulating themselves on their narrow escape and making jokes at our expense. Not that I particularly *longed* to see Stevie right then, I realised that I was far too emotionally fragile to cope with him on top of all the goings-on in the woods, but at least if he *had* shown up I could have had the satisfaction of ignoring him. Archie Patience and his boys shot off the stage to find another nice cold pint of lager somewhere, and Esther immediately leapt up on to it, flushed, excited, but, as far as I could see, still sober. She resembled a big, gold Christmas decoration.

'My lords, ladies and gentlemen!' she honked into the microphone, half-bowing down, with her eyes closed. For a moment I wondered whether she just might be having an orgasm, such was the extent to which the occasion evidently affected her, but anyway, the chit-chatting and hob-nobbing hardly subsided an inch so she straightened up, took a deep breath and tried again.

'MY LORDS, LADIES AND GENTLEMEN! *OI THERE!*'

That shut 'em up. 'Thenk you!' resumed Esther. 'It's wonderful to see you all tonight at our little besh! Now, I'm not going to do a vote of thenks, we'll save that for the end, but we are about to draw the Grend Reffle, which will be followed immediately by the auction of the two *febulous* watercolours we've all been admiring, by the well-known artist, and, may I say, *highly* efficient committee member, Susannah Grant!'

There was a sprinkling of applause, but still no sign of Susannah.

'But just before we do, I'm delighted to announce that this year's total, taking into account the pledges from the sponsored Toddle, ticket, reffle and drinks sales, but not including the auction proceeds, as the auction hasn't taken place yet, obviously, as you'd be thinking there was some sort of fiddle going on, which there isn't, is a truly magnificent six thousand, eight hundred pounds!'

She'd done it. We'd all done it. Hearty applause broke out and Stuart, rather dashingly, I thought, rose to his feet, followed by every other male in the place, and Esther, moved beyond words, which for her was very moved indeed, curtsied.

The Honourable Eleanora-Jane Gordon-Smith, Joffy's niece, was called up to draw the raffle. For a girl with such a large quantity of names, there wasn't much of her. Rail-thin, with a long nose and shoulder blades you could slice cheese with, she stubbed out her fag and wiggled diffidently on to the stage to whoops from the lantern-jawed male young things at Joffy's table.

Now, this kissing thing – just how the *hell* does it work? From the look of things, the more aristocratic you were, the more times you had to kiss Eleanora-Jane when you went to collect your prize. I mean, someone called Digby from the Joffy crew managed about nine – poor Eleanora-Jane resembled a battery hen pecking grain through bars as they dodged around each other's cheek-bones before Digby got his hands on his luxury hand-carved lamp-base. Moving down the scale, someone called Milo Swan from the Honourable Lavinia Crickett's table completed four before trousering his Skibo Castle luxury dinner and golf voucher (to some unfriendly booing from the Gorvaig golfers – *they'd* wanted that one), but the majority of winners seemed to settle for one or two.

Awkwardly, someone called Arbuthnott from the lawyers' table won Stuart's legal services voucher, and he muttered darkly on his way past that Stuart was quite possibly touting for business illegally and that he'd be looking into the matter first thing on Monday morning. I was delighted when he fluffed the Kissing of Eleanora-Jane, mistiming the second one and snagging on her nose.

Lovely little Amber won an ugly luxury padded foot-stool in swirly purple plush – she kissed Eleanora-Jane twice without mishap. Then, trickily, the next ticket out was also hers, and given that *that* prize was a set of six Waterford Crystal whisky tumblers, she swiftly returned the footstool and grabbed the crystal before anyone could decide whether she was being really sporting, or not.

A dressing-gowned Struan Gruber had been prodded out of his Dormobile at the end of the raffle to present Eleanora-Jane with a bouquet of flowers. He offered his hand for her to shake, wisely, rather than enter the fraught kissing arena, and was given a glass of lemonade for his trouble.

Stuart whispered, 'Isn't anyone going to give anything to the person who gave the kid his lemonade for giving the girl her flowers for giving out the prizes? We could be here all night.'

Archie Patience and his band were by now standing to one side of the stage, anxious to get on with the dance programme. Esther shouted 'Shan't be long, boys!' as she frisked back to the microphone, holding a riding crop, ready to commence the auction of the two paintings.

But she didn't get a chance to do a thing. This time the sight of a big gold woman holding a whip quietened the crowd as if by magic, and after a few moments nobody in the marquee was saying a word as the unmistakable sound of approaching bagpipes could be faintly heard from outside.

Everyone turned to gawp towards the entrance. The sound of the reel got louder and louder, until at last the curtain was swung back and a lone piper in full Highland dress entered the marquee, proceeded up the entire length of the empty dance floor and turned to face the guests, playing all the while. It was stirring stuff, and really rather thrilling. Esther was flummoxed and didn't move a muscle, other than to dart panicky looks at Tony. People began tapping their feet in time with the reel, softly at first, then a little louder, using their heels, until the rhythm became the heartbeat of rocks on a riverbed, with the music from the pipes flowing over the top. I clutched Stuart's hand.

It seemed that nothing could interrupt the moment, the sheer unexpected *rightness* of the piper and his music, standing amidst us all, just playing a tune. It was sort of basic, yet incredibly special. So simple, yet somehow nerve-tatteringly poignant, a reminder that where we were, and what we were doing, was actually really, bloody good. I watched Esther fearfully, afraid that she'd wreck everything by pouring water over the piper or something, but she had shrunk to the back of the stage, where Tony had his arm round her shoulders, and they were listening intently, like the rest of us.

No, when the inevitable interruption came it was in the even more unexpected form of the ear-splitting roar of a revving engine from just outside. Everyone turned towards the entrance in irritation, but the piper played on and all of a sudden the curtain swished back for a second time, and into the marquee thundered a huge, black motorbike, ridden by a man in head-to-toe black leather, with a woman, riding side-saddle, clutching his middle. They each wore black crash helmets.

The bike slowed to a halt in the middle of the dance floor and the riders began to dismount. Nobody moved. I clutched Stuart's hand even more tightly, horrified. 'Strange sort of Hell's Angels invasion, this,' he said quizzically. Oh my God. The motorbike. I recognised it. It had to be Stevie and Theresa. Why the *bloody hell* . . .?

But it wasn't. To gasps of utter disbelief from all corners of the room, the riders removed their helmets and revealed themselves as Lord Jonathan Brankin and Susannah Grant. Joffy held his helmet aloft before bowing extravagantly, then he propped up the bike and bounded over towards the stage. Susannah meanwhile ruffled her hair, took off her cape to reveal a gorgeous, tight red sheath dress, and convulsed with laughter. Joffy strode over to Esther, kissed her (three times), and whispered something which flipping well ought to have been an apology, before bounding back to the microphone.

'Good evening, one and all!'

A cheer started up at his guests' table and spread round the room like a rather posh Mexican wave.

'So sorry we're late! Can't trust the buses round here, what?' Laughter. Disproportionate, I felt.

He went on. 'I *heaupe* you'll excuse this frightful intrusion, but I just couldn't resist the opportunity, under these happy circumstances, to announce that gorgeous Susannah ... come here, my sweetheart, has agreed to do me the very great honour of becoming my wife!'

Even Joffy's guests seemed, well, *gobsmecked*, but after taking a moment to digest such a humungous announcement, the entire room, at least those who knew either Joffy or Susannah or both of them, including me, suddenly couldn't think of a single reason why this wasn't the most wonderful news they'd heard in ages, and began to cheer. Joffy and Susannah kissed, and Stuart and I looked at each other and said in unison, 'Awww!'

Archie Patience and his band sprang to their places, and with admirable impromptu ease began to play 'Congratulations', while Joffy and Susannah jumped off the stage and waltzed round and round the motorbike, with the rest of us clapping along like idiots. It was a delightfully cheesy moment, finally brought to an end by Esther, who faced the band and drew her finger across her neck several times until they took the hint and wound it up. Joffy escorted Susannah to his table, where there were dozens and dozens of kisses to be exchanged.

'Well!' she said, stretching out her arms like Céline Dion. 'What can we say? Marvellous! Marvellous! Jolly good! *Right,* the auction. Sit down, everyone. Please. Who'll give me fifty quid for the first picture, titled, oh, bugger, what is it, ah yes, *"Who would have thought it?"*'

A chuckle went round the room as the meaning of the painting was explained. Bidding started in earnest.

'Seventy!'

'Eighty!'

'Ninety!'

Esther tried to keep up by pointing to the bidders with her riding crop but it was hopeless. Seizing the chance to display wealth, blokes from all corners of the room barked the price up, ten pounds at a time, but by the time the price had risen to four hundred pounds, there were only three bidders left in contention: a determined solicitor, a competitive golfer and the Honourable Lavinia Crickett.

A bid of four hundred and twenty was the swansong of the solicitor, whose husband had put his head in his hands and looked as though he might be sobbing.

'OK, we have four twenty, any advance on four twenty? You, sir? Madam?' This must have been how Esther thought it would be – she was suddenly radiant. A gold lamé dominatrix, with a whip.

'Four fifty!' The golfer.

'Four seventy!' The Honourable Lavinia Crickett who, on closer inspection, looked a little odd.

'Four ninety!'

'Five hundred!'

'Fucking hell!' Thus did the golfer remove himself from the bidding.

'Anyone else?' asked Esther, tapping her whip against the side of her thigh. Are we all done at five hundred?'

It seemed as though we were.

'Sold, at five hundred pounds! Yippee!'

Susannah looked shell-shocked, as the Honourable Lavinia Crickett stood up and bowed. Bowed. *That* was what was odd about her – the Honourable Lavinia Crickett was a man in drag.

'I think he's devised a meaning all of his own for that picture,' said Stuart thoughtfully.

'Now, let's see if we can do as well for the second one! *"Eliza's Flowers".*'

And so they were. Stuart and I realised at the same moment that Susannah had painted the posy of flowers held by the statue of Eliza Brankin. We looked at each other.

'Who'll give me ten pounds?' wheedled Esther, 'for this nice little bedroom picture?'

'One thousand pounds!' shouted Stuart.

There was a gasp as everyone turned to gawp towards Stuart, me included. He glanced at me and shrugged. Oh, what the heck. If we gave up food and cut off our electricity for a few months, we'd absorb that, no problem.

'Wow!' gulped Esther.

Silence.

'Um, any more?'

More silence.

'Sold, to, to, Mr Macdonald! My word!'

A few bars from the Archie Patience Band shut Esther up and warned of an imminent dance. Checking my dance card, I saw that it was the Eightsome Reel, in which I was to partner Stuart. He reached for my hand.

'Shall we?'

'Why, Mr Saatchi, I'd be honoured!'

Susannah came rushing over and, before we had a chance to congratulate her, she caught Stuart's hands and said, 'Stuart! Are you sure? A thousand pounds for my picture? I know it's for a good cause, but ...'

'Don't you worry, we're sure,' I replied. 'Hang on a sec, Stuart.' I took Susannah's arm and pulled her over to the side of the marquee.

'Susannah, the picture of Ben – I love it. I ... I ...' Tears were starting up again and Susannah waved away my thanks, her left hand considerably lower than her right under the weight of the antique diamond knuckleduster Joffy had presented to her.

'I'm so glad,' she said. 'It was an honour.' She kissed my cheek and turned to go back to Joffy's table.

'Can I ask you something else?' I called after her, knowing that there would never be a good time to ask what I was going to ask, so I might as well seize the worst one possible.

'Of course,' she replied, coming back over to where I was standing.

'Well, why on earth didn't you tell me about Joffy when I asked you if you were seeing anyone?'

She opened her mouth and looked ready to apologise, then obviously thought better of it. After a moment she said, quite gently, 'Gail, I didn't tell you because I didn't want you to know! It's as simple as that! You'd made your opinion of Joffy abundantly clear, and I knew that I was in the early stages of something truly special. I didn't feel ready for your ridicule.'

Oh boy, did I ever deserve that.

'Well, I was wrong,' I said. 'And I'm really sorry.'

She gave me a huge smile. 'Let's forget it, shall we? Come on, I'm dying for a dance – this is the only one Joffy and I can do!'

Feeling immensely relieved, I rushed back over to join Stuart and the others, just in time for the start of the Eightsome Reel. With Iain and Amber, Otto and Esther and Tony and Sheila making up the remainder of the eight, we launched into the dance with gusto, whirling round in a circle, then executing our teapots, grand chains, *pas-de-basques* and figures of eight with wine-fuelled concentration, before taking it in turns to make fools of ourselves in the centre.

Wasn't it George Michael who sang about guilty feet

having no rhythm? Well, he was right. Guilty feet live double lives; they go through the motions of the dance when all the time their instinct is to run away and hide. That's how mine felt, anyway. Guilty, and aching. No wonder they've got no bloody rhythm, with all that to think about. Opposite, Stuart was looking at me with such love I could hardly bear it, and as the dance progressed, I couldn't have cared less if we were doing the Eightsome Reel or the Twist, as realisation hit me that, at some point, I'd have to tell him everything.

The thought filled me with such a surge of trepidation that I barely noticed when the dance came to an end, with high-fives and rowdy 'Whoos!' all round because we'd managed to finish at the same time as the band. Sliding gratefully back into my seat, I kicked off my shoes, gulped down a glass of tepid water and wiped my damp forehead with the tablecloth. It took a moment to register who was sitting beside me.

'Having fun?'

It was Theresa.

And attached to her, by means of an arm thrown territorially around her shoulder, was the unmistakable form of Stevie Chip. He leaned even closer into her and – *kissed her cheek*!

'Get you a drink?' he murmured in her ear, before removing his mouth from her cheekbone, looking round at me and saying, 'Hello, Gail.'

'Mmm. Champagne, don't you think?' Theresa purred.

'Oh, I think!' He stood up and headed for the drink table. I had to admit he looked gorgeous in his kilt and black jacket – just how a man *should* look in the kilt ...

Having given up all hope of seeing either of them and let my guard drop so completely, appearance-wise, I could only gawp like an idiot, while gasping to get my breath back and think of something to say.

'Where the *hell* have you two been?' was all I managed.

Theresa, looking utterly amazing in the green dress, if a bit flushed, gave me one of her looks. Her *'come off it, stupid'* look.

'You *haven't*!' I gasped.

'I bloody have!' she replied. 'And about time, too! Don't know what's been keeping the bugger! Been driving me nuts!'

Stuart came over. 'Theresa! You look hot!'

Theresa raised her eyebrows and grinned. 'Thanks, tiger!'

'No, no, I mean you look *hot,* like, too warm! Of course, you look *hot* too, but . . .' He sat down and put his head in his hands.

'Good to see you, too, Stuart,' smiled Theresa. 'You OK, Gail?'

No, absolutely not. 'Me? I'm fine! Why shouldn't I be?' *Oh, only about a zillion reasons . . .*

She touched my shoulder. 'Aren't you pleased for me?'

Aha, that was a tricky one. 'Just be careful, OK?' I said eventually, looking at her earnestly. She laughed, looking through the crowds for Stevie's return with their drinks.

'Yes, yes, I know! And if I can't be careful, I'll be good, just like you!'

Chapter Seventeen

The arrival of Thomas's summer holidays, two weeks after the ball, heralded the start of a big change in his routine. Exasperated by his growing obsession with his Game Boy, a passion he shared with most of the other seven-year-olds in his class, I'd made the unilateral decision to confiscate the machine for the duration of the holidays, with the sweetener that he could play with it, for an hour at a time, if it was raining. So far, four days in, it hadn't rained once.

I was amazed, and more than a little disturbed, by how poleaxed he was by this act of treachery on the part of his mother, but my ruthlessness at least gave him a figure on which to constantly vent his fury, rather than concentrating his energies on capturing Bulbosaurs using Water Attack, or whatever it was he'd previously been absorbed in on his miniature screen.

'You're ruining my life!' he sobbed, lifting the phrase from a gritty kids' TV drama which he'd been slumped in front of minutes before. 'I can't go on like this! I'm through with this place!' And he'd mini-stormed outside, slamming the door.

'Isn't there some kind of Pokémon rehab we can check

him into?' pondered Stuart as we gazed out of the kitchen window at our son, who'd thrown himself onto the lawn and begun pulling out clumps of grass. 'I'm not sure if cold turkey's been the right approach here.'

'Maybe I should just give it back to him?' I said nervously. 'This is torture. Perhaps just for a short time each day?'

'What, and undermine our parental authority?' replied Stuart, but sounding a bit unsure. 'But then again,' he went on, 'it is *his* toy I suppose – who says we've got the right to take it away from him?' Now Thomas was gazing forlornly at the cloudless sky. He must have been the only boy in Scotland praying for rain.

I chewed my lip. 'It wasn't healthy, those hours he spent staring at that wee screen. It'll ruin his eyesight!'

'Maybe, but it's meant to be excellent for his hand-eye coordination, apparently,' Stuart countered, rubbing his chin. 'I'm sure I read that somewhere. Look at Japanese kids!'

'Um, why?'

'They don't all have glasses on, do they, and don't they spend their entire lives playing with electronic stuff?'

'But he should be out playing rufty-tufty games! Riding his bike over the flower beds! Kicking his football at the house!'

Stuart was quiet for a moment. Then he said softly, 'But he'd have got into trouble for those things, too.'

Thomas looked round and saw us, then turned away mournfully again. After a few moments he dragged himself wearily to his feet, plodded over to the climbing frame, heaved his way to the top and stood perilously upright on a single bar at the top, stretching both hands out in front of him.

I gasped and rushed outside like lightning, Stuart close

behind. 'Thomas! Be careful! What on earth are you doing?' He looked for the entire world like he was about to hurl himself off the top into oblivion.

He looked down at me, the picture of innocence. 'I only want to catch the rain as soon as it comes, Mum. Then I'll get my Game Boy back quicker.'

Stuart had dodged in front of me and was fielding Thomas at the foot of the frame. He glanced over his shoulder at me, and I nodded.

'Tell you what, big man,' he began, 'maybe we can do each other a favour?'

'Oh yeah? Shoot,' Thomas replied suspiciously. I realised he'd been overdosing on telly as well. Still, we could work on the language after we'd dealt with the zombie behaviour.

'Come down, and we'll talk, man to man.' *Step back from the edge!* I inwardly shrieked.

Stuart grabbed Thomas as he clambered down, bundling him into his arms for an enormous hug, which Thomas resisted for only a second. 'Here's the deal. You play football with me for an hour, and then you can have your Game Boy until bath time. How about it? I could really do with the practice?'

Thomas gave the proposition due consideration, then answered, 'Well, OK then, Daddy, so long as you stop pulling your shirt over your head when you score?'

I turned back happily towards the house, but not before I overheard Thomas confide in Stuart; 'Mum's probably *way* better on the Game Boy than me by now, she's had it for *ages!*'

The phone rang half an hour later.

'Gail?' I jumped involuntarily when I heard the voice. 'It's Susannah. Sorry to disturb you. How are you?'

'Fine! Just great! You?' I told my heart to calm down. *Stop it, girl, she's innocent, I tell you!*

'Fine, thanks.'

There was a silence, which I felt compelled to fill. 'Um, haven't seen you since the ball – got used to that ring yet? It's such a . . . a corker!' Oh, God, when would I learn to just bloody shut up?

She laughed. 'Just about. It's lovely, isn't it? Gail, I know it's short notice, but Joffy and I have decided to take advantage of the lovely weather and have a barbecue tonight – would you like to come? A sort of informal engagement thing – bring the children, of course – Abigail's longing to play with Emma again. Sorry, I know we should have been more organised, but we were just so enjoying the sunshine and thought we'd seize the moment to practise our joint entertaining skills!'

'Oh! Tonight?' I said, playing for time while mentally processing the offer.

'Yes, about six-ish? Very informal, just burgers and beer, that sort of thing. Nothing fancy.'

I looked around for Stuart, who'd put himself in goal and was being pummelled by Thomas's spot kicks, and decided to take a corporate decision without disturbing their game. Now, let me see. First of all, I definitely owed it to her to show up wearing the locket. Second, despite myself I was attracted to the idea of swanning around Invermartin again, acting the big fat memsahib, sniffing the airy halls and finding out what 'tiffin' meant. Third, the Stevie-spotting probability was moderate-to-high – I mean, a girl may still look, even after she has done the right thing, may she not? And fourth, there was bugger all in the fridge for supper.

'We'd love to, Susannah, thank you. What can we bring?'

'Oh, nothing – some wine if you like. You should know just about everyone else who's coming – oh, I bumped into your friend Theresa in Tesco earlier and asked her along too – thought you'd be pleased about that!'

Ah, but I *so* wasn't. Theresa and I hadn't been in touch since the ball. It wasn't unusual for us to go for a couple of weeks without speaking, but this was the first time I'd actually gone out of my way not to contact her. I mean, what would I have said? Or not said?

But it was too late to change my mind and back out of the invitation now, so I just chirped 'Great! See you at Invermartin at six, then!'

'Oh, sorry, didn't I say?' flustered Susannah. 'The barbecue's at my house, not Joffy's. Sorry, is that OK?'

The memsahib closed up her fan. 'Course it's OK, Susannah! Why wouldn't it be? Oh, and by the way ...'

'Yes?' she prompted.

'I still truly love my locket.'

'I'm so glad,' she replied. 'See you later, Gail.'

'Bye.'

Stuart agreed to come along ungrumblingly enough after I promised to drive him home at the end. Thomas was promised as many burgers as he could eat, and two goes with his Game Boy in the morning if he behaved himself. A grown-up barbecue wasn't exactly a trip to Disney World, but at least it would be a diversion for him, and I promised myself that I'd take him and Emma swimming tomorrow. Emma was happy to be off to a party as it meant getting to wear her best white broderie anglaise dress and matching hat.

Clothing-wise I decided to leave the jeans at home and astonish everyone by working a bit of a sophisticated look, so out from its cellophane shroud came the pastel flowery linen Audrey Hepburn shift dress I'd bought during a *'smarten yourself up, slag'* moment in Glasgow two years ago but never actually worn, to which I added my pink embroidered mules, a white silk chrysanthemum for my hair, and, of course, my wondrous locket. The only summery cardigan I owned was stained with Blackcurrant Angel Delight so, because my arms were finally beginning to turn from Highland blue to healthy buff, I left it at home. Needless to say we were followed all the way to Susannah's by what I fervently hoped was only a rogue black cloud.

We arrived early, just before six, as I knew that the behaviour-o-meter would be running down fast at that time of night. The plan was to chit-chat a little, stuff barbecued foodstuffs down the children and then head for home by eight at the very latest. Susannah greeted us warmly and showed us through to the garden. She looked radiant, as though everything she'd ever done in her life had been working up to becoming the person she now was. Now maybe that's true of all of us, but I saw in her a change which couldn't have been forced or faked – it was as though she had *found* herself. I'd never known what the hell that expression was all about up until now.

Just before we left I'd had a flash of genius and gift-wrapped a huge unopened book on twentieth-century art, which had been given to Stuart and me as an engagement present and which had languished in a box in the loft ever since (along with some marble and wire cheese cutters, a few pasta-making machines and the four spare electric carving knives), after remembering to check that it hadn't been lovingly inscribed by the original giver. Susannah's delight upon opening it made me feel that, far from being a slapdash old meanie, I had just participated in a loving and thoughtful act of re-homing.

Informal? Burgers and beer? *Nothing fancy my arse.* Susannah had lain on *staff*, for God's sake! And it was almost an insult to refer to her back garden as anything so common as a *back garden*, such was the abundance of trailing roses, sweet-pea arbours, covered walkways and wrought iron furniture which adorned what I dimly remembered was once a neglected piece of waste ground, so useful in its day for shagging and drug-taking, behind Susannah's hall-conversion home.

'Meet you in the gazebo near the ha-ha, daahling,' whispered Stuart, accepting a tumbler of Pimms from a waitress and surging off to speak to Joffy, who was standing by the barbecue speaking to one of the staff.

Thomas, Emma and I stood at the edge of the lawn and sized up the situation. From Thomas's point of view it wasn't very promising. Not many people had arrived so early and there was no sign of any children over the age of about three, no visible toys or play area, and also no sign of the food being ready yet. He looked up at me with a *'well then?'* expression on his face and I shrugged in defeat and pulled the Game Boy out of Emma's changing bag. Oh, well. I reasoned to myself that if I'd been at a *kids'* party I'd either want some decent grown-ups to play with or else to be given something interesting to occupy myself with, like a gin and tonic, so why shouldn't it work in reverse for him?

Emma decided to head for the house and Abigail's toy basket, and after checking that she was within eye- and earshot, I picked a glass of orange juice from the tray-bearing waitress, which turned out to be some sort of yummy mango and passionfruit concoction, and set about wondering who to delight with my presence first. There were a few stray people there whom I didn't recognise, but I waved to Iain and Amber Moffat, who had three-year-old Jessica and five-year-old Harvey behaving impeccably beneath them, and was just about to go over to speak when a voice from beside me piped up.

'Gail Buchanan! Class swot! How are you doing?' asked the tray-bearing waitress. I jumped and looked closely at her pretty, freckled face.

'Linda Blair! Class ... mate! Not too bad, thanks, you?'

'Oh, surviving – just about getting used to being back in the village again! We only moved back to Loch Martin at the beginning of the year – been in Aberdeen for the last sixteen years!'

'So, what are you up to these days?' I asked, pre-empting an awkward silence. *She's a waitress, you garbling pinhead!*

'Oh, you know, bit of this, bit of that.'

'Any of the other?'

'What, with three kids? What do you think?' She put her free hand on her hip and raised her eyebrows. I racked my brains – let me see ... Linda Blair ... yup, she'd gone out with Stevie in fourth year. In fact she was probably no stranger to this very garden in its previous life.

'Understood. But if you've been here for months why haven't we met up before now, at the school gate?'

'What, the Primary School? Oh, heavens no! My girls are sixteen, fifteen and thirteen, Gail – they're all at the High School! Don't look so shocked – it'll be your turn soon enough – the tantrums, the mood swings, the slamming doors ... '

I thought of Emma. 'I get those already.' Then I blurted out, 'God, Linda, if you think about it, we're both old enough to be grannies!'

'Except we're *not* yet, are we?' she pointed out, a little piqued. Linda was in the mild-to-moderately scary bracket of my school memory bank, and piquing her was the last thing I wanted to get involved with. Wait a minute – didn't there used to be some ancient rumour about her and Caveman Walsh, the happy hippy history teacher? Hmm, couldn't really fling *that* into the chit-chat, now, could I?

'That your husband?' she asked, looking at Stuart, who seemed to be acting out the Catching of Thomas as he Dived from the Climbing Frame. '*Very* cute – so what's your married name now?'

'Macdonald. Very unusual, and I don't think. Yours?'

'Urm, Walsh. Got to go – thirsty punters! See you later, Gail!' She moved away with suspicious haste. *Har!* Linda married the Caveman! Ug Ug! Poor her! Poor him!

Evening out! No no, not an *evening out*, which was what I was having, but even-ing out! That's what life did to you when you turned into a grown-up, which was, I realised, right about now. It evened people out. Not absolutely everyone, obviously, but lots of people. Joffy, Linda, Mary-Bell Ritchie, Stevie, Ralph the gitty writer, Susannah, me – hell, *Esther*, where were the differences? Weren't we all just looking for love and appreciation in our own ways? I sniffed my drink to make sure it wasn't some lethal alcopop responsible for making me feel all introspective and navel-gazy.

'I bloody hope that's got vodka in it, you big tart,' said Theresa, sidling up behind me and feeling my bum. 'My, my, which wedding have we just parachuted in from tonight, then? You look gorgeous, honey!'

I turned round, saw at once that she was on her own, and gave her a hug. 'Oh, T, it's so good to see you!' Yet again I was on the verge of stupid tears. The past few weeks had turned me into one mega-moist mother.

She pulled away in surprise. 'Hey, you, not again! Come and tell me all about it!' Linda handed her a glass of Pimm's and then melted away sharply.

'Where's Stevie?' I asked, gawping nervously at Susannah's back door in anticipation of his arrival.

'Stevie? Stevie who?' she replied, calmly taking her cigarettes out of her handbag. 'Would you be meaning ball-boy, by any chance?'

I just stared at her, letting my mouth hang open like a hooked fish. We sat down on the steps leading from Susannah's kitchen to the garden, and a crowd of people appeared from behind us and had to edge past to get to the party. Claire, Esther, Val and tribe, all paused as though to speak and then presumably thought better of it when they saw the expression on my face. The garden was suddenly full, and with a whoosh of flame, the first of the food was whacked onto the industrial-sized catering barbecue by a Chinese man in a tall chef's hat.

'Of course I mean ball ... Stevie! What's going on?'

'What do you mean, what's going on? *Nothing's* going on, Gail! Why, did you think I've been busy marrying him and conceiving little Chipolatas when I hadn't been in touch? So sorry to disappoint! Smoke?'

I shook my head. 'But ... you shagged him at the ball!'

She grinned. 'No, Gail, I shagged him *before* the ball, if you remember. And immediately after it, come to that. Oh, and the following afternoon. Outside. Against a tree. Standing up.'

'You dog,' I hissed. 'And ...?'

'And then he went home for tea, of course!' she laughed.

'What, and you haven't seen him since?' I asked incredulously.

'Only once. I popped up to Invermartin last week to return his pants, and we had a quick coffee.'

'Why didn't you just leap on him while you were

there?' I asked, *because that's what I'd have flipping well done, that's for sure.*

'Gail,' she said, sounding a little exasperated. 'I don't know why you're getting all hot and bothered! I didn't *want* to leap on him! What's the problem? We just had a bit of fun and moved on! I'm sorry your matchmaking didn't work out, but that's just the way it is!'

'It wasn't matchmaking!' I lied.

She gave me one of her looks. 'Whatever. Anyway, we weren't really all that compatible, and we had absolutely nothing in common—'

'What? Oh, yes you did!' I cut in. 'You've got loads in common! You're both so alike ... You're both ...' I stopped mid-sentence, floundering, like that fish again.

'Single and gagging for it?' she suggested, helping me out.

'No! Course not! I didn't mean that at all!' Oh, God, *didn't I?*

'All we had in common was *you,* Gail, if you think about it.'

I thought about it. Was that one of the reasons why I'd been so attracted to Stevie? Because by being flirty and funny and single and gagging for it he was a male version of Theresa, only with added testosterone and, and stuff?

Then I asked, terrified, 'So did you talk about me?'

'Not really, we didn't talk about anything much, come to think of it. He likes you a lot, though, and I know damn well you had the hots for him ...'

'Rubbish!' I lied again, but with such a huge force of relief behind the word that I must have sounded quite convincing, because Theresa made a backing-off gesture with her hands and smirked apologetically. Thank God, he hadn't told her.

'Anyway, I've got other fish to fry these days, so can

we stop the post-mortem now, please? We're going to have to mingle.'

'You mean circulate.'

'Why don't we simply "mix"?'

'Let's work that lawn, baby!'

We stood up and went our separate ways, Theresa to find another drink and me to check on Emma, who was absorbed with Abigail in throwing a Play-doh tea-party. Literally throwing, as globs of fluorescent dough were attaching themselves to the floor, the windows, and Emma's white dress. A teenage girl, identified earlier as Susannah's new mother's help, had them under close supervision and I waved at them all happily before plunging off to find a new grown-up to talk to.

'Hello, Gail,' said a gloomy voice behind me. I turned round to be confronted by Esther, paling into insignificance beside the vibrancy of Tony's Hawaiian shirt, mirror shades and yellow Lancashire Mutual baseball cap. Oh, shit. I'd wanted to find someone *far* nicer than these two!

'Hello!' I replied, reminding myself not to let my eyes dart about looking for escape routes. 'Where's Magnus?'

'We had to leave him at home,' replied Tony, equally gloomily.

'What, home alone?' I har-har-harred.

'Of course not!' Esther snapped back. 'He's not well.'

'Oh! Sorry to hear that – what's up?'

'Behavioural,' said Tony mysteriously.

'Really?' I mean, what the heck else can one say to that?

'We're waiting for a diagnosis from some specialists,' Esther confided.

'Oh, no!' Suddenly it sounded serious.

'We're convinced it's either reverse seasonal affective disorder, attention deficit disorder, hyperactivity or possibly even early-onset juvenile ME.'

'Perhaps a touch of all four,' added Tony, taking a large green spotted handkerchief from his Bermuda shorts pocket and blowing his nose most fruitfully into it, right in front of me. 'And he's got a cold.'

My goodness, what an unlucky, not to say *unlikely,* combination. Poor Magnus, to have all this, plus Esther and Tony as parents ...

'How worrying for you both! When, I mean how long ...'

'Days, now. He's been simply dreadful. We're beside ourselves. I've stopped giving him dairy products, naturally, to see if that helps at all, but I blame my GP, personally. She should have picked something up *long* before now,' Esther spat. 'We've complained formally, of course.' No doubt using *Debrett's Correct Form,* a little voice inside me snarled.

'Not days, honeykins, it's been *well* over a week! Ever since, well, it started round about the time we told him about the new bubba in Mamma's tum-tum ...' Tony received a smack in the chest from his wife for that one.

'Esther! You're pregnant!' I shrilled.

'*Shhhhhhh!*' they spluttered back, showering me with spittle and possibly tuberculosis.

'That's wonderful news! How are you?' I whispered, eyeing her belly and not noticing any difference from the usual, fairly solid mound.

'Quite hellish, actually. It was such a shock – we weren't planning to have any more, were we, Tony?' She looked at him accusingly, like he'd been the only person responsible for her condition.

'Definitely not. We don't think we could possibly have enough love to give a second child, do we, honeykins?' Esther nodded ruefully.

301

'Oh, don't you worry about that!' I trilled. '*Everyone* thinks that when they—'

'But Magnus is *borderline gifted*, Gail,' cut in Esther. 'You've just got no idea what that's like! He's going to need so much from us in future, what with his behavioural needs, his educational programme, his development ...' She tailed off and clutched her forehead with her hand.

Tony put his arm round her shoulders. 'Come on, honeykins, let's go and get you a drink. Of *squash*.' He began to lead her away then turned back to whisper, 'Pregnancy's the only thing I know which keeps her off the booze,' before rushing to catch her up.

Poor Esther. What a screw-up she was. And poor Magnus! Possibly the least likeable child I had ever encountered, yet suddenly I was compelled to run over to them and say, 'Tell you what, give Magnus to me! I'll look after him!' before deciding that perhaps this would be a sympathetic gesture too far.

I looked over to the barbecue and saw that the food seemed to be almost ready. Thank goodness, the kids would be starving by now. I ambled through the people towards Stuart, who by now was deep in conversation with Iain Moffat.

'Amber and I prefer to mulch,' Iain was saying earnestly. 'It's so quick and convenient, and you've got absolutely no clippings to worry about. Amazing!'

'Yes, I do see that,' Stuart replied, 'but doesn't that leave you with moss problems?'

'Not at all! Although I do spray with a systemic moss-killer and fertiliser once a year, just to be on the safe side.'

'Hmm, sounds like a good idea,' agreed Stuart.

'Stuart's a ride-on man, aren't you?' I broke in, elbow-ing myself between them. 'On the lawn, of course. What

302

else would I be talking about? Hello Iain!'

He glanced down at me. 'Hello. Anyway, Stuart, the only thing we really do miss are the clippings for the compost heap, but Martinside Riding School's an excellent source of well-rotted ...'

I gave up and cruised away, with neither bloke mourning my passing, arriving at Amber at a bad moment, as she was trying to disguise the fact that Jessica had pulled her pants down and was weeing unstoppably in a flower bed.

'Jessica! Naughty girl! You don't do that at home, so you shouldn't do it here!'

'Doesn't she?' I said. 'Thomas wees in the garden at home all the time! I envy kids that freedom, don't you?'

She gave me a wholly inappropriate, under the circumstances, look of distaste before collecting herself and replying, 'Well, it's so much easier for boys – they just unzip and point, don't they?'

'Yup, in so many ways.'

Just then a large raindrop plopped down the front of my dress, and all its little raindrop mates decided that now would be a good time to gatecrash the party. Typical! The first day in about five years when I'd ventured out without any rainproof clothing! But there was no panic-stricken rush for cover – for one thing Susannah, our hostess, had stayed resolutely put, displaying impeccable upper-class stoicism which would stand her in good stead for her future life with Joffy at musty old Invermartin, and for another, the food was beginning to be dished up.

Susannah's mother's help, who turned out to be called Claudia, asked if it would be all right for her to give Emma some food, as she was feeding Abigail and Isabella anyway. More than happy to agree, I called Thomas away from his Game Boy den under a tree and we crossed the lawn to find some burgers.

With the cooking professionally under way, courtesy of the chef, Joffy had now taken over at the helm, blackening items of food with child-like enthusiasm. He came round to the front and double-kissed me exuberantly.

'Gail! You look simply marvellous! Shame about the rain, but I'm sure it's only a shower! Would you care for one of these scrumptious organic ground-steak patties?'

'Hello Joffy – and here was me thinking they were burgers!' I replied.

'Aha, an easy mistake to make, my dear. Thought the same thing myself, until wonderful Boris here put me right!' He clapped his hand on the Chinese chef's shoulder. Then he turned his attention to Thomas. 'Now then, young man, onion and ketchup for you? Marvellous! Is that Pokémon Gold I see in there? Never got past the Red version, myself – too many levels!' Thomas's face told me he wanted to have Joffy as his new daddy.

I sat under the tree with Thomas while we ate our burgers.

'Mum?'

'Yes?'

'Do you know the difference between a Raichu and a Weepinbell?'

'I don't even know what they are, pet!'

'They're Pokémon, of course! I thought you were getting good at it!'

'Not as good as you, it seems.' He looked delighted at getting one over on his old mum, and I was ridiculously touched.

'Mum?'

'Yes?'

'Can I get back to my Game Boy now?'

'Course you can.' I looked round to see who to go and

304

bother next. My dress was interestingly seeped-through with rain, and I could feel that my hair was beginning to frizz. Kissing the top of Thomas's head, I got up from his den, just in time to catch sight of Stevie coming down the steps onto the lawn, arm-in-arm with a thin, sulky-looking girl. I stared at her. It *couldn't* be! Oh, but it was! It was Eleanora-Jane Gordon-Smith!

Looking round for Theresa, I spotted her engrossed in a game of hopscotch with two of the larger Gruber children, so I began to cast frantically about to find someone else to latch onto, put on a show of one sexy girl having one hell of a good time ... but Stuart looked as though he was showing off his invisible strimmer action to Iain, Susannah was handing out umbrellas – I guess she was the sort to have a few spares handy, probably stored in her handbag for just such an eventuality – Amber was heading for her car with her disgraced child and her disgraced child's little brother, Val was holding a rhubarb leaf over Charity to shelter her from the raindrops, singing and rocking her to sleep, and Esther ... no, get a grip, I wasn't desperate enough to rush over and join Esther.

Inevitably, the more I tried to avoid catching Stevie's eye, the faster he caught mine. He pulled Eleanora-Jane away from her intensive round of double and triple-kissing, whispered, no, *murmured* something in her ear, and pulled her towards me.

It's so unfair! Why does wet hair make a man look like the most shaggable thing on earth, whereas it makes a woman resemble a bag lady? A bag lady having a bad hair day, even? My damp dress had taken on the texture of a potato sack and the silk chrysanthemum had slid halfway down my head. I yanked if off and then, looking at it distastefully for a second, tossed it over the fence. Come to think of it, viewed by an outsider the gesture could well have seemed like a bit of a sexy flamenco-esque challenge – whatever, when Stevie reached me he double-kissed me with the practised expertise of any man with a silky-haired thin posh girl on his arm (although did he hold on to me for just a fraction longer than necessary?), before drawing back to make the introductions.

'Ellie, this is Gail Buchanan.'

'Macdonald,' I corrected.

'Sorry, *Macdonald*. Gail, allow me to introduce you to my very good friend Ellie – or Eleanora-Jane for short?'

Eleanora-Jane rolled her perfect little almond eyes at Stevie, leaned forward and offered me a damp, hollow, downy cheek, which I was momentarily compelled to slap, but I took a hold of myself just in time to proffer my own for the most seamless of double air-mwahs the civilised world had ever seen.

'Gail and I were at school together,' Stevie explained.

'Really?' said Eleanora-Jane in the voice of a fag-smoking toff. 'How extraordinary!'

'And, um, why would that be?' I ventured, determined not to let the upmarket little slapper off with anything.

'It's just that you look so much younger than him – doesn't she, Stevie?'

Forgiven! What a charming girl! But hold on – just when did I take the step-up to being pleased when people think I look young?

'She certainly does, not a day over ... seventeen, I'd say,' Stevie replied – was that a wink? And why was I blushing?

'As you two know each other, would you mind *awfully* if I went to speak to Uncle Joff-Joff?'

'Not at all!' we chorused, before looking at each other and saying 'Oh, sorry,' together, then laughing embarrass-edly and saying, 'Stop it!' until a perplexed Eleanora-Jane wafted off anyway. I turned to watch her kiss Uncle Joff-Joff four times.

'Nice dress,' said Stevie.

I looked down at the damp linen. It actually didn't look too bad, considering. 'Oh, an old favourite. I only bring it out when it rains.'

'That why you keep the price label hanging down the back?'

'Oh, God, I haven't, have I?' I gasped, fumbling around my neck. 'I can't believe nobody said anything!'

'Perhaps they've all got better manners than I have. Here, allow me.' He slid round behind me and began gently fumbling at the nape of my neck. I trembled as his fingers brushed my skin. Fortunately nobody seemed to be watching, the barbecue had caught fire and Joffy was flapping around like a grasshopper trying to fan out the flames, which held everyone's attention nicely for a spell.

'You got a bargain there, didn't you?' Stevie said, handing me the label, 'Reduced from a hundred and forty quid to eighty five! Result!'

'Thank you,' I replied.

'Gail, I've been meaning to get in touch, but I've just been so busy ...'

'So I see,' I said petulantly. 'Eleanora-Jane Gordon-Smith!'

'Gorgeous, isn't she?' said Stevie, proudly, watching her sponge ash off Joffy's face.

'So, you're together, then?'

'You mean in the biblical sense?' he asked.

'Well, I mean in the fishing hut sense, if that's the same thing?'

He grinned. 'Looks that way.' Then his face clouded over. 'Gail, can we go somewhere private? I need to talk to you.' He looked into my eyes and against my better judgement, which had taken a sound battering recently anyway, I found myself nodding.

Feeling nothing if not exposed and guilty, I followed him through the crowd, up the steps and into the house. Passing the playroom, I saw Emma and Abigail being read to by Claudia from a huge jungle pop-up book. We came into the airy sitting room, which was spotless, and deserted.

'Here?' I suggested.

'I guess the bedroom would be a bit suspicious ...'

'Stop it.'

'Sorry.'

We sat down side by side on the larger of the two sofas. Susannah had laid the art book I'd given her in the centre of the coffee table, and I felt a twinge of guilt that my slapdash gift had been so graciously received. Yup, Susannah was going to be just fine with Joffy.

'Well?' I asked, as coolly as I could, seeing as how, now that we'd got here, Stevie didn't seem all that eager to start talking.

'Um, I don't know how to start this – don't even know if I *should* start this ...'

'Just tell me,' I prompted, desperate to know what he was going to say, and reminding myself that it might be about Theresa, or, or sending us a bill for taping off the Toddle route, or ...

'Gail, you know when you rang me up to say that you weren't going to see me any more?'

I shifted in my seat. 'Yes, of course.'

'Well, I was, um, kind of gutted about that, actually.'

There was an awkward silence, which I felt compelled to fill, but for once, *just for once in my life*, I couldn't.

'Which means,' he went on, 'all that stuff I'd said to you earlier, about not wanting to mess with your life, about just wanting some fun with you ... well ...'

'What, Stevie?' I said.

'Well, it wasn't true. I mean, maybe at the time I thought I could make it be true, but the fact is, that, um, I think I was falling for you. I think I *did* fall for you – I couldn't stop thinking about you after that day you came up to Invermartin.'

'Oh, Stevie,' I said, suddenly wanting to put my arms round him. 'I . . . don't know what to say—'

'Which means, Gail,' he interrupted, 'that if you hadn't put a stop to things when you did, well, put it this way, I'd probably be making one almighty nuisance of myself round your way by now, and that wouldn't have been right, for any of us.'

He looked downwards, his hands clasped in front of him. My heart was pounding so hard that it was a wonder the whole sofa wasn't jumping up and down.

'Why are you telling me now?' I asked. 'I mean, I'm glad you are, but you didn't have to, did you?'

He looked at me, obviously struggling to find the words. 'I guess I thought you deserved to know what was going on in my head, that's all.' He looked as though he was going to say more, then stopped.

'And?' I said quietly.

He sighed. 'This is going to sound like the most almighty load of crap but, well, Gail, you're *different*. We go back a long way, you and I. I couldn't believe my luck when you agreed to go out with me when we were at school, you were so smart, and kind of *sussed* about everything, I didn't think I stood a chance – and boy did I ever deserve it when you chucked me!'

'Sussed? Me?' I said, incredulously.

He smiled. 'Well, I thought you were! Anyway, I've got to finish saying this before I lose my nerve, or someone comes in.'

'Go on, then.'

'After you phoned to ask me to go to the ball, I charged about, whooping like a lunatic for about ten minutes afterwards, before stopping to ask myself what I was getting into such a state about, you being married, and having chucked me at school, and the fact that you were fixing me up with Theresa, not yourself, and all these small details. But I couldn't help myself. It was a chance to get close to you. I should have realised then that I wasn't going to handle the situation very well, shouldn't I?' He rubbed his head, and looked down again.

'It wasn't just you, though, was it?' I said gently. 'I didn't exactly fight you off.'

'No, but I still deceived you, didn't I? I offered you something I wasn't going to be able to live up to, and I need to apologise for that. You said sorry to me, when you were only doing the right thing . . .'

'Eventually,' I reminded him. 'I . . . well, I really liked you, too.'

'Whatever. I'm sorry, Gail.'

'Don't be. We had a bit of fun.'

'Have you told Stuart?'

I took a few deep breaths. 'No, not yet.'

'So you will sometime?'

'I hope so,' I replied, fingering my locket. *Would I?* Tell my lovely, caring, grieving husband that I'd let myself become involved with an old flame? Did he need that sort of knowledge bothering his head? Was it fair for him *not* to have it? It seemed my mental jury was out on that one and it had been sent to a hotel indefinitely to consider its verdict. My conscience was on hold.

'Fair enough, I guess.' He stood up and stretched, immediately looking a bit more like the Stevie of old. 'OK, should we go back out into the rain? Got your

wetsuit?' He eyed my damp dress. 'Aha, I see you have!
I'd probably better go and find Ellie. She'll be out there
somewhere shaking the dressing off the lettuce.'

'Stevie?'

'Yup?'

'What about you and Theresa, at the ball . . .'

'Theresa? Theresa's a great girl!' he said, smiling wistfully. I tried to block out the images which were probably
running through his mind. Trees, slinky green dresses and
all. 'We had a pretty good time using each other, actually.
Sorry, does that sound like treachery?'

I thumped him, possibly for the last time ever. 'Nope,
but it does sound like Theresa!'

Outside, the rain had lightened to a faint misting drizzle
and the sun was fighting its way past the big black cloud.
The party was in full, chit-chatty swing. Linda was charging around topping up Pimm's glasses, Boris the chef was
handing out plastic bowls of what looked suspiciously like
Thomas's favourite of *jellycreamandsprinkles!!* (as it is
excitedly known in our house), and Emma, mottled with
Play-Doh, ketchup and strawberry ice cream, was tottering around with Abigail and the saintly Claudia. Each girl,
including Claudia, brandished a toy green fishing net
stapled to a cane, and they were noisily pursuing a blame-
less purple butterfly. I watched Stevie and Theresa wave
gaily to each other, before going to check on Thomas in
his Pokémon den.

Only he wasn't there, and after casting around for a few
moments, trying not to become anxious I eventually
spotted him at the far end of the garden, digging in a patch
of earth with Val, Eden and Struan Gruber.

'We're hunting for minibeasts!' he shouted as I
approached. 'Look under that stone, Mum, it's got

311

millions of slugs and woodlice and everything!'

'Val, you're an angel,' I said, as she tenderly reburied a humungous earthworm. 'Thanks for looking after him.'

'Oh, no, Gail, he's been a lot of fun! It's so nice when a child shows an interest in the environment! Thomas tells me he's going to create a minibeast day care centre, don't you, Thomas?'

He nodded proudly, pointing to a plastic beaker which was carpeted with squiggly things. 'Yes, just like in Pokémon Yellow!'

'Well as long as it doesn't come into the house,' I said, shuddering. 'How are you, Val?'

'Oh, we're fine!' she replied, smiling serenely. There was a silence, but it wasn't in the least awkward, and I wasn't in the tiniest bit compelled to fill it. We sat together companionably; happy kids, happy grown-ups. Stevie, his arm draped around Eleanora-Jane's pointy shoulders, was talking animatedly to Linda. I overheard him exclaim, 'what, *Caveman* Walsh?' and giggled to myself, as Linda refilled their glasses and stalked away.

'Why don't you bring the children round to play sometime?' she asked. 'Thomas said he'd love to see Struan's wormery, and it would be so lovely to get to know you all better?'

'That would be really nice,' I replied, meaning it.

There was a yowl which I knew instantly to be from Emma, and I sprang to my feet to find her. It didn't take long; the cries led me to a knot of fussing adults, clustering round the little messy heap that was my daughter, stroking, soothing and brandishing bowls of *jellycream-andsprinkles!!* all to no avail.

Claudia looked distraught. 'She fell on the path! I'm so terribly sorry! It's ... it's her knee!'

I picked Emma up and checked her out. The graze on

her knee was so tiny I had to look at both legs several times to ascertain which one had actually been hurt. Still, it's no fun to fall over at a party, whatever your age, and I held her close and tried my best to soothe her, even though the larger the crowd around her grew, the louder her cries became.

'Don't worry,' I said to Claudia. 'These things happen, she'll be fine in a minute.' Claudia looked ready to find a vase to smash over her own head, like Dobby in the Harry Potter books, so I repeated, slowly and emphatically, 'It's – all – right – Claudia! It – wasn't – your – fault!'

Joffy, meanwhile, had bounded into the house and sweetly returned with a bag of frozen peas to apply to the injury. Stuart and Susannah, who'd been deep in conversation at the other end of the garden, arrived at the same time.

'Now then,' Joffy said tenderly, 'can't have the prettiest girl at the party upset now, can we?'

Maybe it was the flattery, maybe it was the peas, or maybe it was just something a bit special about Joffy, but anyway, the effect was like magic – Emma's crying turned to beaming smiles within about ten seconds.

'Thet's more like it!' he laughed, then he patted my arm. 'The bridge between tears and laughter's really a very tiny one – whatever age one is, don't you think?'

'Mmm,' I agreed. 'Um, Joffy?'

'Yes, my dear?'

'I'd like you to know that I think Susannah here is a very lucky lady.'

He smiled at me, then at her. 'Wrong way round, my dear, wrong way round!'

'Well, lady lucky very a is here Susannah, if you prefer . . .'

Stuart cut in through the laughter, 'I think we'd prob-

313

ably better call it a night, don't you? This kiddie could probably do with a bath and bed.'

Handing Emma over to Stuart, I went off to round up Thomas. He grumbled a bit about having to leave his new friends, but after the promise that he could de-slug my lettuces when he got home, he jumped up and dashed off to find a lid for his trapped minibeasts, high-fiving Theresa on the way past. Theresa looked as though she was heading off as well.

'Need a lift home?' I asked when I caught up with her.

'Me? No thanks, I'm being picked up any minute.' There was an odd look about her, one I hadn't ever seen before. Her eyes were shining, and she seemed curiously jumpy.

'Oh yes?' I quizzed, taking hold of her arms and staring into her eyes. 'And where might you be off to at this hour?' It was half past seven.

Without warning she gripped my elbows tightly and started jumping up and down. 'I'm going on a *date*!' she squealed. 'On my date with destiny! On, quite possibly even, the first date of the rest of my life!' She scrunched her eyes up and hugged me violently.

'Wow!' was all I could say. '*Triple* wow!' emphasised the point a bit. 'Well, who is it? Do I know him?'

She was breathing fast. 'Yes, yes you do, actually ... oh my Lord, here he is! Wish me luck!'

And standing at the top of the steps, jingling a set of car keys and looking like the proudest man on earth as Theresa walked towards him, was George from writers' group.